MINA

MINA

A NOVEL

Jonatha Ceely

DELACORTE PRESS

MINA
A Delacorte Book / April 2004

Published by Bantam Dell
A Division of Random House, Inc.
New York, New York

Book design by Sabrina Bowers

Library of Congress Cataloging in Publication Data
Ceely, Jonatha.
Mina : a novel / Jonatha Ceely.
p. cm.
ISBN 0-385-33690-x
1. Irish—England—Fiction. 2. Administration of estates—Fiction.
3. Italians—England—Fiction. 4. Identity (Psychology)—Fiction.
5. Passing (Identity)—Fiction. 6. Women immigrants—Fiction.
7. Women servants—Fiction. 8. Country homes—Fiction. 9. Young
women—Fiction. 10. Cooks—Fiction. I. Title.
PS3603.E36M56 2004
813'.6—dc22   2003055431

Manufactured in the United States of America
Published simultaneously in Canada

10 9 8 7 6 5 4 3 2 1
BVG

MINA

And I heard a voice. This is what it said:

"Love and Hunger stand before thee—

twin brothers, the two forces that move

all living things."

— *Poems in Prose*
by Ivan Turgenev

PREFACE

SOME YEARS AGO, a friend asked me to assist with the challenging task of cleaning out his grandmother's house. The grandmother had died just days short of her one hundredth birthday, leaving the old family home in upstate New York and all of its contents, accumulated over more than a century, to my friend's mother. She, herself eighty and frail with heart disease, was by then living a restricted life in a retirement community in North Carolina. Much as she wanted to take on the responsibility of her inheritance, she could not manage the trip or the labor involved. On my friend, an only child, fell the work of sorting valuable family treasures from junk before the house was sold. Or then again, he said, he might keep it. He could fix it up and rent it while he decided whether he wanted it as a weekend place, an escape from the city. It seemed a great pity to let it pass out of the family. No matter what, however, he had decided the house had to be cleaned out.

He explained all this to me on the telephone. I must say here that my friend and I were once a couple. We had, it seemed, drifted into love and then out again. After a year or so, I remember, he proposed, I declined. We didn't see each other for a while and then, meeting by chance, we talked and realized that we could be friends. Now we have dinner several times a year, call each other when one of us has an extra theater ticket, that kind of thing—pleasant but no longer romance.

When my friend explained his problem to me and appealed to me for help, I was flattered. I also—the truth here—felt guilty.

I had not known the grandmother; I had met the ill mother just once. I had, in fact, avoided meeting them, drawn back from commitment, imagined the discomfort of being appraised as a prospective daughter-in-law, and resisted. Perhaps I agreed to help now because I felt I owed the old women amends, or perhaps I was glad to be needed—or curious about what I had passed up. Perhaps, if I am honest about it, I had a fantasy that a week together might reignite the romantic spark between my friend and me. Friendship has many virtues, but between a man and a woman—well, sometimes it seems a truce in battle rather than the peace treaty itself, accommodation not heart's ease.

We drove out of the city together. To my surprise the house was lovely; from my friend's description and complaints I had envisioned a ruin. It was instead a sturdy old house, set back from the road. A gingerbreaded wooden porch ran along the front, a wonderful place to sit in a rocking chair after a day's work and watch summer twilight descend. We had no time to sit there, however. The work turned out to be prodigious. My friend's mother had given him a list of items she remembered and wanted. While he worked to identify and to crate and to ship what she had requested—which involved long telephone conferences as well—I was assigned to clear the attic.

I admit it, we initially tried to work together and failed. We talked too much. We began to dream about what it would be like to live in the house, and then we began to argue over what should be kept and what sold. I found myself drawn into discussions of how the rooms might be furnished if a renter was found and, even more time-consuming, what should be kept if my friend decided he wanted the place for himself. Together, we would be drawn outdoors. My friend showed me the apple tree in which he had built a tree house when he was twelve; we walked around the house and barn and speculated on the cost of renovations and landscaping. Simultaneously, we drew back. We agreed that if anything was to be accomplished we must work independently.

The attic scared me at first. One climbed a narrow stair to reach it. My footsteps left marks in the dust on the treads. As I looked about in the dim light, however, I was intrigued. The faint odors of mothballs, cedar, lavender were comfortingly familiar. The place was crammed with stuff. As I sorted objects into the useful and useless, the antique and the merely old and odd, I began to experience the thrill of the treasure hunter. So many things: suitcases and trunks containing shawls; a dressmaker's mannequin propped in a corner; boxes of high button shoes of still-soft leather and the button hook for doing them up; boxes of books—the Harvard Classics, the Hardy Boys series, outdated medical textbooks; a wooden case containing eating utensils and a bayonet that my friend identified as having belonged to his grandfather during his service in the First World War; a glass case in which was a stuffed mink, moth-eaten. There were cooking pots, earthenware, old jelly jars, and—meticulously packed in cotton wool and cedar shavings—a banquet service for twelve of bone china decorated with pink roses and gilt. There were years of tax files to be hauled to the local dump, ledgers, and an old camera in a fraying leather case.

On the fourth day I came upon a square wooden box pushed in under the eaves. I stooped to pull it out and then had to sit down on the floor beside it. My heart was pounding. After I opened the little window in the gable end, I felt better and returned to examine my find. The box was substantial, made of a golden wood—maple, I thought—and fitted with a hasp closure and a padlock. The key that fitted the padlock had been tied to it with a piece of frayed string. During the first days on the job I had consulted my friend about each new discovery, running downstairs and waiting patiently until he finished the current telephone consultation with his mother. I soon discovered that none of the items he had been delegated to rescue was stored in the attic, and that if I were to seek advice on everything I considered valuable or interesting we would never finish the job. One learns to be ruthless with other people's mementos and curios.

So I undid the padlock and opened the box. Inside was a package wrapped in cloth. The cloth seemed a fine cotton lawn that must once have been white but was now somewhat yellowed with age. Inside the cloth was a thick wad of papers tied about with a fancy green ribbon. Threaded on the ribbon and tied into the final knot was a gold ring with a red stone—a garnet, I supposed, was most likely—set into it.

The papers were a handwritten manuscript, complete in itself, but accompanied by no explanatory note. My friend had no recollection of having seen the box, the manuscript, the ribbon, or the ring before. His mother, when he consulted her, had no recollection of anyone in the family having mentioned such papers. No names or incidents, indeed nothing in the pages we examined that evening, seemed related to my friend's family history. When, at my insistence, he called his mother with further questions, she was quite annoyed. She had no interest in people she had never heard of. Had we found her old mother-of-pearl teething ring attached to the silver bell inscribed with her initials yet? she wanted to know.

Curious, I stayed on an extra day to go to the local historical society to research the names associated with the house and its nineteenth-century inhabitants. I could find no connection between that history and the manuscript I had found.

My friend, identifying no family story in the record, felt ultimately quite unsentimental about the trove of papers. He was prepared to throw out all—except the ring, of course—into the box of trash for the dump. He made no objection, therefore, when I claimed the papers as my payment for helping him. Before I left to return to the city, he gave me the ring also—the secondhand dealer who came to appraise the furniture and china that was not wanted but was too good to discard said it was gold and set with a small ruby, eighteenth-century English work. He admired the chased design along the band even though it was very much worn. Since I wanted the papers, my friend said, it seemed only right to keep everything together. I do not wear the ring; it rests in a box with the green ribbon. Sometimes I take it out and look at it and dream of its history and speculate on how it came to be tied to an old manuscript stored and forgotten in the attic of a Victorian house in upstate New York.

Strange how dream and reality interpenetrate. There are times when it seems impossible to disentangle one from the other.

I still remember how I felt as I sat on a dusty trunk in that attic, the smell of age—clean and dry—in my nostrils. Dust motes danced in the sun that sent a pale ray diagonally across the slant-sided room. My friend bustled on the floor below as I read the pages, yellow-edged with time. The quality of the paper was not good; the pages chipped at the edges as I turned them over. The manuscript was in danger of disintegrating in my hands. I seemed to read a dream—my dream or that of another. Now I say another's, but during the remainder of that week as I sat in the attic, now just pretending to help my friend, I would not have sworn to you under oath what emanated from my mind and what was spoken to me across time.

The minuet of motes in the sunbeam reminded me that all decays, all disintegrates, all re-forms into new life. This world is but an infinite contra dance of atoms—what once was may be again in the endless ballroom of time—so why not my dream and another's simultaneously? Why not?

In any case, I took the papers away with me at the end of the week. Over the next few months, as I found moments to spare from my work, I copied the manuscript onto my computer. The author's writing was obscure at times. Evidently she had used one of those old steel-nibbed pens, which had spluttered and occasionally even blotted the pages. Some sections had clearly been written in great haste. Others were labored over with crossings out and revisions. Most of what I have designated Chapter Twenty seemed to have had grease spilled on it. Stains had soaked the paper and smeared words. I labored a long time, reading and rereading, puzzling out the meaning contained in the crumbling pages on which the once black ink was fading to metallic brown. But the reader will—to adapt Charlotte Brontë's words—comprehend that to have reached the public in the form of a printed book the narrative will have undergone some struggles. No need to be concerned with that now. Enough to say that the pages that follow are my transcription of the manuscript I found.

Perhaps some reader will recognize the tale as a family story, or, if not that, then the experience of an individual character, a name, or a detail will strike a chord of memory or meaning.

So circumstantial an account must have roots in some real past. My friend and I—we seem to see each other more often now—discussed it just the other night over dinner in our favorite restaurant. I say the record of a long-dead hand, that faded ink, those foxed pages, survived in the dusty attic for a purpose. He reminds me that 1848, the year the manuscript describes, is long ago and far away in experience as well as in time. We cannot expect to understand people who lived then, he says; our present, our assumptions about how we live, are so different from theirs. I nod—perhaps he is right, but I wonder. I felt a connection to *something* when I lifted those papers from their box in the attic and untied the green ribbon. I feel it again when I slip the ring onto my finger. The little red stone catches the light when I turn my hand. Perhaps, I think—just perhaps—a dream of the past can guide us to understanding who we are.

MINA PIGOT

My Story

What is there in thee, Man, that can be known?—

Dark fluxion, all unfixable by thought,

A phantom dim of past and future wrought,

Vain sister of the worm,—life, death, soul, clod—

Ignore thyself, and strive to know thy God!

"SELF-KNOWLEDGE"
BY S. T. COLERIDGE

CHAPTER I

SOMEONE ASKS: What country, friends, is this? No answer. I open my eyes with a start. In the dim early-morning light, the world returns around me. I lie nestled in straw in the stable loft of a country estate. I look out a dormer window toward the soft hills that rise in a low ridge between the estate and the nearby village.

Below me the horses shift in their stalls. Their safe smell and their heat rises to me. It is dawn, and the sounds of the yards and the house awakening will begin in a few moments. This is the moment of stillness before the lark rises toward the rosy light raying up from the eastern horizon, toward the zenith of the clear spring sky.

My work begins as the lark flies up, singing from its meadow nest to greet the sun. I too rise. I begin not with a hymn to nature but with a visit to the outhouse, ablutions under the pump, a quick ordering of my garments. Then I attend to the horses. They need water, clean straw, and grooming. But first I have something else to do.

I have a dream that recurs. It came to me again last night. I walk from the door of our croft into the field that slopes to the south. The land is green, green, green, like a velvet gown laid over a curving body. In my dream I tread lightly on the soft surface. I feel the spring of grass beneath my bare feet. As I pace down the slope of the field, I feel the warmth of the sun on my face and arms. All is pale blue above, green below, and a fresh wind blowing. I notice something growing in the field. Loaves of bread, golden-crusted. It is as if the corn had grown, been harvested, thrashed, ground, kneaded, baked all in a night—as if the bread grew ready to my hand and mouth directly from the earth. In my dream I smell the yeasty bloom and fall to my knees, mouth watering, guts cramped with hunger. I am eager to pluck and eat these magic mushrooms, brown-gold buttons on the green velvet field. I lay my hands reverently on a loaf and find that I hold stone. Frantic, I rise and run about the field from seeming loaf to seeming loaf. All stone and heavy beyond bearing.

I stumble, weeping, down the slope, and in that sudden translation of dreams find myself in a dug field. A man in ragged clothing stoops over his spade; his face is averted from me and his lowered head is covered with a shapeless blob of felted hat. He looks familiar and yet I cannot put a name to him. He turns the earth, stoops his back into the weight, lifts brown clumps from the soil—potatoes. Here is food, I think; not crusty, fragrant bread but gray flesh formed under dark loam. This man will share with me a potato or two, and I will find green herbs in the field and feed my brother. I hurry toward the man and stand beside him. My heart fails me, for here again are stones. His face turned from me, he delves stone after stone from the ground, brushes away dirt and sets the stone on a rising heap. A cairn is growing in my dream, a monument, a funeral pile. I stoop to see the face of the man who digs. His blue eyes burn with fever. His eyebrows are thick and red. His cheeks are gaunt with hunger, yet glazed with the red-gold stubble of his rough beard. This is my father. He does not speak. My tongue is thick in my mouth, my throat burns. I cannot make a sound. It would not matter if I could; I know he would not hear me.

I turn to look back to the house at the top of the rise. It is tiny in the distance. I have come much farther than I thought. I turn my steps along a path. The green grass lies to my right, the spaded soil to my left. My father will not, cannot, speak to me, for he is dead. I think that I will go back to the house and find my brother. The house is a white toy in the distance, the sky is blue and far above. I am filled with a sense of urgency.

Then, as always, I awaken in a strange country. Above the place where I nest at night in the barn loft, I have rigged a bag that swings away from the beam on a thin string. The string is enough to hold the bag, yet not thick or strong enough to give passage to the mice that might forage here. I let the bag down and check its contents. The mug and the spoon are there and my brother's jacket, folded carefully. The bag would be limp with just those three things, but hard bread packs the cloth too. Fresh bread would mold, flour would sift away. The cook sets out this dry bread for the field hands; for three mornings now, I have managed to filch some. Why I do so, I do not know. There is food enough here at the kitchen door for all the outdoor workers. Even so, I keep this private store. I count the brown-gray squares. Six now, put away against the day of need. I will not eat of this, not even nibble on a corner to taste it. It will not matter if a little mold grows on this bread; that is easily scraped away, the biscuit boiled in water to a sticky dough. This will suffice as food. And my store is secret; I will not be called to share it until I find my brother. When the day of need comes, as come it will, I will be ready. I hoist my cache again to safety and begin the day.

It comforts me to groom the horses. I lead the black, Sultan, out of his stable into the sunshine of the back courtyard, fasten his lead to the iron ring in the wall, and wield the comb until his flanks shine and my arms ache.

As I finish with Sultan, the kitchen maid who peels the vegetables, cleans the pots, and helps the cook as he requires comes out the kitchen door. I have spoken to her just once in the three mornings I have risen here. Yesterday, she handed me a chunk of brown bread and a wedge of cheese and said, "Here, Paddy, I don't suppose you saw such food as this at home."

"No," I said, "not since two years ago. They are starving at home." She did not answer that.

Today, she has her hair tied up in a fancy green ribbon, her skirts down at her ankles, not kilted up as she wears them when she is working. She carries a bundle under her arm.

"Good morning, Mary," I say respectfully, keeping my voice low. "Are you off to the village so early?"

"Indeed, I am," she says, tossing her head in her saucy way. Her face is pudding-plain and marked by smallpox besides, yet her blue eyes are clear lake-blue and fringed with long lashes. "Indeed I am, Paddy. Off to the village and beyond." She winks at me, fluttering her black lashes down to her pox-scarred cheek.

"Beyond?" I ask, puzzled by her way of speaking and her new manner. She seems impertinent and yet fearful of her own boldness. It frightens me that she might be doing something that will involve me in a wrong.

"Beyond, indeed," she asserts. "I'm off across the hill to the village and the stagecoach for London town."

"London?" I feel quite stupid.

"London?" she mimics my Irish speech and my bewilderment. "Yes, London. I had a letter yesterday. My sister has a place for me in a great house, a maid's place, sweeping and dusting the fine things. Mr. Serle will have to find someone else to shell his peas and scrub his pots. Or do it himself, the black foreigner."

"Oh." I can think of nothing to say to this Mary I have never seen before, this bold girl who was hiding all the time inside the lazy kitchen scullion with her straggling hair and dirty skirts.

"Oh?" says Mary. "All you have to say is 'Oh'? You Irish are as stupid as they say."

I want to say that I am not stupid, just surprised by the change in her. She looks almost clean in her traveling-to-London clothes. But I know it is wiser to hold my tongue. "Well, goodbye, Mary," I say. "Godspeed your journey."

"I'm away," she says and hurries out the gate.

And Godspeed to me too, I say to myself under my breath. There will be a place in the kitchen to fill today. I wonder whether Mr. Serle, the black foreigner, will be angry when he learns she is gone. I have glimpsed him walking in the kitchen gardens in the morning and heard him speaking to the gardeners. I do not catch his words when I listen, only a murmur of sound. He is not a man who raises his voice. Where does he come from? I wonder. He is not so black, I think. I have seen darker in Ireland even, and in Liverpool for certain.

I lead Sultan out to the paddock behind the stable. The master will ride this morning as he does every morning. I lead out the gray mare, Gytrash. If the master's lady does not ride her, I will exercise her, following the master in a lazy loop down to the path along the river, across the meadow by the road up to the ridge of hills, and then down along the river again to the copse of great oaks, and, finally, back across the meadows to the stable yard. I hope the lady will be busy with the house today. I love to ride. The master does not speak to me, and I am free to move with the horse and to think of my father and my brother who loved horses and raced them and wagered on them and laughed when they won and drank up the prize money to my mother's despair. But she laughed too and said that it was all gravy money anyway and who could not love the beauty of a clean race. And when they lost, they had a pint for consolation and groomed the horses for longer even and whispered to them to run better next time.

As I run the currycomb down the dappled flank of Gytrash, I dream of the past. *Gytrash* means *ghost;* Mr. Coates, the stable master, told me. As I curry her, I think of the past. I think of the dark bay horse I groomed for my father, the dreams of horses my brother told me as we did the work on the farm. Gytrash brings my ghosts to me each morning, and for that I am grateful. I have nothing now except my ghosts, and the gold ring my mother gave me sewn into my shirttail, my brother's riding boots, and the bag of bread I have saved in the loft.

The clothes I stand in and my brother's boots. The boots he was taking to America. His boots, which are too big, I stuff with straw before I put them on to ride. They hardly show the water stains that marred them; I have rubbed and waxed them until they shine.

Mr. Coates will not allow me, or anyone who works for him, to ride barefoot. I have no proper shoes yet. Working in the yard, I must go barefoot, for shod in the boots, I would trip over myself. Also, the boots are my brother's good riding boots. I will not wear them to muck out stables. His ordinary boots are gone with him. I keep his riding boots well for his return.

Gytrash goes into the paddock with Sultan, stepping daintily and then lowering her head to crop the grass. I close the gate and return to the stable for the pony. I am beginning to feel the day growing as the sun's warmth strengthens. Once the fat pony is brushed down, I will muck out the stables and then wash myself again and seek brown bread and a mug of ale at the kitchen door.

Long after I have eaten my breakfast in the stable yard, the gentry will rise and go to their meal. Soon after that, word will come down to Mr. Coates that the horses are to be saddled for the morning ride. Later, I will polish tack and fill the water pails. I am slowly becoming accustomed to the rhythm of this place. I am beginning to feel safer here.

The cook, that dark-haired man to whom I have never spoken, is leaning against the dairy wall across from the kitchen door. He turns his face into the sun as if he would warm himself. He raises a hand in casual greeting to me as I go toward the stable again. I raise a hand in return. I wonder if he knows yet that Mary has gone away.

The pony lowers its head and swings it sideways at me as I lead him from his stall. He will nip my arm if I am not careful. I do not like this fat brown animal. He stands no more than my shoulder height at his neck. When a child or a young lady is perched on his broad back, the animal is docile enough. The halter and the lead are what annoy him—especially in the early morning. Later in the day, when he has waddled about the pasture and been exercised, he seems happier.

I set to work with the currycomb. Mr. Coates comes through the gate and across the yard. He lives in a cottage down the lane, away from the great house and close to the chapel.

" 'Morning, Paddy," he says in his gruff way.

"Good morning, sir," I respond respectfully. He makes me uneasy, although I know that is not sensible. After all, he gave me a job when I arrived here just three days past, with nothing to introduce myself but a note with his name written on a sliver of paper, my claim to know his niece, and my assertion that I am good with horses.

Mr. Coates slaps the pony on the neck. The pony, startled, sidles toward me. I leap away. Mr. Coates stands stock-still, his fists on his hips.

"Mr. Coates," I exclaim, "sir!"

"You handle the beast well enough, Paddy," says Mr. Coates. The pony reaches its neck toward him, its lips drawn back and its yellow teeth bared. Mr. Coates reaches out to catch the bridle. I know he will jerk the pony's head down to discipline it.

"Comb out and then braid his mane up today," says Mr. Coates, jerking the pony's head around so he can look at its rough mane. "And exercise him well. They say that one of the guests, a timid lady, might wish to ride this afternoon. And clean yourself up too. Douse your head under the pump."

"Yes, sir," I say, moving close in again to the beast's rear quarter with the comb in my hand. My heart pounds in my chest.

Mr. Coates slaps the pony's neck again, and the nervous beast stamps. This time I am not quite quick enough. The pony's rear hoof catches the side of my left foot. I feel as if I have been bitten. I think I hear the crunch of bone.

I stagger back and sit on the mounting block, cradling my foot in my two hands. No tears, I tell myself, no tears.

"Let me see that," says Mr. Coates. He grasps my foot roughly and twists it. I cannot help myself. I cry out.

"It is broken, and it is swelling already," he says. "You will never get a boot over that. And you cannot exercise these horses or ride with the master barefoot."

"I can," I assert, but inside I feel hopeless. Perhaps I could manage to mount Gytrash, but I know I can never ride and control her with my foot hurting like this. "I have ridden with far worse injuries," I claim.

"No, lad, you will have to go. You are puny as it is, and with this injury I cannot trust a spirited horse to you. Remember that I took you for a few days on trial only." The stableman shrugs, looks sorry, turns away from me. "There's work in Milford, no doubt, for a willing boy with a lame foot."

I feel the tears start to come. "I can groom the horses even if I can't ride out to exercise them," I protest. "I can throw down hay from the loft."

"I must have an exercise boy," Mr. Coates maintains. "I must have a lad decently outfitted to ride with the master and the gentry." There is something in his voice that tells me he is not truly sorry to have found a reason to send me away.

The man standing in the sun by the garden wall walks down the courtyard toward us. "What is the quarrel here?" he says. His voice is low and his accent strange to me. Not the country, not London, but some other place.

"No quarrel, Mr. Serle." Mr. Coates seems easygoing; he does not sound offended. "Paddy here has been careless. He has let the pony step on his foot. He won't walk or ride for the week or even two. I cannot keep him useless to me all that time."

"He looks well enough," the dark man says, staring me up and down. His expression is neutral. He neither smiles nor frowns.

"I am well," I say. "I can do the work."

"Draw two pails of water and carry them to the stable door." Mr. Coates is looking not at me but at the other man.

I limp over to the stable to fetch the pails. I put my weight down on the heel only. The movement pains me, but I cannot bear the thought of being turned away. Where can I go? And how can I go if I cannot walk?

"Stop," says the dark man. "Let me see that foot."

I sit on the mounting block again, and he takes my foot in his hand. "Does this hurt?" he asks, moving my ankle a little. His long-fingered hand, which does not look so large, can fully circle my bony ankle.

I shake my head, no.

"And this?" he presses down on the top of my foot.

I shake my head again, no.

"This?" he presses sharply where a lump and a bruise are growing below my two outer toes. The nail of the smallest toe is torn and bloody.

I hold my breath until the pain subsides.

Mr. Serle sets my foot down. "Let me see you stand," he says. "Both feet on the ground."

Gingerly, I slide from the mounting block. I put weight first on my right foot and then tentatively set down the left. It is not so bad if I keep my weight on the heel.

"Now a step," Mr. Serle says.

I can do it if I do not set the left foot down fully.

"The ankle is not broken," he says. "There may be a broken bone in the foot or just a bad bruise."

"It does not matter to me," says Mr. Coates. "The boy cannot work with the horses."

"It does not matter to you," Mr. Serle says in his even, quiet voice, "but it matters to the boy. And I can use all hands today even if the hands do not have feet to match."

"I will do any work, sir," I say, standing as best I can, trying to look fit.

"I am sure you will," he says. "With your permission, Mr. Coates?"

Mr. Coates nods sourly. "You won't get a fair day's work from him, in my opinion, but suit yourself, sir."

"I will, I think," the dark man says. "Mary has run away to make her fortune in London, I learned just now. We are short-handed in the kitchen."

I am glad inside, but my foot has started to throb, and the effort not to cry takes my attention.

"What is your name, lad?" asks Mr. Serle.

"Just call him Paddy," interjects Mr. Coates in his drawling way. "He's one of them starving Irish come to England to make his fortune. My softhearted niece in Liverpool, Susan, sent him on to me. He'll be off soon enough, I'll wager you. They don't stick with a job, I find."

"What is your name, lad?" Mr. Serle says again.

I try to shrug nonchalantly as I used to see my brother do. "Just call me Paddy," I mutter. Why should I care?

Mr. Serle raises an eyebrow. "Paddy it is, then," he says. "We will put ice on your foot, I think, and then find work you can do sitting down."

He is as good as his word. Tom, the cook's assistant, a tall, bland-faced fellow with white-blond hair and faded blue eyes, goes off to the icehouse. Mr. Serle orders me to rinse my foot under the pump in the yard and then to come sit on the bench just inside the kitchen door. My bare foot is wrapped in a clean rag. When Tom returns, I must soak the foot in a pail of ice and water.

"Keep the foot in the pail for as long as you can stand it. Then take it out and let it warm. Then back in again until the water is no longer cold."

I limp to the kitchen, where I must stay on the bench out of the way. First I am set to pick over a peck of rice, looking for the little gray stones on which Mr. Serle says some guest in the great house might break a tooth if I do not do my job well. When I have cleaned the rice, I will use the knife Tom gives me to trim the asparagus piled by the hundreds in flat baskets; then I will shell the bushel of peas that stands ready. After that, they will find more for me to do. There is a dinner party and a supper to prepare for. Mary has gone without warning, and the extra servants from the town of Milford have not yet arrived to help.

I must work steadily, and when I am not soaking my foot in the pail of ice, I must prop it on the bench, says Mr. Serle.

"And do not cut yourself with that knife," Tom says kindly. "We keep our tools sharp in this kitchen."

"Here," says Mr. Serle, setting a piece of bread and a mug of cider beside me on the bench. "When you are recovered enough from the pain to feel hunger, you must eat."

My head whirls and my foot throbs. Cautiously, I set to work, sifting rice grains through my fingers into a clean bowl. I am out of the way by the outer door of the kitchen, which is a good thing, for Tom and Mr. Serle move swiftly about the room, armed with great knives and hooks for shifting pots upon the fires. I glance about as best I can while getting through my own tasks and resisting crying for the pain in my foot, and for the danger I am in of being thrown out into the fields and lanes defenseless. I realize with horror that perhaps I cannot even climb to the hayloft for my bag and blanket. I will be better, I tell myself, and plunge my foot into the pail of ice again. I will do the work set me and find my way as best I can.

After a while, the pain in my foot eases. I can look about me with more accurate perception. In this one room there is more food and more equipment for preparing it than I have ever seen in my entire fifteen years on earth.

The bench I sit on is just on the right inside the main door of the kitchen. The great room lies before me, with fires on each side glowing behind iron grates and the looped chains that I will learn later are part of the apparatus for turning roasts. Pots are set on iron counters let into the walls beside the visible fires. From the steam I see rising, there must be fire under these too. Great metal cupboards on wheels obscure my view of what is cooking. There is a long table in the center of the room laid out with white cloths and wooden chopping boards and knives and cleavers. Against the far wall is a counter that is also heaped with foodstuffs and, beside that, dressers with rows of basins, forms, and other cooking utensils.

To my left I can see a stone passage and the door to another room. It must be the scullery, for clouds of steam billow out from time to time and pots are taken in and brought out again. There must be space in that room too for other work; Tom goes in and out with roasts to set on the spits and plucked poultry. A man wearing a great shiny apron carries in a fish as long as a two-year-old child. He disappears with it into the scullery door. Later, two of the helpers, who have at last arrived from Milford, carry it out laid in a long pan. The fish must have been scaled, for it does not gleam as it did when the man brought it. Mr. Serle directs the servants to place the long copper pan on one of the range tops. I learn that the iron counters are the range tops, because he says, "Place the fish steamer here on this range top. The fire is right for it." The sight of the flames flickering up from the fire box when the metal cupboard is moved aside makes my heart beat faster. I hold my breath for a moment and calm myself.

To my right is a longer stone-flagged passage. There are several doors letting into this hall, which has high windows on its right-hand side. In the rooms in that direction, the baking and dessert preparations must be taking place. Servants with flour-smeared cheeks hurry in and out with closed dishes, pie plates, and—when Mr. Serle or Tom demand something—bottles of bright liquids.

Ordering them all about is Mr. Serle. Mr. Serle is thin and dark. He moves with the strength of flexed wire. His black hair curls back from his face. His skin is clear olive with a flush high on the cheekbones when he is annoyed or warmed by working at the fire. He is of medium height. He has a high-bridged nose and black eyes with long, black lashes. His eyebrows are thin and arched. I am afraid of him, I think. When he attended to me earlier, he seemed to know something about me that I had not told him.

Moving about the kitchen—his kitchen—he looks quick, impatient. There is a list of dishes written up on a slate that is attached to the wall near the passageway that leads to the main house. Tom consults it from time to time when one of the assistants hired from Milford asks him a question. Mr. Serle never has to look. He seems to have in his head exactly what needs to be done and the order in which he wants the others to work. He stands at the long, scrubbed-pine table and his hands move deftly with the great chopping knife. The men and women come to him and he gives them their directions simply and clearly, his hands working all the while.

In the course of the day, as its golden track across the kitchen floor tells me how the sun moves, the two men, Mr. Serle and tall Tom, helped by Mrs. Bennet, the pastry cook, by the two regular kitchen maids, the boot boy, who has been temporarily promoted to cleaning pots because Mary has disappeared, and by the six extra helpers from Milford, turn crates and baskets and barrels of meat and fish and shellfish and vegetables and rice and cream and butter and fruits and sugar and herbs and spices into a great dinner for twelve people and a supper for thirty. Of course, as I will eventually understand, it is not all accomplished in that one day. The supper dishes, especially the cold meats and the pastries, had been in process of preparation for several days.

But that knowledge comes later. Through that long first day in Mr. Serle's kitchen, my senses swim and swoon in the odors of meat and fish and pastry and vegetables being baked and broiled and roasted and steamed. When two of the assistants wheel past me on a trolley a haunch of beef that they have taken down from its spit and I see the brown crackling fat and the red juices oozing out onto the platter, tears come to my eyes. My village in Ireland—all two hundred souls of us—would have shared out a portion each of such a meal and considered ourselves well fed.

But I have little time to look about me. Mr. Serle constantly directs work to me. Heaps of washed things are piled beside me or placed in baskets at my feet. Basins are handed to me with quick instructions to stir or to beat. I shell peas, I pick over spinach, I shred lettuces, I hull strawberries, I grate orange peel, I stir a custard until it is cold. Sometime in the late morning, after I at last nibble the bread and drink the cider, I forget to feel hunger. Soon I even forget my foot. There is so much to see and to smell and to do.

No one seems to eat. Indeed, Tom and Mr. Serle pick up a spoon occasionally and taste a sauce, but no one actually eats a meal. I think, with so much food piled about them, they forget what it is for. In the late afternoon, when the footmen come down with trolleys to take the made dishes away through the stone corridor that leads to the main part of the house, Mr. Serle dismisses me.

"Here, lad," he says, noticing me, it seems, for the first time since he plunged my foot into the pail of ice and gave me bread just after dawn, "here's a bowl of sorrel soup for you and a cheese tart. Eat, and then get yourself some water at the pump and be off to your bed." He thrusts a bowl and a spoon into my hands. He sets the pastry on the bench beside me before he turns away to his work.

I spoon the gray-green soup into my mouth. It tastes like lemon and fresh grass and potato and cream. For a moment I am hungry again. Later, as I limp off toward the stable, he calls after me, "Be here at dawn, lad. Be back at dawn."

CHAPTER II

I LIMP TO THE STABLES and make my way up the ladder, holding tight and dragging up with my arms to keep the weight as much as possible from my foot. Although I fall asleep almost as soon as I have curled myself into my nest in the hayloft, I soon awaken again, startled, believing that I smell smoke. My heart pounds in my chest. I sit up and sniff the air. Nothing. It must have been a fearful dream that roused me. After that, I have a restless night. The moon hangs a round lantern in the sky. All is silver shadow and black recesses in the straw where the stable cat rustles, hunting mice.

My foot aches. I get up to check that my bag is hanging from the rafter where I left it. It is there, but that does not comfort me as it did yesterday. My foot aches the more for the movement.

When will I feel safe? I wonder. I try to remember when I last was myself. I fall into an uneasy doze but waken again with a start. I have begun to dream of the whitewashed cottage by the road with the green pasture beyond. The door is open and I am about to enter. Fear wakes me.

I find the lump in my shirttail that is my mother's ring sewn securely into the hem. With that in my fist, I find a small comfort, comfort enough that I can allow myself to search the past for a good moment.

The picture that comes is of my father leading the gray mare up the lane to the cottage. The sky shines Madonna blue, and light wind blows in the spicy scent of roses blooming by the cottage wall. My brother shouts a high "Hurrah!" and comes tumbling out the door behind me, running toward my father and the horse. Startled, the mare tosses her head, whinnies, and pulls against the lead.

"She has spirit, she does," my father cries.

My brother laughs and says, "She does. A fool could see it."

Below me, Gytrash shifts in her stall, and the odor of horses and hay helps me to rest. When the moon sets, I sleep a little.

At dawn, I rise and brush my clothing well. In the quiet of the hayloft, I rub my hair over with the little rag I keep to blacken it. Outside at the pump in the yard, I wash my hands and face. I hold my foot under the cold water before I wrap it again in the rag that Mr. Serle tied on. The swelling has gone down along the side of the foot, although the little toe is twice what it should be still. A black bruise shapes the crescent of the pony's hoof upon my flesh. But already I can put a little more weight down. The cobblestone yard is cool and damp under my feet as I limp to the kitchen door.

In the kitchen, the light is gray and pale. The great metal cabinet on wheels that yesterday shielded the heat of the fires from the room has been thrust aside. Tom is emptying ashes into a bucket. He will lay fresh coals and light the fires. I see now that there are grills for roasting and ranges for boiling and baking on both sides of the kitchen. I spent all day here and did not realize all that the metal walls hid.

"Good morning, Tom," I say.

"Good morning," he replies gruffly. "Is that foot better, Paddy? I could use some help carrying out the ashes."

"No, Tom." Mr. Serle has come down the corridor from the left-hand side of the kitchen. He must have been in the scullery or the cold room. "The lad will help me set the dough for the manchet rolls and then sit for the rest of the day. In a week or so you will have help."

"Humph," Tom grunts as he lifts the ash-laden bucket. "His head is sooty enough already. Did he sleep in the coal hole?"

"In the stable loft—" I begin.

Mr. Serle cuts me off. "Leave the lad alone. Here, boy, I won't have you cooking in your horse-tending clothes."

Mr. Serle has brought a pair of trousers for me and two blue smocks that will cover me from neck to knees. "One to wear and one to wash," he says. He has shoes and stockings for me too. "I can't have you dripping boiling soup on your feet," he says. "Wear these in the kitchen. Roll up your pants and jacket and put them away later. You can wear your shirt under the smock if you are chilled. But wash it before you wear it again in my presence."

I feel relief that I do not have to take off my shirt. I wonder if Mr. Serle can see my anxiety. When I look at him, however, he is busy measuring out flour into a great wooden trough. He has set a white hat over his black curls.

"Go to the cold room," he says. "Down at the end of the corridor there. Bring me the jug of milk that is on the marble slab under the window. I brought it over from the dairy. Tomorrow that will be your task."

I limp down the corridor. Although they were snug to put on, the stockings and shoes comfort my sore foot and make the walking easier somehow. I push open the door of the last room. It is dim and cool there. A dead rabbit hangs from a metal rack that runs the length of the room. I grasp the heavy brown milk jug in both hands and carry it carefully back to Mr. Serle.

"Good lad," he says. "Now listen carefully. You are going to learn to make breakfast bread for the gentry."

So begins my education as a cook. The hearty loaves of brown bread that the servants eat and the more delicate white loaves for the upstairs gentry come every morning from the bakery ovens in the village. Mr. Serle also dries the white bakery bread for crumbs that are needed for pastries, puddings, and for thickening sauces. The hot manchet rolls that the ladies and gentlemen eat with their breakfast at ten o'clock in the morning are made in this kitchen.

"French rolls, they are called nowadays," Mr. Serle tells me. He pours milk into a pan. He warms it at the range where Tom has already lit the new fire. I watch as Mr. Serle shows me how to spoon the yeast from its crock and to replenish the yeast mother so it will continue to grow. He pours warmed milk over two spoonsful of yeast in a little bowl and stirs it gently.

"Slowly," he says. "Haste kills yeast, which is a living thing and must be respected." He pours the rest of the warmed milk over the white flour that he has sifted into a wooden trough. He mixes all to a thick mass with a long wooden spoon. He adds the bowl of milk and yeast, which has bubbled itself into a froth and sends out an aroma of comfort and home that makes tears start in my eyes at the same time as my mouth waters. It is the first time since I left my home that I have remembered food as a pleasure and not just a duty.

"This is the kneading," Mr. Serle instructs. "The dough must be turned and folded and pressed down until it is silky smooth and all of the flour has disappeared."

He looks at my hands, which I washed at the pump this morning. "Go into the scullery, Paddy," he says sharply. "Scrub your hands with the brown soap you will find there. And never come into this kitchen again without first cleaning yourself."

I hurry to do as he bids. It is the first time he has spoken roughly to me, the first time he has called me Paddy. In the scullery, I scrub my hands and wipe my eyes on my sleeve. When I return, he looks at my hands suspiciously but directs me to try the kneading. The table is high for me and the bread trough is large. Carefully I fold and push the dough, turning it always clockwise as my mother taught me.

"You know how to knead," Mr. Serle says.

I bob my head down. "My mother taught me," I murmur. "She worked in a great house and learned their ways before she married."

Mr. Serle reaches a dark hand across the board and presses the lump of dough with his index finger. His fingers are long, thin, vibrant with strength. "Wheat flour was not so common in your house."

He says it not as a question but as something he knows about me, about who I am.

I stiffen my spine and lower my voice as best I can. "We

were not so poor," I say. "We were not so poor while my father was working for the gentry that we could not have wheat bread for a holiday."

Mr. Serle scoops white flour into a sieve and shakes down a cloud of white onto the dough. Motes of white catch in the dark hairs on the back of his hand. "Here," he says, "let me give the lump a final turn. You knead unevenly; you are a child still and not strong. Sit by the door again today. When we are finished here, begin by picking over the bowl of dried beans and the peck of rice that are set out for you."

I am afraid to speak lest my voice shrill.

Mr. Serle leans over the table, kneading the bread with his strong hands. I stand by silently watching his firm, sure strokes. When he is satisfied, he stops, pats the plump mound tenderly, and then sighs deeply. "See how I set the dough in a proofing bowl, lad," he says. "Treat it gently, for it is a living thing. And clean up here." He moves on briskly to the scullery, where he will prepare kidneys for a dish of kidneys in gravy.

"Get to work, Paddy," Tom rebukes me as he brings in another scuttle of coals for the fire. "If you have nothing to do, I can find plenty for you."

Later he shows me how to clean raisins by setting them in a bowl and pouring boiling water over them. When they have cooled, I rub each one between thumb and forefinger until the seeds drop away. Then I put the cleaned raisins into a measure. It takes me all the afternoon to complete the task.

The next days are filled with new experience. I am up before dawn now to set the bread. The gentry always have the soft white manchet rolls for their breakfast. Mr. Serle shows me the canisters of spices that he uses. One morning half the breakfast rolls are flavored with the black spikes of caraway seed that look to me like mouse droppings but give a savory, salty odor to the rising dough. Another morning he directs me to add anise seed or the grated peel of orange and a handful of currants. Today as I knead the dough, he speaks in a longing voice of a substance called saffron that he says colors the bread a deep gold. It comes from little flowers that grow in the field, he says.

"Nothing else is like it, child," he tells me. "But it is expensive and hard to find. Not the kind of thing the merchants of Milford favor."

"One of those damned India curries," sneers Tom.

"No," says Mr. Serle in his calm voice, "saffron comes from Spain. Curry is entirely a different dish. It is very popular in London now."

I wonder if I will ever eat such a thing as saffron or curry. Already I know that if Tom despises something, it might be interesting. Mr. Serle seems to know everything and to despise nothing. He advises Mrs. Bennet, the pastry cook, on the use of leaves from the garden to flavor jellies and custards. I learn the words *rose geranium* and *nasturtium* and *sorrel*. Violets I already know, for my mother loved them. She had a handkerchief with a violet embroidered on it. But that is gone, burnt—no, I will not think of it. I knead the bread with all my might.

"Slow and steady." Mr. Serle has noticed my haste and rebukes me softly. "Find a rhythm, treat the yeast with respect and kindness."

They expect more work from me every day now. I retreat to the stable loft dead tired. The licking fires of the grill and the range and the stock boiler flicker in my mind as I ease myself into sleep. My foot aches still, and often that too keeps me awake even though my mind would sleep. It is harder and harder to be up as dawn breaks. One rainy morning I am fast asleep when day comes. Mr. Serle, I learn later, sends Tom over to the stable to rouse me.

I awaken to the sound of angry thumping on the ladder to my loft.

"Paddy! Hey, Paddy!" bawls Tom down below.

The horses stamp and turn in their stalls. Tom has found a metal pail and bangs it against the ladder. Sultan whinnies, a high, anxious sound. He will rear and kick in a moment. If he hurts himself, there is no knowing what will happen to us.

"Get down here," shouts Tom.

"I am hurrying. I am hurrying," I call in agitation. What if someone came up here? I thrust my legs into the trousers that I pulled off last night. It is too warm now to sleep in all my clothes. I pull my clean kitchen smock over my singlet and scramble down the ladder with my shoes and stockings in my hands.

"Lazy slob of an Irishman," Tom growls at me. "Making me come across the yard in the rain." Before I am aware it will happen, he lashes out with his hand and smacks me across the side of the head. I cry in pain. My ears ring.

Mr. Coates comes hurrying from the tack room at the other end of the stables. "Here, here," he intervenes. "Take your quarrels elsewhere. You are bothering the horses." He begins to soothe Sultan.

I limp across the yard behind Tom. In the warmth of the kitchen, Mr. Serle is kneading the manchet dough—my job. He looks at Tom and then at me as we come in. His gaze is steady as he turns his head slowly from Tom to me.

"Wash up before you work," he says to me in his quiet voice. His tone is neutral. I wonder what he is thinking.

I hurry to scrub myself in the scullery and then fall to work washing lettuces that are heaped in a wooden basket. When they are clean, I will shred them. Then Mr. Serle or Tom will cook them into soup. It will be on my poor head if the grit of sand rubs between the wooden stirring spoon and the bottom of the pot. My hands are soon red and aching in the icy water of the scullery sink.

Later in the morning we go out into the courtyard to sit in the sun for a few moments while we eat our breakfast. The rain has cleared, and I am ordered to wipe down the bench by the dairy so that Mr. Serle can sit in the sun. Mr. Serle loves the sun, I think, for he turns his dark face toward it and closes his eyes. It seems as if his face smooths out somehow when he turns it into the light. I look at the bread in my hand. The upset of the morning, the sting of Tom's hand, make it impossible to eat.

"Dreaming of the south?" says Tom in his rough voice. He takes a pull on his mug of ale.

"Perhaps," says Mr. Serle. "It is never warm enough for me."

"Lucky you work in a kitchen, then," Tom says. "That's warm enough, I hope."

"Indeed." Mr. Serle speaks absently, as if thinking of some other subject. His black eyes snap open and look at me. "It will not do," he says.

"What?" says Tom.

"The boy will have to sleep in the corner of my room. He won't be earning his wage if he is not awake to help at the beginning of the day."

I wonder that he uses the word *wage*. The place to sleep in the stable and food to eat were all that Mr. Coates offered when I came to this place. I suppose that is what Mr. Serle means too. There is so much food here. The servants eat as much as they want. The master would not give money as well.

"What do you think, lad?" asks Mr. Serle. "We will take you out of the stable loft and put you on the cot in the alcove of my room. I will wake you in the morning in good time to wash yourself and fetch the milk and knead the breakfast bread."

"But where is your room, sir?" I manage to squeak out. I had not thought of Mr. Serle sleeping anywhere. He was just there every morning in the kitchen, clean shaven, dressed in a spotless white jacket. Like a god in an old story, he happens when and where he is wanted.

Tom is looking from Mr. Serle to me with a strange smirk on his face. Then he laughs. "Not so smart, Paddy. Stupid as well as dirty-looking, aren't you?"

"Stop that," says Mr. Serle without changing his voice. "I sleep in the attic room above the scullery and the cold room, lad. It is a good space. It's quiet and the dawn light comes in. The kitchen chimney warms it. I will show you the stair that goes up beside the cold room when we go in. Which we must do." He rises abruptly. Tom and I follow him back inside. As I go, I put away into my smock pocket my chunk of bread. I will add it to my bag later. My appetite is gone, and I will choke if I try to swallow a morsel.

Tom, laughing at me, points out the narrow stair that goes up to the attic at the north end of the kitchen wing. The kitchen itself is a double height, so there is another stair to the longer room above the pantries where the women sleep. Tom has a bed in the men's attic with Mr. Serle, but he does not use it. He goes down to one of the cottages every night, where I think he must have a woman, for he says Dorcas's bed is warmer than any kitchen attic and winks at me. I am glad to learn that he will not be there. It is hard enough to think how I will manage.

When the valets have come to take the dinner down the stone passageway and up the stairs to the gentry, Mr. Serle tells me to go fetch any of my things that I have left in the stable loft. "Best go before dark, lad," he says. "I suppose you have a bundle there? You will want it with you."

In the stable loft I lower my bag from its hiding place in the rafters. I have nothing but my blanket and that. I hope that Mr. Serle will think my bag stuffed with clothing. I worry that it will be prey to mice in the new place, for I will have to hide it under the cot where I will sleep.

I worry less about how I will manage myself when I see the corner that will be my place. As Mr. Serle said, the attic is large, with windows along the eastern side and the great brick chimney on the southern end. Beside the chimney is my alcove. There is a cloth strung on a rope that turns the space into a little room. In the alcove is a cot with a straw mattress and a blanket over it. I will have two blankets now, I think. On the wall are two hooks for my things. That is all. It is enough.

There is a matching space on the other side of the chimney, where Tom can sleep if he stays here. I am relieved to see that Mr. Serle's bed is at the far end of the room under a dormer window. The first light of the sun must strike his face at dawn.

That night, we clean the kitchen as always and then climb the stairs to the attic. "Good night, lad," says Mr. Serle politely as if I were his guest in his great house. Perhaps I am.

The alcove is dark, and I miss the window of the stable loft through which I could watch the stars in the night sky. In the velvet black of this new space, I sink to my knees beside the bed and clasp my hands before me. My prayers come slowly. It is hard to be thankful, and yet this quiet corner, this bed, this place to work and earn my food are gifts. Under my fingers, the rough edges of the chipped glass beads of my rosary remind me that I am poor and a sinner. I arrange my brother's pants and jacket neatly on one hook. Before I hang my work trousers and smock on the other and climb into the bed, I check that my bag of bread is safely stowed. I pull my blanket over me, then settle on the straw mattress of my cot. I hear a soft murmuring sound. Mr. Serle must be talking to himself, I think.

I sleep, and the bad dream comes to me again. I walk from the door of our croft into the field that slopes to the south. The land is green, green, green, like a velvet gown laid over a curving body. In my dream I tread lightly on the soft surface. I feel the spring of grass beneath my bare feet. As I pace down the slope of the field, I feel the warmth of the sun on my face and arms. All is pale blue above, green below, and a fresh wind is blowing. I notice something growing in the field. Loaves of bread, golden-crusted. It is as if the corn had grown, been harvested, thrashed, ground, kneaded, baked all in a night—as if the bread grew ready to my hand and mouth directly from the earth. In my dream, as always, I smell the yeasty bloom and fall to my knees, mouth watering, guts cramped with hunger. I am eager to pluck and eat these magic mushrooms, brown-gold buttons on the green velvet field. I lay my hands reverently on a loaf and find that I hold stone. Appalled, I hold the heavy gray lump in my two hands. I will the stone to turn to bread again. But now instead I see the flesh wither away from my grasping fingers. Now the flesh is transparent, now gone completely. My hands are bleached skeletons, white bone. The stone I hold is a tiny tombstone. I scream and awaken in the dark.

"What is it, child?" The curtain between my corner and Mr. Serle's bedroom is thrust aside.

"Nothing," I say. "A bad dream." My face is wet. Perhaps I am crying.

"Come down into the kitchen," Mr. Serle says quietly. "The fire is dying yet. It will be warmer. Keep your blanket around your shoulders."

I follow him down the stairs and past the scullery. In the kitchen, he draws the hastener away from the fire and pulls two low stools from under the table by the east windows. He sets them before the fire and adjusts the screen behind us. Coals glow red in gray ash at the bottom of the firebox. We are in a small, protected world with warmth before us and the metal reflective screen of the hastener behind us, holding in the heat.

Mr. Serle goes away for a moment and returns with a mug. "We will warm some milk for you," he says, setting the mug on the range top to the left of the fire.

"I am not hungry," I tell him.

"You ate nothing at supper," he admonishes me quietly. "You will sleep more soundly if you have nourishment."

"I ate at noon dinner," I protest.

"A crumb of bread and a corner of cheese," he says. "You are thin as a broomstraw."

"I am sorry I cried out," I tell him. "Did I scream?"

"You shouted," he tells me. "You cried, 'Don't die! Don't die!' "

"I am sorry," I say. "Forgive me." I do not remember crying out in my dream, only the horror of my skeleton hand holding the tombstone.

I think I hear Mr. Serle catch his breath, but he speaks quietly to me. "And now," he says, "you awakened me from sleep. Before we rest again, you owe me a story."

"I do?" I am abashed. What can I say that will not multiply my danger?

Perhaps Mr. Serle senses my fear, for he speaks kindly to me. "Trust begins with knowledge," he says. "Begin at the beginning. Tell me of your family. Perhaps you need to speak of them."

My family, I think, and their faces rise to me. A picture comes into my head of my mother, sitting in her low chair by the turf fire, knitting and talking to my brother and to me as we sit at her feet. Her bright blue eyes look down at me, and in my mind I again touch the rough brown linen of her skirt. I will tell a story to satisfy Mr. Serle, I think. He is kind to me and I should offer something. Surely, it cannot be dangerous to talk of the distant past and of my parents. Retelling the stories they told us children brings them closer. And then a great need to speak presses on me. Words tumble out.

"My mother was born in the south of England," I say. "She grew up in Falmouth, raised by her aunt. Her own parents died of a sickness when she was very young. Her aunt was her mother's older sister, a fussy old maid who supported the child and an ancient grandfather by dressmaking and fancy needlework. My mother went to school and studied faithfully. Her aunt took her also to the houses of the gentry and taught her the craft of sewing and the refinement to talk to her betters with dignity. When my mother was fourteen, the grandfather died, and soon after the aunt took sick. There was no other family my mother knew of. Her mother's relatives were all scattered and gone, and her father's folk were seafaring people, she told me; she thought they left for the Americas as they could over the years. Certainly, there were none of my mother's name left in Falmouth when she wrote to the parish priest there three years back, searching desperately for friends who might help us in our time of trouble.

"My mother told me that her aunt was consumed with worry that, after her death, my mother would be left unprotected in the world. She appealed to the ladies of the family that had most favored her with their dressmaking trade. Just before the old aunt died, the family found a place for my mother as lady's maid to the oldest daughter, who was being married. The aunt gave my mother a teacup painted with roses that had belonged to her grandmother. My mother said she cried because she knew then that the aunt was really dying. She stayed with her to do what she could to ease her illness, but it was a hopeless case. So her aunt passed away easy in her mind, and my mother had a place."

I stop. Perhaps I am telling too much. I look at Mr. Serle.

"The aunt sounds like a good, conscientious woman," Mr. Serle says gently.

"Indeed, my mother thought so all her life," I reply. I want to tell someone that I treasure the gold ring with the red stone that my aunt gave to my mother as she lay dying and that my mother gave to me in like circumstance. I have the ring hidden about me even now. I remind myself I dare not, must not, say such things even to a man with a gentle voice and dark eyes that moisten with emotion and sparkle in the firelight.

Mr. Serle reaches over to see if the mug of milk is warm yet. "Tell me a little more," he says, "and then your drink will be ready."

"My mother did not greatly like the life of a lady's maid," I continue. "She was skillful enough in the sewing and washing and pressing and hairdressing that was required, but it was lonely. The woman she served was just in her ways but cold in manner. The household was a small one, just another maid with whom my mother shared a room, the valet for the husband, and the cook and her three assistants. My mother always said that the hardest thing was that she had no one to visit on her afternoon off. She would walk in the town and then go to the vespers service at the church. That gave her pleasure. She suffered also because the people she worked for were Protestants, and they required her to attend their morning prayers and to go to Sunday evening service at their church with the other servants. It made her angry, but she dared not speak for fear of losing her job."

I pause. Perhaps Mr. Serle is insulted or shocked. What do I know, after all, of the people in this household?

Mr. Serle says only, "It must have been hard for her. Go on." I look at him but I cannot see his face, only the dark crown of his head.

I pull my blanket tighter round my shoulders. The image of my mother talking rises in my mind again. I hear her words as if she herself speaks through me. "Her priest counseled her, she said. She must bear silently what she could not change, he told her. He asked her to visit a sick woman for him and read to her. My mother was glad to have a purpose beyond mending lace and visiting the graves of her dead family. The woman was educated, and so my mother read the Bible to her and history and improved her own mind.

"Just when my mother had begun to make a little life for herself, the family she worked for told her that they were going to live in Ireland on their estate there. At first my mother was heartbroken. No one would be left to tend the graves of her grandfather and her aunt, and she had become fond of the woman she read to. Her priest encouraged her, however. She was going to a Catholic country, after all. My poor mother believed she must go, for Falmouth offered little choice of work; in any case, she could see no way to seek another position without angering her present employer. They had helped when she was desperate. She believed it would be ungrateful to leave them."

"It is hard to leave one's native land," Mr. Serle says, "even if one was not always happy there." He stands suddenly, startling me, and stirs the milk. "It is almost ready," he says; he seats himself again.

I sigh and continue. "And so—she helped to pack the family's trunks and put her own few possessions into a lidded basket that had belonged to her aunt. To her surprise, she liked the land she went to. The country was green and beautiful and she found the native people kind. But the woman she served had bad luck there. She died giving birth to a daughter. The husband was angry. He blamed the Irish doctor. He blamed the Irish midwife. He conceived a hatred for the land and for the people. But he did not leave. My mother said that when he hated the place it was easier for him to make money there, to bleed it white.

"The man asked my mother to stay and to bring up the little girl. He said that at least she spoke like an Englishwoman and not in a barbarous country brogue. My mother was afraid that it was not right for her to stay in the household of that man, but what choice had she? She had only six months' wages due her and no one to go back to in England.

"In a few months she discovered that caring for the child gave her more freedom. The baby was healthy and grew robust. The wet nurse was, therefore, soon dismissed by the master, who refused to have Irish servants in his home unless there was dire need. He would have sent the child out to the nurse's cottage, but my mother told him that the place was dirty and that the baby would have slept with the pig and learned the local dialect at her nurse's breast. That was enough to make the man keep the baby in his house and to forbid the nurse to speak in the child's presence. And he instructed my mother to prevent the infant's crying at all costs. He said it hurt his ears."

"A hard master to serve," says Mr. Serle.

I shake my head. I see my mother's kindly, smiling look rebuking the thought that Mr. Serle has expressed. I feel I must say what she would say. "We children would cry out and say, what a bad man, but my mother said he was angry at the loss of his wife, not at the wet nurse. Only it was easier to curse those around him—maybe he wanted to curse God but dared not. The crying of the baby hurt his heart, not his ears, but he could not say it."

"I see," Mr. Serle murmurs.

"And it benefited my mother. She felt guilty about telling the tale of the wet nurse and the pig, even though it was the truth. But she could not be sorry at the result. It kept her with the child and gave her reason to be often out of the house. All the summer she would bundle up the infant and take it out of doors into the gardens and green byways of the estate. That is how she met my father. He was the head groom and was out at all hours. He drove the cart to the village for supplies too. So they would see each other and talk a little. And then he would take her into the town to buy things she needed for the baby. One day, she got up her courage and asked him if he would wait for her by the shops while she slipped into the church for a few minutes. She was afraid, you see, that her employer, who assumed she was a Protestant, would find out the truth.

"After that they were fast friends, and soon he asked her to marry him." I stop myself. I remember that the next thing my mother always said was that she loved him for all his kindness even though he had the reddest hair she had ever seen. Blazing it was, she would say, like the sun coming up on a hot morning before a thunderstorm. But this I dare not say aloud to Mr. Serle. Instead, I hurry on with my story.

"Her employer was angry at her for marrying. My mother had hoped that she might stay on as nursemaid to the child, for she loved the baby and the wages would have been welcome too. But her master was very angry. Angry that she wished to marry an Irishman and angrier still when he learned that she was a

Catholic. He tried to deny her the wages she had already earned on the excuse that she had lied to him, but there my mother bested him. She told him she had never lied, only not said all she knew, which was virtue in a servant; and she said he should be ashamed to treat the person who had cared for his own child like a mother in such a way. She reminded him that it was his dead wife who had hired her, not he. She said it was an insult to his wife's memory to treat her servant so.

"The man relented enough to give her her wages, but he gave nothing else. Of course, my father was still employed to care for the horses on the estate. He was needed too much then to be let go. After my parents were married by the parish priest, they were allowed to live in one of the estate cottages."

"And you were born soon thereafter," says Mr. Serle.

"Oh, no, sir," I respond. "My brother was born and then my sister. I am youngest of we three but taller than my sister." The memory of us standing back to back and laughing comes into my head. "No," I say and swallow hard to keep back the tears, "youngest of two. My sister died last year."

Mr. Serle sighs, a light breath, and says, "You were right as you first spoke. Youngest of three. The lost ones are never gone while we live; they stay with us."

His tone comforts me even though I am not sure what his words mean. Perhaps he believes in ghosts.

"Tell me more about your family," he says. He is looking at the dying fire; his eyelids are lowered, hooding his eyes from me. "Were you once happy, child?"

His question puzzles me. There is a longing in it that I do not understand. This man seems kind, but I have made mistakes before. And yet, despite my sorrows, his question makes me smile. Pictures rise between my tired eyes and the softly glowing grate. I am running eagerly after my brother and my sister and helping in the house—and the yard too, I remind myself. This childhood—it feels a hundred years ago although it is but two—seems safe to talk about, and so I tell him, "Yes, I was happy. We had a cow and later a horse. We all worked to grow the pota-toes and oats in our field. We grew wheat too for the estate. My mother sewed for the gentry after the master she had worked for married again. Even though the master was angry still, his wife liked my mother's skill. So there was money for my brother's schooling, a piece of stew meat, or good bacon for Sunday dinner.

"And then—" My voice catches in my throat as the pictures rise unbidden before my eyes. The hilled potato vines with their white and pink blossoms. Summer and heat and rain and the vines withering. My brother, his spade in his hand, shouting for my mother to come quickly. My mother seizing the spade and digging and digging and the black masses that we could not eat, stinking in the turned red-brown earth. And later my mother crouched, weeping, by the hearth with Eliza's head cradled in her arms while I sat in the doorway with my hands clenched tight to my belly to stop the ache there.

"Then?" Mr. Serle speaks doubtfully, as if he does not want to hear what then.

Suddenly I am angry. "Then?" My voice has risen, but I do not care. "Then the full force of the famine was on us. The potatoes in the earth and in the storage bin gone black and putrid. At first we bought food. There was little enough for sale, but we managed. Only the need grew around us. We were not the only ones frightened by it. The gentry who owned the estate on which we lived sold their horses and fled back to England, leaving my father a pittance for all his years of toil and the empty promise of work if they returned. Now we had nothing to eat and my father desperate. My sister ill and dying and no medicine to help her. The estate manager at the big house doled out thin soup on Tuesdays and demanded the rent same as ever. When the people gave up and left for America, he was glad. We saw it."

"America," Mr. Serle says in his quiet voice. I wonder if he is listening to me now or deep in some dream of his own. He sighs and, rising, pokes at the fire to start a flicker of orange flame. He shifts the mug of milk to catch the dying warmth. "It is almost ready," he says, and then repeats as if to himself, "America." He sits. He turns a little toward me. His face looks kind in the dim light. "Your people thought of America?"

"Everyone in the village talked of America," I tell him.

"There was food there and land for the asking, they said. Letters came back from the brave ones that ventured first. One by one the families began to pack up their things and to go. There were more and more empty cottages along the lane. When at last the priest himself began to talk of taking the rest of his flock and beginning new in New York City or Boston maybe, my parents decided we must all go too. Only my mother was so weak, you see. Nursing Eliza and grieving for her had worn her thin as thread. When my brother and I talked about it later, we understood too that she had starved herself to save us."

"A good mother," Mr. Serle interjects. I nod, speechless, as the tears stand again in my eyes.

"My father gave up his pint of ale on Saturday night, my mother sold the sheep to buy us food. And then, just when we were packed to go, the cow sold away to my mother's sorrow, my parents both fell ill with fever." I stop. I cannot go on. My mother, her beautiful face sunk in, her eyes wild, holding my hand, crying to me—promise me, promise me—but what it was I can never know.

"They died," I say. "My brother and I could not save them." The image of my brother holding a cup of water to my father's lips rises to me. My brother's hand is shaking. The water spills on my father's throat. My father's red-gold hair that blazed with life is dull and dingy gray.

"It is too terrible to say," I whisper. "We buried them, and the landlord's men came and burned the cottage."

The pictures in my mind flicker and flame. I try to turn my head away from them, but they persist. I can shake my head frantically and squeeze my eyes tight shut, but still the flames burn up through the thatched roof and smoke spreads a black hand out from the empty doorway. Mr. Serle's hand on my arm brings me back to the kitchen and the hearth. I am trembling and tears run down my cheeks, but my heart steadies. I take a breath and sigh.

"Enough for one night, child," says Mr. Serle. "You are tired and the milk is hot for you. Drink it and you will sleep. The world serves the bread of affliction to us all. Rest. Sorrow will keep until tomorrow." He takes the mug from the range beside the dying coals and a fork from the hearth where he laid it ready. He whisks the liquid to a froth.

I bow my head and drink the sweet, hot milk. We are silent in the firelight for a space of time. The fire is all but dead now. In a few hours it will be tepid ash, and Tom will sweep out and polish the grate and build a new fire. Mr. Serle rubs his cheek where black stubble shows and then speaks.

"Our griefs take time to mend, lad. Let it rest for now." Mr. Serle stands and stretches. "To bed. You are young, but I am old and need what sleep I can still steal from the night."

"Yes," I murmur, sleepy now at last, and drain the dregs of sugar in the bottom of the mug.

We climb the dark and narrow stairway, and I sleep sound behind the curtain until Mr. Serle calls me back to work in the gray light of the dawn.

CHAPTER III

SOME MORNINGS I awaken only when Mr. Serle calls to rouse me. Sometimes I awaken on my own and lie still under the blanket listening to the sounds of the outer room. Mr. Serle talks to himself in the morning. It sounds like a foreign language to me. The rhythms of the speech are like the pattern the priest makes mumbling the prayers in Latin perhaps, but when I listen for a familiar word—a *gratia Deo,* or an *ave Maria,* or an *in nomine Patris*—I hear strange sounds only, nothing familiar. Sometimes I think I hear an *amen* just as the sounds cease; I am not sure.

One morning at dawn, as the words begin, I slip from my bed and creep to the cloth that protects my corner. I will twitch the hanging aside, I think, and see what Mr. Serle is doing. To my disappointment, there is little to see. Mr. Serle stands facing the window, his back to me. I think he may hold a book in his hand, but his body is turned so that I cannot be sure, and the ray of summer sunshine striking into the room makes his form a silhouette. His face is turned to the light, which gilds his throat above the open collar of his shirt. Perhaps he is praying or speaking his thoughts to the morning sun. There is a private feeling about him, and I am ashamed. His secrets are not my business any more than I would have mine be his. When he calls me to get up, I am curled in my bed pretending to be asleep.

"Wake up, child," he says in his usual voice. "Wake up. The day is fine and clear. When the breakfast bread is made, you have new lessons to begin. One of the maids left yesterday; you must begin to assist Mrs. Bennet with the pastry-making."

"I am ready in a moment," I say, trying to sound sleepy. As his footsteps retreat to the stairs, I peek under the bed to be sure my bag is where it ought to be, safe with its freight of bread. This is my ritual every morning. I have not added to my store for several days, but still I look first in the morning and last at night to be sure of it. There is no sign of mice. And so I pull on my smock and hurry down to wash and begin my tasks.

I learn this morning that I have a gift for sugar. Over the next month under Mrs. Bennet's tutelage, sugar becomes my love, my passion. The great cone of the stuff rests on its own tray in the pantry. I go in with my basin and use the steel pincers to gnaw off some lumps. Then with my knife I chip and chop until the basin is filled with crystalline pebbles. In the pantry, I crush the sugar to a fine powder using the tray and the roller designed for the purpose.

At the stove, I work alchemy. I see sugar dissolve; I smell its change from sandy grains to white glass to molten caramel; I pour it out onto a square of white marble set into the pantry counter and let it cool; I pull it into ropes of taffy, color it, cut it, set fancy twists in little paper cases; I mix cakes, drizzle flavored syrups into the warm crumb, and ice the tops with a glossy polish of sugar and egg white; I sugar fruit peels and violets and rose petals. The fruit and flowers remain sweet and tender in their crystal coats. Sugar and I understand each other.

And yet, I cannot bear to eat the stuff. Mrs. Bennet insists that I must taste what I make. She says that I must learn to judge the balance of sweet and salt; the texture of custards and syrups must be silky smooth on the tongue. The only way to learn, she says, is to know with the mouth as well as with the hands. I resist more than the merest drop. The aromas of the stuffs I work with delight me; to eat as well would be a surfeit, gross and unnecessary.

The pantry where I work with Mrs. Bennet is quiet. We hear the clatter and movement in the main kitchen as distant action even though it is just next door. The pantry has a range with a small fire under it, but the great grills and the turning spit jacks of the main kitchen are not needed here. I am glad to be away from the roar of the fires and the whistle of wind and heat in the chimneys. Even though the hasteners shield the working areas of the kitchen from the heat of the fires and the sight of the licking flames, I feel fear there when I must help to shift a roast or set a baking pan in a hot oven. Indeed, if it were not for Mrs. Bennet, I could be content with my new work.

Mrs. Bennet is a stout woman who bulges in her clothes like sausage stuffed into a casing. Her small features are pinched in the center of her broad face. She moves swiftly and efficiently about the room, light on her feet and breathing through her mouth. When she rolls the sleeves of her blue work dress to keep them away from the pastry, I can see that the skin of her forearms is smooth and hairless, but freckled faintly. Her hands are pink and plump, her fingers deft and strong as she crimps the fancy crust around a pie.

When the morning's work is done, she sighs heavily and eases herself down into a chair. She fans herself with her apron even though the room is not hot.

"Now, lad," she says, motioning me to pull the three-legged stool from under the counter and to seat myself on it. "Now, lad, we deserve a little refreshment before we make the cakes."

Leaning sideways, she makes her chair creak as she reaches in to a shelf where baking tins and fancy molds are kept. She brings out a squat dark-brown glass bottle. "Here, Paddy," she says, pulling the cork. "Here's our reward for a good morning's work." She tips the bottle at her lips.

"You worked hard enough, lad. You deserve a nip," she says, and passes the bottle to me.

I sniff at it suspiciously. Strong fumes rise to my nostrils. It smells like the whiskey my father drank to celebrate when his horse won a good race, but it is not whiskey. This is stronger, more pungent even. "It's good black rum, lad," Mrs. Bennet says impatiently. "If you don't want it, I won't waste it on you. What are you? One of them Evangelicals?"

The anger in her voice makes me feel that I must join her or risk her rejection of me. I tip the bottle cautiously at my lips, thinking to take the least possible taste. My caution is my undoing. A quick, short pull would have been smarter. The liquid spills from the bottle—a little into my mouth, a little on my smock. The hot strength of it makes me cough and sputter.

"What!" exclaims Mrs. Bennet, seizing the bottle from me before I can drop it. "You are wasting the good stuff, boy."

"I never had spirits before," I say as meekly as I can between gasps. "It took me by surprise." I do not like the taste of the rum in my mouth and, therefore, summon courage. "Best not to waste it on me in the future," I say boldly.

Mrs. Bennet thinks this is funny. She laughs loudly and then rocks back in her chair and tilts the bottle to her lips again. "Never fear, Paddy. I'll not waste a drop. But I thought you Irish had a liking for the stuff."

"Perhaps some do," I say, "but it is sorrow that draws them to the spirits as much as a liking for the taste of it." My mother used to say this to me, and now the thought of her and my loneliness in this strange place fills me with sadness. The sweet smell of the baking makes an emptiness in my heart.

Mrs. Bennet must notice my expression, for she says sharply, "Don't be so down in the mouth, boy. And don't you go tattling that I need a drop of medicine now and then to help the pain in my legs."

I learn quickly that Mrs. Bennet needs the help of her bottle all day long. First it is to prevent the pain from coming in her legs and then to counteract its presence. By the afternoon the bottle helps her to forget the intensity of the aches that assail her. The more she takes, the more unpredictable she becomes. What she finds uproariously humorous at noon causes her to flush red with anger at sunset.

"The Lord preserve me," I exclaim when a boiling syrup spits a hot drop onto my hand. I move the pot from the heat and run to plunge my hand into cold water.

"What Lord is that, you young blasphemer," says Mrs. Bennet. "You're one of these Papists, aren't you?" She rocks in her chair and takes another nip from her bottle. "I don't like your kind. Sell us all to the priests and the Pope, you will."

"I don't think—" I begin timidly.

"That's it," she interrupts me. "Not allowed to think. Did your mother teach you these wrong ways?"

I want to say my mother taught me only good, but Mrs. Bennet is not listening.

"I have a good mind to take you along to the chapel with me on my next afternoon," she grumbles. "That'll show you good Christian worship."

I think I have an answer for this. "I don't have an afternoon off, Mrs. Bennet. Only Sunday mornings, and then I have to go to the chapel with the other servants."

This statement does not mollify Mrs. Bennet. She begins a long complaint about the Papists and the price of corn, which I do not understand. She is angry also that Mr. Serle is chief cook, not she. A foreigner, she calls him. Perhaps a Papist, perhaps something worse, she mutters, tilting her bottle. I open my mouth to question her and then think better of it. I must stay quiet. Suddenly she is in a good humor again. When I pass close by her chair, she reaches out and pinches my arm.

"You are getting stronger, boy," she says, "and a very little fatter. Feeding on the fat of the land and hardly doing a day's work for it."

Tears sting my eyes, but I know better than to argue with her. Mrs. Bennet has good days and bad days. This afternoon she will pull on her bottle and then fall into a snoring sleep until I waken her to look at the pies. Tomorrow she may be bustling and jovial, teaching me new recipes and cursing her bunions only occasionally. I must let her be and do the work as best I can.

One afternoon, as I stir the custard that will fill a pie, she notices—or pretends to notice—that a flake of black has fallen from my hair onto the pastry she is rolling out.

"What is wrong with you, Paddy?" she shouts at me. "Do you have lice or some scrofulous disease that you must grease your hair? I could swear, indeed, that you rub soot in it, it's that filthy. Here, come here."

She takes the wet cloth she keeps at hand to wipe up spills and reaches to seize me. I think she wants to wash my face and head. I dodge away quickly. Pans clatter as I bump against the counter. Mrs. Bennet shouts "Stop!" at me.

"What is the trouble here?" Mr. Serle is standing in the doorway.

"The nasty lad is dirtying my clean pantry." Mrs. Bennet is red-faced with anger. "I won't have it any longer."

Mr. Serle looks at me appraisingly. "Indeed, he is dirtier than usual today. Come with me, lad."

I follow him out of the pantry, relief at escaping Mrs. Bennet mixed with fear of what Mr. Serle will do to me.

"This way," he says mildly, and leads me through the kitchen toward the scullery. Tom, ladling stock over a pair of ducks turning on a spit, looks curiously at us as we pass. "I will be right there," Mr. Serle says. "Reset the bottle jack, please; it's almost run down."

We pass the wet larder, where one of the maids is washing vegetables. "Here," Mr. Serle indicates, and we go into the scullery, where water simmers in the great boiler.

"You must take more care to be clean." Mr. Serle faces me, his fists on his hips. "Mrs. Bennet is a sot, but she is a great pastry cook when she is sober. Learn from her and do not distress her with your slovenly personal habits."

"I—" I want to speak in my own defense, but I can think of nothing to say that will not betray me.

Mr. Serle eyes me sternly but speaks gently. "I think you need more than the cold water from the pump in the mornings. Come in here and take warm water and soap in a basin. Then use this cloth to rinse your face and neck." He hands me a clean rag, which I take stupidly, not knowing what else to do. He does not seem to expect me to speak. "And if you are not willing to wash that dreadful spiky hair of yours, bind it up in a clean head cloth."

"I do not have such a thing," I say in despair.

Mr. Serle sighs deeply. "You are a sad case, lad. Now, wash while I go find something for you."

Tentatively I choose a basin and draw some hot water from

the spigot of the boiler. I temper it with cold water from the sink and rub the rag on the cake of yellow soap on the scullery sink. I am wiping the back of my neck when Mr. Serle returns.

"That's right, child," he says approvingly. "When you are done, rinse your washing cloth and hang it here behind the boiler. I have found you a cloth to wrap your head." He hands me a dark blue kerchief.

"Like this," he says impatiently, and shows me how to fold and tie it. "Now go back and get to work."

Mrs. Bennet makes a sort of "Garumph" sound in her throat when I return. But she does not mention my dirtiness again. Not so with Tom, who comments on my new head cloth and pretends to check my neck for a dirt line when I come into the kitchen with a meat pie to be baked in the big range.

"Let me just check that pastry for soot," he says, seizing my arm to stop me. I almost drop the heavy pie dish. "The gentry won't want to eat the nits from your head."

"Leave the lad alone," Mr. Serle says. "You have your own work to attend to, Tom. I need the fire stronger in the south grill. You have the north one going well. I need the other as hot."

The kitchen is flanked by the two great fires with their chimneys and their smoke jacks that turn the spits and their ranges set into the wall. The tall hasteners, with their compartments for dishes that are being kept warm, shield the room from the heat of the fires. Often, only the fire on the north wall is lit. In the warm weather many of the dinner dishes are cooked early in the day and served cold. The meat pie that I carry, for example, is to be baked today and kept overnight in the cold room. The gentry will carry it with them to eat at a lunch by the river tomorrow. They are having a fishing party. Or so Mrs. Bennet tells me.

Tom has laid the fires early in the morning and lit the north one at dawn. Now he fusses with the damper in the chimney on the south wall.

"Did you bring in apple wood?" Mr. Serle asks him. "I need a sweet-wood fire to grill ducks."

Tom mutters to himself and goes out to the yard to bring in

a fresh load of wood. The coal fire burns hot for roasting beef, but Mr. Serle likes wood for cooking poultry, he says. I set the pie carefully into the range oven, turning my face to the side to avoid the heat. When I step back my heart is racing. I walk carefully toward the pantry.

"Note the time, child. Note the time," Mr. Serle reminds me. He keeps a slate on the wall and three big hourglasses in the center of his worktable.

"Where the devil are the lucifers, Paddy?" growls Tom, who has returned with the wood.

"Lucifers?" I say, turning to him in panic. I feel stupid. What does he mean? The name frightens me; I have not heard it spoken since the priest at home shouted sternly from his lectern one Sunday service about the fall from grace. What can Tom mean? What does he want? I am already afraid of Tom, with his cold blue eyes in an egg-white face. If he were in league with the devil himself, it would not surprise me.

"He means the lights for the fire, lad," says Mr. Serle. "The tin box and the sandpaper should be always in the drawer of the dresser by the left-hand window. Go fetch them."

I do as I am told and hand the things to Tom, who takes them without speaking to me. Of course I have seen the tin box in Tom's hands before. I just never thought of what he was doing. Now I watch as he drags the end of a wooden splint along a coarse sand-coated paper. The wood flares into fire and a strange, pungent smell comes to me. Tom, holding fire at the end of his fingers, sets the straw and kindling alight in the grate under the logs he has laid there.

Mr. Serle laughs at me. His fine brows arch and his black eyes sparkle. "Your mouth is wide open, boy," he says. "Have you never noticed the lucifer lights before?"

I shake my head. "Never," I admit.

Tom laughs loudly. "Let me show you the miracle," he says, and drags another stick along the paper. It makes a scratching sound like a mouse in the wall and then flares alight with a pop. Tom moves toward me with the fire in his hand. "I'll wager that greasy hair of yours will make a fine torch," he says.

"God save me," I cry.

"And what god would that be, Paddy?" says Tom. "The Pope? Or are you seeing the fires of hell in this flaming stick?" He moves it toward my head.

I cower to my knees, covering my head with my arms. "The saints spare me," I cry. Tears wet my face.

"Paddy wants a priest," jeers Tom. "Confess your sins to me, boy. I'd like to hear what a sly sprout like you could be up to."

"Enough," says Mr. Serle.

"The lad's a coward and a dirty Papist," Tom sneers, but, to my relief, he turns and drops the burning stick into the fire behind him.

Slowly, I rise and retreat toward the door. If Tom lights another of those lucifers, I will flee to the yard outside. But Tom seems to have lost interest in me for the time being. He is busy adding the apple-wood logs to his fire now that the kindling has caught.

"Don't forget to come back in half an hour to check that the pie is baking evenly," Mr. Serle says. "Tom will see that the fire is kept up." Then Mr. Serle, to my relief, wheels the hastener between Tom and me. I slip off to the pantry to help Mrs. Bennet crimp the edges of the almond tarts.

That night, after the scullery is clean and Tom has gone off whistling to his bed in the village, Mr. Serle and I set out the clean utensils ready for the cooking of breakfast.

Mr. Serle is silent for some time, and then, "You are afraid of fire, aren't you, lad?" he asks suddenly.

My heart turns over in my chest. But before I can speak he says, "Or perhaps you are afraid of Tom?"

I am relieved. This does not have to lead into dangerous paths. "I am afraid of Tom," I say, relieved to put it into words. "I think he does not like Irish people."

"I think you are right," says Mr. Serle dryly. "Have you met many such in your short life?" he adds.

"Not so many," I say. "There was the man my mother worked for before I was born. My father worked for him too. It was cruel when the master took away his work. The master came by our cottage once, riding his black horse, but he never spoke to me. I peeped from behind the door and saw him. He was dark as the devil himself. He could have been a Jew or a gypsy even."

Mr. Serle sighs and sets his knives out in a row before the wooden board he uses for chopping. "Do you miss your religion, lad?" he says.

"Yes," I say. "I do not like the prayers with the gentry here. We just stand like cattle while the master reads the scripture. It does not seem real." My mind reaches out to the stone-built church and my parents' graves beside it. Perhaps green grass is grown over the raw earth there. "I wish I had a priest to go to as my mother did when she was young."

"Perhaps you can go into Milford one day," says Mr. Serle.

I look at him suspiciously. "I would not tell the gentry here that I only pretend to listen to their prayers. They might send me away, and then how will I eat?"

"Perhaps one day when I have business in Milford, I will take you with me." Mr. Serle is looking at me in a considering way. His black eyes gleam. "You can see the town and find a priest if that suits you. I will not tell what you do if you keep my secrets in return."

I wonder if he is joking. What secrets would I keep for Mr. Serle? He is looking at me. I must speak. "I am afraid of the town," I say. There are reasons for that I cannot confess to Mr. Serle, so I cast about for some explanation that will satisfy him. "There are bad people in the town," I say. "Gypsies, or worse. Even Jews." What are his secrets? I wonder. What does he want of me? I must be careful.

"What do you know of Jews, lad?" Mr. Serle seems to be looking dreamily at the dying coals of the fire. His eyelids droop down, and his dark eyelashes rest against the line of his cheek.

"They killed our Lord," I say earnestly, remembering the words of the priest telling the story of the crucifixion. "And my father said they do all manner of evil. They hoard money that they get by cheating and stealing. They pretend to be good, but in secret they mock religion. They say that they even kill babies for their rites."

"Did you ever see a Jew?" Mr. Serle speaks mildly. His face is turned further away; I cannot see his expression.

"Once," I say. "My mother warned me about him. And to stay away from the gypsies at the fair also." And then I wonder. "How can I know if I saw others?" I feel like crying. "I never heard of anyone complaining that their baby disappeared." I realize suddenly that this is true. "Perhaps no Jews live in Ireland."

"They only visit for the fairs?" he says. I think Mr. Serle might be making a joke, but I don't understand it. He picks up the poker and breaks apart the last coals in the grate. The fire is almost dead now. "Do you ever feel a doubt that—" Mr. Serle stops abruptly. "Never mind," he says. "Never mind. It is time to sleep. Go to your rest, lad. I will call you at dawn."

I am relieved to leave an unpleasant subject. Mr. Serle lets me climb the stairs alone. He has to stir a marinade for a spiced beef, he says. He does not speak to me again that night.

CHAPTER IV

SOME PEOPLE have a foolish way of not minding, or pretending not to mind, what they eat. For my part, I mind my belly very studiously, and very carefully; for I look upon it that he who does not mind his belly will hardly mind anything else." Mr. Serle tells Tom that is a quotation from Dr. Samuel Johnson. Tom grunts and plugs his mouth with a slice from a great ham that has just been taken from the meat keeper in the cold room and will go up to the dining room to sit on the sideboard for the gentry's breakfast. Tom takes his breakfast on the move, and Mr. Serle does not rebuke him. Indeed, the kitchen is so busy that all take their meals as they can find a moment.

Mr. Serle himself drinks coffee mixed with hot milk in the mornings and eats a manchet roll from yesterday sprinkled with sugar and toasted at the fire. When the weather is fair, he crosses the dooryard and sits on the bench against the dairy wall to feel the sun on him as he drinks his coffee.

Each morning, after I have set the dough for the manchet rolls, I usually eat bread with a morsel of cheese. Sometimes, if the bad dreams have plagued me all the night, I have no appetite for anything at all. Like Tom, I drink a mug of ale in the morning. The servants eat their dinners at noon at the big table in the housekeeper's room. Tom says that when the family is away, the servants who are left often eat in the kitchen because it makes less work. Mrs. Bennet eats well at noon and so does Tom, but Mr. Serle does not join them. I must go sometimes, for Mr. Serle sends me to carry the stew or the meat pies, but I usually slip away to be outdoors. I do not desire anything to eat until evening when the work is done. Then I cut a wedge of pie or drink some soup left over from the gentry's dinner. Sometimes the image of my mother's starving face rises in my mind, and then I am too sad to eat. Even so, I can see that I am gaining flesh. My arms are rounder; the bones of my wrists no longer make great knobs under thin skin. I notice even that my legs are lengthening; I will be almost as tall as my brother soon. I roll my trouser cuffs two turns now, not three.

In the morning while Mr. Serle sings his muttered song by his window, I look at my foot to see if it is better. The bruise has faded to pale yellow, but the toenail on my little toe seems twisted. Often the foot hurts in the evening as I help to scrub the pots and clean the tables. But it is true also that I forget the hurt for hours each day. Perhaps I will be ready to ride soon and can ask to try my old job again. I slip out sometimes to pet Gytrash. I miss the smell of the stable. I lean my head against Gytrash's smoky flank and think of my brother. After, I must be sure to wash my hands well under the pump in the yard or Mr. Serle will scold me.

"Clean yourself, lad. Keep the stable in the stable. Bring only clean hands into my kitchen."

"Your kitchen," Tom snorts rudely. "The gentry upstairs would have you out the door if they heard you say that."

"Good cooks are not so easy to find these days," Mr. Serle replies mildly. "And it is my duty to make the rules here." There is a silence, and then he adds, "Good cooking depends on consistency, and consistency is achieved by setting down a rule and obeying it."

Mr. Serle keeps a book in which he writes each evening what he has cooked that day. Tom laughs behind his back and says that Mr. Serle wants to be famous like Soyer. I have never heard of Soyer, and Tom says he is a famous London cook who wrote a book and is a fool for thinking he can feed the poor. "The poor are always with us and always hungry," Tom says. "That is their fate."

The kitchen is warm and full of life but not so safe for me as the stable. There are too many people in the kitchen, and they look too sharply at me when the work is slow. While we are waiting for a syrup to boil, Mrs. Bennet nips from her bottle and questions me about my family. I avoid answering her as best I can. I do not like to lie outright. Usually I can deflect her into complaints about how hard she works and how her legs are swollen again today. I am more afraid of Tom, who teases me every day now about my dirty hair even though I bind my head carefully in my kerchief.

The truth is, I do take grease from the rendering pot that Mr. Serle keeps on the back of the range. In a small square of cloth that I keep for the purpose, I rub a pinch of soot from the brickwork above the fire and a daub of grease together. Alone in the privy every morning, I rub the cloth thoroughly over my head. Next, I bind my blue kerchief carefully about my head. Then I wash my face and hands under the cold water of the pump. When I come into the scullery, I take the cloth that Mr. Serle gave me from behind the boiler and moisten it with hot water. Again I wipe my face. I rebind the kerchief about my head. I wipe my face again; this time I can go right to the edges of the kerchief. Finally I wash my hands and forearms in the hot water at the sink. I have to be careful that no trace of soot remains on my hands.

Susan, the girl at the inn in Liverpool—Susan, to whom I owe my freedom—showed me what to do and gave me the little cloth, which first had soot from her lamp. "Your hair will give you away," she said. "That red-gold flames like sunset on a summer evening. Everyone who has seen it will remember it and you. Walnut juice is better to hide it than soot," she told me, "but where can we find walnut juice in the middle of the night at an inn by the Liverpool docks?" She comforted me when I cried that the soot would rub off and I would be found out. "The soot is better," she said. "It will be easy to find wherever you go. Also, you can wash it from your hands. Walnut juice stains what it touches, and then your hands would give you away."

I wonder if Susan would tell me to trust Mr. Serle. She told me not to tell Mr. Coates the truth, and he is her uncle. He will not understand, she said; best to work and gain his trust. When she comes to the country for her days of rest in the late summer, she will help me find a next step, she promised. I think that I will be glad to see Susan again, and I wonder when she will come.

It is strange, I think, that I knew Susan for just a few hours of one night. We did not even speak as normal people do; we conversed in whispers. Yet she is as vivid in my mind as anyone I have known. Her thick brown hair pulled back into a plait, her blue kerchief, her brown eyes clear and flashing almost golden in the firelight, her bristling eyebrows—she had a fierce, frank look. With the poker in her hand she might have been a knight ready to go into battle.

My mother once told me that we all have angels in our lives; some we recognize, some we never see. She said that such angels are a gift to us to help us find the way to safety. The priest at Falmouth was an angel to her, she said, helping her to keep her faith and to find hope through service. She thanked him in her prayers always. It strikes me then that I have not said my prayers in at least two weeks.

So before I climb into my bed, I kneel beside it and clasp my hands. I pray that the souls of my mother and father and my sister, Eliza, will watch over me from heaven. I think that heaven must be warm and sweet-smelling, like a kitchen where cakes are baking. I pray that I will see my brother again in this world. I pray that Susan is safe and well and that I may see her to thank her for helping me. I hold my rosary and say a Hail Mary and ask for a blessing.

Afterward I fold my shirt and place it under my pillow. I lie under the blanket, sleepy, holding the lump in the linen that is the ring my mother wore. To hold it is to touch her hand in thought. I hear Mr. Serle come up the stairs and move about the room beyond my curtain. Tomorrow night I will pray for Mr. Serle too. Can I trust him? I wonder. It would be like drinking clear water to sit with a friend and tell what has happened and ask for advice. How can I search for my brother? Mr. Serle might know what to do. Or Susan. And Susan would know how I can best protect myself from Tom and his teasing. Thinking of her flashing eyes under the thick eyebrows and her decisiveness as she tells me what to do and where to go, I fall asleep. In the morning I awaken from a dream in which her voice whispers in my ear, *Hope!*

It is raining. The sound of water tapping on the roof and dripping from the eaves blurs everything. Heard under the pour of water, Mr. Serle's voice mutters in the room. The sound rises and falls like a song. Mr. Serle is saying his prayers. The thought comes unbidden into my mind. I know this and have known it for some time. What will I do with the knowledge? I ask myself. The answer is easy. Nothing. The strange language puzzles me, but I will not dare to question him.

Perhaps Mr. Serle is suspicious of me, for he looks at me oddly when I come into the kitchen from the scullery.

"You are not clean, lad," he says. He sounds annoyed, which is not like him. I have become accustomed to his calm and neutral tone.

"But—" I begin. I want to tell him that I have washed, just as he told me to.

"You have a smudge on your forehead," Mr. Serle says. "One would think you rolled in the ashes during the night. Go back and wash properly. Use hot water and soap this time."

I stomp out in a sulk. Mr. Serle does not like me. When I return, Tom is in the kitchen, wielding a butcher knife to mince beef for rissoles and complaining loudly.

"Rain, I hate the rain in summer," he says. "I was soaked coming up the lane."

"The farmers will be glad," I say. It is tiresome to agree with Tom no matter what he says. I hate myself for being afraid of him. I want to say that he is the better for a good rinsing off in the rain, but that would be provoking him too much. My little daring does not matter anyway, for Tom is not listening.

"They say that the gentry are going up to London soon," he says greedily. "They will take some of us with them."

"Why is that?" says Mr. Serle. He does not sound very interested; I guess he is being polite. Not that Tom would notice or care. He is wrapped up in his own thoughts.

"They need all hands for dinners and entertainment parties and such. The daughter is all of seventeen now and the old folk are looking out for a husband for her."

"And you are going to help?" Mr. Serle snorts derisively and stirs his sauce. I watch him make a deliberate pattern: twice around the edge going right, then a figure eight across the middle, then twice around going left, then repeat. He catches my eye and, to my surprise, his dark lashes flicker down over his bright right eye. Startled, I realize he has winked at me.

"London," says Tom. "I must see London. Think of the fancy carriages and the people and the heaps of food and money. I could ride around on the back of the carriage when Miss goes calling. They might give me a livery. I am tall enough to look well in a livery." He straightens his back and sucks in his stomach.

"May you have joy of it," Mr. Serle says, still stirring the pot on the stove.

"Don't you want to be in London instead of in this dead place?" Tom demands.

"I have seen London," Mr. Serle says mildly. He seems to be in a good mood now. "And Paris too."

"Is that where you were born?" I cannot repress my curiosity.

"He was born in Rome," says Tom, interrupting. "You would not know it from the smooth way he speaks; people around here think he's a Londoner, or a French cook, but I know better."

"Rome?" I make myself breathe slowly. "Did you see his Holiness the Pope himself?" Once, when the bad times began at home, I asked my mother why the Pope, who is the shepherd of us all, did not send food to help us. She answered in an angry voice that I must never be disrespectful of the Church. We are its children, she said; we do not question the wisdom of those who speak to God.

"The Pope?" sneers Tom before Mr. Serle can speak. "What would Mr. Serle care about a pope?"

Mr. Serle knits his brow and glowers. I am afraid that I have put him back into a sour mood. Yet when he speaks there is a sadness in his voice. "I am no Papist, Paddy. Not all the people of Rome have reason to love your Pope."

I feel hurt, but it takes a moment for me to absorb why. Then it strikes—he rarely calls me Paddy. He must be very angry. I tell myself not to think about it. Mr. Serle is not a bad man. It does not sound as if he hates the Pope even if he does not exactly love him either. I wish I could ask him, however, if he is English born in Rome by chance or native to the place, and if so, why he would not care about the Pope.

"You love the Pope, don't you, Paddy?" Tom is staring at me.

"Why, I do not know," I say, surprised into honesty. "I hardly know about him. Only he did not send help to us when we were hungry at home. Perhaps he did not know."

Tom and Mr. Serle both laugh at this. I do not know why it should be funny. It is just the truth.

When Mr. Serle moves the pot he has been stirring from the range to the table and goes down the corridor to speak to Mrs. Bennet, Tom begins again. "Did you serve in the church, Paddy?" Tom asks. "You look innocent enough, but I'll wager you were the priest's fancy boy just the same." I am bewildered by the anger in his voice and by his words, which make no sense to me.

Mr. Serle returns and spares me more teasing by asking Tom whether the forcemeat is ready for stuffing the fish. "Pay attention to this way of preparing the whole pike," he says. "It is fashionable in London."

"London," Tom sighs gustily. "What I would give to see London."

"You can see Mary in London," I tell him. "She said she was going there to work in a great house."

"Mary!" jeers Tom. "What would I want with her?" And then he turns to his work.

"Doesn't Mrs. Bennet need you, lad?" says Mr. Serle. Obedient to the command that I hear underneath his mild question, I hurry to the pantry.

I find Mrs. Bennet making a short paste. Usually she likes to do this herself, because the pastry must be rolled and then layered with sweet butter and then rolled again and allowed to rest. While the pastry rests between the turns of rolling and buttering, Mrs. Bennet rests too; she nips at her bottle as she tells me what cream custards and pie fillings to prepare. The rain has made her grumpy, however.

"No sugar confits today," she says, "and no Italian meringue for the queen cake. They will have to have powdered sugar and be done with it."

"Why not?" I ask. I like boiling the syrup for the meringue and beating it into the egg whites in the copper bowl. It is slow work that passes the time quietly.

"The rain, idiot, the rain!" says Mrs. Bennet, pulling on her bottle. "You can never make the sugar come right in this damp. The icing would be grit in their teeth. It's as much as my job. And them taking me to London to be the pastry cook for the big parties."

"So you and Tom will both go?" It seems too much to hope for.

Mrs. Bennet snorts derision at the suggestion. "Tom?" she says. "They don't want that lad after the maids. You know they only hire the pretty girls in London. No, our Tom will be here as usual."

"And Mr. Serle?" I ask.

"Mr. Serle was asked to go and refused them, I hear," says Mrs. Bennet. "He gave the excuse that he was ill in London, and the doctors told him to stay where the air is good. He threatened he would find other employment, I heard, if they tried to force him. A good cook like that could work for a duke, you know."

"Really?" I am doubtful. Mr. Serle does not seem proud enough to work for a duke.

"Lad, lad," says Mrs. Bennet. "Mr. Serle is a great cook. Don't you go doubting it. If you were not such a sad barbarian, you would be able to tell that no one can flavor a soup or a sauce as he can. And what he does with oranges and lemons! It is the southern blood in him, you see. He may not be one of your good Christian gentlemen, but I know a great cook when I taste his work."

For emphasis she takes a long pull on her flask. I hurry about my work. Very soon, I know from sad experience, her mood will darken again, and I want to be well out of her way when that happens. The main kitchen is not much more pleasant when I return there. Tom is still complaining that the village is dull, that the woman he sleeps with is nagging him to post the banns and marry her, that no one has a spark of life to them anymore.

"London," he says. "The town is full of doings and gaiety. Only the pretty girls get to be maids in London town. All the servants have Sunday afternoon for holiday every week and none of the nonsense they have here about being back for evening prayers."

"It wouldn't hurt you a bit, Tom, to say your prayers." Mrs. Bennet has come into the kitchen. The mention of prayers reminds me of what Mrs. Bennet said: that Mr. Serle is not a good Christian gentleman. I have little time to ponder this, however, for Mrs. Bennet is staggering. Mr. Serle rescues the pie dish from her hands and hands it to me. He guides her to the bench by the doorway and sits her down.

"Come, come, Mrs. Bennet," he says firmly. "You must rest here."

"It is my feet again," she says. "I can hardly work for the pain."

"I do not doubt it," says Mr. Serle. "Sit here. The lad will bring you a cold cloth for your head, and I am going to make you coffee. It takes the fumes off from the liquor."

"I could go to the coffeehouses in London," says Tom. "I could drink my coffee and read the newspapers with the other bon tons."

"You?" says Mrs. Bennet. "You one of the bon tons? Why, Paddy here would make more of a gentleman." She laughs so hard she gets the hiccups.

"Set that pie dish down and get Mrs. Bennet water," Mr. Serle orders me. I realize that I have been standing there with my mouth agape.

"The lad's a goony," Mrs. Bennet says. She thumps her knee with her fist and rocks with laughter and hiccups.

Tom joins her whoops. I fetch cold water in a stoneware pitcher and set it on the table with a mug. Mr. Serle pours water for Mrs. Bennet. "Here," he says. "Drink this in sips, or I will pour the jug down your neck."

Tom laughs loud at that. I go away to clean vegetables and lettuce in the scullery. When I return, all is quiet again. Mrs. Bennet has gone back to her pantry. Mr. Serle is standing at the open doorway, looking out at the rain streaming down into the courtyard.

"I hate the rain," he says as I pass him.

"Why, sir?" I pause with my bowl of carrots in my arms.

"It rains too much and then the floods come."

He seems to be speaking to himself more than to me. I respond nonetheless. "Floods do not always follow rain. We are on high ground here."

"Floods follow rain," he says. Then he shakes his head and turns briskly. "Where was I?" He crosses to the worktable and picks up a knife. "Bring that here, lad," he says.

After all, it is a busy day like any other. When the dinner is sent up, the rain stops, the sky clears, and Mr. Serle walks in the courtyard with his hands behind his back. I take a piece of bread to chew and follow him.

"No fear of floods now," I say as cheerfully as I can muster. Perhaps he will talk to me about the real things in his mind. If we know each other, he might help me.

"No, no fear now," says Mr. Serle.

"Were there many floods in Rome?" I ask.

He looks at me sharply and seems as if he would rebuke me for speaking. Then he sighs and shrugs his shoulders. "Do you fear fire, lad?" he says.

"I do," I answer. "Yet it is not the fire in the grate that cooks the meat and warms the kitchen on cool nights. It is the fire that might spill from behind the bars and burn my clothes. I am afraid not so much of what is as I am afraid of the danger that might be." I stop. I wonder if he can understand me.

"As you fear the fire, I fear rain. Not water, you understand. When we pump it into a jug, it is nothing to care about. Indeed, it is necessary for our lives. But when it pours from the sky and when the rivers rise, then—" He shudders and stops. "We will not talk about it," he says. I think he does understand me. "Trust begins with knowledge," he told me when he asked about my family. When he speaks of his fears, he gives me knowledge. Perhaps that means he wants me to trust him.

We are quiet for a space. Mr. Serle speaks again, so low it might be to himself. "Rome is a city by a river. The river clasps it in an embrace that sustains and strangles. I hate Rome and I long for it. The tumbled stones and the olive trees, the savory smell of chestnuts roasted in the street at charcoal braziers and the stink of cesspools." He stops.

"Perhaps you miss your family?" I ask timidly.

"I left Rome," he says harshly. "I went to Livorno, where there was no life for me. I went to Paris and learned to cook. I went to London and lived in a cellar, cooking at coal fires. I am here in the country to strengthen my lungs. When I feel strong enough and have saved my passage money, I will go to America. There is no looking back."

"You will not go to London with the gentry?" I have such a need to know that he will not go that my voice trembles.

"I will not, lad. London is not for me." He walks by the wall of the dairy and is silent.

The last of the sun glitters on the raindrops still hanging in the clematis vine that grows against the dairy wall. The cobbles of the yard have begun to dry, and their white surfaces show pale like the white ash forming on the black coals of the fire.

I am silent too. What can I say? Does he have a family? Perhaps they are all dead or lost, and the pain of speaking of them is too much. I search in my mind for something to say. I am so glad that he will not go away to London. But he says he will go to America. Maybe he will take me with him if I ask. Something inside me wants to tell him everything, yet I cannot think what might be safe or wise to say next. We stand silent in the courtyard, where the wet still glistens on the bench and on the garden gate and on the orchard trees beyond.

Tom calls from the kitchen doorway. The housekeeper has brought down word that the pike is a great success. The master and the mistress congratulate Mr. Serle for the dinner. We walk in to clean the kitchen.

CHAPTER V

MRS. BENNET IS VERY EXCITED. She rolls the paste for a pie with a flourish. It is true that the gentry are going to London. Everything will be in an uproar for the few days, Mrs. Bennet tells me. After that, she says, it will be quiet as the tomb for a month or more.

"There will be no need for you to be learning fancy cakes anymore until I get back," says Mrs. Bennet with satisfaction. "Maybe Mr. Serle can help you learn to put up preserves. The gardener, Mr. Plumb, says that the apricots and the peaches look promising this year."

I notice that Mrs. Bennet has forgotten to complain about her legs. When she has done her work, she bustles off to look over her things. She has mending to do and her trunk to pack, she says, leaving me to mind the oven temperature so the tarts don't burn. Meanwhile, I must look over the currants for a cake and soak them in a little brandy, which she has set out. She has forgotten to drink from her flask, I notice. When she returns from her room, she is humming a tune.

Going to London has a good effect on Mrs. Bennet. Tom, in contrast, must stay here and is miserable. He teases me mercilessly until both Mr. Serle and Mrs. Bennet tell him to stop. Then he contents himself with pretending to slash me with a knife whenever I pass close to him. I avoid him as much as possible, of course. Luckily, he leaves as early as he can in the evenings. He does not dare arrive late in the mornings because he knows Mr.

Serle will send him off to find another job if he does not have the fires lit and ready. Mr. Serle told him so.

The gentry are ready to leave at last. The hamper is packed for the journey with cold roasted chickens and boiled eggs and raspberry turnovers as well as all manner of other edibles. Mr. Coates, who is supervising the stowing of luggage on the carriage and the cart that will follow it, sees Mrs. Bennet's box placed to her satisfaction and herself on a seat with a cushion under her. She has refused to travel to town by the train with the other servants. Too dangerous, she asserts. The carriage rolls out of the stable courtyard. It will go to the front of the house for the family. Sultan and Gytrash are led out and saddled also. They go to London as well. The family will ride in the great park in London, Mrs. Bennet informed me. Young Miss will show herself off on Gytrash to attract a good husband. The lady's maid has told Mrs. Bennet that Miss ordered a blue riding dress chosen to look well against the smoke color of the horse. I will miss Gytrash, although the man who notices her will be a good husband, no doubt, since he will have an eye for a sound horse.

All of the kitchen work is finished and the baskets are gone. I am feeling relief that the bustle is over, when Mr. Coates returns, leading Gytrash. She has thrown a shoe and cannot be ridden until the blacksmith comes.

"Here," says Mr. Coates, handing me the reins as if it were the most usual thing in the world. "Take off her saddle and put her in her stall like a good lad. You know what to do. We will stop in the village to tell the smith to come up as soon as ever he can. He will shoe her and take her down to his stable until I can send my lad back to get her."

Mr. Coates is going to London. They need him to care for the horses and drive the carriage. The lad from Milford he hired when I hurt my foot will drive the cart with the trunks and boxes and Mrs. Bennet. I think that I could be the one sitting on the cart, tickling my whip over the back of the plow horse that pulls it. I would see London. No, I think, it is better here. Except that I wish I could be the one to care for Gytrash.

Mr. Serle, who is leaning against the stable wall with his hands in his pockets, must be able to read my thoughts. "Leave the horse here," he says. "The lad will have little to do in the kitchen with everyone gone. His foot is better. Let the blacksmith come and do whatever he needs to. The lad can care for the horse until your stable hand comes back."

I am so happy at the thought of caring for the horse that I want to put my arms around Mr. Serle and thank him. "Oh, please," I say, and Gytrash, hearing my voice, swings her head to me and tugs at the reins.

"Well, Paddy," Mr. Coates says to me abruptly. "She's a valuable horse. Can you do it?"

"Oh, yes," I say.

Mr. Coates nods and gives me instructions about feed and getting the smith's opinion on exercise. He hands over the reins. "Lead her easy," he says, and then adds abruptly, "I will be off. The gentry will be getting impatient at the delay. Miss will be in quite a temper that Gytrash cannot go with us. I had best get the delivery of the bad news over with. I'll send the smith." He hurries off, stiff in his polished high boots, to the gentry and the waiting carriage.

I lead Gytrash to the stable and unsaddle her and hang up her gear in the tack room. When the smith comes, he gives her a new shoe but tut-tuts at length. The old shoe must have been awry for days, he says; she is gone somewhat lame in the leg. He gives me salve and directions. He will send word to Mr. Coates, he says, not to hurry to take the horse to town.

And so life becomes simpler and yet is busy nonetheless. I rise early—sometimes even before Mr. Serle is awake—and go down in the dew-washed summer dawn to tend the mare. I do the kitchen work all morning and then slip away with a nuncheon of bread and meat or a piece of fruit, to sit on the pasture fence. Mr. Serle has set the servants' meal at noon, with a supper just before sunset. There are at most ten to feed and no need for fancy dishes. Tom is more content. He does not have London, but the work is lighter and he goes off to fairs and market days with Mr. Serle's permission. Sometimes Tom has orders to find a special fruit or to purchase mushrooms for the ketchup we must bottle; sometimes he just goes. It is peaceful in the kitchen then.

Yet just when I am sure that all is well, Mr. Serle falls ill. It begins slowly. First he looks tired and asks Tom to set out the cold meat for the supper; that night he retires early. The next morning he complains that he has a chill and, after consulting with the gardener, brews up sage, rosemary, and plantain in water with honey. The kitchen is heavy with the sweet odor of it. But rinsing his throat with this medicine does not seem to help him. That night I awaken to hear him tossing and turning. His cot creaks under his restless movement.

In the morning, I awaken to a silence. There is no creaking cot, no muttered prayer. I lie still in horror. Eliza fell sick at first with a painful throat. Did Mr. Serle die in the night? I hold my breath to hear the least sound. The rooster crows in the stable yard and then, to my relief, I hear a rustle of movement. I hurry into my clothes.

Mr. Serle is lying on his bed. He has clutched the clothes up under his chin. His black eyes are like wet pebbles in his head, his skin is pale, he is shivering even though the room is warmed already by the morning sun. I go back to my corner and take the blanket from my cot and bring it to him.

"Here, sir," I say. "You look cold. I think you have an ague."

He looks at me as if he has never seen me before in the world. "I am cold," he admits. "I will rest awhile. Tom must set the fire and make a stew for the dinner."

"Yes, sir," I say. "Shall I bring you soup to eat?" I will hurry and groom Gytrash, I think. Then I will tend to Mr. Serle.

He turns his head as if the thought of food disgusts him. The growing beard shadows the side of his face and stubbles his chin. "Later," he says.

"You must have water," I say, trying to remember what my mother would do for me when I fell ill. "I will bring it."

Tom seems not to care very much that Mr. Serle is not well enough to come downstairs. He stuffs himself with slices of meat from yesterday's boiled mutton and complains about the extra work. Much of it he assigns to me. After I fetch the milk and cream from the dairy as usual, I have vegetables to clean and chop. There will be soup as well as stew for dinner, so it will be easy to get some for Mr. Serle. Tom tells me to make pastry also. He wants a fruit pie; I know enough to realize that such things are eaten as leftovers from the gentry's table, not made fresh for the servants. There are plenty of bottled cherries on the shelf, however. One jar is not likely to be missed, so I do as he asks without arguing. Obedience to a bully is easier than fighting, even though I know it means that next time I will have to fight twice as hard against him. It is almost noon before I can climb the stairs to Mr. Serle. I carry a jug of cool water and a mug.

"Here is water," I say.

"Thank you," he whispers.

At first I think he must be better, because he looks at me so attentively. Then I realize that he does not know who I am. With a shaking hand, I pour water into the mug. "Let me help you," I say.

I assist him to sit up against the pillow and hold the mug to his lips. He swallows a sip. I see his throat move even though the drop of the liquid in the mug is not perceptible. "Thank you," he whispers again.

"I will bring you some soup," I say.

He looks into my face. "Where is your yellow veil?" he says. "Did you wear it in the street?" He becomes agitated, and his hands move restlessly over the blanket. "Is the water rising?"

I am puzzled by his words and remain silent. I want to re-assure him, but what can I say? It comes to me that it does not matter whether I speak truth. I should soothe him.

"There is no danger today," I say in the quietest voice I can muster. "No need to worry. Drink another swallow of water and rest until I bring the soup."

It seems to calm him, for he nods, sips water again, and lies back against the pillow with a sigh. His eyes flutter closed. Boldly, I pull the blankets straight around him. My hand brushes his, and I feel that his skin is burning hot and dry.

I hurry down to the kitchen. When Eliza was ill, my mother

bathed her face with cool water, I remember. I fetch a basin and a clean cloth. Tom is busy by the stove, stirring something and talking to one of the housemaids, who must have sneaked off from her work. With the family in London, Mrs. Bennet gone, and now Mr. Serle ill, the work is slighted. I am glad that Tom is distracted, for it means that I can slip into the scullery and away again without his questioning me.

Upstairs I find that Mr. Serle has pushed the blankets awry again. His eyes are open, but he still does not know me. He nods without interest when I speak to him. I set down my basin and carefully smooth everything. I help him to lean up again, and he drinks a little water.

"I am going to bathe your face, sir," I say, and to my relief he nods again. I dip the cloth into the basin and carefully wipe his forehead. He smiles at me and, emboldened, I wash his cheeks and then his neck. A little water trickles down to the opening of his nightshirt on his chest. I wring out the cloth and blot it away.

"I will go to get some soup now," I say. "Can you eat a little?"

To my dismay, he shakes his head. "Just water," he manages. After I help him to drink a little, he speaks again. "Be sure to wear the veil," he says anxiously. "I am worried for you."

"I will wear what is necessary," I say. "You must rest, not worry."

"Paddy! Paddy!" bellows Tom at the foot of the stairs. "I need you!"

I set the mug of water where Mr. Serle can reach it if he wishes and pull the blankets more neatly about him. I hurry off to help Tom with tasks he could as easily have finished himself. Finally, the servants are settled to their meal. When Mr. Serle is asked for, Tom says he is sick with an ague. He nods at me and tells them the lad is taking Mr. Serle food. They shrug and dip their spoons in their bowls. I wonder that they can feel hunger, eat, when someone is ill in the house. I ladle some broth into a dish, take a spoon from the drawer, and climb the stairs again.

Mr. Serle is sweating. Water beads on his forehead where his dark curls spring at the pale skin of his temples. The fever has broken and he knows me again. I bring a basin and a cloth and lave his face and shoulders. His nightshirt is wet.

"Do you have another nightshirt?" I ask. It cannot be good for him to lie in damp clothing.

"You must bring my box over by the bed," he says.

His trunk is a black box, banded with metal. It is not very large and not very heavy, although it is too much for me to lift and carry by myself. I drag it across the space from the wall to the bed.

"Turn it so that I can see into it," says Mr. Serle. He seems very weak, but the strange stare is gone from his eyes. He is himself.

I do as he asks, turning the trunk so that the hasp faces Mr. Serle. There is no lock, just a piece of cord tied through the handle and knotted. Mr. Serle fumbles with the cord.

"Shall I untie it, sir?" I ask.

He nods and I stoop. The knot is complicated and it takes me a moment. When it comes free, I step back to let Mr. Serle raise the lid. He shoves at it and then looks at me apologetically. "I can't do it," he says.

"Let me," I answer. It is no difficulty to lift the lid while standing behind the box. Once the lid is up, I step back. I do not wish to appear a busybody, poking my nose in where I am not wanted. Mr. Serle seems oblivious to me as he peers into his things.

"Ah," he murmurs, lifting out a nightshirt and laying it on the bed by him. "And this," he says, as if only to himself. He has taken out a linen bag with a cord knotted about the neck. "Now close the trunk and push it back," he says. He fumbles with the bag and then pushes it away. "You must undo this," he says.

Carefully, I unloose the cord and open the neck of the pouch. Inside are several packets of oiled silk. "Shall I set these out?" I ask.

Mr. Serle nods and I lay them one at a time on the blanket next to him. As I do so, he picks each up and sniffs it. He sets the packets aside in turn until he finds the one that he is looking for.

"Put those away," he says, gesturing to the packets he has rejected. He unfolds the end of the little envelope he is holding and wets the end of his finger with his tongue. He dips the finger into the packet and then tastes. He makes a sour face. "It is as bitter as I remember," he says, "but it must serve."

"What is it?" I cannot hide my curiosity.

"I was sick with this same fever in Paris a year ago," he says. "I lived above a chemist's shop, and when I staggered down the stairs and fell into his shop, burning with ague, he did not throw me out. He had a powder that he had bought from a trader in the market. It comes from one of the Spanish colonies, he thought, and the man that sold it swore it would break any fever. It is the bark of a tree that does not grow on this side of the ocean."

"Oh, I pray it will help you," I say.

"You are kind, lad," says Mr. Serle. "Now, help me to take my medicine. A pinch in water will do."

I shake a little of the reddish-brown stuff into the mug and pour cool water in with it, two fingers high. The stuff floats, and I take the spoon from the cooling bowl of broth to stir it. I run down to the pantry and fetch sugar, thinking it may make the medicine easier to swallow. When powder and sugar have been well stirred into the water, Mr. Serle drinks it.

"It is so bitter," he says, almost petulantly. He folds the packet with the remaining powder and hands it to me. "Keep this," he says. "I must take it morning and evening until the fever stops."

"I will guard it with my life," I say.

"No need to be so dramatic, child," he says.

"So this strange drug will cure you?" I ask as I close the lid of the trunk and prepare to push it away to the wall across from Mr. Serle's bed.

"The fever will come back," he says sadly. "First I will feel cold, then I will burn. Then the sweat will come and I will feel relief and great weakness. It will happen for six or seven days. If the powder works, the fever will be less severe each day. If it does not work, the fevers will be greater and greater until I die of it."

I feel angry. If Mr. Serle sickens and dies, who will protect me? I want to shake him and tell him to get up and go down to the kitchen.

"You must drink and eat to keep your strength," I say. "Do not let the fever win." I want to cry and plead and tell him he must live, but what is the use? I cried when Eliza was ill and it was no use. It makes me angry that the people I need desert me.

"You are right," he says. "You have a good heart, lad. Bring me broth and make me drink it even if I say not."

"I will," I say, "every morning and night."

"No," he says, "it will be no use to urge me when the fever rages. I must take what I can when the fever eases."

I vow to myself to do as he asks. I help him change from his sweat-soaked shirt to the fresh one. When I go down to the kitchen again, I wash the shirt in the scullery and make beef tea. Luckily Tom is busy, and luckily too he has not locked up the meat keeper. I hang the wet shirt in the sun to dry and climb the stairs with a covered bowl of broth.

Mr. Serle is dozing on his bed, the blanket drawn up around him. His eyelashes flicker as I approach, and then his eyes open wide. I help him eat the broth I have made. He is so weak that his hand trembles, and I hold the spoon to guide it to his lips. When he is finished, he thanks me. I offer to fetch more, but he refuses. His pale face breaks my heart.

"Did others in Paris have this illness?" I ask.

"Do not worry, lad," he says. "This is not a disease you can catch from me. It is an old Roman fever that comes back on me at times. It will be over soon and then I will be tired for a week. After that, it will be as if nothing happened—until the next time."

"I am glad it does not make others sick," I say, but think silently that I would not care if I were ill and died. To make the conversation last I ask, "Is it only those born in Rome who suffer from this illness?"

He smiles a little. "Bad air causes it, they say. If one is born where swamps and standing water breed infection, it is a danger."

"The air is good at this house," I say. "I do not understand that you should be ill."

"I think that the infection hides in the body somewhere," says Mr. Serle. "I was sick in Rome for many months and then was well a year. When I fell sick again in Paris, the apothecary gave me the powder you saw to bring the fever down. I was sick a week. It has been a year since then. With the powder to help cure me, I think I will be sick a week or even less this time."

He lies back, exhausted. "It is hard to rest when I know that soon the cold and then the fever will come again," he says.

"What can I do?" I respond.

"Ask the gardener, Mr. Plumb, for leaves and flowers of chamomile," he whispers. "He will know. Infuse the leaves in boiling water and leave it for an hour. Strain the liquid into a jug and bring it to me." He lies back on his bed as if exhausted just from speaking. Glad that there is something for me to do, I hurry down the stairs.

"Please, please," I beg the gardener when I find him forking over a heap of dirt. "Show me chamomile and let me pick it."

"What for?" he asks suspiciously.

"Mr. Serle is ill and has asked for chamomile," I say.

"Yes." Mr. Plumb nods, his battered and shapeless felt hat shades small, white-lashed eyes in a moon face. "Chamomile tea is good to soothe a fever. Or dandelion. You can pick dandelion in the pasture, lad."

"He asked for chamomile," I say staunchly. Mr. Serle needs me to be brave for him, I tell myself. I must take him what he needs. "Show it to me and I will pick it. You do not have to trouble yourself, Mr. Plumb."

The man bumbles slowly across the garden, talking to me as he goes, or perhaps to himself. "There's violets," he says. "Violets is good for hoarseness in the throat. I use that myself. Or creeping thyme. See the little purple flowers there. The leaves and buds are excellent against headache and the nightmare. Do you have nightmares, lad?"

I want to shake the man. "Chamomile," I insist again. "Which is the chamomile?"

Mr. Plumb stops and points the handle of his rake at a clump of gray-green weedy-looking stuff behind the purple-flowered thyme. "There it is, the chamomile, *Anthemis nobilis.* Pick what you want, lad. It hasn't bloomed yet. Tell Mr. Serle I wish him better health." The man goes stumping back to his heap of black dirt, trailing the rake.

Quickly I pick handfuls of the ferny stuff. The smell is sharp and pungent. I carry the fragrant armful into the scullery. It will be easier to work there, out of Tom's way. I find pleasure in the action of washing and stripping the leaves, chopping all fine, pouring on boiling water and setting the herb to steep. When the maceration is cool, I pour off the green-gray liquid and stir in a few spoonsful of honey. It is good to do something. I think of my mother hunting the field for herbs to ease our hunger when there was nothing but a handful of oatmeal and a cup of ale for soup. The trying helps to make the burden bearable.

Then the supper must be laid out ready and Tom's orders attended to. Finally, the servants are settled to their meal and I can climb the stairs again. Mr. Serle is dozing. As I wonder whether to awaken him or leave him be, his eyes snap open and he sees me standing at the foot of his bed.

"Is it time for the medicine?" he asks.

"Yes," I say, "first the medicine and then you can wash away the bitter taste of it with chamomile tea."

"You made it so soon," he says wonderingly.

I mix his medicine and help him hold the cup to drink it. After he has taken it and some tea also, I muster courage to mention a subject that has been worrying me. "Have you need of the chamber pot, sir?" I feel bold asking it, but he is sick, after all. Our bodily needs must be met whether we will or no.

Mr. Serle grimaces. "The sweating takes the water out of me," he says. "But you are right. I must use the pot. Will you help me stand?"

I think my face has flushed red, but I will not think about it. I find the chamber pot under the bed and remove the cover. I pull the one chair in the room close to the bed and set the pot upon it. I help Mr. Serle to put his feet down and sit on the edge of the bed. He grips my shoulder, and I brace myself to help him stand. Somehow we manage, even though I am not sure whether I am more afraid that he will fall in a heap at my feet or that I will see his private parts and shame him without his knowing.

In the event, I am so busy holding him up and steadying him so that he does not water the floor instead of the pot that I have no time to notice anything I should not. And Mr. Serle is a naturally modest man who lifts his shirt as little as necessary. When he finishes, he falls back into the bed, a rag doll. I cannot help but see as I cover the pot and set it at the stair head that his water is dense and pungent. But there is no blood in it and that, I know, is good.

And so for six days I rise earlier than ever to tend Gytrash and to toil up and down the stairs with jugs of fresh water, bowls of beef tea, mugs of barley water, sippets of toast, warm water for washing. I help Mr. Serle to stand and relieve his needs. I take his chamber pot down every morning and empty it in the privy and wash it at the pump. Meanwhile, Tom takes advantage of Mr. Serle's absence from the kitchen to demand heavier work from me. After I fetch milk in the morning, I must carry in buckets of coal from the storage shed. Tom wants me to watch the stews and stir them to be sure the bottom does not stick, as well as make pastry for meat pies. If I take on the main work in the kitchen, he is free to eat and to talk to the maids or the gardener. He drinks ale now in the middle of the morning as well as with his breakfast and dinner. His temper suffers for it.

The first three days are terrible. I find I cannot eat when my mind is filled with the picture of Mr. Serle lying helpless, racked with shivering and fever, his face a mask of pain. Morning and night, I hurry from attic to kitchen to stable. The second day I almost faint as I help Tom to move a stew pot from the range. I have to eat, I tell myself. I have to be strong enough to do my work. Mr. Serle and Gytrash both need me.

I kneel beside my cot and pray into the night that Mr. Serle will be delivered from his danger. My sleep is disturbed by dreams. A house is burning. I pick handfuls of chamomile and throw them into the fire as if that would quench the flames. A voice calls, "Water! Water!" and I sit bolt upright in my bed and listen. I hear Mr. Serle's labored breathing, the only sound in the silence of the night. He is still alive.

Again and again, I go to sleep with hope and waken with despair. Mr. Serle does not know me when the fever clouds his mind. He raves about the yellow veil and the danger of the rising water. On the fourth day the fever strikes as usual after his morning chills, but this time he does not lose his mind. He eats a little more. The next day the fever passes more quickly, and later he can hold the spoon himself to eat the soup while I steady the bowl. On the seventh day Mr. Serle is not in his bed when I awaken.

To my relief, I hear him on the stairs. He mounts slowly, holding the railing and resting on each step. When he is in the room, he smiles at me.

"I have been down to the privy on my own," he says triumphantly. "I washed myself in the scullery. Now I will take one more dose of medicine and rest. Tomorrow I will work again. And shave," he says, rubbing the curly beard that shows on his gray cheek.

I want to shout with gladness. He is not going to die. I help him to the bed, mix his dose of powder, and leave him to sleep. When I bring up soup and toast, he eats with appetite. When he is finished he looks at me with a return of his old sharpness.

"You look thin," he says. "This has been too much for you, climbing the stairs and nursing me. When did you last eat?"

"This morning," I say. I do not tell him that an end of bread and some water were all I had.

"Leave me to rest," he orders. "I require you to go and eat something nourishing."

I obey him, of course. I eat some cheese and a bowl of broth for my supper. Because Mr. Serle is better, I can take more joy in tending Gytrash the next morning. My appetite for breakfast is better after an hour in the stable. That evening Mr. Serle comes down to the kitchen after the others have eaten and all is quiet. Tom is cleaning up without demanding that I do most of it. I bring Mrs. Bennet's chair from the pantry and set it near the warmth of the fire for Mr. Serle. He sits with his blanket about his shoulders. It hurts to see him so thin and weak. But he takes toast and boiled fish to eat when I offer it.

"Thank you," he says to me. His smile makes my heart jump with happiness in my chest. "Tom," he says, "you have let the spits get crusted with fat. Be sure to polish them well before you light the fire tomorrow."

With Mr. Serle in charge again, the work is shared more equitably. Tom must carry the heavy hods of coals as he did before. Not that I have little to do. We bottle sauces and make preserves as the various fruit of the estate and the surrounding farms come into season. After a day spent stirring sugar and fruit at the hot range, I go tired to bed at night.

Now that Mr. Serle is recovering, I eat a little more. It seems to encourage him if I sit nearby in the evening and have a spoonful of stew or a wedge of meat pie. He tells me to make rice pudding for dinner and eats it with relish. After a week, it seems almost usual to eat both morning and night. I watch Mr. Serle gain color and strength. The haggard look, the sunken cheeks his illness gave him, is fading.

"You're getting fat, Paddy," says Tom to me, speaking thickly through a wedge of pork pie.

"Leave the lad be," says Mr. Serle peaceably. He is sitting with a book. Supper is over, and the few servants who came for the meal have gone. They say there is to be dancing tonight at a fair in the village of Hay.

When we are cleaning the range on the other side of the kitchen, where Mr. Serle cannot hear us, Tom returns to the attack. "The English have wasted too many good men in Ireland," he snarls. "A poor country with a populace of lazy dunderheads. They cannot even feed themselves, we hear."

"It is not the fault of the people that the potatoes failed," I protest.

"I'll wager it is their fault," says Tom. "They should grow a better crop. They must be bad farmers."

"No, that is not true," I cry.

"It is too," grins Tom, laughing at my discomfort.

"The people are starving, and the landlords send food away to England," I say, the image of ships I saw in Dublin harbor before my eyes.

"The Irish are a lot of traitors to the crown," Tom asserts. "Why should we send help when the Irish do nothing for us?"

"My father fought against bogey Napoleon," I shout at him. "He was a boy, and they took him to fight. He fought for the king and for the English people. It's nothing you did for him in return when he had need of food."

"I doubt you are telling the truth," says Tom insultingly. "I have heard the Irish tell tall tales. Why would I believe a girly boy like you?"

"If my father were here, he would stop your bullying," I say with a defiance that I do not feel inside. "You would not stand up to a true soldier."

"A true soldier," scoffs Tom. "I'll wager the Popish pawn was driven to fight by his betters."

"At least he was not a Jew or a gypsy," I say. "Or an Englishman," I add under my breath.

"Enough quarreling," says Mr. Serle. He looks tired and gray-faced again. "Finish your work and be done."

"I'm off," says Tom, hanging his smock on a peg by the door. "Tomorrow I have a day's holiday, remember?"

"Indeed," says Mr. Serle. "You will want it after dancing tonight. Don't drink too much new beer or get yourself in too deep with the lasses."

Tom grunts his good-bye and goes. Shaking with anger still, I wipe the table one last time and take the cloth into the scullery to give it a good rinse in hot water from the boiler. When I return, Mr. Serle is still reading. The currant cake that was served for supper is on the sideboard still. I should wrap it in its cloth and put it away in its tin in the pantry. Perhaps I will have a small piece before I do so. I was down at the stable with Gytrash when the others ate. It was early this morning when I had breakfast.

"May I take a piece of the cake?" I ask Mr. Serle.

"Of course, child," he says, looking up. "You do not eat enough."

I cut a piece and come to sit near him. "What is the book?" I ask. "Is it your Bible?"

"No, it is a story. It is a novel, child," Mr. Serle says. "Like the Bible, it tells a story, but the tale is of men and women who live now."

"Are novels good?" I ask. "At home we read the Bible and the plays of William Shakespeare. Sometimes my parents took the parts. I remember my father speaking the great words of Marc Antony to the citizens of Rome. His voice was thrilling. I never saw a novel." I wonder if Mr. Serle knows about Marc Antony and the death of Caesar. He must if he was born in Rome.

Mr. Serle is talking not about Rome but about his book, this novel. "Indeed," he says. " 'A novel shows us a picture of natural human existence; it exercises our imaginations; it points out to us the path of honor and teaches us a knowledge of the world. We can gain the lessons of experience without its terrors.' "

I ask him to say it again. "How beautiful," I say. "I would like to learn the lessons of experience without terror."

"I read that somewhere," Mr. Serle says, and laughs. He sounds happy almost.

"What is the picture in your novel?" I ask.

"This? This is a story of the wilderness of America. It is about a brave Indian girl and a young man and a girl whom she helps. It is set in Massachusetts years ago, in Boston. I have just read about the trackless forests in the western part of that colony."

"Who wrote this novel you are reading now?"

"A woman, Catherine Sedgwick. They put their names on their stories there."

"They don't here?" I am puzzled.

"Here they hide behind a false name or they say *a lady* or *a gentleman.*"

I can tell from the contempt in Mr. Serle's voice that he does not think this hiding of names is good. I like to talk to him.

Since he was sick and thanked me for helping him, I feel safer. I want to tell him my name.

"What is the title of your book?" I ask instead.

"Hope Leslie," he says.

"What?" I say, confused. "Hope what?"

"Hope Leslie," he says. "The title of the book is the same name as the heroine of the story."

"Is it the Indian girl?" I ask.

"No," he says. "Her name is Magawisca, a strange name to us. She is a very noble savage."

"Will you really go to America someday?" I must summon my courage soon to ask if I can go with him. Mr. Serle might help me search for my brother.

"Yes," he says, and he snaps the book shut. "I read the novels written by James Fenimore Cooper also. I am going to America. I will see the trackless forests. But there are cities growing there beside the forests. Workers and all kinds of folk who are busy and thriving populate the land. And the land is bountiful in grain and fruit. I am going to make a place where people come to eat good food."

"Is everyone in America rich enough to hire a cook?" I ask doubtfully.

"Have you never seen a restaurant?" Mr. Serle asks.

"I do not know," I say. "What is it?"

"It is a place with comfortable chairs and tables and a great kitchen. People come to eat their meals there and pay generously for a well-cooked dinner."

"I have been to an inn," I say, thinking of the house in Liverpool with its damp walls and warren of rooms. I think of Susan bustling in the warm sitting room with a table for guests to eat at near a great fireplace. It was Susan who made the place welcome to me. Mr. Serle does not have so welcoming a manner— even though he is always kind, I remind myself.

"An inn is not the same thing." Mr. Serle is firm on the point. "An inn sells a bed for the night, a slice of meat, a piece of bread, and a mug of ale to stave off hunger. No—I mean a restaurant where people eat with dignity. They have them in Paris everywhere now. I worked for the famous Monsieur Beauvilliers at the most famous restaurant in all Paris. Monsieur had a magnificent kitchen and waiters trained to address his clients' every need. I remember the bill of fare had twelve soups and twenty entrées of veal alone. How we worked in that kitchen! But it was a privilege; the platters went to the tables as works of art. The waiters upstairs told us that the richest people of Paris went to eat their dinners there. Word would come down to us to make a capon in cream sauce garnished with truffles look especially elegant for a banker or a noble and his friends come to dine after the races. Monsieur Beauvilliers knew each of the patrons by name and remembered what he ate the last time he dined there and what dishes and flavorings he liked and which wines he preferred. They said Monsieur knew the incomes of each patron also and how many lobster salads and foie gras *truffée* each could afford."

I sit in amazement. I am sure my jaw has dropped open and my eyes are round as hoops. Mr. Serle never talks so much or with such passion. What can I say? But he has only paused to take breath. He continues.

"I would begin simply, of course," he says, "but the restaurant would be quality from the beginning. I will not have your English chop house or sleazy inn in a back street with its gray mutton and flat beer. 'Animals feed themselves; men eat; but only wise men know the art of eating.' Brillat-Savarin said that." Mr. Serle pauses again.

"It is a wonderful dream," I say.

Mr. Serle sighs deeply. "You are right, lad," he says. "It is a dream. Who knows how or when I can make it real."

I feel suddenly that it is the most important thing in the world that he should have his dream. "I will work in your restaurant," I say. "I will learn the art that makes wise men happy."

"Thank you," says Mr. Serle, and bends his head over his book again. I sit idly, looking at the dying fire. Perhaps the restaurant will be real, I think, and famous. My brother will have made his fortune and he will come to eat a fine dinner. I will hear his voice and know him. Then I will make him a crisp oat cake, just the way I used to. Who made this? he will ask. Mr. Serle will tell him and he will demand to see me. Only one person in the world could have made an oat cake as perfect as this, he will say, and I will throw my arms around him and never let go.

Mr. Serle coughs and startles me. "Oh!" I say.

"Lost in your thoughts, lad?" says Mr. Serle.

"I was thinking of my brother," I say.

"I hope it was a good thought," he responds kindly.

I want to tell him everything then, but caution stops me again. I do not know him really. He might betray me.

"Good night," I say. I rise.

"Good night," he answers. His book must be exciting, because he does not look up but leans in toward the light of the fire and turns a page.

The full moon makes the room upstairs glow with a pale light. I am glad to climb into my cot behind the curtain. I hold the lump in the tail of my shirt that is my ring, sewn away in safety. I think of my mother. My heart swells with the sadness of it all. Someday I will have a friend to whom I can say anything—anything—without fear or shame. Maybe Mr. Serle. Maybe.

CHAPTER VI

LIFE RETURNS to its safe rhythm. I rise before dawn. I wash myself. I go to the stables, where Gytrash whickers her good-morning welcome and nuzzles my shoulder. She moves strongly now. The smith looked at her again a few days ago and advised that she was ready for riding. Now she spends her mornings in the paddock, and I can take her out in the afternoons. When my work with the horse is done, I wash again and go to the kitchen, where Tom is lighting the fires and grumbling.

I am so glad that Mr. Serle is getting better that it takes me a day or two to see that Tom does not share my feelings. Mr. Serle's return means for Tom being prompt to lay the fire. He cannot tell me the night before that I must do it so that he can sleep. He cannot order me to move the stew pots on the range by myself while he makes eyes at the maids. Mr. Serle insists that the boiling pots be moved always by two people. The return of Mr. Serle also means a higher standard of cleanliness throughout the kitchen. No quick sweep with the broom and swipe with the cleaning rag will suffice now that he is back demanding that the worktable be scrubbed white at the end of the day. Tom was getting used to being in charge and having his own way, I think. He does not like being second again.

The kitchen staff and the few servants who are left eat together, except for the housekeeper, who has asked to have her meals served in her sitting room. Tom carries the tray to her and complains every time. I suppose he has tried to make her interested in him and has failed. She must be nervous of her authority, for she orders the two housemaids about in a peremptory way. They imitate her behind her back. I think she likes Mr. Serle. She comes into the kitchen at least once a day to ask him a question. Is comfrey good for making a skin lotion? she asked yesterday, and Mr. Serle just shrugged and said he did not know. He advised her to ask Mr. Plumb. Her manner with him could be said to be inviting, but he does not seem to notice. I feel sorry for her because she seems so alone in her position.

She would not want to make me her friend, and, in any case, I am too busy. With Mrs. Bennet away, the task of making pastry and sweets is mine. In addition, I help with the other preparations. Mr. Serle tires quickly. If he stands at the worktable or the range too long, he grows pale. He does not say a word but goes to sit by the window for a moment or two and then resumes his work.

Because the weather has been growing warmer every day, we do most of the hot work as early in the morning as possible. Salads and cold meats with mustard make dinner many days. Of course, things still must be cooked every day, for nothing keeps long in the heat, even though the cold room stays cold and the ice remains solid under the sawdust layers in the icehouse. Mr. Serle is insistent that we take care that all is fresh and good.

Mornings start out smoothly, for each of us has a routine of work that is accomplished independent of the others. When that first round of daily work is finished and the tasks specific to this day at hand are to be set and begun, Tom starts to grumble.

"You favor the lad," he says to Mr. Serle. "Just because he was a devoted little nurse when you were indisposed, you lighten the work for him."

"Tasks should be done according to the skills of the workers," responds Mr. Serle in civil tones. "You are a fine butcher and carver, Tom. I would not trust the boy to trim or truss roasts yet. He is better off picking over the cherries; that is work suited to a quick eye and nimble fingers."

"Nimble fingers indeed," mutters Tom as Mr. Serle goes out to the cold pantry. He casts a glowering look my way. "Do you know what *toady* means, Paddy? You look to me like a kind of toad."

I open my lips to defend myself and then think better of it. Tom is more than twice my size and rough in his language. I will pay tomorrow if I quarrel with him today. When Mr. Serle returns, he instructs me to divide the cleaned and washed cherries into two basins. One heap will be layered in stone crocks with brandy and cinnamon sticks added, and the other heap must be stoned. These stoned cherries will be stewed with plenty of sugar for a preserve.

"Where is the cherry stoner?" Mr. Serle asks Tom. "The lad will need it."

Tom shrugs and roots through the drawer of the dresser where implements for special tasks are stored. He seems annoyed. Perhaps it is that I have caused him to expend extra time to look for the tool.

"It is not here," he says. "Mrs. Bennet carried off her favorite tools with her. No doubt she thought that we would not be doing fancy cooking here while the family is away. We usually send the best fruit to London."

"And we still do," says Mr. Serle. "A great basket of cherries and a crate of apricots went this morning. The direction came yesterday to send the best for eating fresh and to preserve as much as possible of the rest. It is a bountiful crop."

"Well, Mrs. Bennet will have her hands full, and Paddy must make do with a knife," Tom says.

He passes me a small-bladed knife. I look at it doubtfully. I have never stoned a cherry in my life, but I determine that I will not ask for help. It will give Tom yet another chance to sneer at me. Mr. Serle must have noticed my doubtful look, for he sets down the book he was consulting.

"Set out a basin for the stoned fruit and a cup for the pits," he says. "Slice the fruit like this." He picks up a cherry and the knife and with a quick twist frees the stone from the flesh and drops the stone into a cup and the cherry into an empty bowl. "Pull a stool to the corner of the table and work neatly," he admonishes. "Cherry juice stains."

I discover that indeed it does. My fingers are soon red with the juice. It is hard to find the right rhythm for the task. I am constantly dropping a stone into the basin with the pitted cherries and having to fish it out. Also, the knife seems to grow duller and more awkward to use each time it scrapes against a cherry's pit. It seems as if I have worked for hours, but the mound of unpitted cherries is hardly reduced and the mound of pitted fruit is pitifully small.

"You are slow, Paddy," says Tom, coming behind me suddenly. "Just like a lazy Irish boy to make an easy task last the morning."

Startled, I cut myself. The knife slips against my thumb. At first I feel nothing, and then a sharp pain. Welling blood mingles with the red juice on my finger. I cry out and rush to the scullery to run cold water on my hand. Mr. Serle is there, filling a pot with stock from the boiler by the hot-water reservoir.

"What happened, lad?" he asks.

"I cut myself," I reply. Now that the blood and cherry juice are cleared away, I see that the wound is hardly mortal—a gash perhaps half an inch long on the ball of my left thumb.

"Let me see," says Mr. Serle.

"It is nothing," I say. "The knife slipped. It is dull, I think."

"A dull knife is more dangerous than a sharp one," Mr. Serle says. "Here, I will show you a trick."

He pulls a thin strip of cambric from one of the clean rags that are stored on the shelf. He binds that over my thumb tightly. Then he takes a candle end and softens it until he can spread a layer of wax over the bandage. "There," he says. "Your wound is protected and so are the cherries."

"Thank you," I say. I am not sure that this waxed bandage will last very long in actual use, but it is ingenious.

Later in the morning when there is a pause in the work, I notice Mr. Serle laying out knives on the end of the worktable. He seems to be giving the organization of them some thought. Finally he calls me over.

"A serious cook must have his own knives," he says. "I have set these aside for you. You must sharpen them and keep them clean. I will show you the technique for using the whetstone. When you are finished each day, wrap them with the sharpening stone in this cloth and store them in the drawer."

"Thank you," I say, looking at the three knives and the rectangle of gray stone he has set out on a piece of flannel. There is a small square chopper, a long triangular blade, and a small triangular blade. I am amazed. "I will try to take good care."

"Don't think they are really yours, Paddy," growls Tom. "Your Mr. Serle can't give away the things of the house."

"True," says Mr. Serle without rancor, "but I can make the lad responsible for learning to maintain his own set of tools while he is here."

"I will do my best," I say.

"When you are grown and earning a good wage by your skill, you will buy your own set of knives from the best cutler in London," Mr. Serle tells me. "True cooking is not possible without knives. Knives kill the living thing, so they are dangerous, but they create too. Knives separate, divide into parts. They chop into large or small pieces or mince to paste. Such division makes the mixing of ingredients possible. The purpose of the cook is to unite and meld, to balance and recombine flavors, to make fresh combinations of taste and reveal the myriad sensations available in the world—" He stops.

"Poetry about cooking," sneers Tom. He rolls his pale blue eyes toward the ceiling and makes a sour face. "Cooking is feeding the gut. Just like a foreigner to make a fuss about a piece of dead cow. Kill it, roast it, slice it on a plate, eat it with bread and mustard. Why bother talking about it?"

"I like to hear it," I protest without thinking before I speak.

"I imagine there is a lot you like," says Tom.

"I like to learn," I say. "Mr. Serle has much to teach me about cooking. I have never been to London and Paris." I realize after I say it that it would be more polite to have included Tom also as a teacher. Perhaps, I think, I can win his tolerance by appealing to his vanity. But it is too late.

"So beloved Mr. Serle is your teacher? Teacher of what? Be honest now!" gibes Tom. His forehead knots in anger and his face mottles red along the cheekbones. In contrast, the rest of his face and his hair look whiter than ever.

"Mr. Serle is considerate of us. Why should we not be considerate of him?" I say. Tom is unreasonable.

"Considerate?" Tom shouts in anger. "Considerate of you, a puny thing who shirks the heavy tasks. And it makes all the more work for me."

"I do my share," I reply indignantly. "You are stronger than I am for some tasks, but I grow stronger every day. You are wrong to complain."

Tom seems to decide that my anger is funny. He laughs roughly and turns to Mr. Serle. "Your catamite is feisty today," he says in a strange voice.

Before I can blink and wonder what *catamite* means, Mr. Serle leaps from the range to the worktable and lunges at Tom. He holds a long thin boning knife in his right hand. He seizes Tom by the front of his shirt, twisting it in his left hand. The point of the knife is pressed to the tender flesh under Tom's chin. Tom reaches for a knife on the table, but Mr. Serle jerks him away to the center of the floor. I gasp and move to the rack where the pots are stored.

Tom seems taken by surprise as much as I am. Fear shows in his face. "Graa—" he says, a strangled inarticulate sound without meaning.

"Take back your words," says Mr. Serle. "Take them back."

"I—" Tom begins. His shoulders are hunched as if he would flinch away from Mr. Serle if he could.

"Do not think that I am afraid to kill you." Mr. Serle's voice expresses his contempt. He is not so tall as Tom, but his tight, wiry strength makes Tom look flabby, weak, and slack in his grasp. "I do not take insults from anyone."

"Don't kill me," gasps Tom. "I spoke in jest." His arms stretch out as if he would grapple with Mr. Serle.

"I did not hear a jest," says Mr. Serle. "I heard an insult, not a joke." He twists Tom's shirt with greater force. I hear a button rend from the cloth. Tom's arms drop to his sides. He makes a frightened, groaning sound.

"Apologize," demands Mr. Serle. "Apologize to me and to the lad. Say you are wrong and that you beg forgiveness." He presses the knife under Tom's chin, and I shudder as a bead of blood drops.

I am afraid of them both. I pick up an iron frying pan from the pot rack and hold it ready. I will hit Tom if he tries to hurt Mr. Serle. I will hit Mr. Serle if he starts to kill Tom. The two men stare into each other's face.

Tom mumbles something.

"You are wrong," says Mr. Serle. "Say you are wrong. Loud so we can hear you."

"I am wrong," says Tom in a strangled voice.

"Yes, you are wrong and you know it," says Mr. Serle with a note of triumph. "And now say that you are sorry. Say 'I apologize.' "

"I am sorry," Tom says. "I apologize." His eyes look down. He is no longer trying to outface Mr. Serle. I am surprised that he gives in so quickly. Perhaps he is just empty wind inside. I would not apologize so fast if I had only meant to joke and had it taken wrongly.

Mr. Serle lowers the knife and releases Tom's shirt, pushing him away as he does so. Tom reels backward. His face is red, whether with anger or shame I cannot tell. His blue eyes are bleary with fear or tears. His knees seem about to give way under him, and he steadies himself with a hand against the table. Blood is beading under his chin but not enough to fall and stain his shirt. Mr. Serle is breathing heavily. Sweat stands on his forehead. Will they fight now? I wonder. I do not know how men behave and if their quarrel is over.

Tom sees me standing with the great black pan in my hand. "Look at the brave lad," he snorts. "Which of the two of us were you going to brain, Paddy? Let me guess." He seems subdued, ready to let the fight go, I hope.

"You can put that down, lad," says Mr. Serle. He even smiles.

"I would hit you both," I say defiantly. "I would hit you

both if you tried to kill each other. I would hit you both even though I do not know what your anger is about."

"Go away, lad," says Mr. Serle, breathing hard still. "You have not had a holiday for weeks. Go away and ride that horse. It must be ready for exercise."

I am glad to escape the kitchen. I run up the stairs to the attic to hang my smock on a peg and put my head cloth with it. I put on my shirt and pull my old felt hat about my ears. When I pass through the kitchen, hurrying to escape the anger there, Tom is slumped on the bench by the door, holding a wadded cloth to the slack flesh under his jaw and looking sour. I stay as far from him as possible and avoid his eye. He mutters under his breath, but I can see that the fight is gone from him completely. Mr. Serle is leaning against the table edge. His arms are crossed across his breast, and he is looking down at Tom.

"Go away," says Mr. Serle again, noticing me. "Tom and I will settle our differences with talk."

I hurry away out of doors. The sun beats down in the courtyard. If I were to take off my shoes, I would feel the heat of the stones. That is what I most want at this moment—to take off the heavy boots and stockings that bind my feet, to shed the woolen trousers that make my legs itch, to throw away my hat and go free. Of course, such freedom is not possible, but after I lure Gytrash from the paddock and set her bridle and strap a blanket on her for a saddle, I take off my shoes and stockings and set them on top of the fence post at the paddock gate. This much freedom I will claim.

Gytrash goes eagerly out of the gate and down to the path along the river. It is cool there where the shallow water runs flickering in the sunlight, but soon the trail turns away from the stream and crosses the meadow. We climb up toward the ridge of the hill. The sky opens up, and the town of Milford is a smoky smudge in the distance. I rein Gytrash in and sit for a long time looking out at the western horizon. I think of the place where I was born and wonder whether I will ever see it again except in dreams. Gytrash shifts and swings her head back. She does not understand why we are staying here when we could be moving. I kick her into motion and she goes gladly down from the ridge to where the path returns to the river and the silence of the oak grove.

Once we are out of the wood and in the meadow again, I dismount and throw her bridle over a bush. It is too soon to go back. The kitchen will be close and warm. The supper will be laid on the table and the servants will be laughing together. Perhaps Tom is telling what happened earlier. I wonder if he will say that Mr. Serle threatened to kill him. Perhaps by now they have killed each other. I think that I do not really care. I am tired and their anger tires me even more. I lean back on the soft grass. Gytrash lowers her head to crop a wildflower. Her lips move delicately as she mouths a small pink flower. Lethargy overtakes me.

I sit in the meadow as the light fades and night falls. The moon peeps up, a round silver coin behind the trees. I do not want to be caught outdoors under the full moon. It is not healthy, and I feel such lassitude even now. I look at my hands. The bandage that Mr. Serle made for me has disappeared. Where or when I cannot remember. I did not notice its loss. It does not matter, for the gash of the knife is barely visible now.

My hands are long-fingered. They are like my father's hands, strong and adept. I think of my parents' faces: my mother's rounded chin and straight nose and thick eyebrows that I have inherited; my father's long face with its broad nose and high forehead. Horse-faced, my mother used to tease him, saying he looked just like the animals he loved. My father's people are all slim and lanky folk, with narrow heads and big, capable hands. We grow tall quickly. I remember my brother's arms coming out of his sleeves, his bony wrists and the felt hat he favored that he would pull down about his ears so that only his wide grin and the length of his jaw were visible. I remember Eliza, slim and pale and brown-haired with a boyish figure even though she was full fifteen as I am now, and Mother remarking that the family comes late to womanhood.

A warm breeze blows from the woods, bringing the scent of

ferns. Usually a ride on Gytrash makes me feel alert, but tonight I feel sleepy and heavy. It seems hard work to remount and to ride back to the stable. I remember my shoes and reach for them from Gytrash's back as we pass the gate on the way to the stable. It is easy enough, and yet I am clumsy and drop a shoe and have to dismount and find it in the failing light. At the stable, I fumble with the straps and buckles. Gytrash tosses her head impatiently and whickers at my incompetence. By the time I have combed her and forked fresh hay and filled the water pail, it is full dark and I am yawning. "Good night," I tell Gytrash, and kiss her velvet nose. She nuzzles my hand and turns away.

Mindful of the smell of the horse clinging to me, I stop in the scullery to wash with warm water. I have to light a candle end and carry it from the kitchen so that I can see what I am doing. The moon is not yet elevated enough in the sky to illuminate the windows here. The kitchen is clean and orderly. Whatever passed between Mr. Serle and Tom after I left did not leave further chaos.

I creep up the stairs in the dark. Mr. Serle is already asleep, for I can hear him breathing deep and even. In my corner, I shed my shoes and stockings and remove my trousers. Fumbling in the darkness, I hang them on a peg. I should take my shirt off also, I think. The night is warm. I do not like to have it so far across the room. I settle the matter by taking it off but folding it up and setting it under my pillow. I say my prayers and compose myself for sleep.

CHAPTER VII

I SLEEP and then awaken abruptly. My heart is racing. Perhaps some noise startled me; perhaps a dream frightened me. The air around my bed in the corner is heavy and close. The darkness, which usually comforts me with its blanket of privacy, oppresses me tonight. I rise and draw aside a corner of the curtain that shields me from Mr. Serle's part of the room. Moonlight floods through the windows, making the shapes of the bed, the chair, Mr. Serle's trunk against the wall silvery against a shadowed background.

I cannot see Mr. Serle. I stand still, my hand on the coarse weave of the curtain. Then I hear a little snort of uneven breathing and a creak from the bed as Mr. Serle moves in his sleep. His anger has passed and he is at peace. All is well, I think. I should return to my bed. Still, I stand there watching the shadows waver in the moonlight. At this hour of the night the real world is insubstantial, melting, changing its shape from moment to moment. I feel as if I might step into the moonlight and melt away myself.

The night presses in on me, warm and close. I feel uneasy suddenly, as if my skin is too tight for my body. I am wearing only a cotton singlet that was my brother's. A month ago it came to my knees and I bunched it up about my waist when I put on my trousers; now the garment covers me from shoulder to just mid-thigh. I consider taking even that off. I want to tie the curtain back to allow more air into my corner, but think better of it. When I lie down, the bed feels cool for a moment.

I doze again and dream that I am in the garden with the gardener, Mr. Plumb, who showed me the chamomile. He wears the same shapeless felt hat. He carries a spade with a narrow blade. I ask him where he found it and he answers me gruffly that he found it beside the cemetery wall. I ask him where the cemetery is. He gestures with the spade. Following the direction he has indicated, I walk through a lush garden. Soft, thick grass underfoot makes my progress silent. On either hand rosebushes droop under damasked-pink blooms that send out their heavy fragrance on the night air. The perfume cloys with its sweetness and makes my head ache.

The dream path takes me out of the rose garden. The air is clearer now, and I feel refreshed. I pass into a grove of white birch trees. The trunks are yearning arches of paleness canopied with lacy patterns of pale green. Under the trees all is dim and verdant, smelling of fern and a musky sweetness of lilies hiding under the swords of their foliage. I want to stay here and rest, but the path compels me forward. Beyond the birches there is a clearing where moonlight pours down like water onto velvet clipped grass and ancient tombstones.

The stones are tipped this way and that. Some are fallen completely. There is runic writing on the stones, impossible to make out in the shifting shadows cast by clouds blowing across the moon and trees tossing their branches. I stoop to the marker closest to me. It is tilted on its side, but I can trace with my hand engraved letters. I am sure I can read a name, a place, dates, if only the light would steady for a moment. Just as I am sure I can form a comprehensible word, the letters change and meaning vanishes. It is as if some malicious force is taunting me to understanding and snatching it away whenever I approach.

I sigh and sink down to sit upon the fallen stone. What is the use of trying to read an ancient tombstone anyway? There is no significance in it for me. An answering sigh shocks me. I look up from the gray stone and the wavering grass. My hand clutches the rough granite. My heart is pounding in my chest. A woman is seated on the stone next to me. She is veiled and draped in some soft material. I cannot see her face. She raises one hand in a signal of greeting to me, but she does not speak.

I am standing now, looking out at row upon row of stones. On each is seated a silent figure, head bowed and veiled. Apprehensive, I walk down a grassy path. Figures nod or raise a hand to show that they are aware that I am passing. I raise my right hand in respectful greeting. I recognize no one by gesture or posture. All is silent, all is withheld. And yet this is not a desperate or threatening place. There might be peace in this silence.

I raise my arms above my head and twirl myself in a dreamy circle in the center of the graveyard. The stones and shadowy figures wheel about me. When I am still again, I see what I had not seen before: About the periphery of the cemetery stand files of shrouded figures. They are cloaked in gray; hoods hide their faces. I move to them, and as I do so, one here, another there, pushes back a hood to reveal a dead face I recognize.

These are not peaceful spirits. They do not salute me with the benedictory gesture of a hand. They are silent and yet their mouths open and close as if they would speak. Eliza pushes back her hood. Her face is thin and gaunt, transparent in the moonlight. Her lips open like the beak of a little bird begging food. Children I played with, people of the village, the sailor, who was kind to me when the terrible voyage began, show their faces. Old Aileen reaches out to me, her drowned eyes streaming tears. I want to turn my face away, but I cannot.

Then I see my parents standing together by the trunk of a great beech tree. The gray of their cloaks seems part of the smooth bark, and a down-sweeping branch arches over them. I know them from their stance and the loving way they link their arms even before I see their faces. Simultaneously, they unhood themselves.

I strain to cry out. It is as if earth blocks my mouth. There is no air. I cannot breathe. My parents' faces are ravaged and destroyed. Through the lower part of my mother's face, the bare bones of the jaw and a broken tooth are visible. A worm clings to a lock of my father's red hair and then falls to the ground, taking hair and skin with it. I will die of the terror of it, I think, and then I see that their eyes look through the veil of mold and decay with love. Forgetting all else, I look into their shining eyes, turning from one to the other. The eyes become larger and larger until all I see is the slate blue of my mother and the piercing blue-green of my father. Love flies from each black pupil to my heart. My chest is filled with longing. I am about to burst with joy and despair.

My mother wants to tell me something. She forgot a secret. Something important that I need to know. I strain to understand, but now the eyes recede. The shades of blues and greens and black are shards of color swirling past me like the ripple of waves in the wind. The draped figures of my parents have transformed themselves into hawks. They fly away, wheeling higher and higher, my mother the smaller, following my father's soaring turns. They are beautiful against the moon above the beech trees, and then they are gone.

"Come back," I cry, knowing as I strain to speak that this is dream speech and I can make no sound. "Come back. I promise that I will go home and tend your graves forever." I strive to make the words into tangible things. They are stones in my mouth that I will spit out into my palms as if they were cherry pits. There will be something to place in the hands of the sorrowing spirits. I form the words, I bend my head into my joined, cupped hands. Triumphant, I raise the words and see blood pouring out between my fingers. My cry of horror awakens me.

I lie bathed in sweat, my heart racing. The straw of the mattress on my cot, the roughness of the blanket that covers my legs irritate me. I feel my skin prickle. I am hot and thirsty and afraid. My cheek is damp from tears or saliva. I must have made a noise when I awakened, for I hear Mr. Serle turn restlessly on his bed. The slats creak under his shifting weight. He murmurs something as if he is half awake and asking a question. I must be very quiet. It is not fair to deprive him of his sleep.

I rise silently and pull my bedclothes straight. My singlet is twisted up above my waist, and I set that in order too. I shake out and refold my shirt and replace it under the pillow. When I lie down again, I turn on my side with my hand tucked under the shirt so that I can hold the little round of the ring inside the linen. Now I feel calmer.

The moon must have risen higher, for now a pale, uneven band of light shows where the curtain does not quite meet the wall of the alcove. It is less oppressive when it is not completely dark. I hold the ring and think that tomorrow I will pick thyme in the garden. The fat gardener with the pale eyes said that thyme is good against the nightmare. I wonder how one prepares the thyme. Inventing a recipe—thyme, of course, water, honey— I sleep again.

Another dream takes me. I am lying in a room on a low, hard bed. This is not the bed on which I am asleep and dreaming; I know this even as I dream. This dream bed is made of dark heavy wood, carved at head and foot with twining vines and flowers. Instead of lying on slats and a rough straw mattress, I am stretched on a hard, even, polished board with a thin pallet of goose down underneath me, just thick enough to make lying here possible. My head is cradled on a feather pillow.

I am wearing a long velvet dress. I can feel the soft texture of it under my hands, which are crossed at my breast. I cannot see the color, yet I know that it is a deep red, the luminous red of claret wine in a crystal glass. The dress covers me to my ankles, and the skirt tails across the polished wood of the bed. The room is paneled in mahogany, rich and smooth with years of polishing. Above me, the ceiling is coffered; darkly painted scenes of subjects that I cannot decipher are inset among carved mahogany frames.

The light in the room is diffuse, warm and flickering. Perhaps there are candles in brass sconces on the walls, but I do not turn my head to see them. No compulsion holds me where I am. I could sit up, move about, if only I had the will to do so. A deep lassitude overwhelms me, however. I have no desire to change my position, not even to turn my head.

The room where I lie is silent, empty of all sound. The room is clean, neutral in temperature; no odors either pleasant or unpleasant intrude. The room is neither large nor small. Nothing oppresses, nothing stimulates. The air is quiet because nothing moves here.

Outside this room is bright light and a bustle of activity. The gay voices of people chatter. I can hear the sounds of male and female, the shrill cries of children, the cough of an old man. I listen passively. If I need to know what is spoken, the words will become clear to me. The voices talk on, but no words bloom like flowers from the foliage of babble. There is a world of business and social intercourse and play outside the room where I lie, but there is no meaning and no need for meaning.

If I lie still with my hands folded across my breast and my feet, which are shod in black satin slippers, turned up to the ceiling, all will be well. Nothing will harm me. I need not struggle, I need not think. I will lie here in this safe space and dream forever.

I feel as if I am floating. This is peace, I think in my dream, this is enough. Yet just as I think that I have reached a journey's end, the room begins to change around me. The ruddy light flares up. The room becomes warmer. I can see that indeed there are candles in brass sconces along the walls. As I watch them, the candles grow in girth and height. They blaze brighter and brighter, hotter and hotter. Soon the room will be on fire.

I want to sit up, to find the door of this room that is about to burn. And now I find that when I have the will to get up from the carved bier, I cannot. I am bound to my bed with bands of iron. Afraid, I twist from side to side. I will call to the people in the corridor beyond this room. Someone will rescue me. I lift my head, and now I can see that the room has no door. Perhaps there is a secret opening with a latch hidden in the carved paneling, but it is invisible to me.

I open my mouth to call, and no sound comes. Even if I could cry out, I can tell that no one would hear me. The busy voices outside are quarreling. Shouts and angry curses drown all other sounds. I strain against the bonds that hold me, I will my throat to make a sound. I am trapped and lost. A feeling of shame overwhelms me. I was unable to lie still enough to keep peace hostage in my breast. I thought I was safe and I was in the greatest danger.

The room is really on fire now. I cannot breathe. My velvet dress grows ever more voluminous. The iron bands may break, but the dress wraps me like a shroud. It is wet now and heavy as lead. I will never escape.

With a gasp, I awaken. My blanket is tangled about my legs. My undershirt is twisted almost backward. The place is hot and airless, and a pungent odor assails my nostrils. The bed feels damp about my hips. For a moment, I think with shame that I have wet the bed. I reach down with a cautious hand. Something slippery is on my fingers.

I climb from the cot and go to the curtain. The moon is sliding downward now and the light is not so bright as it was when I last awoke. I look at my hand in the moonlight. There is a dark smear on my fingers. And now I recognize the smell; it is blood. It must be my blood.

I stand by the curtain, rigid with fear. I feel a tickle of something on my inner thigh and am afraid to look. Perhaps an animal has bitten me. Panic overtakes me.

"I am dying," I cry. "Help. Help." It is a feeble, strangled sound, but it is enough to rouse Mr. Serle.

"I am coming," I hear him respond. His bare feet make a hollow sound on the floor. "What is it?" he asks with a sigh when he sees me standing by the curtain. I have awakened him from sound sleep. He is barefoot and yawning in his nightshirt.

"God save me. I am bleeding," I say. "Some animal has come in the night. I am afraid it is still on my body or in the bed."

"Let me see where you are bitten," Mr. Serle says.

"Oh, sir, I cannot," I cry to him. I hold the bottom of my singlet down in front of me between my legs. I have made a terrible and dangerous mistake. Tears wet my face and spill down my chin. I am shivering with cold and fear.

"So you cannot show me?" He looks at me curiously. He pulls the curtain aside and goes over to my bed. He drags blanket and pallet out into the attic space where he can see them. There is a very small, dark smear on the cloth of the pallet.

soothes me. The soap makes bubbles about me, winking iridescent in the candlelight, and then froths away in the gush of water from the taps as I turn and stretch each part of me to be rinsed.

It is a relief to scrub my head free of the grease and soot that caked it. I will pay the cost of not pretending no matter how harsh the penalty. The reward is that I am becoming myself again, I think. Naked and clean, I am myself. And yet myself transformed somehow. This is not death, I realize, although it felt like it for a time. We know who we are, but we know not who we may be.

Standing in the sink, I look down at myself in the trembling candlelight. My arms are slim and strong. They are freckled golden about my bony wrists where the sun warms when I ride Gytrash. In the last two months my breasts are grown, not much but enough to see the mounds of them. The nipples are no longer a child's bumps on a flat chest; they are golden brown coins turned just a little to the outer sides of my chest. Between the jutting hipbones, my stomach is smooth, interrupted by the pucker of the place where the cord that tied me to my mother's heart before I was born was connected. Below my stomach is a thin haze of red-gold hair that I have not noticed in these months of fear and secrecy. The new hair glistens in the candlelight. I like it.

My thighs are straight and slim, with just a hint of gold hair on them. My feet, like my hands, are long and strong, except the little toe where the nail is growing in thicker and twisted. I am not perfect, and yet, I am complete and whole.

I am not afraid anymore. I climb out of the sink, take a clean rag, and rub myself dry. I tear a rag and make a pad to put between my legs. I take my smock, which I had hung beside the boiler, and button it up. I turn the sleeves back so that they do not drag over my hands. I smooth my hair and feel that it is still wet. Even so, it is soft and springing into curls already now that the soot and grease do not stick it down.

I start to go into the kitchen and then turn back again to the water tap off and to take the candles. The rag I used has the barest smudge of dark blood on it. I put it into the

"See," I say pointing, "there is blood on my bed."

Mr. Serle stands looking down at the mattress, and then he looks at me sharply. His eyes are narrowed and his brow is creased. "Is there blood coming between your legs?" he asks me.

I nod, speechless.

"Lad," he says briskly and with emphasis. "*Lad,* the first thing is to clean you and this bed. Then we will pursue the question of animals that bite in the night. Can you walk?"

"Yes," I say meekly.

"Good. Chances are you are not dying. Wait here."

I stand shivering as Mr. Serle hurries off down the stairs. He returns in a moment with a lit candle in a dish and a rag.

"I am going down to the scullery to build up the fire under the boiler," he says. "When I am down the stairs, hold this cloth between your legs so that no blood drops. You will come down and wash yourself. For now we will turn your pallet over and I will find you a clean blanket. Do you have a shirt to cover yourself when you are clean?"

"Yes," I say.

He hands me the rag, sets the candle down on the floor nearby, and goes away. I think he looks at me with pity. I take the cloth up and with trembling fingers fold it small and press it in between my legs against the private place. I remember my mother admonishing me when she set out the washtub of warm water and the scouring cloth for me on Saturday afternoon to "wash my private place as well as the rest of me." The house would be warm and my father and brother off on their own business. First Eliza and then I and then my mother would wash. My mother would comb out our hair and braid it. Eliza and I argued for the privilege of combing my mother's hair. "Now we are clean and fresh for chapel on Sunday," my mother would say when all was done. After supper Eliza and I would sit out by the doorsill while my brother and father had their wash. My brother would join us, his hair wet, and then we knew to stay out until my mother called us. "I must just wash your father's back for him," she would call. "Enjoy the evening 'til I call you in. And stay clean," she would add.

I shudder and take up my clean smock from the hook and then pick up the candle. The safe days are gone. If I am dying of some bleeding disease, I must do so with courage, I think. I do not want my parents to be ashamed of me. I make my way down the stairs where the moon throws shadows to the scullery.

CHAPTER VIII

ON THE DRAIN BOARD in the scullery is another candle. Water is running into the big sink where we wash the pots and soup cauldrons. When I first saw the place, I asked Tom why the sink was so big. He told me at least one sink had to encompass the kettles that serve to make stews for fifty people when the hunting season comes in the fall. I stand shivering on the stone floor, feeling like a rabbit myself.

I hear Mr. Serle's voice. "Climb into the sink. We will leave the water running through." Mr. Serle sets a handled pot of steaming hot water from the boiler on the drain board beside me. "Here, child," he says. "Wash all of yourself with soap and warm water. Then rinse yourself."

"Where will you be?" I ask hesitantly. I do not want him see me and at the same time I am afraid of this dark room, e ing with the sound of running water, lit only by the fli candles.

"I will be in the kitchen," he says, reading my mi you are afraid. There are clean rags on the shelf. one to burn when you are washed." I feel him rath looking at me through the flickering light. "Wh cleaning yourself, wash your hair properly enough of pretending." He turns and goes.

I climb into the deep sink and cro ment, I realize that it is foolish to was still on. I take it off and use it as a wa my head all over. The hot water

still-burning fire under the water boiler and see it reduced to ashes. Now I am ready to talk to Mr. Serle.

Mr. Serle sits on a stool by the embers of the grate. His head is bowed into his hands. I think that his posture is one of sadness, and wonder why he should be sad when I am alive and strong, not dying.

"I am here," I say. I stand in the kitchen with a candle in each hand.

He starts at the sound of my voice and turns to look at me.

"Your hair is very red," he says.

"It is still wet," I say. My voice is a squeaky treble pipe, which seems to complain although I meant only to state a fact. "It is lighter when it is dry—my hair, that is."

"Sit here," he bids me, pulling another stool beside the grate. "The coals are still warm."

I obey, and we sit silently. I feel remote from my body again. Mr. Serle must have questions for me. I would not be surprised if he were angry. The silence hangs between us. The settling of ashes as the fire dies sounds like thunder in my ears.

"I never told a lie," I say finally.

"No, you never did," says Mr. Serle. "But you never told the truth either."

"There is a reason I have to wear boy's clothing," I say.

"I am sure there is," he responds. "Do you wish to tell me what it is?"

I think about it. "I cannot," I say reluctantly. "It would not be right. My danger is my own."

Mr. Serle makes a noise of surprise in his throat, but says nothing for a time. Then, "Danger? Are you sure?" he asks.

"For now I have to keep my secret," I say.

"Does that mean that I must keep your secret too?" he says. "What are you asking of me?"

"Please, please," I beg him. "What will I do if they find me out? How will I live and eat?"

Mr. Serle looks at me as if he is considering something that is me and also some larger thing that stands behind me. I almost turn to see what it could be. "I think she does not know what she is asking of me," he says as if to himself. He is silent for a longer moment, and then, "For now your secret is safe with me," he says in a louder voice. "I will not betray that you are not a lad. But I will not lie for you either. If you are challenged, I will not pretend."

"Thank you," I answer. He must be a good man. "You are fair. I cannot ask more."

"Really?" he looks at me, considering something, and then looks away at the red of the embers in the grate.

We are silent again for a space. The moon streams in on the floor at the other end of the room, and the clock ticks on the wall.

"I have to ask you something," I say.

"Yes?" he encourages me.

"Do you know what happened to me?" I ask meekly. I feel a fool. There is some explanation, there must be, that I should know but do not.

"What happened to you? Oh, you mean the blood?"

"Yes," I say.

"How old are you, child?" Mr. Serle asks me.

"I am fifteen, I think," I tell him. "I will be sixteen in the autumn."

"That is old enough for it," he nods.

"Old enough for what?" I ask.

"Old enough to show the signs of womanhood," he answers. "Did you not know?"

"Know what?" I ask, bewildered.

"Each month a woman sheds some blood. It is the sign that she is grown and ready to marry. I do not know a word for it in English."

"But I do not want to marry," I protest.

"Not that you have to marry," he says, "but that you are ready if you wish to."

"Yes," I say doubtfully. I wonder if he is right. "My mother was not fifteen but twenty-five when she married. Why did she wait so long if she was ready?"

"Where I was born, men and women marry by the age of twenty. It is considered right to do so. Perhaps your people think differently, or perhaps your mother was waiting to meet a man such as your father," Mr. Serle says. He sounds a little impatient.

"That must be it," I say, relieved. "She was waiting for my father." My mother's voice comes back to me unbidden. "The family comes late to womanhood," she says softly to Eliza, who is sniveling in her bed. My mother's voice is just loud enough for me to overhear.

"But what does it mean *really*?" I wonder out loud. "Womanhood and ready for marriage. Why did no one tell me about it before?"

"I have no idea." Now Mr. Serle sounds annoyed. "Perhaps it is against your religion to talk about it."

What does he mean, I think, and what is making him angry? "I am sorry," I say. "You have been kind to me, and I am bothering you with questions."

"I am tired," he says. "Ask what you need to know."

"Why blood?" I ask. "I do not understand it at all."

"Nor do I, truthfully," says Mr. Serle. "You will have to ask a woman. Or a doctor of medicine. It has something to do with making a woman's body ready for a man."

"A man?" I am confused again.

"A man goes to a woman," he says. I can hear the patience in his voice. "They make a baby. The baby grows where the blood came from."

"But a baby grows under its mother's heart," I cry. "Love puts it there. When it is time for the child to be born, the midwife calls to it, and it comes."

"Indeed it comes," says Mr. Serle. "It comes from between the woman's legs. It comes from the place where you shed blood just now. Did you think you came out of your mother's mouth?"

"How do you know these things?" I demand. It is not natural that a man would know so much about a woman.

"I had a wife," he says. "We had a child."

"A wife? A child?" I exclaim without thinking. Why has

Mr. Serle never spoken of them? I wonder. I look at him, amazed, and something in his face makes me afraid.

"But your wife?" I squeak out. My need to know presses on me beyond all. "Your wife told you such things? I am sure my mother never talked to my father so."

"Maybe not when you were near," admits Mr. Serle, "but believe me that your father would have known where a baby is born."

"The midwife called it," I say stubbornly.

"Next you will be telling me that babies are found in cabbages," he says.

"I know better than that," I say. "That is a fairy tale."

"Indeed?" he says.

"I will tell you what happened to me," I say. Suddenly I want to talk about it, to make another person understand.

But Mr. Serle has changed his mind. "Not tonight," he says. "We are both too tired for stories now. Besides, there is a problem we must solve."

"What?" I ask.

"I found this under your cot when I turned the pallet over," he says, and holds up the bag bulging with bread that I keep against the day of disaster.

"That is mine," I say. "You have no right to take it."

"The bread is moldy and there are insects in it," Mr. Serle tells me. "If you leave it much longer, there will be mice."

"But I have to keep it," I say, stretching out my hand for it. "I have to."

Mr. Serle makes no move to hand the bag to me. "Did you go hungry for a long time?" he asks somberly.

"Two years," I whisper. I feel such shame to talk about it.

"That is a long time," says Mr. Serle. He seems to withdraw into himself for a moment. "I knew three months of living without enough to eat and years of want. But two years starving. Two years is a very long time."

"Two harvests of nothing," I say. "Two years with the grain going to pay the rent and nothing left." In my mind I see my sister, my parents, and my brother wasting thinner and thinner. Without willing it, I look down at my hands. I remember the bones sharp under the skin. It seems not right that flesh sheathes them now. "Two summers of herbs from the pasture edge boiled in water, and the oatmeal the priest bought and doled out to us. Charity and despair."

"I understand," he says. "It is terrible when hunger cramps the gut and clouds the mind. And terrible when the dawn brings a return of pain and no hope. But a bag of moldy bread will not save you if bad times come again. Indeed, this decay may kill you."

"I do not care," I protest. "I will eat that rather than beg. The bread is dry. I can soak it in water. You are lying that it is moldy. You want to save it for yourself."

"No." Mr. Serle seems sorry for me rather than angry at my impudence. "You cannot keep it. I will stand for many things, but not for a room infested with vermin."

I begin to cry. "I cannot just throw the bread away," I say. "What if the crops fail? What if there is no food?"

"I will give you a choice," he says. "Burn it in the fire now. You can think of it as a sacrifice to the gods of famine. Or leave it with me, and tomorrow I will scatter it in the pasture for the birds to eat."

"Let me keep it a few days more," I beg.

Mr. Serle shakes his head. He looks sad. "Believe me; it will be worse if you wait. Make your choice now, and then you must sleep. And so must I for what remains of the night." He yawns widely. "I do not want to be cruel. I wish to be kind to you, but you must let it go."

My heart leaps in my chest. He wishes me well. "Will you scatter it for the birds tomorrow?" I ask. I am going to trade bread for kindness, I think. Is it a good bargain? And then, suddenly, I too yawn, so widely that my jaw cracks.

We both begin to laugh, then stop, awkward. The candle gutters and only moonlight casts shadows in the room. I can see Mr. Serle only dimly.

"What am I come to?" Mr. Serle says as if to himself. "A nursemaid and a harem eunuch perhaps. Nothing surprises me anymore."

I cannot imagine what he is talking about. I say nothing.

"Enough of change and sorrow. Time to sleep," he says to me.

We walk up the narrow stairs. He gives me the blanket that hangs at the end of his bed.

"Thank you," I say.

"Are you calm now? Can you rest?" he asks.

"I think so," I say.

"You do not sound entirely sure," he says dryly.

"There is one thing I wonder about," I admit. "What is a catamite?"

Mr. Serle's face crumples into lines of laughter. He stops himself and passes a hand across his jaw, wiping away the signs of mirth. "A catamite," he says, "is a boy used by another man for sexual purposes."

"What?" I say. I will have to think to get my mind around such a thing.

Mr. Serle seems to understand. "Think about it some other time," he says kindly. "It is hardly my problem now, no matter what poor Tom has decided to think."

"Yes," I agree sleepily. I feel very tired. The moon has set and the faint light of dawn shows in the window above Mr. Serle's bed. There is nothing to be done except to close my eyes. Without my willing it, my eyelids seem to be shuttering my sight of their own weight.

"Sleep through the day," Mr. Serle tells me. "You tended me kindly when I was sick with the fever. It is your turn to rest. When Tom is gone this evening, you will come down and sit by the fire and eat and talk to me. Rest now. I think you did not sleep much during the night."

He turns away and draws the curtain of the alcove. As I sink into sleep, I hear his footsteps recede across the attic floor. Mr. Serle is married, I think. Where is she? Sleep is brushing clear thought away like mist rising through the trees. My brother's shirt with the ring sewn into the tail is under my pillow again.

Mr. Serle must have replaced it when he turned my mattress. I think of the gleam of the red stone set into its gold band. The ring given to my mother by her aunt and then from my mother to me. Woman to woman to woman, I think. The ring is safe. Am I safe? I wonder, but I am too tired to think about it.

CHAPTER IX

I SPEND THE DAY SLEEPING, too lazy to feel hunger, and now evening has come. Tom has gone to his mistress's bed. The kitchen is clean and quiet. It is safe for me to come down and sit on a low stool by the dying embers of the grate. I feel strange with the rags tied round me. I have made a sort of belt with a thin strip of rag. I tie a doubled cloth that passes between my legs to the front and the back of this belt. It feels odd and awkward and yet comforting, somehow. If what Mr. Serle told me is true, all women do this, my mother before me and maybe Eliza too, although I do not think so. Eliza would have told me about it.

"Drink this," Mr. Serle commands, handing me a mug of hot liquid. "It will warm you. And when you are finished, the time will be right to tell me your story." He sets a plate with bread and cheese beside me.

I taste the liquid in the mug. It has a strong salt flavor. I recognize beef tea. Mr. Serle has made for me the same nourishment I made for him. I drink and am grateful.

"My sister died and then my parents died," I say. "I told you. My brother and I set out for America."

"It is time for you to tell the rest of the story," says Mr. Serle. "What is your name, child? Certainly it is not Paddy."

"My name is Mina," I say.

"Mina?" he says as if he is considering whether this might be the truth or not.

"Mina. Mina Pigot." I repeat it firmly. "I did not leave my village in these clothes."

"That I believe," he says.

"How can I tell you?" I ask. "How can anyone know the sorrow of it?"

"Say it and I will try to understand," he says.

So I begin, and as I speak, the kitchen, the warmth, even the dark face of Mr. Serle fade into the memories of my lost home. "I told you of the hunger and the sickness. Did I tell you that the landlord's men came and burned the cottage? It was a place of disease, they said. Three people had died there. After the roof was gone from over our heads, my brother and I stayed for a few days with an old woman in the village whose children were all gone to America. My brother consulted the parish priest about what we should do. The priest wrote letters for many of the old people in the village. He—the priest, that is—had received a letter from old Aileen's son asking the priest to find someone to bring her to him in America. The landlord would give her passage money in exchange for her signing away the rights to her tillage, the priest said. My brother thought we should have the same, but when the priest inquired about it, he was told that all of our land was forfeit because our father had been dismissed from his job and not paid the rents for two years. By rights, the factor said, we should have been evicted from our cottage a year before. We knew that was a lie, but what could we do? Father was dead and any papers he had were burnt up.

"We counted up the money we had left. My parents' savings had gone out coin by coin to get us food as our need became ever more desperate. I should tell you that when my father lay dead and our mother beside him dying, she made us swear on her prayer book that we would take all of the savings hidden behind the stone in the wall beside the hearth and use it to go to America. We were not to put a penny of it toward burying them, she said. We could take the two good sheets and use them for winding clothes, she said, nothing more. 'They were good enough for our marriage bed, and they will do to bury us beside your sister,' she whispered in her fever. 'Promise me!' "

I stop and swallow hard. If I stop now to weep my sadness, I will never have the courage to continue. Mr. Serle sits silent, his face turned toward the fire. His calm and the warmth of the mug in my hands comforts me. I lower my head to drink for strength and then hurry on.

"So we buried them and counted the savings and made our plans. The priest thought that old Aileen's son might help us to find respectable work in New York; he might not be very rich, but he had said he would find the money to send for a passage if the landlord would not do right by his mother. He must have a heart, the priest said, and if we brought his mother to him, he would be kind to us. To tell you the truth, it did not look like such an easy task to shepherd the old lady to Dublin and across the water. She declared herself afraid to go, and then, after the priest read her the letter from her son yet again, when she would go, she wanted to take every pot and pan, every stick of furniture, and every rag and button with her.

"My brother and I needed little time to prepare. All we possessed went into two sacks, one for each of us. The money I sewed into the sleeve of my brother's coat, except for two silver coins that we agreed I should have against a disaster that separated us. Those I sewed into the hem of my petticoat.

"It took much more effort to help Aileen choose what she might take and what she should give to her neighbors or to the priest for those in need. Once she made up her mind to go and began to pack her bundles, she changed her mind completely about taking her possessions with her. She thought only of the dire distress of those she was leaving behind. One must have the churn even though her cow was sold, and another the spinning wheel for wool even though there was not a sheep left among all the cotters. 'Times will be better for them soon,' she said. 'They will be ready with the things they need when times are better.'

"Now we were hard put to make her understand that she would need a blanket for her bed on the ship and a pot to cook her food as well as such warm clothing as she could find. She would have left all behind, saying that her son in America would give her what she needed, and the poor souls of the village had greater need than she.

"She was hard of hearing, old Aileen, and stooped with age

and hunger. Our conversations with her had to be carried on at a bellow that the whole row of cottages must have heard. And in the excitement of preparation, she began to forget who was alive still and who dead.

" 'Just run across the road with this iron skillet for your mother, Mina,' she said. 'It is too heavy for us to carry to America, and she will value it when we are gone.'

"Tears came into my eyes. From the cottage door we could look out and see the burnt shell of the house and the heap of chimney stones. Seeing me brush tears away, Aileen came to the present again and hugged me and cried herself and asked me to forgive her. How could I not?"

I stop. My hands are trembling. Mr. Serle looks up and, reaching over, takes the half-full mug of broth I have been holding. He sets it on the range.

"It is getting cold," he says. "We will warm it again for you."

He stirs the coals and sits again, head bowed, hands clasped before him. He is waiting for me, I think. It is up to me to go on or to stop. I blink back the tears that blurred my eyes at the thought of my mother.

"Poor Aileen. At last, the one object she must take with her to America was her crucifix. Her son had carved it for her from linden wood when he was a lad, before he left to make his fortune. She fussed and fussed that she would lose it. At last, my brother made a little hole in the top so that she could put it on a string about her neck. Then she was happy. My brother cut a stout walking stick for her too. She could use it as a cudgel, he shouted at her ear, if anyone dared to bother her. She laughed and laughed at that.

"So we were soon ready to depart. We would walk to Dublin and there find a ship to carry us to New York. The priest had heard that they were leaving almost every day. We joined a group of people from our village going to Dublin. A bedraggled, sorry lot we were.

"All of the animals had been sold to pay the land rents or to raise passage money. The last morning came, and we assembled in front of the church. The priest came out. The people who were leaving stood weeping. Those who were staying stood around us, gaunt, silent wraiths of themselves. The priest spoke to us for the last time. He blessed us for the journey. That comforted many."

"And did it comfort you?" interposes Mr. Serle.

I am surprised at his question. "Of course," I say. "Faith always comforts the afflicted."

"I see," he says.

I wonder if he does. He must have no faith to question that a blessing did not give us courage for our journey. It flashes through my mind to ask him what he prays for every morning, but I think I had better not. I am dependent on his goodwill if I am to stay here.

"Eat some bread," he suggests. "You must be hungry."

I shake my head no. "I will go on," I say.

"We piled our bundles on an old cart and made ourselves the mules to draw it, taking turns about. Most of us, worn out with care and starvation, or recovering from illnesses made longer and more wasting by our hunger, tired fast. For many folk it was all they could accomplish to carry themselves along at a creeping pace.

"It took us three days to walk to Dublin. The first night we sheltered in a little church by a crossroads. It was empty but clean. Perhaps someone had swept it before leaving forever. There were withered flowers on the altar. It had not been so long since people were there, and yet, the life was drained out of the place. It did not feel haunted, though. We found water in a brook nearby and pot herbs in the meadow beyond the little graveyard. We made a fire by the entryway and cooked what we had as soup to share among the lot of us, fifteen or so. So we sheltered there and were glad of it, for it rained that night.

"The next day dawned cold and drizzling rain. The road was rough. Not many folk had passed this way. One of the men said that it showed a great change, for this had been a route to the markets that many cotters used. The countryside seemed empty now. As we plodded our slow way, we came down a hillside and into sight of a village below us. The men in front of the file came hurrying back and shouted at us to stop. They could see bodies in the street, they said, and dogs. We should stay away from a place of disease and evil omen.

" 'But what if there are living in the cottages?' asked one of the women. 'What if there are souls too weak to come out?' She began to tremble at the horror of it.

" 'We dare not risk the illness that has felled them, so that none are left to bury the dead,' argued the man who had turned us back. 'Besides, the dogs are dangerous. We must turn and go back to the last crossroads, or else make our way to the south across the fields and well away from this accursed place.'

"The people stood silent. We knew he spoke in sorrow and in fear. What right had we to expose ourselves to fevers? There were little children among us. They might be orphans soon enough no matter how we tried. It was not right to seek danger. But my heart still hurts when I think of the unburied dead and someone ill and helpless and alone and the dogs barking in the street. I cannot help but feel that we argued for saving the children, but what we most truly felt was fear for ourselves."

We sit silently a moment, Mr. Serle and I. Then he says, "You and your people did right, Mina. The living must go on as best they can."

I sigh. "What's done is done. It cannot be changed now except in wishes of the heart, and, there, I will pray to be forgiven all my living days."

"I understand," says Mr. Serle. We are silent for a space.

Mr. Serle gives me the mug of beef tea again. I curl my hands around the warmth of it. "Drink," he says. "You must tend to yourself."

Obediently, I take a sip of broth. Mr. Serle says he understands. I hear his words and wonder what is in his heart.

"You were on your way to Dublin," Mr. Serle reminds me to go on with the story.

"Rather than turn back to retrace our path, we moved out into the sodden fields and made our way around the dead village. We each took a stone in our hand in case the dogs scented us and came out. The wind was for us, and we made our circuit unscathed back to the high road. We hurried on for many miles before we felt safe to stop and rest. Just off the road someone had begun to build a sod house. A yard was cleared and stones piled ready to make a chimney. A well had been dug and a stone wellhead set in. On a small handcart, turf sat waiting to be unloaded and used to build the cottage walls. We shouted and hailed, but no one appeared.

" 'They must have gone,' said my brother. 'There are no tools, no signs of a recent fire. This turf has been rained on more than once. See how the edges are frayed and spreading, no longer sharp-cut from the spade.'

"The drizzling rain had stopped. The sun was setting among long streaks of rose-red clouds on the western horizon. Because the well water seemed sweet and good, we decided to stay the night. The sky had cleared and we were on a rise. None of us had the courage after what we had seen behind us to push on in search of another village. If there was worse ahead, we could wait until tomorrow to face it. So we camped there in the lee of the half-built sod hut for the night. We cooked the oatmeal the good priest, Father Fintan, had given us for the journey. That was little enough to eat, but we could build a good fire and be warm.

" 'Indeed,' my brother whispered to me, 'we are better off in the open than in some place where pestilence lingers in the dark corners.'

"My brother looked over the handcart and carefully unloaded the turfs, piling them neatly to the side. 'Look here,' he said, 'this is a good enough cart. You and I, Mina, can push it together. We can put our things and old Aileen on it. It will ease the burden for the others if we divide our load from theirs.'

"Perhaps it was theft, but it did not seem so. The cart answered a need for us, and no one told us no."

"Nor would I," says Mr. Serle quietly.

"The next morning it was hard to go on. We ate a little barley bread and drank water to ease the cramps of hunger, and then we walked again. We passed abandoned fields and a gang of ragged men breaking stones. They were being ordered at their work by two men on horseback. No one spoke to us as we hurried by, our faces averted from their shame.

"Later on that day, we began to see the signs that we were drawing near a great city. There were cottages with poultry in the yard and flowers. The road widened out and became smoother under our feet. The cart became easier to pull. In our joy to have our end in sight, we hurried beyond our strength. I stumbled. The cart almost went over. When we stopped to rest, Aileen, who had been riding, insisted then on getting down and walking.

"It was easier pulling the cart without Aileen perched on it, even though her old bones made her as frail and as light as a house wren. It was easier work, but famished as we were, we moved more and more slowly. Aileen hobbled gamely enough, but her fastest pace was less than our slow plod. The group we had traveled with were slow too, but even so, they moved ahead of us. Soon we lost sight of them.

"We must have taken a wrong turning among the confusion of streets, for after a while the road began to run not into the city as it should have but between low stone cottages with a fruit tree or two and gardens behind. My brother knitted his brow and looked about as he does when he is worried. Aileen was walking so slowly now that she was almost at a standstill.

" 'We are on the wrong road,' my brother said morosely. 'This cannot be the way to the docks.'

"As my brother and I stopped, old Aileen tottered to a stone by the road and sat down on it. She leaned forward on her stick. 'I must rest awhile,' she gasped. 'Water.'

" 'I will go ask at a cottage,' my brother said, and he went off down the path to the door of the nearest place. I heard the barking of a dog and then a voice bidding the dog be still. My brother returned and said we should come down to the dooryard, there was water for us.

"We helped Aileen to her feet and made our way to the cottage. The handcart we left by the road. Truthfully, we could not have pulled it a step farther. In a way, we did not care about it anymore. My head was swimming, and I could see that my brother staggered when Aileen leaned heavy on his arm.

"As we approached, a stout woman came out of the cottage. She held a mug in her hand. 'Here is water,' she said. 'Sit on the bench by the door and rest your bones. You must have come a weary distance today.'

" 'Weary indeed,' said Aileen. 'Thank you for your hospitality.' She drank eagerly from the mug, and then my brother and I swallowed our share in turn.

"We must have looked as sorry and famished as indeed we were. When my brother, who had drunk last, handed back the mug, the woman weighed it in her hand and regarded us thoughtfully.

" 'I have just finished the milking,' she said at last. 'Rest here and you will have a basin of milk to share.'

"When she came out again, she had a bowl in her hands and three spoons in her apron pocket. The bowl held not just milk, but milk with potato rough mashed in it. Aileen's eyes grew round when she saw what it was.

" 'Christ bless you,' she said. She would have seized and kissed the hem of the woman's skirt if the woman had not moved back a step.

" 'Eat slowly,' the woman admonished, and stood with her fists on her hips, watching the three of us bend our heads eagerly over the bowl.

" 'I did not think there was a good potato left in all Ireland,' said my brother shyly when we were done.

"The woman's eyes widened. 'There is food enough here for those who have money to buy it,' she said. 'Is it true that they are starving still in the countryside?'

"Aileen let out a cry. 'Starving?' she said. 'They are perishing of hunger in the villages. We have seen dead lying unburied in the streets.'

" 'I thought it was better,' the woman said slowly. 'They say corn has come from America, and the soup kitchens and workhouses answer the need. Indeed, the landlords complain that the workhouses eat up all their profit in taxes.'

" 'Profit?' said my brother scornfully. 'They talk of profit when the people are dying of starvation and fever?'

" 'Fever?' The woman drew back in alarm. 'Are you coming from a place with fever?'

"I could see from the expression on my brother's face that he thought it would be wrong to lie to her after she had given us her food. Before he could tell all, I said reassuringly, 'There was fever in the village we came from several days ago, but no new cases for a week before we left. The danger passed.'

"The woman did not look reassured, and her words showed us she regretted having us in her dooryard. 'I hope you are rested,' she said. 'Your companions must be wondering where you are.'

"We understood she wanted us gone. We thanked her for the food and asked the way to the docks, which she gave willingly. As we rose and my brother gave his arm to support Aileen, the woman seemed to hesitate. 'Wait just a moment,' she said, and went back into the house.

"When she returned, she had something wrapped in a paper. 'Here,' she said, thrusting the packet into my hands. 'You will want food, and there are many who cheat travelers on the docks. Here are scones and a bit of ham. I can't spare more from my man's supper.'

"We took what she offered with words of gratitude, even though in our hearts we felt the shame of need. She gave to speed us on our way and to excuse her own guilt for fearing us."

"You are hard on her," says Mr. Serle. "Fever is a fearsome thing."

"Yes," I sigh. "Charity must be accepted with a humble heart, and it is hard to be humble."

"The food must have been welcome no matter how it came," Mr. Serle notes.

"It was," I admit.

" 'She is a rich woman,' said Aileen as we made our way

back to the road and our cart. 'Imagine, ham for her man's supper on a weekday even.'

"I think all our mouths watered at the thought. None of us had eaten meat for months. Indeed, when we had turned the corner to go the way the woman had directed us, we stopped and opened the packet and shared the bit of ham into three pieces. For a long time we sat by the road and chewed and did not speak. At last my brother said, 'Perhaps we should have saved it for a later time.'

" 'No indeed,' Aileen said. 'A dog might have smelled it and attacked us, or someone seeing us eat it might have tried to steal it from us. Better to have the food safe inside us than risk losing it.'

"We agreed. Besides, it was too late to change what we had done. I wrapped the scones carefully for later and put them well down in my bundle."

Mr. Serle moves suddenly and makes a sound in his throat.

"What is it?" I ask him.

"I should tell you I scattered the old bread from your bag," he says. "The birds were glad of it."

"Oh," I say, desolate at the thought of food, defense against the future, gone.

"I am sorry," he says, and, indeed, he looks sad. "I begin to understand your need of it."

For a moment I feel anger. Who but one that has shared starvation can feel the ache of belly and mind, the need and the shame?

"I am sorry," Mr. Serle says again. "I did not mean to halt your story."

"Of the walk through Dublin to the docks, I remember little," I tell him. "The streets were crowded and confusing. My brother asked the way a hundred times. Some strangers hurried by without answering him, while others were kind. Some stopped and pretended to help but told us nothing, only laughed at our country accents and country clothes. There were beggars on the corners and people lying up against buildings. We could not tell whether they were dead or sleeping. As we drew near our destination, we could see a perceptible stream of people moving to the same place. When a woman washing clothes spills soapy water into the clear brook, it makes a cloudy stream within the stream. So the people coming from all directions of the country-side became visible among the Dubliners going about their ordinary business as we converged with our bundles and carts upon the ways to the docks.

"The quays were frightening. People and baggage and animals all together. Ships great and small were berthed at the dock-side or moored out in the river, bobbing at anchor. Tangles of ropes threatened to trip us. The bustle of sailors and bewildered country folk made a shifting picture in which we could not tell which way to turn or whom to ask for help. There were bags and trunks piled everywhere and people poking about them, whether in search of something to steal or hunting for their own possessions, we could not tell.

"We agreed that it was wiser for Aileen and me to sit in a corner out of the way while my brother went down to inquire about the next sailing for America. He was gone a very long time. Aileen dozed in her place, but I dared not for fear of what might happen. At last, my brother returned, discouraged.

" 'They say there is a ship preparing for Canada in two weeks,' he said. 'And the week after that several more will go, one to New York. Two ships sailed yesterday. We came to the city too late and too soon. How are we to live for two weeks as well as buy our passage?'

" 'We can go back to the cottage,' ventured Aileen hopefully.

" 'It will be burnt by now,' said my brother brutally. I could see that he did not know what to do next.

"We sat, helpless, listening to Aileen bewail that she had ever left her home, when a man stopped beside us. He seemed to be a laborer on the dock, a rough-looking man. He stared down at us crouched beside our things.

" 'Where are you from?' he inquired.

"When we told him, he smiled a great gap-toothed grin and said, 'I thought I recognized the accent. I have a cousin lived there who left just yesterday for the New World. Stop your wailing, granny, and tell me what is wrong.'

"We told him that there was no ship for two weeks, and we had little enough to buy our fares and have something left for lodging and food when we arrived. To live on the dock for two weeks would kill Aileen, and yet, we could not pay for a boardinghouse in a city like Dublin. He took off his hat and scratched his head and hemmed a little.

" 'There's two choices here. You can come home with me and sleep in the shed, which is crowded but dry. I can give you that shelter but not food, for I have a wife and children to feed. The other way is to take the ferry today to Liverpool across the sea in England. There is a great packet ship bound for America sailing from there the day after tomorrow. We have just been loading cargo to go over to it.'

" 'Can we be sure of getting passage?' asked my brother.

" 'I cannot promise for sure,' the man said, 'but two and three ships a week are sailing from Liverpool now. Your chances are good.'

"So we thanked him and he showed us where the ferryboat was and helped my brother to buy the tickets. He gave us advice about what to do in Liverpool and to beware of those who would cheat us. After despairing, we were full of hope again."

"The world brings us good as well as evil," says Mr. Serle. When I look at him, he is gazing not at me but at the coals glowing in the grate. I have the feeling that he sees something far away from this place. Something in me wants to know what he is thinking, but the need to tell what I have seen pushes everything away.

"The ferryboat was preparing to sail when we boarded her," I continue. "We found a small space on the deck and settled Aileen out of the wind. As we put out from Dublin Bay, we saw ships sailing away to the southeast.

" 'They will sink,' I cried, excited by this new feeling of sailing across the water. 'They are low in the water; a wave will wash over the deck.'

" 'What do they carry?' That is my brother—curious and practical too.

" 'Wheat,' said the man beside my brother at the rail. 'Wheat grown in Ireland for the London folks. And that ship over there has cattle fattened on our good grazing.'

" 'But they are starving in the villages,' my brother said, his voice strangled.

"The man shrugged his shoulders. 'What do the rich London folk care about that?'

" 'But justice—' my brother began.

" 'The landowners must sell their produce and pay their taxes,' said the man. 'Who in Ireland can pay the prices?'

" 'It is wrong to let a people starve when there is bread to be had,' my brother argued. 'They should not allow food to leave the country while the folk suffer famine.'

" 'Tell that to the Protestant landowners and the lords in England,' the man returned, and spit over the rail into the water.

" 'Unjust,' cried my brother.

" 'There is no justice, lad. Forget that. And take my advice and watch your words. There is fear of sedition here.' The man moved away.

"My brother turned to me. I see the anger in his eyes still. 'We starved for nothing,' he said.

" 'Perhaps they did not know—' I began.

" 'Nonsense,' he said. 'They knew and did not care. I will not trust the gentry ever again.' "

I glance at Mr. Serle to see if he is shocked by such defiant words. He does not stir where he sits. He might even be asleep except that I see his eyelids flutter and his hand move on his knee. The fire is almost dead now. I sip tepid broth from the mug in my hands, and then I see the ship and stand beside my brother once again.

"We stood silent at the rail as the wharves and ships of Dublin fell from sight behind us. It was cool on the deck as the night closed in. We made a sheltered place between the bundles for Aileen and settled down to rest. I drew my shawl about me.

The sea chopped and the ship rocked side to side and up and down. None of us was hungry for the scones we had in our packet. The kindness of our meal of milk and potato and the ham was still with us, more than any of us had eaten in one day for many weeks. Perhaps in the morning we will want bread, we agreed.

"As we settled ourselves, my brother tapped my hand. 'Imagine, Mina,' he said. 'We are crossing the sea on a boat.'

" 'I would be gladder if we were already sailing west to America instead of east to England,' I told him.

"I could not sleep and sat huddled with my legs drawn up to me and my arms about them. I thought of Aileen, old and bent, hobbling across Ireland with courage and hope. I thought of my brother, who believes that to point out the right to people will inspire them to act according to it. He is so strong and so innocent. I thought of America, where I will work as a servant perhaps until we have money to buy land and horses. I wondered if I would find a kind mistress and a welcoming house. If we are lucky, we will prosper, I thought. We will find our own cottage as soon as ever we can. There, I will help my brother train the horses and keep the gardens.

"The sea smoothed itself, and the ship moved steadily on, sails creaking in the light winds."

CHAPTER X

THE QUIET in the kitchen stretches itself. In the grate, one red ember glows still within its winding sheet of ash. Mr. Serle rises. "Rest a moment," he says. "I am going to fetch some wood for the fire." He pushes back the hastener screen and crosses to unbar the door.

The open door lets in a rush of damp night air. The heavy heat of the last few days has dissipated into the chill of summer showers. I shiver and set down my empty mug. Mr. Serle had put bread and cheese for me on a blue and white plate. The round of it, the brown crusted roll, the yellow cheese, the silvery glow of the knife blade are beautiful.

Mr. Serle returns with an armload of logs. Raindrops glisten in his dark hair. He rebars the door and makes a little bustle of building the fire again. He fetches himself a draft of cider from the cold pantry. Before I can tell him that I am not hungry, he takes down the toasting fork from its hook, splits the roll, and says, "You must eat something more. I will make cheese toast for us as soon as the fire burns down a little."

"Yes," I say despite myself.

"Will you go on with your story?" Mr. Serle's voice invites me to speak.

"I *must* go on," I say. It eases my mind somehow to tell it.

"In Liverpool," I continue, "we found a greater version of Dublin. More wharves, more people, more confusion. Aileen and I sat patiently half the day while my brother walked hither and yon to discover what we must do and where we must go. At first, it seemed a little time to us, for there was so much to watch. There was much to be wary of also. Ragged men approached to ask if we needed our bundles carried to a ship. Women with bread and gray-looking cakes asked us to buy their wares. Two men stopped and demanded that I go with them to a tavern.

" 'Anyone with hair so red must have a fire inside,' the taller one said. 'Let us quench it with English ale.' 'Her head is as bright as a new copper,' said the other. 'That coin will pay for our ale,' laughed the first, and thumped his friend on the back. They smelled of drink and would not take no for an answer. One tugged on my shawl until I was near tears. Finally, they left us when Aileen shook her stick at them and shouted at them to be gone. I pulled my shawl over my head after that, so that the brightness of my hair would not attract attention.

"We were at the point of despair that my brother was lost or hurt, when he returned. He had brought a fresh bun for each of us, as well as hard biscuits and our bottle filled with clean water. He had good news. We had vouchers for passage on a three-decked packet ship sailing for the city of New York in two days. We eagerly ate the buns as he told us of his talks with kind people as well as with scoundrels.

"With our passage paid and an understanding of what we would need for extra provisions on the voyage, we knew we must make decisions about how to allot our resources. The coins in my petticoat and in Aileen's must be saved for America, we agreed. For the meager remainder we could choose shelter for tonight or food to carry with us. In a way, I suppose it was a comic conversation. We scanned the sky to try to decide if it would rain. We examined the docks about us to see if there was a sheltered place. We worried that the prices for biscuit and meal were the highest at the docks, but if we strayed too far, we might be lost in the faceless city.

"My brother argued that Aileen should have a bed for the night while the two of us could sit out. Aileen refused to be parted from us. She was fearful that we would lose each other. Truth be told, I feared the same if we separated from my brother.

"There were inns that took in travelers for a night for a

high price. Moored in the river were hulks of old ships. My brother said that these were inns of a sort also. Folk waiting for passage crowded in there below the rotting decks. A priest he encountered on the dock and asked advice from told him to stay away. They were cheap shelter, he said, but overrun with rats and pestilence. Many of those who waited there would never live to take their passage west.

"In the end, we exhausted ourselves with talk and stayed where we were for the night. There was a little overhang from a shed and we were out of the wind enough. We ate our biscuit— gnawed on it, that is. My brother finally hit upon the idea of soaking pieces in water in the bowl he carried in his bundle. It made a bland mush but filling enough to keep hunger quiet for a while.

"All up and down the docks, small groups of travelers were doing the same as we were. On the water, lights glowed red from ships. As we settled ourselves on our bundles, the dank smell of the docks overlaid with the sharp smell of the sea came to us on the night air. Later, I awakened from a restless doze to hear angry shouts in the distance and then a shrill scream, cut off. Then silence.

" 'Are you awake?' I whispered to my brother.

" 'No,' he grumbled. 'Go to sleep, Mina. It's all right.'

"In the morning we picked ourselves up and shook ourselves into wakefulness.

" 'Like dogs,' complained Aileen.

"My brother insisted that we take our things and go down the dock to where a brazier was glowing. A gypsy-looking man was selling tea from a steaming kettle or a thin, greasy soup from a black pot. We spent a very little of our money for a mug of tea each. It was cheaper if you had your own mug and did not have to make use of the battered tin cup the man offered. The hot liquid with a little more biscuit dipped in it heartened us for the day.

"First we waited in a line to see a doctor who would stamp our passage tickets that we were fit to go to America. Hours it took, not because the doctor was taking time to talk to the people but because there were so many of us and just the one of him. We talked to those before and after us. There was a tired mother with her two little girls, who looked very sickly. She kept warning them not to cough. 'You won't get to America to see your papa if the doctor says you are ill,' she said severely to the poor things. When a hawker came by selling bright-colored little candies, old Aileen bought them one each because she felt so sorry for them.

" 'My son will meet me at the dock in America,' she said. 'I will not need my coins then.'

"When at last our turn with the doctor came, it was over in a minute. 'You're a fine lad,' he said to my brother. 'Let's hear you cough.'

"My brother gave a sort of *ahem,* and the doctor laughed and stamped his paper. The man looked at me and then at my brother. 'Your wife?' he asked.

" 'My sister,' answered my brother. I like to think he said it proudly.

" 'Indeed?' the doctor said, as if he did not believe it, although why he should not seemed strange to me. 'Guard her well. There's many a sailor out there who would like that red-gold hair despite her grimy face.' He stamped my paper and pushed it back across the desk. 'And this is your granny, I suppose,' he said, and stamped Aileen's paper too. 'Next,' he called, without waiting for a reply or looking at us again.

" 'Why did he talk about my hair?' I asked my brother. 'Yours is as bright.'

" 'Pull your shawl over your head,' my brother answered, and we hurried down the stairs as best we could with our bundles and Aileen leaning on her stick.

"Farther down the wharf we found the store that sold food and supplies for those that had the money to take extra on the voyage. The people my brother had talked to the day before had warned him to have something by him for the rough days. Our contract tickets said that we were to have water and rice and tea and oatmeal and molasses and pork meat too. My brother wondered how they could say that was not enough. The food they give out must be cooked somehow, his informant pointed out. When the weather is rough, no cooking fire is allowed. Perhaps if you are seasick, you will not care, but if there is a week of bad weather, you will suffer indeed without food or only raw oats to chew.

"We stood in line again. Now we bought hard biscuit in a sack. After much deliberation between salt fish and cheese, we bought a very little fish and some oatmeal for a supper that night.

" 'We will be light-headed and weak by tomorrow if we do not have something more than biscuit,' my brother pointed out. 'Look how the bit of ham gave us strength for two days.'

"For the journey we bought a cheese in a rind and a piece of soap for washing. Indeed, when we had finished in the shop and packed our stuff away carefully, we found a pump and washed our faces for the first time in many days. Then we went in search of the ship that was to carry us over the ocean to our new lives.

"We had little money left, but we felt rich in resources and ready to face the hardships ahead. We were even happy though we faced another night on the dock and four weeks or more on the sea with who knows what dangers of wind and waves. The night was mild enough again. We thought our luck was with us that it did not rain. The salt fish and biscuit soaked in water from the pump made a nourishing soup. The oatmeal for the next day we kept to eat aboard the ship. We felt our strength increase for the days ahead.

"Above us the ship towered dark and sturdy. Her name was written on her, the *Abigail*. Other travelers assembled near us to wait for dawn and the time to board. A rough man, seeing us set down near the gangway of our ship, tried to argue that he could take us to an inn that would cost us almost nothing for a night with hot food. Afraid that he was looking for a way to cheat us, we assured him that almost nothing was too much for us who had nothing indeed. At that, he lost interest in helping us.

"Early the next morning we carried our bundles up the gangway. My brother and I each shouldered a sack. His contained a china mug, a pewter bowl, a horn spoon, his good linen shirt, two old singlets, his Sunday pants and jacket, and, most important of all, his riding boots and my mother's little prayer book. My bundle contained my mother's good shawl, a woolen skirt, a linen blouse, my pewter mug, an iron pot for cooking, and a big wooden stirring spoon that was my mother's and my father's mother's before her. Each of us had also a blanket to wrap ourselves against night and cold. My brother carried his knife, which was my father's, in his pocket. I had a housewife—a packet of needles and thread on cards and a little scissors—that I kept in the pocket of my skirt with my rosary. With our food, that was all we had of our lives, and that was enough to go on with."

"It was enough." Mr. Serle startles me by repeating my words. I have been far away from the kitchen. Now, as my mind and senses return, I see that Mr. Serle has toasted bread and cheese together for me. "Eat a little," he says, "and drink before you speak further."

I obey. The food is good. The sweet, rich smell makes my body crave it, and yet the taste is ashes in my mouth. I chew a morsel dutifully. Mr. Serle tips back his head to drink his cider, and I watch the strong column of his throat glow red and brown in the reflected light of the fire beyond him.

"It was a warm day when we boarded our ship," I say, "for spring was growing on us, but the wind from the water snapped the lines against the masts and blew the women's skirts about their legs. I remember I felt happy as I stood beside my brother on the deck. We had climbed to the top, even though the man who looked at our paper had told us to go first to the bunks—one way for men, the other for women. But when we asked if we could go up and look around first, he had shrugged.

" 'Suit yourselves,' he said, 'but don't say it was my fault if you find yourselves with a cramped corner above three squalling seasick brats.' Aileen said we must hurry and have all set. And he laughed and told the old lady not to hurry herself, the tide's turning would be hours yet.

"Aileen insisted that she and I must have a good place even if my brother did not care about himself. So we went down and claimed bunks beside each other. The space was cramped and

dark but clean enough to begin from. With our bundles and ourselves it was going to be crowded, but we did not worry about it.
The excitement of traveling had caught us. I found Aileen's
blanket for her and spread it. Aileen lay down on her place. She
was tired, she said. She would watch our things and guard our
food and talk to the women coming in. It would be wise to know
right away who was good company and who not to trust. I
should go up to my brother, she said, and see the sights.

"I think it was a good ship really, only unlucky. That day
she was beautiful. For hours we watched as men toiled about
her, loading barrels and boxes into the hold, mending ropes,
hoisting and then lowering sails. People streamed up the gangways and onto the decks, where their tickets were checked and
names were written on a long list just as ours had been. Then
they were directed this way and that to the places where they
would sleep.

"That night we gathered on the deck to cook our food. Only
after the ship was sailing on the ocean would the shares of meal
and bacon and molasses we had paid for in our tickets be given
out. Those who had more divided their food with those who had
not had the means to provide for themselves with extra. We were
glad that the people on the dock had told my brother what to do
and had not cheated him out of all he could pay. A family of a
man and woman with their puny baby girl had a share of the
gruel we cooked. Aileen cooed and chucked the child under the
chin and told the mother to keep it warm in the night air.

"After eating, the people sat about the deck. The light, warm
breeze rattled the many ropes that dangled from the masts.
Someone from the west country had a pipe, and so there was
singing and a little dancing and much quiet talk of where people were from and where they hoped to go. No one said a word
about the death and deprivation in their home villages. Food
and loss seemed forbidden subjects. Once in a while, a speaker
would be overcome by hidden thoughts. Sorrow would flow in a
broken voice or tears. Then the person nearest would pat the
griever's sleeve in a tentative way and murmur a hopeful word
for the future."

I hear Mr. Serle sigh. "What is it?" I ask.

He sighs again and leans forward. His hand shades his face. A log crackles and breaks behind the bars of the grate, startling me even though I know it is safely contained. I wonder if Mr. Serle will answer me.

"It is nothing, child," he says at last. "Your story brings back old thoughts." His voice is thickened as if hiding tears.

"Perhaps I should stop?" I say doubtfully.

"No, no," he tells me. "You tell it so I see it with you. That is good. Go on."

"My brother and I slept on the deck that night," I tell him. "We wanted the air and freedom while we could have it. One of the sailors told us that when the ship was under sail, the passengers would be required to stay belowdecks except for an hour to cook a meal. When the weather came on rough and stormy, even that would not be allowed.

" 'You have hard biscuit laid by, I hope,' he said to us. 'If you do not, there will be days with no way to eat. I can sell you some if you like.'

"Perhaps he meant to gull us, but he said it in a kind enough way. We thanked him and said we were provided for, and he went off for a last night on shore, whistling gaily. In our corner, we talked of the future. How we would work and own land as they say everyone can in America. We would make our parents proud of us.

"Below us, the dark water pushed and gurgled between the ship and the wharf. The lamplights of Liverpool shone through open windows and at tavern doors. Above us, for a while, stars towered in their myriads, stair upon stair of light leading to heaven. Then the wind shifted and died and clouds crept higher and the stars winked out. We drew our blankets round our shoulders and rested.

"The morning was a tumult of excitement. A last tumble of people were pushed aboard. The gangways were drawn in. The thick hawsers that roped the ship to the dock were loosed and pulled, dripping, to the decks. People stood below on the dock, waving their white handkerchiefs. On the decks about us were families clinging to each other, waving at the land, even though they knew no person on the dock below, and weeping. There were single people too, some of them looking joyously at the blue sky and swelling sails of the ship, some standing alone, gazing sadly at the wharves and sheds and dark houses of the city we were leaving.

"My brother explained to me that ships sail down the River Mersey from Liverpool when the tide is at the full and about to turn. The water ebbing from the land would carry us out to the Irish Sea. Then we would be away to the south around Cork and across the Atlantic.

"The day was fine, the wind was fair. The city and the riverbanks slipped off behind us. The captain ordered all the passengers mustered on the deck. They called a roll to see that all were present and not one extra. Anyone trying to hide to steal a passage would be sent ashore again in the pilot's boat when we cleared the mouth of the river, they said. When all was done, one of the ship officers said we could, as a special favor from the captain, stay on deck until dark fell to see the coast of Ireland as we passed away to the south. Some wept at that and sat down to stare through the ship's railing at the clouds to the west. Aileen crossed herself and said a prayer for our safe passage.

"God was not listening to Aileen that day, for lovely as it was, it held destruction." I stop. Tears choke me. "It is terrible to remember," I say.

Mr. Serle's face looks comfort. "Sometimes pain rises like a wave from the sea and overwhelms us," he says. "Let the tide ebb."

I sit silent for a moment, swallowing my grief. The flames are whispering still about the logs that Mr. Serle brought in. The pictures of the past rise up in them. "I must tell," I say.

Mr. Serle nods and looks down at his clasped hands. The tilt of his head is sad, I think. I want him to understand.

"The ship cleared the mouth of the Mersey River," I continue, "and the pilot's boat cast off and returned to port. A steady wind carried us south and west. Other shipping made the sea busy with motion close by and farther out at the horizon. Their

masts were a forest clad not in green leaves but in fluttering, bil-
lowing white. I wondered what it would be like to be out where
only the waves rolled and no other life could be seen. Now, the
white sails lit the dark of the waters all about us. On our ship,
people sat quietly on the decks or organized their places below.
Sailors went about their business. I felt sleepy in the salt air.

" 'Look, Mina,' says my brother, pointing to the left of the
ship. 'That must be the coast of Wales on the horizon. Soon we
will see Ireland over to the right.'

" 'And that will be the end if it,' I say.

" 'Perhaps not,' he replies. 'We may make our fortune in
America and return to do good in our village.'

" 'Only if the English have left us to rule ourselves,' I say,
remembering many conversations by the firelight. 'If not, our
fortune will be wasted in taxes sent to England.' At that my
brother laughs and says he thinks I am in the right.

"It is pleasant on the deck, but I think of Aileen below. She
may want water or help arranging her things. I make my way below, climbing cautiously down the narrow ladders. I carry my
brother's bag with me. He used it as a pillow during our night on
deck, and now he wants me to guard it until he has looked over
the companions with whom he will be sharing the space allotted
for single men.

"In the front of the ship are the bunks for women. The
space is cramped because it is a triangle, narrowing at one end to
the bow of the ship. We consider ourselves lucky, however, for
the bunks we have claimed are in the middle of the space. We are
back from the narrowest part but forward from the ladder that
goes down to yet a lower level. At that lower level the sleeping
quarters are even darker than ours, and already malodorous
smells rise from them. There are no windows—or rather port-
holes, as I should call them—in our room. Light comes from the
hatchway that opens to the deck. When the weather is fine, as
it is now, we have some light and air. I shut my mind from what
it will be like to be confined here in bad weather.

"As I climb down the narrow ladder from the deck, Aileen

welcomes me. We have wood-slatted beds, one over the other. In the space below the bottom one, she has stowed her sack of household goods. She has put her chamber pot there also. Somewhere she found a string, and she has used that to tie the handle of the pot to a slat of her bed. 'It will prevent it sliding about when we are on the high seas,' she explains to me.

"It makes me laugh. From the next bunk a black-haired woman with a dirty blue shawl and a comb in her hand says that when the ocean is rough we will not be allowed to use the pot at all but will have to hang from the edge of the rail outside to do our business. 'Else we will all be awash in ordure,' she says sharply.

" 'I prefer that to being swept overboard,' says Aileen.

"I am about to add my say on the subject when the black-haired woman stops combing her hair, raises her nose, and sniffs. 'Do you smell smoke?' she says.

" 'No,' says Aileen. 'But I am old and my senses are weak. What do you smell, Mina?'

"Dutifully, I sniff the air. The air is close compared to the freshness on the deck. I smell unwashed flesh, the whiff of chamber pots, cheese and salt fish and the raw-wood smell of the bunks. There is the hint of smoke. 'Perhaps some people are using the firebox,' I say. 'On the deck I saw an iron box filled with sand. We are allowed to make a fire for cooking there on calm days.'

"The woman shrugs. 'Perhaps,' she says, and returns to her task of combing and plaiting her black hair.

"I shake my blanket out and arrange it on the rough slats that are to be my bed for the coming weeks. What dreams will I dream here? I wonder. I arrange my brother's bag as a pillow, pushing the softer clothing and his blanket inside it over the knobby boots. I lie back to try the bunk. I remind myself that I must take the bag to my brother in a few moments. Above my head is rough planking; beside me the shell of the ship. At my feet and behind my head are my neighbor's bunks. We will be like sprats salted in a barrel when we are all packed in at night.

Lying there, I can hear the timbers that hold the ship together creak as she moves through the water. I fall into a reverie, perhaps a doze. Many nights have passed since I lay on a bed to rest. The slats feel rough and hard beneath me but not so hard or so rough as the stones on the wharves at Dublin and Liverpool. In my doze I dream of my mother building up a turf fire under her black cooking pot. 'I am going to make a currant pudding for your father's dinner,' she says in the dream. 'Fetch me the currants from the stone crock, Mina.'

" 'I am certain I smell smoke,' the black-haired woman says loudly, bringing me out of my doze. She stands in the center of the cabin, arms akimbo. 'I am going on the deck,' she says. 'Something is wrong.'

"At that moment, shouting erupts and feet pound above our heads. A bell clangs wildly and then rhythmically. The shouting becomes words. 'All hands on deck! All hands on deck!'

"I jump down to the floor. Aileen rises from her bunk and grips my arm in both her hands. 'What is it, Mina?' she cries. She can hear the bell perhaps, but not the words the sailors are shouting.

"I put my mouth near her ear. 'We must go up to the deck,' I bawl.

"Aileen clings to my arm. She points to the ladder to the deck below. 'Fire!' she cries.

"A thin curl of smoke rises toward us. My brother's bag! I grasp it from the bunk where I was leaning against it as a pillow. No matter what, I will hold it, I promise myself. Then I seize Aileen's hand and pull her to the ladder that will take us to the deck. Below us I can hear a child wailing and fearful shouts.

"On the deck, all is confusion. A sailor is directing men toward the group that has begun to fight the fire and women and children to the stern or bow of the ship, out of the way. Aileen and I stumble forward, since that is easiest for us. Beside us comes the woman with the two little girls. They have climbed up from the lower deck and are coughing great gasping coughs, as if their lungs would turn themselves inside out.

"Smoke rises from the center of the ship. A line of men has

formed a chain. At the rail a bucket is let down on a rope and then hoisted full and passed along from hand to hand until it disappears out of sight below. An empty bucket returns along the line of eager hands. They do not have many buckets—five, perhaps. It takes long moments to send each on its way and get an empty back to be dipped again.

" 'There is your brother!' cries Aileen, pointing, and I am relieved to see his bright head.

"I am about to rush toward him when a sailor blocks the way. 'This way, miss,' he shouts. 'Away from the fire. This way.' He herds us back to the rail and toward the front of the ship.

"Thick smoke streaming from the hatchways pushes us back. Shouting sailors rush past us. Men, women, children, crying out the names of those they have lost in the confusion, crowd along the deck. Aileen and I help each other to stay on our feet.

" 'Look over there, Mina,' says Aileen, pointing to the west. 'There are ships coming. We will be saved.'

"I peer out, coughing. The ships look small and far away. Far below us on the water is a rowboat. A sailor is pulling on the oars and gesturing up to the people. He wants us to jump into the water. I clutch Aileen's arm and point. 'Jump down!' I cry into her ear.

"She looks at me in terror. 'I cannot swim,' she wails.

"A man helping people over the rail hears her. 'Here, mother,' he says. 'Hold this and keep your head out of the sea.' He tears a piece of the railing away and pushes it into Aileen's arms. Then he rushes off to someone else. Aileen looks at me in confusion. She drops the wood and turns to move farther into the front of the ship. There is no use calling to her. There is so much noise that even I, who can hear, cannot distinguish words. The screams of people and of the animals trapped below make the very sounds of hell."

Without thinking, as I speak, I put my hands up over my ears. The past echoes in me, tears at me. I hear my own voice grow harsh, as if I breathe smoke again and not the calm air of this quiet kitchen. I draw rough breath. I must say it. I must.

"Flames lick up through the deck at the base of the central

mast. I cannot see my brother anywhere. Smoke swirls away, and then I can see that Aileen has crept out toward the bowsprit. A gust of wind blows a sail flapping across between us, and I lose sight of her. Then she is visible again. Others have joined her, inching out from the beaked front of the ship atop the great pole that will take them away from the burning hull and masts and out over the water.

"Aileen pushes one of the little girls I saw earlier ahead of her. I cling where I am, coughing in the smoke. There is no fire where I am. I can see what those in the bow cannot see. The ropes that hold the rigging above the bowsprit are on fire now. The little girl screams and points to the water. She slips sideways. Aileen reaches out to catch at her. She is too late. The child's pinafore string catches on a metal cleat, causing her to dangle for the bat of an eyelash. Then I see rather than hear the rending of cloth, and the child drops away and is gone."

I am sobbing now and cannot stop. Perhaps Mr. Serle does not understand my choking words, but he is silent. Even if he spoke, I would not hear him. Nothing but the agony that I witnessed lives in me now.

"First Aileen is a stone figure paralyzed in a gesture of horror. Then her head moves. Her gray hair has come loose from the knot she binds it in, and the thin locks blow like smoke across her face. Ash and a bit of burning sail brush past her cheek. Her shawl catches fire, the fringe flares up. She sees it and sheds it as one lets drop the peel pared from an apple, letting it go to the water. Warned by the ash showering down, she turns her head upward and sees the burning ropes and sails above her. Now her lips move as if in prayer. One hand goes to the crucifix at her breast. She brings it to her lips. And then she plunges from the ship. I am praying too. May she live, may the sea spare her.

"I hear the cries of human voices on the sea like the chirping of birds from a distant forest. A silence begins to grow around me. Mercifully, the animals no longer shriek and bellow. I hear the crackling of the fire eating the ship. A monster is disemboweling the creature that carried us across the surface of the sea as a horse carries the rider across rich pasture. The skin of the ship rolls lightly in the licking little waves. The masts are three great torches above me. The deck is warm beneath my feet.

"I scream my brother's name and listen in the burning silence for his answer. The burning of our croft and the burning boat mix in my mind.

" 'Mina! Mina!' My brother's voice carries to me on the wind like a whisper from a dream. I make my way along the rail, holding tight. Billows of smoke blow this way and that across the deck. The wind seems to be ever shifting. I cannot see where I am going nor where the little boats are below me.

"The ship wallows in the waves. The wind shifts and blows the smoke, which had cleared for an instant, back over me again. My eyes sting and blur. I remember the piece of wood the sailor thrust at Aileen. It is lying where she left it at my feet. The railing is broken here. The sailors must have torn away many pieces to make a place for the people to jump from the ship.

"I hold the wood and the bag with my brother's boots tight to my chest. In just a moment, I think, I will leap clear of the ship. But I do not move. Perhaps the devil is in the burning hold beneath me. He wants me here. I stand at the broken rail.

"Perhaps I would have stood like a statue or a witch at the stake until I was burnt to a scatter of embers, but the fire itself broke the spell. I hear the snap of a rope burned through and the roar of flame. I look up. A burning sail like a sheet of red gold floats down to envelop me in its hot embrace. I run forward along the rail to escape it. The flaming cloth falls apart as it wafts down. A great piece floats to the water, where people cry out and the men in the boats pull frantically this way and that on their oars. A smaller piece grazes me. I feel its hot breath on my neck and smell the acrid stench of burning hair. My braid has come unwound from my head, and now it too is alight. The edge of my skirt is burning.

"I do not want to stand, a human torch, at the rail of this vessel. 'Virgin Mary, Mother of God, help me,' I pray. The devil lets me go. I jump for the water. As I plunge, my skirts balloon out. The canvas sack with my brother's possessions puffs with air too. I think I will sail to America with my skirts and my bag.

Then the cold of the seawater numbs my legs. My skirts begin to absorb the wet and I feel the drag of them. I scream for help.

"Strong arms haul at me. Someone curses because I have the straps of my brother's bag wound around my arm and cannot be freed from it. Somewhere inside me, where I am not wet and cold and burnt, I am glad I have not let go of it."

I stop speaking, breathless from the rush of memory. My hands are clutched at my chest as if I still hold my brother's bag. My skin burns. My face streams with tears. I look about me, bewildered.

"Here," says Mr. Serle gently. He hands me a clean kitchen towel to wipe my face. He brings me a cup of water. "Here," he says again. "Rest a moment."

It takes many minutes for the tears to stop. When I wipe my face and look up at last, Mr. Serle is sitting with his chin on his fist, staring into the embers in the grate.

"Are you tired?" I ask timidly.

He gives me a startled look. "No, no," he says. "It is I who should ask if you need rest."

I sigh a deep breath. The story wants to be told. I hear my voice again in the quiet kitchen. "I am saved by the sailors in a skiff put out from a passing pleasure boat. As the burning ship drifts to the west on the tide, they row about in the chaos of wood and bundles and struggling people, pulling in all that they can help. Nearby, other small boats ferry the saved and the dead to the ships that help us.

"After they haul a load of living and dead into the boat, they row back to the larger ship that waits for them. We, the saved, sit humbly, crowded in together—the closeness is necessary but it is also comfort and warmth. We draw up our feet so as not to step on the drowned laid on the floorboards. One woman sits weeping over her child. She calls his name—Thomas, Thomas, Thomas—over and over without ceasing. Finally a sailor speaks roughly to her, telling her to stop. 'But he is asleep and does not breathe,' she cries. 'I must wake him to breathe.'

"The sailor seizes the child from her arms and holds him upside down and taps his back. Water pours out of the tiny thing's mouth and nose. Then the sailor rights him and sets his own mouth against the child's mouth and blows in. The thing gives a gasp and begins to wail thinly. 'There, mother,' the man says gruffly. 'There is your Thomas.'

"The woman does not speak aloud again. She stares at the sailor with great, round, frightened eyes, from which tears leak. She holds the child tight and whispers in its ear, sobbing all the while. The child gasps at her breast.

"Our little boat draws up to the side of its mother ship. The sailors help us up a ladder. When the living are aboard, the dead are hoisted after. Men in smart blue coats and gold braided hats shout orders to the sailors. Gentry stand staring at us. One lady steps back so as not to soil her shoes in the streams of seawater that drip from our clothing. Then she smiles a kind and pitying smile and comes forward to help the mother and child to a place on a bench. She seems to have forgotten her shoes.

"Ladies in white summer dresses wrap blankets about the shoulders of the saved. I lie on the deck of this glistening ship, a sodden, dirty bundle of clothing and trembling flesh, holding the wet bag that is all I have left of my brother, weeping and weeping.

"In the distance the ship is a black line of hull against blue water and three spires of flame. The wind blows puffs of white smoke toward the southwest. The water is littered with the debris of poles and blackened planks and gray floating rags that may be dead animals, or the bundles thrown overboard by the desperate people, or the people themselves adrift on the tide. Tears choke in my throat, and I lose all consciousness."

CHAPTER XI

I WIPE MY EYES with my fists. Mr. Serle is watching the fire. "You survived the *Abigail*," he says. His voice is gentle; his face seems kindly in the flickering light. "You survived the *Abigail*," he repeats. "I am in wonder. I read reports of the tragedy. Now you have made the horror of it real to me."

I nod at his words and begin to tremble. "I live it still," I say.

Mr. Serle rises. He stretches out a hand as if he would touch me and then lets it fall. "You need warmth," he says. "I will heat more broth."

While he pours the dark liquid into a pan and sets it where the fire is still hot, I sit breathless still. The burning ship, the sea, the falling child, the screams of pain—my mind cannot let go of them. As if he reads my thought, Mr. Serle speaks quietly. "It is not so long ago you suffered," he says. "In time you will find ease. You have told me of courage and humanity as well as disaster."

His hand touches mine as he gives me the mug again. I drink the warm broth and think of what he says. "Perhaps someday I will say you are right," I tell him. "Good happened as well as evil, but I feel the pain of loss no less for that." I sigh. My tears have dried and the drink strengthens me. But the past still holds me and my story pours from me again. "I was rescued," I say, "and I must have fainted. When I come to myself, the sun is lowering in the west and the pleasure ship that rescued me and others is approaching the wharves of Liverpool. A ray of light strikes full in my face, blinding me almost. I am aware of stirring about me, but it is hard to see more than dark figures. My throat hurts.

"When someone comes between me and the slanting light, I can see again. A woman is stooping over me. Her skirts sweep about her as she bends. Her face is shadowed within a bonnet decorated with pink satin ribbons. Her hand touches my cheek. 'Poor child,' she says in her English voice, 'poor child.'

"I sit up and look into her face. 'Poor is not what I am,' I declare. My voice in my own ears is coarse and hard from weeping. 'I am fortunate. Fortunate to have left a place where want and illness strike the good and spare the bad. Fortunate to have my life saved by brave men who dared to bring their little boats up to a burning ship. And I have two coins sewed into my petticoat, see.' And I grasp her hand to show her where the money is hidden. I think I must have been mad in that moment. Perhaps it was her voice that reminded me all at once of my mother's accents and of the injustices of smooth-tongued English landlords that made me speak boldly without thinking."

Mr. Serle nods and says, "There are times when one has no choice but to speak."

"Yes," I respond eagerly, "I discovered it was not so wrong to say what I felt. The lady did not seem shocked or insulted. She gave me clean water to drink, and then she held my hand in hers and looked into my face carefully.

" 'Tell me who you are,' she says.

"I feel ashamed then for being angry at her. She cannot help her fine clothes, pale skin, and satin ribbons any more than I can help my sodden skirts and salt-rimed face. A lady must look like a lady, after all. It is her role in life. So I say yes, I will tell who I am.

" 'Mina, Mina Pigot,' I tell her. I tell her also about my brother and how I must find him so that we can start again to seek our fortunes in the New World. Perhaps I tell her more than she wants to know about the deaths of my parents and the deserted village and the grain ships sailing out from the starving land. After a while, she pats my hand and advises me to rest.

" 'You are a brave girl,' she says.

"When the ship reaches the port of Liverpool, she and her husband will conduct me to a respectable inn where I can rest for the night. As the saved leave the ship, the master writes down the name of each person. Tomorrow a list will be posted near the harbormaster's office on the wharf. Tomorrow I can search for my brother, they say. The lady and her husband and their servant walk with me from the ship up the twisting byways of the city to a comfortable inn of several rooms.

"There they summon the housekeeper, Susan Coates, and give her instructions to care for me. They pay the innkeeper for three nights' lodging and give me something extra for new shoes, for my old ones were lost in the sea.

" 'Please,' I say. 'Who are you? How may I thank you for your care of me?'

"The lady laughs and pats my hand. 'A gift means more when the giver takes no payment,' she says. 'We wish you well in finding your brother and your fortune, little mermaid.'

" 'But how can I thank you?' I insist. I would like to stroke the pink satin ribbons that make a shiny bow under her round chin.

"The lady takes a stern look on her face. 'By being a good girl,' she says, and turns away to climb the stairs to her chamber. Her husband bows without speaking to me or to Susan and goes along behind her.

"I like Susan as soon as she speaks to me. Her voice is low and has a throaty tremble that gives it character and depth. She is dark and ruddy. Dark hair with a red tint where the light catches it is tied up in a coil at her neck. Little curling tendrils of hair escape at her temples and ears. Her brown eyes flash with feeling. Her clear, olive skin flushes red across the cheekbones when she works by the fire or speaks of difficulties. Her person is ample like her voice. She would make three of me at least.

" 'Dear me,' she says, looking at me in the light of the fireplace in her small sitting room. 'We have some work to do. You look like a half-dead sparrow dragged in by the cat. And put that wet sack over on the hearth away from my good rug.' She speaks firmly and yet her eyes look kindly on me, and her face glows. I set my brother's bag down gently where she has indicated.

"The first thing that Susan does is to remove my sea-bedraggled clothes, all of them, down to my skin. She gives me a basin of warm water and bids me sponge away the salt. She finds an old wrapper of her own to cover me and orders me to sit by the fire and warm myself. I shudder and turn away from the glow when she pushes a stool next to the grate. Without speaking, she nods to herself and moves a screen to shield me from the red heat and the smoke. She understands my fear without my saying a word. In that moment I know I will love her forever no matter what else befalls.

" 'And now,' she says, as she puts my stained clothing into a pot and pours hot water over all, 'now we will soak the salt out of your skirts and petticoat and camisole. While that is setting, I will cut your hair.'

" 'My hair?' I whisper. I am hoarse still from weeping. I put my hands to my head. Startled, I understand that the right side of my hair is a ragged tangle. Black, frizzled ends of singed hair rub off in my fingers. The ache I have been aware of without thinking of its source is the burn along the outer shell of my right ear. My braid hangs still from the left side, but when I bring it across my shoulder I can see that it is all red and black and eaten into until it is half gone. I would weep again if there were any tears left in me.

" 'I am going to cut it so that it is more even,' Susan says. 'You will look a thousand times better. Don't worry,' she says in response to what must be fear in my eyes. 'You will not have that rope of red-gold to your hip, but you will still have plenty of hair when I am done.'

"Susan is as good as her word. When she finishes with her scissors, she has trimmed the longer, unburned side of my hair to shoulder length. The other side has been shorn of the burned ends. She has noticed the burn on my ear and soothes it with salve from a little jar she keeps in the hutch across the room. Finally she combs my whole head so that the longer hair blends with the shorter. She gives me a scrap of mirror so that I can see that I appear to be a normal girl. Now that my hair is dry, the strands about my face have sprung out in a fine haze of curls.

"Susan looks at me thoughtfully. 'You look like an angel with your hair a halo about your head. You must do as the lady said and be a good girl. Your heart should copy the beauty of your head.' "

I stop and look at Mr. Serle. Perhaps because the flow of my voice has ceased so suddenly, his face is turned to me, not to the fire.

"Yes?" he says.

"No one before ever said the word *beauty* to me. I wonder if it is good or dangerous?" I raise my hand to touch my hair. It is a relief to feel it soft again, not stiff with dirt. It must look now as it did that night when Susan cut it.

"Good or dangerous? You ask me difficult questions, child." Mr. Serle shakes his head slowly and murmurs in a voice I can barely hear, "Beauty is truth."

I think about that but can make nothing of it. I feel as if I am not myself but someone who lives in an alien world and must weigh each thing that happens, each word that is spoken, to find whether it means safety or threat for me. If my mother called me beautiful, my heart would leap with the knowledge that she loved to see me, but Susan's words frighten me even though she seems kind.

"Well," I sigh, "I do not know. It seems a danger to me, but I forgot it until now. I remember the hearth littered in scraps of hair and the dead snake of my braid. Susan does not study me again. She takes a broom and sweeps the hearth. She wrings out my clothing, rinses my brother's shirt and trousers, the blanket, and even the sack itself, and sets all on a rack to dry by the dying fire. She offers me food: ham and cheese and bread. I want to eat but I cannot. The smell sickens me. I have no appetite.

"I worry about the things in the sack. Feverishly, I put my brother's boots where I can see them. They are water-stained, but Susan promises me that she will give me grease for them in the morning. The pewter bowl, the china mug, the horn spoon I set reverently by the boots. These things my brother held and used. My mother's prayer book is ruined with water. I put it beside the boots to dry. I will keep it, but it may never be opened again. I am beyond weeping over it. I am so tired now that I cannot hold my head up to speak.

"I sleep that night on a trundle bed in Susan's room, well content to rest and be warm. Nightmares of the lost souls floating in green water turned crimson by the red of a blazing fire seem a small price for a night in a quiet room. Awakened by the fear, I lie and think that I did not see my brother's face among the drowned. That must be good, I think, and settle my mind for sleep again. Surviving makes one hard. The heart can hold only so much before the mind says stop, no more feeling."

"Ah, yes." I hear Mr. Serle sigh. He is not looking at me now, but sitting as he was with his legs stretched before him and his hands clasped at his knees. I wait for him to speak again but he is silent, and so I plunge on.

"In the morning Susan gives me soup of bread and warm ale and tells me the news. My benefactors are gone. Their coach took them away before dawn broke.

" 'Will you tell me who they are?' I ask.

"Susan shakes her head decisively. 'They did not tell me,' she says. 'If the lady wished to be known, she would say her name.'

" 'But I would say her name in my prayers,' I tell Susan.

" 'You can remember her in your prayers without her name,' says Susan smartly. 'God knows who she is.'

"I put my head down sadly.

" 'Do not sulk, child. And names being the subject, what is yours?'

" 'Mina,' I tell her.

" 'I am Susan,' she says. 'You look better this morning, although you are still a broomstraw of a thing. You have been starving, I think.'

" 'Myself and others,' I say sadly. 'And now many who dreamed to go to a land where there is work and food have lost their lives in trying.'

" 'But the news from the docks is better than anyone

hoped,' Susan says. 'The ship is lost, burned up and gone to the bottom with perhaps fifty souls, God rest them. But two hundred and more were saved. They say the crew, and the captain, and the sailors, and even the gentlemen on the ships who saw the smoke and came to help behaved like heroes. Lord Nelson himself could not have been braver. The baker brought the news this morning.'

" 'What of the dead and the living?' I ask. 'How can I discover where the old woman from my village and my brother might be?'

"Susan's face shows sympathy, but she shrugs her shoulders. 'The dead that were fished up by boats coming into Liverpool are on one of the hulks. They put the bodies of the drowned there to guard the city against disease. They will keep the dead a day or two apart and then bury those who are not claimed in the Potter's Field. You can go to the hulk to see if there is the body of anyone you know. I would go with you, but there is work to do here that I cannot leave to others.' I think that Susan's eyes brim with sadness even as she says the harsh words.

" 'What of the living?' I ask. 'Are they all scattered about, or are they on one of those hulks also?' I feel despair. The grim dilapidation of the hulks we saw in the harbor as we left Liverpool weighs on my thoughts. They are coffins indeed. And yet, if everyone is in different inns or lodging places, how can I begin a search for my brother and Aileen?

" 'The living may not all be in Liverpool,' says Susan. She is setting up a tray with baker's rolls and tea in a brown-glazed pot. It must be for one of the gentry upstairs. 'They say that the tide carried some of those clinging to timbers away toward the coast of Wales. There may also be survivors who were picked up by ships going to other ports—to Dublin or even to America. A captain who took in one or two poor souls would not turn back his ship. They say that the pleasure boats that came in yesterday afternoon and in the evening made a list of the names of those they rescued. It will be posted up somewhere on the docks. The priest of the church at the port may have knowledge also.'

"When I am dressed in my dried clothing, Susan finds me an old shawl to cover my head. My hair is not long enough to make a braid, so I have tied it back as neatly as I can with a bit of string. I am shabby but respectable enough, I think. I have directions to the hulks where the dead lie and to the church where I may learn news of the living.

"I am stepping out the door when Susan exclaims and calls me back. 'You cannot go out in the streets with bare feet,' she cries.

" 'But I have no shoes,' I remind her. 'And the money the lady gave me will be better saved for my passage to America or to nurse my brother if I find him ill.'

" 'You will cut your feet or be treated like one of the beggars if you go out in the city unshod. Here,' she says, and pulls out clogs and rough stockings. 'Use these for today.' She looks at me sharply. 'If you like them, you can use the money the lady gave you to buy them from me.'

"I pull on the stockings and push my feet into the clogs. Then, shod for the city, shawl pulled modestly about my head and shoulders, I set out to find the only people in the world who know me.

"I make my way through the streets to the wharf. I stay close to the wall, for there is much bustle and traffic. I am constantly afraid of being pushed out under the wheels of a passing wagon. The clogs that Susan has given me are a little too big. I am awkward and slow until I am used to them. It is good she insisted, though. The streets are filthy with garbage and dirt. I am very glad not to be barefoot here."

I stop to drink some broth. My throat is dry. The story is hard, I think. I will not go on. The kitchen is so quiet that I hear the light touch of rain against the window. Mr. Serle is silent. He does not seem to question that I have paused. I wonder if I can bear to relive what follows now, and then I remind myself of what Mr. Serle said. There is humanity here as well as disaster, even though I did not see it at first.

"At last I find the wharf. I stand on the end of the pier and look out at the broken hulls tilted on the water. I have no idea what to do next, until a man sitting on the dock edge with a fishing pole in his hand looks up at me.

" 'Ring the bell, miss,' he says. 'Ring the bell on the post there good and loud. Make a good bang.' He nods to the post at the end of the wharf by a ladder that descends to the oily water.

"I ring the bell vigorously several times. 'Good job, miss,' the man says. He grins up at me and then turns back to his fishing. I wonder what sad creatures he pulls from the dirty river and whether he is glad to eat them.

"I shade my eyes and look out. A small figure appears on the deck on the nearest hulk and waves its arms. I wave back. The figure disappears with jerking steps. Soon a skiff pulls out from behind the boat and dances toward me across the rippling water. Someone is rowing fast and efficiently.

"When the skiff comes to the ladder, the rower loops a rope into a ring below and calls to me in a shrill voice. 'Are you come to view the dead from the *Abigail*?'

" 'Yes,' I call to him.

"He grins up at me, an empty, toothless smile. 'Come down the ladder, missy. Down the ladder easy. Hold tight. I will keep her steady,' he cries in a voice like the mewling of the gulls that fly across the river and perch on the sodden posts of the wharves.

"Gripping the slimy steps, I back down the ladder. I am startled when the little man grips my ankle firmly to guide me to a steady footing in the rocking skiff. He holds my elbow tight in one hand and pulls on the rope with the other until I sit down. Then the rope flies loose from the ring, and he whirls the oars about. Seated facing him, I can see that he is a wizened little man with short, bandy legs and broad, muscled shoulders. He cocks his head oddly to one side as he looks at me.

" 'Brewster, eh,' he says in his high voice, tipping his head to the side.

" 'What?' I say. I realize that he turns his head to see me. He has a great scar across the left side of his head. The socket above his left eye is caved in, the eyelid partially gone, and the eye itself white and dead with a smear of blue iris off center.

" 'Brewster,' he repeats. 'My name. I lost my eye at Waterloo. Thirty-three years ago that was.' He tips and turns his head, grinning. 'Took a shot to the throat too. Never spoke the same since.'

"His right eye, which fixes me with a bright gaze, is blue like water reflecting a summer sky. His right eyebrow, a bushy clump of black mixed with gray, bristles with energy. It seems his one eye and eyebrow have taken on all the work of two. 'Well?' he says impatiently.

" 'Mina, my name is Mina,' I reply.

" 'Well, Mina, it's a sad world. Lost someone in the ship-wreck, did you?' he shrills at me.

"I dislike his shrieking voice. I dislike his curiosity. I regret that he knows my name. 'I hope I will not find my friends among the dead,' I respond, trying to keep my tone civil. 'Yet I was separated from them and must begin my search somewhere.'

" 'Best to begin in hell and climb up to the light, eh?' he says.

"I do not know what to make of that and so am silent as the skiff slides under the great cable that moors the bow of the hulk to an anchor in the river. We climb a short ladder to the deck. I stand, fingering the stuff of my shawl and adjusting it on my head, waiting while the man, Brewster, secures his rowboat. Three large cats, two tabbies and an orange tiger, sun themselves on the deck. They sit up and stare at us with unblinking eyes.

" 'Nervous, eh?' Brewster says, wheeling about on his bandy legs and tipping his head to look into my face. 'Try not to take it to heart, missy. The ones you'll see? Think of them as asleep. It will distress you less.'

" 'I have seen death,' I say, rather stiffly perhaps. 'I am anxious to know if my brother is among the dead or to be searched for among the living. Of course I am nervous.'

" 'Of course,' the man says, as he leads me toward the stairs that descend below the deck. The ship smells so of decay and pollution that the odor in the large space below, where twenty or so bodies lie, seems only somewhat closer, more intense, not different in kind.

"I walk slowly down the line of the dead. They are laid

neatly, with their heads to the wall and their legs extended toward the center of the room. The sea has stained them gray and brown. I can see that some once wore brave red skirts or vests, but even what I know were bright colors yesterday are muted. The bare feet at which I stand are milky white or mottled brown. One pair of legs, half bare, are darker. I look to the face and recognize the sailor who tried to give Aileen a piece of wood to sustain her in the sea. His face is smoothed of feeling, blank. His clothing is burned, and the flesh of his arm too; I can smell the ugly odor under the heavy, rotted smell of the hulk.

"I continue, looking deliberately at each face. Cold grips my chest despite the warm closeness of the space. The faces look familiar and yet strange to me. Here is the man who sang a song of lost love that first night on the deck of the ship. Here is one of the little girls whose mother warned her not to cough in front of the doctor. On her chest is a stick doll. She must have had it in the pocket of her pinafore, and now someone has laid it on her body. I notice now that several of the bodies have objects on their chests.

"The man, Brewster, sighs beside me. 'I try to lay them out respectably. Some of the people who come can hardly stand to look at the faces, so I put anything I find in the pockets right out there where they can see. It helps some if they can say they recognize a pocketknife or a bit of finery instead of the face.'

"I do not like it. I imagine this wizened man, hopping about the bodies, tipping his head this way and that to see with his one eye as he searches the drowned for their private things. Probably, I think, he steals whatever is not claimed. Or he may steal even from those whose families come to claim them. He can always say that anything that is asked after must be lost in the ocean.

"As if he can read my thoughts, Brewster says, 'It is all done as the gentlemen in charge say it must be. Everything found on the bodies is sold to pay toward the burials. I do not know who it makes feel better, but the money from the things and the charitable subscription pay for the priest to say a prayer at the graveyard. Do you think the dead would like it so, missy?'

"I do not answer him—as if I could. The last body in the

line is that of the black-haired woman with the blue shawl who sat combing and braiding her hair that hopeful morning that was only yesterday. Her shawl is gone, but her long hair, sea-tangled, lies like kelp on the rough boards under her head. Her body is twisted; one arm is flung out above her head, the other reaches to grasp at nothing as if she still struggled to save herself. Her comb has been placed beside the streaming inky river of her hair.

" 'Do you know her?' Brewster asks me as I stand beside the woman's body, my head bowed.

" 'Not really,' I answer. 'I exchanged a few sentences with her. She smelled smoke on the ship before any of us.'

"Brewster is staring down at the face of the black-haired woman. 'I would have liked to know her,' he says in his strange, whistling voice.

"I do not understand his meaning. I cannot tell if he is making fun of her or making some obscenity of her death or whether he means to express regret of some kind. 'Why?' I respond finally. I do not want to waste time here with this dreadful person. If my brother and Aileen have escaped this end, then I must search elsewhere.

" 'Why?' Brewster squeaks at me. 'Why, because she looks a fine woman of strong character.' He looks at me with his tip-tilted stare. 'How else will the dead live except we think of who they are?' he says.

"I look up at Brewster, startled. I am standing to his right and so it is his right, whole profile that I see. The attitude of his head and body speak reverence and concern. Perhaps I have been misled by his unpleasant voice and dead eye to think his mind deformed.

" 'Did you find the ones you were seeking?' he asks me.

" 'No,' I say. 'My brother and Aileen Magrett are not here.'

"Perhaps Brewster hears the despair in my voice, for he pats my arm. 'You will ask the priest at the mission house by the wharves,' he says. 'And then you can look at the lists posted down by the shipping offices.' His voice squeaks and whistles in his throat. I nod and tell him I have directions to the places.

" 'Did the woman have a friend with her on the ship?' he asks me, nodding to the body at our feet.

" 'I am not sure,' I answer honestly. 'I do not remember. She had her berth with the single women, though.'

" 'You should take the comb,' he says. 'Take it to keep her memory alive.'

" 'I cannot,' I object. 'Someone may still come for her. It would not be right.'

"Brewster shrugs and twists up his face and looks at me, but he does not insist. We turn back and make our way to the narrow stair that leads up to the deck. I am relieved to be out-of-doors again even though the river and the ship smell of ordure and the rank rows of the tenements and the dark warehouses slump along the mucky riverbanks.

"We pause on the deck and breathe the heavy air. 'You keep cats,' I say, nodding to the trio, which has been joined by a fourth animal, a smaller patchwork cat of orange and black and white.

" 'I keep cats,' Brewster agrees. 'They keep the rats away, eh.'

"I shudder. 'Now I have seen the dead,' I say. I feel a deep sadness that I cannot express. Perhaps the man who sang his song, the child with her crude toy, the woman who wore a blue shawl are at peace. Perhaps they are in a safer place than I am. I turn to the man who has conducted me past the row of corpses. 'What of the living? Where are they?'

" 'Many of those who survived the *Abigail* set sail this very morning on another ship,' Brewster tells me. 'They were not afraid but eager to get to their new lives.' He shakes his head and looks his one-eyed wonderment at me. 'Was it despair that made them brave, or was it faith?'

"This is a question that I cannot answer. I am numb to emotion. I want to escape the rotting smell of the hulk and the pathetic relics that were once human beings. I want to find my living brother. Perhaps then it will be safe to feel again.

" 'They will bury these dead tomorrow,' Brewster tells me. 'The medical inspector will order it in the morning. Tell those you meet to come soon to find their friends.'

" 'I will,' I say.

" 'Come here at dawn if you wish to attend the rites,' he squeals. 'You could sing a hymn at the grave. Your voice is sweet. I sang once, but Boney's muskets ended all that for me.'

" 'I am sorry,' I say. I feel helpless and tired.

"The strange little man looks into my face. His one eyebrow twitches. 'Do not fret about it, miss,' he says. 'I am long past grief for what cannot be changed.'

"The little skiff dances across the waves, taking me back to the wharf. The little man leans on his oars and bids me a courteous good-bye. I am sorry to have judged him harshly at first. He has been kind enough to me.

" 'Well, good-bye, then, Mina,' he says. 'Hope, eh? See if the priest has good news for you. Climb into the light.'

"Before I can answer, he whips the rope from the ring, pulls sharply on his left oar to point the bow of the skiff back toward the hulk, and plows both oars into the slimy water. The skiff is almost out of hearing distance as I part my lips to say good-bye. I wave and shout my thanks. Brewster does not answer but tips his head to one side. I think he is smiling his toothless smile, but the light reflects around him and I cannot be sure.

"I stand on the pier with my hand over my eyes to shade them from the light and watch the skiff until it disappears from sight behind the coffin hulk.

"When the skiff and Brewster are gone, a cloud drifts across the sun and the light no longer glitters and plays on the moving river. I turn back toward the town. The man with the fishing pole looks up at me as I pass and nods. We do not speak. As I toil along the street in my ill-fitting clogs, I see a woman and a little girl walking slowly toward the wharf that I have just left. I know what they will find when they go out to view the dead. I am about to turn to go to them when someone jostles against me and a rough hand jerks the shawl from my head.

" 'Here's a flaming head,' a male voice says. 'Who stokes your fires, sweetheart?'

" 'Leave me alone,' I cry. 'I am going to meet my brother.'

" 'Your brother?' jeers the man. 'Let me introduce you to the brotherhood of man.'

" 'Introduce her to me,' says his friend beside him.

"I run then, as quick as I can in the awkward clogs. Behind me I hear laughter.

"The day is wearing on. Everything in this place seems dark and confusing to me. The houses lean into the street, shutting out the sun. People crowd everywhere, selling or begging. Women hang laundry from windows. It must be grimy again as soon as it leaves the washing water—if that water indeed was clean. Whey-faced children huddle in cellarways. Slops trickle in the street.

"I ask two women sweeping before a great building where to find a priest. They lean on their brooms and look me slowly over from head shawl to clog-shod feet.

" 'She's a gawky pole of a thing,' says the nearer one.

" 'And bold as the red hair on her head,' says the other.

"I realize that my shawl has slipped back. I adjust it over my head before I speak again. 'I need your help,' I say. 'For the love of Christ, tell me where I can find the priest.'

" 'She needs our help,' the nearer one says to the other. 'The city is overrun with the starving Irish. What would we have left to feed our own if we helped everyone that begged to us?'

"I grit my teeth to keep from screaming at the old biddies, clucking away to each other like the hens when the hawk circles. 'I do not ask for food,' I say as politely as I can. 'I do not ask for food nor money. I wish only to know where the priest can be found.'

" 'The dear priest,' says the one to the other. 'Such a kind young man, even if he is half Irish himself. He's making himself sick ministering to the slobs and sots he finds on the docks. Why should we send him another one? And not respectable, by the look of her. They say red hair is the devil's gift.' They exchange sly glances.

"I leave them nattering to each other and appeal to a woman carrying a basket of laundry. She directs me to the mission on the docks.

"At the mission house I am bid to take a place in line. No one will answer my questions about where lists of the survivors of yesterday's disaster or messages from one immigrant to another are placed. The people about me seem bewildered to mindlessness.

"When I at last reach the priest, I find a boy, not a man. He has mud-colored hair, blue eyes, an open face that should have been round with life and laughter. Instead, he is drawn and exhausted. His eyes dart here and there as voices call his name joined to prayers or imprecations. Perhaps the ranks of the destitute who have come to him day after day stand between us, but I cannot feel his eyes seeing me.

" 'I have survived the fire on the ship,' I begin, but before I can open my mouth to tell him my need, he speaks. 'God in His mercy spared you. Pray to Him in gratitude.'

" 'I do,' I say eagerly, 'and—'

" 'Father! Father!' says a man rushing up and kneeling at his feet. The priest looks down at him in dismay.

" 'Bless you, daughter, for seeking the safety of the poorhouse rather than a life of sin on the streets,' he says to me in a distracted manner. The man is tugging at his cassock hem. 'Accept charity with a humble mind.'

" 'Thank you,' I say. 'But I seek information, not charity. I have lost my brother, and—'

" 'Bless you,' the priest says again. 'Accept the will of God and pray for your brother's eternal soul. The sister at the door will tell you where to go.'

"I open my lips to speak and then close them. What use is it to ask help where it is clear that help cannot be found. 'You cannot wring blood from a stone,' my father would say. I make my way out to the open air, and a relief it is to be out of the crowd and the smell of despair. I will not be going to the poorhouse, that I am secure in. My parents and the other crofters of our place had many tales of the hunger and the cruelty and the illness that awaited those who took charity from the county. I know in my heart that I will steal and sin rather than lock myself in a prison to pick rags.

"I make my way along the dock. A man speaks to me in a language I have never heard. I see women at the doorways of the dark buildings that tumble along the streets to the waterside. They lean against the doorposts, jutting their hips forward, tossing their unbound hair, and calling out to the men who pass by. I am glad that I am thin. If these women are what men seek, they are not so likely to bother me. Still, I am afraid.

"I avoid looking anyone in the eye, for I do not know who they are or whether they are dangerous to me. The sun is high above. I feel light-headed and confused.

"A line of about ten men is walking toward the end of the next dock over from where I stand. They stumble against one another and waver as if they are not sure where they are going. Two men with muskets come behind the line, urging them on.

" 'Move ahead, move ahead,' a stentorian voice carries across the water. 'Move ahead.'

"A cloud drifts over the sun and suddenly I can see more clearly. The men are not just silhouettes gesturing and pointing, but individuals. There is a tall, shambling fellow at the front of the line, and after him a stout man with narrow shoulders and a thick waist—'a barrel of a man,' my mother would have said. The third in line—my heart turns over in my chest—is of medium height, with broad shoulders and a head of blazing hair. I cry out I know not what words or sounds and begin to run back along the dock.

"I rush frantically through the people working to load and unload baggage. I fall over sacks, but no one helps me up. I have lost a clog in my tumble and must scramble to retrieve it from close by the wheels of a rumbling wagon. By the time I come to the end of the dock where I saw the line of men, they are gone. I look this way and that, shading my eyes with both my hands, for the cloud has passed and the light dazzles on the water.

"At last, among the weavings of ships and barges and small craft on the water, I make out a heavy dory with men pulling on oars along each side. Clinging to a post and leaning out to the river as far as I dare, I scream my brother's name.

"I think that someone in the boat looks up and shades his

eyes to look back to where I stand. His oar drags in the water and, the rhythm of the rowing broken, the boat slows. A man with a musket in his hand stands up and, reaching forward, strikes down the hand of the man who paused to look back. The boat moves steadily away.

"I scream my brother's name again and again. The shouts of men working on the ships and the docks and the mewling of the sea birds are my only answer.

" 'Forget the farewells, girl,' growls a nearby voice. 'He's gone and left you.'

" 'Where are they going in that ship out there?' I ask the man who spoke. He is lifting sacks from a wagon. He pauses and looks out at the boat pulling steadily for the center of the river. Then he looks at me and smiles an inward smile.

" 'It's a gang of men pressed to service on the government's ships,' he says. 'They say there's a couple of packets bound out for Australia tonight carrying prisoners. There's the *Ocean Queen*, a government gunboat, standing outside the harbor too. The word is that she's shorthanded and looking for sailors. The captain won't care that some of them were found in the gin hall.'

" 'My brother would never be found in a gin hall,' I say indignantly.

"The man slings another sack from the wagon to his handcart. 'Come along with me, missy,' he says, 'and I'll give you a bed for the night. You can look about yourself in the morning.'

" 'No!' I say. 'I have a place. How can I get word to my brother on one of these ships?'

" 'The truth is, you can't,' the man says. I wonder if he is telling me the truth. Tears begin to well in my eyes. I pull the shawl farther across my face.

" 'Don't cry, miss,' the man says in a voice that tells me he wants me to cry. 'Your brother will be fed and get his grog too. It's you who will be on the street.'

"The man picks up the handles of his cart and goes away. Perhaps he does not care if I cry or not, for he does not stay to watch me weep. Through the haze of tears I see the boats pull out into the center of the river and make their heavy way to the great packet anchored there. I stand like a post all that afternoon watching for a red head on the deck, but I can make out nothing however hard I strain and squint my eyes. As the sun declines in the west over Ireland, turning the river to blood, the ship draws up her anchors and shakes her sails free and slides away on the outgoing tide.

"I think of throwing myself into the river then; my hand is on the last post of the wharf. Only I remember that it would be a sin. I think of my parents and Eliza. If I die by my own act, I will not see them in heaven, where they surely are. I think too of my brother. Wherever he is, my heart tells me he is not dead. The water lapping at the pilings of the wharf below me looks cold and dirty. I do not want to die here. And so I make my stumbling way back along the docks."

"Are you sure the man who said the ship was bound for Australia was telling you the truth?" Mr. Serle asks.

"I do not know," I say. "Why should he not tell me the truth?" Tears overtake me. I mop my face with the towel Mr. Serle gave me earlier.

"Does your brother have a name?" asks Mr. Serle gently.

I answer reluctantly, "Daniel. Daniel Pigot. My father named him for Daniel O'Connell. My father said O'Connell was a famous man who would liberate Ireland if he could. But he died and never liberated anything that I heard of. Still, my brother was proud to be called after him."

"Perhaps he tried," says Mr. Serle in a tired voice.

"Perhaps," I concede. I do not like to say my brother's name even to myself. By saying it I distance him. Giving his name to someone is giving him away. Better to see his face and to hear his voice without separating him from my thought with a name. I want to explain this to Mr. Serle, but it is too difficult and I am too tired. I do not forget my brother by not saying his name. I hold him closer.

There is a silence. I feel my eyelids heavy with sleep and my head nodding down to my breast. I catch myself with a jerk and look over at Mr. Serle. He sits with his hands clasped between his knees and his head bent.

At last he speaks. "You lost all," he says softly.

"No," I protest. "I have my brother's boots that I cherish for him. I wear his shirt and his trousers. I have my mother's prayer book even though it is swollen from the seawater. I can hold it and remember it in her hand." I am silent. Why should I tell this man more? I ask myself. He does not need to know of the ring. If I tell him that, I will have given him everything. Not everything, I remind myself. The rest of the story is still mine. "No, I have not lost all," I say into the silence of the kitchen. "I have my brother's boots, and I will see him again in this life."

"I believe you will," says Mr. Serle.

"I will," I answer. "He had the little money that remained after he bought the tickets and supplies for the voyage to America sewed in his sleeve. He is cleverer than I can ever be. No one will cheat him as I was cheated. If only I can go to America, I will find him."

Mr. Serle nods his head slowly. He does not speak.

"I am so tired," I say.

"Yes," says Mr. Serle. "You have suffered much."

"It hurts to think of those days," I confess.

"Of course," he responds. "The pain of the past dies slowly, slowly." I nod at his words, but he is not looking at me. He gazes into the shadows of the chimney place. He does not turn his head to see me rise and go. The chains of the smoke jacks jingle in the draft. Outside, the night wind whispers. It is very late.

"Good night," I say.

"Good night," Mr. Serle says. He still stares into the shadows. His voice is distant and kind.

"Good night," I say again, looking at him. I wonder if he is thinking of his wife and where she is. Has he too seen the dead? A scatter of rain taps the window. The stones in the courtyard will be wet and dark in the morning. I leave Mr. Serle staring into the dying embers in the grate and climb the stairs.

CHAPTER XII

I SETTLE MYSELF in my bed and sleep. The telling of my story has eased me. That Mr. Serle does not assume, as the priest in Liverpool did, that my brother is gone forever gives me courage. Wrapped in my old blanket that still smells of home, I dream not of stones or coffin rooms and velvet gowns but of my brother sitting by the hearth, whittling a wooden boat for me to sail in the brook. The rain blows itself away in the night. I awaken to the clear dawn and the sound of Mr. Serle murmuring his secret prayers.

The thought of those I have lost stays with me all the hot summer day, however. Despite my good sleep and calm awakening, the images of sickness, fire, and death come creeping over and over again between me and the living sun. I shake them off with work.

The day moves slowly through its familiar routine of bread and broth and sweets. The usual tasks are interrupted only by a notice sent to Mr. Serle from Mrs. Bennet in London that I should be instructed to obtain rose petals from Mr. Plumb, the gardener, as many as can be had. I am to make rosewater for cooking and to scent a skin lotion; a recipe is included with Mrs. Bennet's note.

When my other tasks are done in the kitchen, I go out to the garden. The roses must distill their essence overnight, so once I have begun the process, I will be free to tend to Gytrash.

I find the gardener, Mr. Plumb, bent over a border of pink and white flowers. He appears at first to be weeding, but I realize, after observing him silently for a moment, that he is inhaling the sweet scent of one of the plants.

"Ahem!" I say.

Mr. Plumb straightens up in a leisurely way and turns to look at me. "Yes, Paddy?" he says mildly. His moon face beams at me, pale under the high-crowned straw hat he wears pulled low about his ears. The backs of his plump hands and his forearms are weathered red by the sun under which he toils, but his face in the shade of his hat is always pink and white. "Yes, Paddy?" he repeats. His little eyes with their stubby lashes twinkle at me.

"Mrs. Bennet has sent word from London," I tell him. "She wishes roses picked and the petals stripped for making rosewater. She says I am to tell you that it should be the same amount as last year. She says no cutting corners. She has seen the basket of the white Madame Hardies you sent the gentry two days ago, and she knows that there must be a quantity of the scented roses this year and just in their prime now."

"She knows that, does she?" Mr. Plumb grumbles. But he grins at me amiably enough. "You brought the tub, of course, Paddy," he says.

"A tub?" I ask. "What tub?"

The gardener sighs. He hitches up his earth-stained pants and then settles his hat more firmly about his ears. "This way," he says, and gestures me to follow him. From the shed beside the vegetable garden, he produces a very large and very ancient tub and two pairs of clippers. "Bring these and follow me," he says, leading the way to the cutting garden that runs in two long beds from the orchard to the river's edge. I struggle along after him with the tub in my arms.

"Mind the thorns," Mr. Plumb instructs. "And shake each blossom to be sure no earwigs nor no bees are inside. Milady Bennet will not like an earwig in her rose lotion."

I follow his rotund, slow-moving figure from bush to bush, picking the roses as he tells me and shaking each one gently. At each clean flower he nods with satisfaction. "There's no ugly earwigs in my beds," he grunts happily.

At last the tub is overflowing with pink and white and red sweet-smelling roses. The heat in the garden and the rich smells of vanilla and clove make me light-headed. The gardener, however, pauses every few minutes to sniff the air appreciatively and to repeat, "There's nothing so sweet as a midsummer rose."

"Now I have to take the petals off, I think?" I ask him.

"A great shame it is to ruin beautiful flowers," Mr. Plumb says. "Yes, strip the petals and do as Mrs. Bennet has told you. And bring the tub back as soon as you are done. You saw where it belongs. Mrs. Bennet always borrows the tub. With her borrowing ways, you would think that she has nothing at all in her kitchen."

"It is good of you to lend your things," I say.

"In the summer, my grandmother used to make sugared mint leaves. A rare treat we thought that was," he says meditatively, and then gives me a disquisition on the preparation of sugared mint leaves. I listen with proper respect and thank him. Mr. Plumb nods ponderously, hitches up his trousers, tugs down his hat, and returns to his work—or perhaps to smelling his flowers again. I do not loiter but lug the tub of roses to the kitchen door, where I sit in the sun and strip the sweet petals into a clean kettle. The mound of whole flowers seems surprisingly small when reduced to petals. Nevertheless, I follow Mrs. Bennet's receipt and set all to steep in the proper way.

The next few hours are mine to groom Gytrash, to ride her down through the meadow to the riverbank, and to spend a little time in reverie. Then, with the summer sunshine still bright on my neck, I turn back. Tom and Mr. Serle are in the kitchen working on the supper and arguing about the best way to make a great pie for the harvest dinner that the master has ordered for all hands when the corn is brought into the barns. I slide behind Tom's back into the scullery; there I wash and tie my head scarf over my hair, careful to hide it all.

"Here is Paddy, the noghead, at last," says Tom. "We have been waiting for you to clean the new potatoes. Back to the scullery with you. They are waiting in the sink."

I am glad to escape his notice. It is cool in the scullery, and the water runs softly over my hands as I scrub the potatoes and the beets too. When I bring the basins of clean vegetables out to the kitchen, Tom is boasting of his women.

"I have my pick of them," he crows. "At the dancing the other night, Jane and Maggie came to blows and hair-pulling over who would dance the second reel with me. Tell me, Mr. Serle, do you like them dark or fair?"

Mr. Serle is making a dish of something he calls salmagundi. He instructs me to prepare and pass the ingredients to him. He does not seem to be listening to Tom. The inward look of his face suggests that his mind is somewhere far away. Meanwhile, his deft hands line a bowl with strips of the lettuce I have washed. He layers boiled chicken, minced yolks of egg, anchovies that I have rinsed free of the salt in which they were packed. Onion and parsley minced together are heaped into a depression in the center of the bowl. I blanch green beans at the range and these garnish the sides. Then I am sent off to draw good oil for a salad dressing of tarragon, vinegar, crushed peppercorns, and oil.

"It would look even better in a clear glass bowl," says Mr. Serle, regarding his handiwork thoughtfully.

"It's too fancy as it is for the servants' supper," grumbles Tom, who usually does not seem to mind luxuries. "The master will be surprised to see meat on the bills for both dinner and supper today."

Mr. Serle shrugs. "They didn't want poultry sent to town this week, but word came late. Two hens were already killed. I will not waste good food."

"I think the women will welcome a special supper," I say. "They have been hard at work today washing and refreshing the feather beds."

"Now we know the reason for the special dish," Tom teases. "Our Mr. Serle has his eye on Grace. Her hair is thin, but her bosom is abundant."

Mr. Serle does not answer. He looks annoyed as he sets the bowl on the supper table. I wonder at Tom's choosing Grace to tease about. She is a mouse of a housemaid who says not a word but looks about her with wide eyes and eats as much and as quickly as she can. She has been in the house only a few days, hired to help with the extra work in refurbishing the linens. I observed her on the first night slip a good slice of bread and a piece of cheese into her pocket. There must be hungry mouths waiting for her at home in the village. The thought of it makes my stomach clench with the old feeling.

Having drawn no answer from Mr. Serle about Grace, Tom returns to his earlier question. "Do you like them dark or fair?" he asks again. "The red rose or the yellow? Or is it breasts or thighs? Or do you go direct to the twat?"

Mr. Serle looks over at me. "Spare us," he says.

"Paddy has heard worse, I would wager," Tom laughs. "And done his share of fiddling about the sex. Unless—" Tom looks meaningfully at me and then makes a face at Mr. Serle, who is turned away. I guess that Tom is thinking of catamites again but does not dare to say it. He sneers at me instead. "We all know what they say of the Irish: underfed and oversexed. It's the religion does it."

I open my mouth to argue, but Mr. Serle anticipates me, shaking his head severely at me and saying loudly, "Enough. Tom, ring the bell for supper. We are ready except that Paddy must go to the cool room for a pitcher of raspberry shrub."

And so the bustle of supper and the gossip of the day take Tom's attention and he forgets his teasing for a while. When the food is eaten and the kitchen and the scullery are clean, everyone hastens away to their homes or to stroll in the warm evening air. Mr. Serle and I are again in sole possession of the place.

It is comfortable to settle by the grate after the work of the day is done. Behind me, the scrubbed pine surface of the great worktable gleams like a bone. The fire is out tonight, for there are no stews simmering for tomorrow's dinner. In a few days we will be busy all day cooking for the harvesters. The master will be back from London to supervise, Tom says. For now, everyone is satisfied with salads, bread, a few boiled vegetables, and cold meats. We do the hottest work of baking early in the morning. By evening the kitchen is cooled and airy again. Still, we sit across from each other where the fire has died. It is an instinct perhaps to seat ourselves by the heart of the place.

"Where did I leave off my story?" I muse.

Mr. Serle hands me a cold drink, sweet cherry syrup mixed with water. It is welcome, for I have had no appetite all day. Remembering pain seals my lips against food. When I recall those with whom I shared deprivation and despair, eating and drinking deny their suffering. To indulge myself is to forget them.

Mr. Serle raises his cup in a salute. "We drink to the thought of those we wish were with us," he says. "Our fortune is shared with them in spirit."

"Yes," I say, and sip the cool fragrance of summer fruit. Mr. Serle has an instinct for soothing me, I think. He finds a road past my fears to affirmation.

"Where was I?" I say again.

"On the dock in Liverpool, dressed in petticoats," says Mr. Serle.

I nod my head. The look of the light on the water ahead of me and on the dark tenements behind me comes back in a rush. "I stood on that dock weeping and calling for a long time," I say. "Longer than was rational. Even if the red head and broad shoulders I saw were my brother's, my weeping could not bring him back from a government ship. At last, the clouds drifting across the sun change the light, and that seems to bring me to myself. I hold the image of the young man I glimpsed and try to examine it again. Its fading makes me question the truth of what I saw.

"Then I remember that I have not even found the lists of survivors yet. Perhaps, I tell myself, I am bidding good-bye to my brother sailing for Australia or India when he is dead or lying ill here in Liverpool. Perhaps he is searching for me and is this very moment standing under the lists looking this way and that for my red-gold plait of hair and ragged skirts, I think. I find the lists of those who sailed on the *Abigail* posted not very far from where I wasted so much time in mourning."

"Surely not wasted time," interposes Mr. Serle.

"Yes," I say. "It was time wasted when I could have been searching and planning."

There is a brief silence between us, and then I continue. "I make my way down the treacherous wharves until, at last, I find the offices and the lists posted on the wall facing the water. There are several, and I read slowly through each. The first is a copy of the list that I saw them writing as we boarded the *Abigail*. I find my brother's name and my own and Aileen Magrett's. There is writing next to the names. Beside my own is written: picked up by *Prince of Wales*, landed. Beside my brother's name is written: picked up by the *Washington*, bound for New York. So I was mistaken in thinking I saw him. All those tears were wasted. Beside Aileen's name it says: unknown. Beside some of the other names there is no writing, only little black crosses. Next to the lists is a large notice about seeking information from Mr. Smith in the office of the *Abigail* and help from Father Boyle at the mission house.

" 'How long will it take the *Washington* to get to New York?' I ask a respectable-looking man who stands nearby with a box at his feet and papers in his hand.

" 'The *Washington*?' he says. 'I heard a rumor this morning that she picked up some survivors of the *Abigail* but would not turn back with them. The captain sent word by a packet going into Liverpool to the owners of the *Abigail* that he would deliver those he had found to New York. They say that he offered to let the poor half-drowned men he picked up change over to the boat for Liverpool, but they refused.' The man knits his brow in sympathy and sinks his voice. 'Was a friend of yours on the *Washington*?'

" 'My brother,' I say. 'And now I must follow him to New York in America. I must find a ship as soon as possible.'

" 'There I can help you, miss,' the man says, all smiling and kind. 'I have been standing here wondering what I should do, and now you are dropped from heaven to both our benefit. Now, don't look puzzled,' he says. 'I am going to explain.'

" 'Yes, please,' I say.

" 'My wife and I and my wife's cousin were to travel to-gether to New York on the *Adelaide* tomorrow morning. We have all our tickets and our baggage packed and ready. My wife and I came on from Wexford, and the cousin from Clonmel was to be following us. We have been here in Liverpool two days at an inn, and now a letter has come saying the cousin is dead of a fever and will never join us.'

" 'I am sorry,' I tell him.

" 'My wife is in our room weeping her poor eyes out,' the man says, drawing down his mouth. I think I see the glint of water in the corner of his eye. 'And I came out to see what to do with the extra ticket. We had the passage all arranged, you see. I have been to the office, and they won't take it back. I must sell it myself if I can. I have asked about for several hours now and no single person has come by, until you. A family of four would have bought it, only there are not three other places to be had. The boat is full, you see, and just this one ticket left. She sails in the morning from the wharf over there. There won't be another ship for New York for a week.'

" 'Is it a high price?' I ask.

" 'Not at all,' the man says, beaming at me. 'I am prepared to take a loss on it. And, then, you remind me of my wife's dear cousin who is so sadly gone.' He names his price, which is less than what my brother paid for our passage on the *Abigail.*

"I had in my sleeve the money that the lady gave me for shoes and in my petticoat the two coins left from our savings. The passage takes it all, with none left for extra food. I do not care about that if I can follow my brother across the ocean, I think. And so I tell the man yes, and he gives me the ticket and shows me where the *Adelaide* will be in the morning. She is moored out in the river just now, he explains, because there is not space for her at the wharf until the packet for Dublin sails. There is no need to wait in line for the doctor today, he says. The doctor promised to be at the dock tomorrow to stamp the tickets of those boarding. All I need do is to be there at dawn. The man smiles and pats my arm and tells me that I am a brave young thing. He wants me to meet his wife as soon as possible.

"I count the coins over to him with care. He gives me a ticket and I can see that it is just like the ones my brother got for our passage on the *Abigail,* only this one has a little picture of a ship and the words 'The Adelaide, a gem of a ship.' I put the precious thing in my sleeve and ask the man his name so I can inquire for him in the morning.

" 'Johnson,' he tells me. 'Mr. Samuel Johnson is my name.'

" 'Thank you, Mr. Johnson,' I say. 'My brother and I will be forever grateful to you.'

" 'Save your thanks for our landing in New York,' he says. 'Now I will be off. My wife will be missing me.'

"I hurry through the darkening streets to the inn and Susan. It is exciting to tell her of my day, of the sadness of Brewster and the dead and the hope that the ticket on the *Adelaide* gives to me. It is hard to sleep that night. I can eat no supper either but rather store in my bag the bread and hard cheese that Susan gives me. I will eat it the next night on the ship, I promise myself. I rise before dawn and leave the still-sleeping Susan. Barefoot again—for I have spent my money and will not take Susan's clogs from her—I make my way to the wharf that Mr. Johnson pointed out to me.

"The sun rises into a pale sky of pink and gold. A barge is loading coal at the wharf where Mr. Johnson said my ship would be. There is no *Adelaide* at the next wharf either. The sailors laugh at me when I demand to know where the ship for New York is docked. Everyone knows that the next ship to go will be the *Lord Nelson* in three days. There is no *Adelaide.* No such ship exists in all the port of Liverpool and never has. When I describe the smiling Mr. Samuel Johnson to them, they laugh and laugh. They know him well. His name is not Mr. Johnson but something else. They are not sure what. He has a new name and tickets for a new imaginary ship every day.

"I drop to a coil of rope and pound my breast and scream. Tears are useless. I am beyond weeping. I have been cheated out of all I had. God must be against me, I cry. Even though I am saved from the ocean depths, even though I can believe my brother alive, I am separated and lost. The smiling devil destroyed my hope.

"I crouch, weeping, all in a heap, cursing the beauty of the day that is so foul. The men shrug their shoulders and turn back to their work. At last the numb horror of it fades a little. Then I feel anger and shame to have been such a fool. At last, I remember that I do not have to sit there on the dock forever. I can go back to the inn. I have spent only two nights there of the three the lady paid for. Perhaps Susan will let me work for my keep for a few days more. I take the bag of my brother's things that I so hoped to please him with when he saw me in America and trudge my way through the dirty streets to the inn again.

"Susan comforts me and bids me wash my feet and rest and drink a mug of tea. All will work itself out, she counsels. My good fortune has yet outweighed the bad, she reminds me. I will find a way. Cleverer and older people than I have been fooled by the Mr. Johnsons of the world. My luck will return. Exhausted, I do as she says. After promising to confer with me after dinner when she will have a little time, she bustles off about her work. In the meanwhile, she sets me by the hearth to polish the brass tankards that have been dirtied by the smoke of the fire. I have a place to rest for a day and a night, and that will have to do."

"So that is how you came to stay in England?" says Mr. Serle.

"Yes," I say. "I lost my chance of going to America."

Mr. Serle seems about to ask me another question. There is a clatter in the passageway. One of the women is coming down from the attic where the maids sleep. She interrupts our talk, and by the time she has taken her cup of water and gone, the moment has passed for whatever Mr. Serle was about to say.

"What shall I do about my hair?" I ask him. "It is getting longer again, and the color will make Tom tease me. Besides, it makes anyone who sees me able to describe me."

Mr. Serle looks at me sharply, but he does not question me about why I do not want to be described. He is patient that way. Perhaps he knows that the story will be told when it is time for it.

"No more soot and grease," he says. "Walnut juice would cover it, but that would take time to prepare. Hair grows and the root color will show again soon, drawing more attention to the disguise. It is a pity to cover what nature has given you. Leave it and wear your kerchief or your hat."

"I think it will be better if it is cut very short," I say. "I have tried as best I can, but it is very ragged, and the back is longer than the front."

Mr. Serle bids me sit on a stool by the grate. He finds the scissors he uses for cutting herbs and clips my hair short all over. When he is done, I sweep the ends up carefully and burn them in the fire. I feel free and clean, with no soot and grease making my head itch.

"Thank you for your help," I say to Mr. Serle.

He replies by handing me the scissors and telling me to go wash them.

"You should dress as a woman," Mr. Serle says when I return from the scullery. "It is easy enough for you to move to the women's sleeping quarters."

"I will lose my job by it," I argue.

"Why should you?" he responds. "Or you can quit today as Paddy and return tomorrow to work as Mina. They will not even notice."

"Tom will notice," I say.

"Tom may notice, but there is even more danger in what he will say if he guesses what you are and finds you sleeping in the men's garret with me."

"He thinks worse of us now that he believes us both male," I say, remembering the quarrel between Mr. Serle and Tom. To my surprise, the recollection makes Mr. Serle laugh.

"Indeed, he thought the worst of us and may still do so. You are right that Tom has the morals of a tomcat. He will think better of me if he knows you are female. But it may be worse for you."

"That is just the point," I insist. "I am safer as I am, not just because of Tom, but because of another danger that I dare not tell you about."

"What?" says Mr. Serle. I am afraid that he is angry.

"Please do not ask me," I beg him. "I promise I will tell the truth when the need comes."

Mr. Serle looks at me. Doubt and appraisal show in his face.

"Will you keep my secret?" I ask humbly.

"Why would I not?" says Mr. Serle. "But since I do not know the secret that makes you believe yourself in danger, I have no secret to reveal."

"But you know my name and who I am," I remind him. "Will you keep that secret safe from Tom and others? Can we continue as we are a little longer?"

"Yes," he says, and sighs deeply.

"I am so tired now," I say.

"Then go to sleep," says Mr. Serle. He sounds impatient but not unkind.

I climb to the garret and fall asleep on my bed behind the curtain, where I dream of running barefoot in green fields. In the hedge the hawthorn is in bloom. I slow to a walk. My brother strolls beside me. He chews on a stem of grass and tells me something important in a low voice. In my dream I strain to hear him. "New York," he mutters. "In America ..." His words fade away into silence. When I turn to question him, he is gone. Fine rain wets the fields. I can feel it beading in my hair as I run back down the path to the cottages. My bare feet fly over the clean, wet grass. I am going home, I sing to myself in my dream. I am going home. I run and run, and yet the cottages are no nearer. The clean grass becomes the dirty stones of Liverpool. I have cut my foot. I am lost. Rough hands clutch at my shawl. A coarse voice calls to me to stop and give an old sod a kiss. I awaken, sweating, to the pounding of my own heart and stare at the dark for a long time before I am calm enough to sleep again.

In the morning I lie awake in the dim light of my corner, thinking that perhaps I should have told Mr. Serle more about the danger I fear. He has been good to me. I can see that he does not like my boy's dress. I do not like it either. But it is necessary, I tell myself. If I give it up, I will give up being the assistant in the kitchen and be sent to mend linen. Or I may be kept on as a kitchen maid, but I will sleep with the other women instead of in this private corner. I will have to give up Gytrash too. No one will let a girl exercise a valuable horse.

There is not much profit in being a woman, I conclude. The bleeding that so frightened me a few nights ago has passed and the heavy, tired feeling that went with it. Now I have the nuisance of finding a safe time and place to wash the rags I soiled. I must keep a supply for next time too. I hope the next time will not be soon.

When I descend to the kitchen, I find Tom already there, in a surly mood. The two women he has been courting have stopped fighting each other and turned against him.

I bring the milk from the dairy and begin to make rolls. "Good morning, Tom," I say. "It is a grand morning."

"Were you sick these past few days, Paddy, or just avoiding work?" asks Tom with his usual sneer.

"I am better now," I respond. "I like to work."

"Your head scarf is untied," says Tom, seizing an end and tugging sharply as he passes behind me.

The scarf comes away in his hand. I wheel about to retrieve it before he can throw it into the grate or out the door. He is standing still with the cloth in his hand, staring at me. Startled, I remember that my hair is no longer soot-black but its natural red-gold. I am grateful at least that it is shorn. No one could think the length girlish.

"Now we see why Paddy was trying to cover up that thatch," Tom said. "The devil himself would not have a more blazing head."

"I am no devil," I cry. I want to seize the knife by my hand and stab Tom. Anything to stop his hurting words.

"You see why he hid his hair," Mr. Serle says, helping me. "He knew that oafs like you, Tom, would tease him for it."

"And tease I will," Tom laughs. He drops my kerchief to the floor and turns to the fire to baste the mutton roasting on the spit. "I'll tease him about his passionate hair since I am forbidden to mention his passion for other things." He looks at me from the corner of his eye. There is a question in his face. I have much to fear from him.

Later, I ask Mr. Serle why Tom torments me so. We sit on the bench by the dairy, our faces turned into the westering sun.

"Why does Tom hate me?" I wail.

"He does not hate you. He hates the idea of you he has made in his own mind."

"Then why does he hate that idea?"

"No one hates us as much as the person who has done us wrong without cause," said Mr. Serle.

"I do not understand," I complained.

"Tom wrongs you, and he knows he has no reason for it. You do him no harm. So he feels something amiss within himself. He turns on you to shout down the voice inside himself that whispers, 'This is not just.' "

"I don't care what he says to himself," I say. "I wish he would stop tormenting me out loud."

CHAPTER XIII

THE SUMMER hurries on. In the early morning the air is soft and sweet-smelling. The dew hangs in tiny pearls on the grass blades and on a spiderweb in the morning-glory vine that twines up the post of the gate to the gardens. As I cross the courtyard to fetch a pitcher of fresh milk from the dairy, I see a figure sitting bowed on the bench against the dairy wall. I am surprised. Perhaps it is a country woman looking for work, arrived before we were risen and dozing now after her walk. Certainly it is a female, for her skirts drag about her legs, and her head and shoulders are wrapped in a shawl. She seems asleep. "Good morning," I say as I approach. The woman raises her head with a start. Her shawl drops back from tangled hair. I recognize the lake-blue eyes with their thick fringe of lashes and the pockmarked cheeks.

"Mary!" I exclaim in surprise. She is surely changed from the jaunty girl who set out on the road to London and a maid's job in a great house not two months ago.

"Paddy," she says, and clutches at my arm. "Thank the good Lord someone is awake at last. I thought you were all dead in there and did not dare to test the door. I must have dropped asleep waiting here. Is there food? I am that starved from my journey, Paddy."

"Wait here," I say. "I have to fetch the milk from the dairy. I will give you milk and some bread. Will you come into the kitchen?"

"You work indoors now, Paddy?" she asks. She sounds surprised.

"Oh, yes," I say. I do not add that it is all because she left. Perhaps she thinks to claim her job again.

"Is Tom there?" she asks.

"No," I reply. "Tom sleeps in the village these summer nights. He has a friend there."

Mary looks startled and then bows her head in acquiescence. "I will wait here," she says, "and then come in with you." She is not so bold as when I last saw her. When I return with the milk, she comes with me to the kitchen, stumbling a little on the threshold in her weariness.

She sits on a stool while I set out a mug of the warm milk and a slice of yesterday's bread. She eats greedily as I go about my morning business. In her uncombed hair is the green ribbon she wore when she left on that gay spring morning that brought me pain and a change in my fortune. Her ribbon is stained with use and crumpled from being tied and retied. I think that if I had such a ribbon in such a green as glows on a teal's neck and dared to wear it, I would keep it clean and fresh. It would shine against my red hair. Stop, I warn myself. I must think always like the lad I am. Paddy does not yearn for green ribbons unless to give to a lass he fancies.

Mary has finished her food. I offer her more, and she accepts it. Tom is late this morning. Mr. Serle was up even earlier than I and is now away in the storerooms making a list of supplies against the return of the family and the preparations for the harvest meals. He must go to Milford this morning. He told me so when I came down to find him drinking tea at dawn.

I am making a syrup of black currants that Mr. Plumb brought in. It does not take long to boil fruit and sugar, strain and bottle it, but it must be stirred as it cooks. The rich odor fills the kitchen. I stand by the range, half hidden by the hastener. Mary has eaten her second piece of bread when Tom appears in the doorway. I hear his footsteps and look over from my work. Tom looks bluff and happy. He must have hurried from the cottage where he sleeps, for his cheeks are pink and his breath comes a little short.

"Good morning, Thomas," says Mary demurely.

"Mary," says Tom. His tone is smooth and he says the name without expression. I imagine that his pale eyes slide sideways and his face shows his surprise. "Back already? I thought you would have liked the city."

"Yes," Mary says. "I did. I served in a fine house with beautiful things to clean and care for. The mistress was kind enough, and the servants were well fed. I would not be here except that I must talk with you. You can imagine what about."

"No," Tom says. "I cannot imagine."

It is as if I am anchored to the range by the long wooden spoon I stir with and the bubbling pot, and by the voices that fill the room with anger. Tom has not noticed my presence, and Mary seems to have forgotten it. They are intent on each other only.

Mary is silent for a long moment and then speaks with heavy emphasis. "I had to leave because of what we did together in the icehouse in the spring."

"What was that?" says Tom with a sneer in his voice. He seems less frightened now. I think that he recognizes something he knows how to deal with.

It is Mary's turn to be afraid. "You know," she says in a strangled voice. "It was just before I left. You kissed me and begged me to stay. You promised love. Now I am two months gone."

"And did you stay for me?" Tom speaks coolly. "Look to your London beaux," he says. "I am amazed you did not find some witch in the alleys of London to rid you of your trouble. Don't think to come whining to me. I have my choice of women. Why should I fancy you?"

Mary gasps. "You cannot deny me," she cries.

"You are mistaken," says Tom. "I do deny you. You cannot blame your bastard on me. Who knows what whoring you did in London or before?"

"I never," Mary gasps. She is crying now. The dark lashes tangle about her eyes.

I think that Tom revels in his cruelty. "A pocked lass like

you will do anything for the boys," he says. "I have met your kind often enough."

"So you will not pity me," Mary says in a hopeless voice.

Tom shrugs. "I will not waste my time," he says. Mary wails like a steam whistle at a Liverpool factory.

The noise brings Mr. Serle from the storeroom. "What is the matter here?" he asks.

Their voices rises louder as the two of them speak at once. Mr. Serle beats down the noise with a flattened palm. "Enough," he shouts. "I see you are returned, Mary," he says as he looks searchingly at her streaming eyes and uncombed hair. "Since your voice was raised the loudest just now, I will ask you to explain what is going on."

I must move the currant syrup from the range to the table now. No one seems to care that I am there, straining the black currant liquid into a clean basin. Tom looks at me and shrugs— one male to another, deprecating the foolishness of women, I suppose—and moves away from Mary and Mr. Serle.

Between sobs and looks of hatred at Tom, who lounges by the range, cleaning his nails with his pocketknife, Mary tells her story of love promised, of her journey to London all unknowing of her condition, of her being sent home with her fare and her two months' wages when she confessed her situation to her previously kind mistress, of Tom's cruel denial of her when all know what he is and what he has done to her. Mr. Serle listens and sighs.

"I suppose you are come back to marry him?" he asks when the sad tale is done and the loud cries of injustice and despair are stilled.

Amidst fresh tears, Mary confesses that indeed she does not know what else to do.

"Will you marry her?" Mr. Serle looks direct at Tom.

Tom shakes his head vigorously. "Of course not," he says. Mary wails anew at his words.

"You have family hereabouts, do you not?" Mr. Serle asks Mary. She nods, too choked with tears to speak. "Then you had best go to them," he says briskly. I think he is a little relieved that a quick way is open to get her out of his kitchen. "Who do you have? A sister? A mother?"

"My mother lives in the village," Mary concedes between hiccups. "She will kill me when she sees me. I left without telling her."

"We will take you to her," Mr. Serle says. "No doubt she will be glad you are back alive."

Tom snorts with laughter. Mr. Serle looks at him with contempt. "You will be silent. There is work to do. You will make the dinner today. Paddy and I must go to Milford."

It is news to me that I am going to Milford. Mr. Serle sends Mary to wash herself and to comb her hair. "You will not wish to frighten your mother," he says. He tells me to put a clean cloth over the currant syrup—the *cassis,* he calls it—and set it in the still room to bottle later. While he gives Tom his directions, I am sent to put the harness on the cart horse and hitch him to the wagon. The driver is away and Mr. Serle has a large order of supplies to be collected in the village.

I realize when I bring the cart to the door why I am needed. When I offer Mr. Serle the reins, he shakes his head in a firm negative. "No, lad," he says, "I have never driven a horse, and I will not begin today." Then he circles far around the patient nag, which stands quietly, and climbs onto the seat beside me. I look down and see that his hand holds the edge of the seat as if we are about to take off on a wild race. Mr. Serle, I guess, is afraid of horses.

I get down and help Mary climb into the back of the cart, where she seats herself on the hay that I have spread to soften the hard planks for her. She does not speak to me but sits with head bowed as I put up the little gate at the back and take up the reins again.

"It is a quiet horse," I observe to Mr. Serle. "See how he does not stir until I bid him go."

"I see," he says through clenched teeth, and I do not dare to tease him further.

We make our way down through the park to the high road

that leads into the village and beyond. Mary directs me to her mother's cottage, which is very little out of the way. We set her down at the end of a path that winds across a meadow to a thatch-roofed place that from the look of it is a single room. Mary thanks us faintly and trudges off, her head shrouded in her shawl.

"I feel sorry for her," I say. Perhaps Mr. Serle will tell me what he thinks.

"One must feel sorry for any young woman who puts her trust in Thomas Grey," Mr. Serle comments. He has relaxed his grip on the wagon seat just a little. "She would have been wiser to deny him."

"What can she do now?" I ask.

"Perhaps her mother and father, if she has one, can make Tom do his duty. Only I doubt it. Perhaps the master might have made him marry her if she were still working for him. Perhaps the vicar at the village church will have some influence. I do not know." Mr. Serle sighs deeply and falls silent.

"I am so sorry for her," I repeat.

"You might marry her yourself, Paddy," Mr. Serle says dryly.

I am startled and laugh uncertainly. Mr. Serle does not add to his joke. I concentrate on urging along the cart horse, which, docile though it is, would rather pull grass from the banks along the way than hurry us to Milford. The empty cart rattles, making further conversation a labor, and we desist. Neither one of us seems inclined to use this expedition together for private communication. The rattling cart, the open air, the hail from the occasional passing carriage, whatever thoughts we have of Mary's dilemma, all seem to act to separate us into our own isolations.

On the edge of town, Mr. Serle directs me to the yard of a large inn. "The horse can be stabled here for a few hours," he says. "There is some arrangement with the head groom. Mr. Coates's stable lad always takes care of it for me when we come to town. You will know what to do."

"Yes," I say.

"I have business to transact," Mr. Serle says. He has

climbed down from the cart carefully and is standing well away from the horse. "Can you find your way back to this place in two hours?"

"I found my way about the dirty alleyways of Liverpool," I say. "I believe I can find my way in a country town."

"Indeed," says Mr. Serle. "I believe you. How will you know the two hours are passed?"

At that moment the church bell chimes ten. "I will hear the noon bell," I say, and Mr. Serle nods approvingly.

"And so will I," he says. Mr. Serle goes on his way, and I turn to care for the cart horse, which does my bidding amiably.

I find the groom, who tells me where to stable the horse. It is lucky that we came into Milford today, he comments, for the great fair will begin in a few days. There will be visitors from all over the county and beyond, he tells me. Even lords and ladies come to see the athletic contests and the horse racing. I evade the groom's questions about who I am, how I come to be working for Mr. Serle, and whether I hope to meet a pretty lass at the fair. When I have seen the horse settled to my satisfaction, I ask the girl sweeping the dooryard of the inn to direct me to the Roman Catholic chapel in the town. With a toss of her head and a superior smile, she points the way.

I find the chapel on a quiet street. The door stands open, and inside, a woman in a black dress is arranging a little pot of flowers near the altar. I dip into the holy water to bless myself, bend my knee, and say my prayer in one of the back benches. I pray for a long time. The woman watches me from the corner of her eye, although she pretends she has not noticed me when I approach her.

"Oh!" she says with a self-conscious start when I say my *excuse me, ma'am*. "I did not notice you. What do you want?"

I tell her that I wish to speak with the priest of the chapel. She looks doubtful. "About a private matter," I say.

"Well, lad," she says, "Father Foxe is in his study. But if it is charity you need, you must apply to the Church or the town for admittance to the poorhouse."

"No, no," I say. "I am not here for charity. It is a matter of conscience I must consult about."

Still doubtful, she takes me to the door and points out the little priest's house on the other side of the graveyard. The Father will be in his study at this hour, she says. I must just tap on the door and he will come. She rustles in her long skirts and smells sweetly of orange water. For a moment I am wistful at the thought of being a woman. Remembering to keep my voice low, I thank her as gracefully as I can for her help and cross the yard by a raked gravel path.

I tap on the door, and after a moment the priest himself opens it for me. He is a small person, half a head shorter than I am, and plump. His round belly pushes out his black coat. He wears a very white neckcloth over which his clean-shaven chin folds. In his hand is a black-covered book in which he keeps his place with his finger.

"Yes?" he says in his English voice.

"Father Paul Foxe, sir?" I reply. "I am not one of your parish but a traveler who asks permission to consult you on a matter of conscience."

"Let me think," he says. His plump little lips purse in and out as he considers my request. This man resembles a shorter, fatter Father Hugh Fintan, the dear priest of the village at home who consoled and counseled us in our troubles. Yet where Father Fintan's voice was lyrical and warm, this man's voice grates on my ear. Where Father Fintan's eyes open wide with alarm and concern when he hears of a problem, this man's eyes squint and calculate. I am close to weeping with homesickness and anxiety when Father Foxe nods sharply, setting his chins aquiver, licks his lips, and says, "I suppose you must come in, lad. Some problem with a girl, hmm?"

"In a manner of speaking," I say.

This man makes me feel stiff and uneasy. As I enter the house, I take my hat from my head in courtesy. I think he glances critically at my hair. We enter the priest's study—at least, I suppose it is his study, because it has a desk with a chair before it and books in a case. Mr. Foxe sits down on the one chair, leaving me standing before him. He looks me up and down, pouting his lips in and out, in and out. I stand awkwardly, wondering why there is no place provided for a visitor to sit. He does not seem to notice my discomfort.

"Irish, hmm?" he says at last. "But not one of the starving ones, I think. Although you are scantily fleshed, you do not look hungry. What little problem brings you here, boy?"

I summon up my courage. "I have a friend," I say all in a rush, "who had some trouble, not with the law exactly, but she was afraid it would come to law and she would be treated unjustly, for she is very poor and without friends to help her, and so she disguised herself as a lad in order to leave the place where she is without attracting notice, and now she has a place and work, only in her disguise as a lad so that she feels safe, but, oh, sir, is it wrong for her to live in such a way? Is she in sin?"

Father Foxe has set the little black leather book he was holding on the desk beside him. Now he taps it with a plump forefinger as he considers what I have said.

"So now she is with child by you?" he says blandly.

"No, no," I cry. The man must be mad. What can he think I have said? "She is a good girl. I have no other interest in her than to be her friend. She asked my advice as a fellow in religion, for where we live is isolated. There is no Catholic priest to turn to. I told her since I was coming to Milford today, I would seek the chapel and set her problem before the priest."

"She lives in man's dress only?" the priest asks.

"Yes," I reply.

"And where does she sleep?" he inquires, wetting his full lips.

"In a private corner," I say.

"Are there men in this room?" he asks sharply.

"Just one. An older man, who sleeps at the very far end of the attic while she is behind her curtain in her corner."

"Does she watch this man undress himself?" The priest is watching me closely. His eyes are bright with interest.

"Oh, no!" I cry.

"And she wishes to know if she is committing a sin?" he says.

"Yes," I say.

The little man looks up at the ceiling. His chins stretch out somewhat but do not unfold completely. After a pause he lowers his head and looks at me severely. "Yes," he says, "she is in sin. She is living contrary to the natural order. What reason can a young woman have for pretending to be a lad except a desire to escape a crime or a lascivious interest in invading the privacy of her male companions? None, I say, none. The crime she claims to be escaping must have been dreadful to drive her to such unnatural action. I will not even dare to imagine what dreadful acts of lust she has committed while hidden in her male disguise. She is in sin. Tell your friend that she should reveal her situation to the mistress of the house and beg her forgiveness for her deceit. Then she may come to me and I will hear her confession and give her penance. She should come soon."

"But—" I begin.

Father Foxe interrupts me. "Now, you sought my opinion and I have given it. Off you go to tell your so-called friend. Remind her that I said she must come soon." He makes a sign of the cross to me. "Bless you, lad. You may show yourself out." He picks up his book. He wets his finger and finds his place, his lips pursing in and out again.

"But—" I cannot give up so easily.

The priest looks up at me, visibly annoyed. "Evening service is at five o'clock," he says. "I will hear your confession then if you are still in Milford and still calling yourself a Catholic. Show yourself out, boy. Show yourself out."

Seeing it is hopeless to attempt to talk to the man, I follow his advice and let myself out. I sit in a shady corner of the churchyard for a while. My head whirls. Mr. Serle advised me to give up my boy's clothing. The priest has told me I am committing a sin. Neither one of them knows why I have chosen to wear my brother's clothing. The priest would not listen, and I am afraid to tell Mr. Serle in case he should be forced to lie on my behalf. I would not ask that of him. Only Susan and I know what happened.

I look down at the sleeve of my shirt, my brother's shirt.

Even if I changed my trousers for a skirt again, I think, I would wear this shirt. It comforts me to have something of his against my skin and the little lump of the ring sewn into it against my thigh. My family is with me. That cannot be a sin, I know in my heart. Yet, I wish I could talk about it quietly with Hugh Fintan, who blessed me when we began our journey and told me to be true to myself and to hold what I love in my heart and never let it go. I think I might write him a letter, yet when I try to form in my mind the words I would use, I stop. I despair of the skill to make him understand.

The clock in the English church strikes the note for the hour. I rouse myself and trudge back to the inn. I find Mr. Serle waiting by the gate to the stable yard, where we agreed to meet. He is gazing at a paper pinned to the gate post, his hands behind his back.

"Look at this, child," he says as I come up and greet him.

The sheet he is examining is a smeary handbill printed in red and black. There is a sketch of a woman's figure in ragged skirts and a shawl about her shoulders. She wears laced boots such as I am wearing. The figure is inked in black, but her hair and shawl are bright, staring red. Her hair is wild as mine would be when it escaped the plait and frizzled in the damp weather. She looks a scarecrow of a figure. Above the picture it says in large black letters REWARD. Under the picture it says:

BOUND SERVANT RUNS AWAY. MR. AND MRS. GREGORY HATTON OF LIVERPOOL APPEAL FOR ANY INFORMATION ON THE WHEREABOUTS OF THE IRISH IMMIGRANT MINA PIGOT, BOUND SERVANT TO MRS. HATTON, WHO RAN AWAY DESPITE KIND TREATMENT AND WORK IN EXCHANGE FOR PURCHASE OF PASSAGE TO AMERICA. SUSPECTED OF STEALING A PAIR OF BOOTS FROM MRS. HATTON. MINA PIGOT IS EIGHTEEN YEARS OF AGE, GREEN EYES, RED CURLY HAIR, SLIM. IRISH ACCENT. ANYONE WITH INFOR-MATION IS ASKED TO FIND MR. GREGORY HATTON AT THE COCK AND KETTLE INN, FOUNTAIN LANE, MILFORD. APPROPRIATE REWARD.

I stand there, mouth agape.

"This is you, is it not?" says Mr. Serle.

"Yes," I admit, "but kind treatment and stealing shoes are lies. And I am not eighteen yet either. I am fifteen, just as I told you. Please, please believe me. I would not steal."

Mr. Serle sighs. "I believe you would not steal. But we cannot talk of this here. We must finish our business in Milford. Is the cart ready?"

"Will you go to the Cock and Kettle to collect the reward?" I ask in my bravest voice.

Mr. Serle shrugs. "Not I," he says. "I will hear your story first."

I reach out my hand to tear the bill from the gate. Mr. Serle stops me. "You will only attract attention to yourself," he says. "In any case, there are several other bills like this posted about the town."

Terrified that Mr. Hatton will pass by and see me, I go to harness the old horse, who, happy with his oats and restful corner, would shake me and the harness off if he could. I keep my hat pulled well down to hide my hair and eyes as I wrestle with the straps and buckles. Luckily, the maid who swept the dooryard earlier is gone and the groom who wished to chat with me before is busy changing the horses for a fancy carriage. I lead the horse and cart to the gate.

"We must be away," I cry to Mr. Serle. "Be seated in the cart, please, sir."

Mr. Serle circles away from the horse and climbs into the cart beside me.

"Do not think ill of me," I say. "I never stole. You know I had no shoes when I first came. You gave me what I wear yourself."

"I believe you," Mr. Serle says again. To my anxious ears his voice is cold.

"I can explain," I say eagerly.

"But not now." Mr. Serle seems to be making an effort to be patient. "We will talk when the moment is right."

"I have done nothing you will think wrong," I say. I cannot seem to let speech go.

Mr. Serle must see that I am trembling beside him. "Control yourself," he says, in what sounds to me a hard voice. "We must pick up the supplies I have arranged. Can you keep this animal calm in the bustle of the town?"

"Indeed, yes," I say, jamming my hat about my ears and picking up the reins. There is no use in trying to make the old horse hurry, so I keep my head well down as we move through the town. Mr. Serle directs the loading of sacks of sugar and dried legumes and I know not what else. In a yard where there is much bustle, I jump down to hold the horse's head and soothe him against the noise. Steadying him helps me to steady myself.

The last place that Mr. Serle directs me to is a warehouse on the edge of town. Mr. Serle descends from the wagon and goes into the building. He is gone for some time. I sit waiting for him impatiently, hunched on the seat, my hat pulled to my ears and my head down so that no passerby will see my face. When Mr. Serle emerges from the dark doorway of the warehouse, another man accompanies him. They are both smiling, at ease with each other. Mr. Serle carries a sack.

"You will like the cinnamon bark," says the stranger. "It is a good lot." This man is taller than Mr. Serle and blacker. His eyebrows are thick and bushy, almost meeting over his beak of a nose.

"My thanks to you," Mr. Serle says. "And for the prayers also."

I relax a little. They are not talking about taking me to Mr. Hatton or the sheriff.

"Of course," the man says. He gives Mr. Serle a hand up into the wagon. I can see that he is not afraid of our horse. "And who is this likely lad?" he asks, peering up at me from under his shaggy brows.

I hunch down even more, afraid to speak. Mr. Serle says in his neutral way, "An Irish lad who is apprenticing in my kitchen."

"A good boy, I hope," the other responds.

"Indeed, he learns well," says Mr. Serle. My heart leaps. He is not so cold to me after all.

"Here's a sweet for you, child," the big man says. He reaches over to put a paper twist in my hand. "Sugared almonds for a treat."

"Thank you, sir," I mutter. I wish we could hurry and go. I want to be free of Milford with its posters and crowds and prying eyes. Mr. Serle and his friend exchange a few words more. I put the paper of almonds in my coat pocket. I can barely sit still.

At last they are finished. I cluck to the horse, and we are soon on our way out of the danger of the town on the country road. Happy to be turned homeward, the old horse jounces us and the full cart along over the ruts. Mr. Serle sits balanced with his arms crossed over his breast. We do not speak on the journey and arrive just in time to help Tom set out the supper. Afterward, Tom stays on and on, drinking ale and talking to Mr. Serle about the workers' demonstrations in the cities to the north of us. They ignore me, and I have nothing to say in their conversation anyway. I go at last to bed, disappointed of any moment of quiet for talk.

CHAPTER XIV

I SLEEP POORLY. The images of the fatly smiling Mr. Johnson, the wet-lipped Father Foxe, and the filthy alleys of Liverpool haunt my dreams. Little waxy-faced children squeak like mice from cellar doorways. Their shrill voices urge me to come down and help my ill brother. When I make my way down into the rank darkness, Father Foxe frowns at me from a black throne. Beside him is a candle stand with a single candle on it. As I beg him to let me tell my story, he wets his thick fingers at his pink, pouting lips and pinches out the light.

In my dream I attempt to cry out, but my throat will make no sound. I can see nothing in the dark, only feel the little fingers of the dying children pluck at me. I hear the voice of Mr. Serle. I have a candle, he says, but I will not light it for such as you.

I awaken and toss again. No one understands. How can it be sin to protect myself? I try to pray, but the words will not form. I am comfortless. At last, I fall into an uneasy, dreamless sleep. In the morning I am very tired. The routine of the day moves forward as always. The master of the house will be arriving soon to supervise the harvest. Mr. Coates is back already, Tom reports. He must see that the draft horses are harnessed properly and shod to pull their heavy loads from the fields to the barn and the mill. Mr. Serle is stowing supplies and making lists to be in readiness for the great meals that the house will serve to the laborers. There will be beer to be made also in the weeks after the main harvest is in. Everyone seems full of energy except me.

I eat a little without appetite and do my duty with the baking as best I can. When I go down to attend to Gytrash, Mr. Coates greets me brusquely, thanks me for my care of the horse, and tells me I can be off to my work in the kitchen. I am no longer needed in the stable. The only good I can find in the day is that Tom is so excited about the coming bustle that he forgets to tease me. I am thankful also that no one seems to have seen the posted bills in Milford. Or if anyone except Mr. Serle and I have seen them, they are not considered worth mentioning.

At last the evening falls. The kitchen is in order for tomorrow. As Tom goes out the door, I remember the currant syrup in the still room. I put the pewter plate I have been rubbing on the plate rail in the dresser. Mr. Serle sits at the table, making some notes in his book of recipes.

"I forgot to bottle the *cussas*," I say, trying to say the strange word he used.

He looks at me, puzzled, for a moment and then smiles. "The black currants? *Cassis*," he says. "Well, you had best do it now. We will want Mrs. Bennet to be happy with our work when she returns."

I fetch the pan and set it on the range. The fire will be just hot enough, I think. The bottles are ready from Mrs. Bennet's shelves. "Wash them well," Mr. Serle tells me when he sees them set out on the table. "I will watch the syrup for you."

In the scullery, as I scrub and rinse the bottles, I think of what I will say to Mr. Serle about the posters in Milford. I remember his silence of yesterday and wonder if he is tired of my woes. Perhaps I should keep my secrets to myself. Why should anyone else want them?

When I return from the scullery, Mr. Serle has laid the funnel ready on the table and seen the syrup to a boil again. It is quick work to fill the bottles.

"They should cool a little before you close them," Mr. Serle says. "While we are waiting, perhaps you can tell me what you wished to say yesterday about those posted bills in Milford."

"You must think me a criminal," I say.

Mr. Serle looks surprised. "Indeed no, child," he says. "A

girl who has run away from her bond perhaps. That is common in these times, I hear."

I do not want him to think me common. "It is not so simple," I say. "I had reasons to flee danger." I shudder again with the fear I felt in Milford. "I thought you were angry with me when you would not let me speak of it yesterday."

"I thought you did not want me to pry into your secrets," Mr. Serle says. "Besides, your feeling was not for the public street or an inn yard. There was a danger to you in that."

"I thought your silence yesterday meant anger," I say.

Mr. Serle looks at me. His face is full of thought. Something in his dark eyes makes me feel a child. "Perhaps I think of my own life and my own sorrows, not of yours, when I am silent," he says quietly.

"I am sorry," I reply. His words make me feel alone.

"What happened?" Mr. Serle asks. He closes his book. "Tell me." His voice is warm again and beckoning.

I sit across from him. "I want to tell," I say. "Remember I was cheated of my money. After I returned, crying and ashamed, through the dirty streets of Liverpool, working in the kitchen of the inn helped me to calm myself. There is so much to do at an inn as evening falls. Parties of travelers arrive, demanding beds and food. Susan, busy running up and down, asks me to help to carry dinners from the kitchen to the room set with several tables where the guests dine.

"Willingly, I work with her until the rush is over. Just as I think we will stop and sweep up and retire, a tall woman hurries into the room.

" 'Am I too late to order a dinner?' she asks. Her words are mild, but her manner suggests that she expects to get what she wishes.

"Susan accommodates her. 'No, madam, it is not too late,' she says. 'What will you have? There is beef or ham with salad. Mina here will go to the cook for you.'

" 'Beef for two,' the woman says, seating herself at a table near the fireplace. 'My husband will be here in a moment or two. Beef and bread and two tankards of your best ale.'

" 'Mina, go tell cook, and then set up the table as I showed you before,' Susan says to me.

" 'A new girl?' the woman asks Susan. She glances at me with shrewd, dark eyes. Her fat cheeks each have a round daub of red on them that surely cannot be natural to her.

" 'She's a new girl, learning how we do things,' says Susan, excusing me for mistakes I have not made yet. 'I am just teaching her a little.' I wonder that she slips into a half truth so easily.

" 'Training a servant takes patience,' says the woman. She has a hoarse, rough voice.

" 'Mina is a good, biddable girl,' Susan replies. In front of this stranger she has changed. She seems stern and distant. I am no longer a guest in the inn whose bed for the night is paid for. Suddenly, I am a servant to be spoken of as if I am not really present. I think that when I allowed myself to be cheated, Susan's opinion of me changed. I feel like a crumb on the floor about to be swept up into the dustpan and tossed in the fire. I grit my teeth and do as I am told. When I return from the kitchen, Susan is still talking to the woman. They fall silent as I enter.

"Then, 'I am looking for a servant to help me on the journey to America and in my house in the city when I arrive,' the lady says in her voice that sounds like a crow calling. 'Do you know someone who looks to go to America?'

"I am speechless with desire. Here I am, I want to say. Susan answers for me. 'Mina here is looking for a passage. She has been cheated of her purse and must find a way to earn money.'

" 'Are you willing to work, girl?' the woman croaks, staring me up and down with a bold look. She has a heavy, jowled face and forward-thrusting jaw. She looks like an English bulldog although her voice is that of the raven.

" 'Indeed, she is a worker and an orphan.' I wonder that Susan gives me no opportunity to speak for myself.

" 'What happened to your hair?' demands the woman. She startles me by reaching out a hand to touch the curls that twine on my neck.

" 'She was in the great fire on the ship that burned two days ago,' Susan explains. 'She was lucky to escape with her life and no burns except for the blister on her ear and her braid gone. A lady paid her board here while she looks for a way to go to America.'

"I am ashamed that I am content to let Susan speak for me. Perhaps if I had to tell my story myself just now, I would only weep. There is something about this woman that makes me not want to weep before her. Besides, Susan's words push the pain away, make it a tale that happened to another Mina. This woman whom I do not like has something I am desperate for, a passage to America. If I am strong and hide my feeling, I can get what I want. Susan is showing me the way. Surely, I tell myself, I can be a servant for a few months if that takes me to my brother.

"The woman continues to stare boldly at me. 'Her hair is an unusual color. Some would think it deforms her pretty features. Some would consider it adds piquancy to her looks.' I hear the distaste in her voice. 'She would do,' she says to Susan but more to herself, and then louder and more briskly, 'She will have to come with me as a bound servant. I will not pay a passage without the assurance that she will work for me to pay back the passage itself and also her training. I suppose those are all her clothes she stands in.'

"Susan says yes. I do not speak. The woman's scornful tone makes me angry. She treats me as a thing, a damaged chair or a chipped plate.

" 'Then I will have to find her less-ragged garments as well as everything else,' the woman says. 'She will have to bind herself to service with me for three years.'

"I am appalled. What about my brother? I am relieved that Susan objects. 'Three years?' she says in a bargaining voice. 'Three years is a long time to work for a passage and a few cast-off clothes.'

" 'Little you know, my dear,' the woman says. 'It is cold in the New World. She will need stout shoes and a thick wool shawl. Besides, she will have a bed and food and training suitable to her position with me. And at the end, of course, if she does not stay in my employment, a letter from me and a small gift of money.'

"My mind races as she speaks. My brother and I had not thought much of the cold in America. It makes me worry for him. Perhaps if I am well clothed and shod and have some money when I join him, it will be easier for us both. If only this woman had a kinder face and voice, I would be easier in my mind.

" 'Fair enough,' says Susan. 'I think you should take it, Mina.'

"My mouth is agape at the speed with which these two are settling my life. I am less sure that I should take this work than Susan seems to be. The woman does not look like one who would be my friend in trouble. Although she sits stout and prosperous in her corsets and purple stuff gown, her face is sour, and her thin, tight mouth stretches over her jutting yellowed teeth. The round red spot on each cheek stands out against her chalky skin. I do not have a chance to voice my doubt, however, for the woman speaks again to Susan.

" 'My husband must look her over before we decide. He will be in shortly.'

" 'Yes, ma'am,' Susan says. 'Only I think you would do well to take her.' The warmth of her voice and her smile to me make me feel better in my heart.

" 'I will consult with my husband as soon as he arrives,' the woman says.

"She speaks as if she is contemplating buying a horse or a cow. Susan directs me to clear away the debris from the tables where earlier diners have finished their meals. 'This is a great chance for you, Mina,' she whispers to me as I load my tray. When I return from the kitchens again, the woman's husband has arrived. Susan has evidently been talking to them, for they all three stare at me as I enter the room from the passageway.

" 'So this is Mina,' says the man. 'I am Gregory Hatton, my dear, and you have met Mrs. Hatton, my wife, Fanny, I suppose.'

" 'Yes,' I manage to get out of my mouth. Mr. Hatton,

Gregory Hatton, is a small man. His wife makes two of him. His thinning hair is drawn back in the old style with a ribbon at his nape. Across his shiny, freckled dome, long strands are slicked as if that would hide his baldness. His dress is neat: a black frock coat, a black waistcoat in some figured fabric that has sheen to it here and there, and white linen. On the little finger of his right hand, he wears a gold signet ring. His hands are white and clean but freckled on the backs with brown splotches. Despite his sober dress, he has the strut of the rooster in the hen yard.

"He seizes my hand and shakes it firmly. Then, to my surprise, still grasping my hand, he spins me around in a turn. When he releases me, I retreat a step. He smiles, baring an even row of small, gray teeth.

" 'A thin creature, isn't she?' he says. 'Don't they feed you here?'

" 'She is just come from Ireland,' Susan says quickly.

" 'I see,' says Mr. Hatton. He appeals to his wife. 'Will she fill out or stay as flat as a plank?'

"Mrs. Hatton snorts. 'She will fill out, of course, when she is fed better. But not by much. This is a lean and lanky type.'

"Mr. Hatton shrugs. 'Are you a good worker, girl?'

" 'I try,' I manage to say. 'I am just come from home, where I helped my mother.'

" 'And how did you help your mother, my dear?' Mr. Hatton shows me his teeth again.

" 'I swept the house. I cooked the potatoes. I milked the cow when we had her.' The unbidden memory of the smooth flank of the cow and the scent of warm milk and dung makes me catch my breath. I tell myself that these are not people to cry before. I go on. 'I helped with the mending of clothes. I can do plain sewing and crochet.' I pause. I feel hopeful. The important thing is to get to America and to find my brother.

" 'Very good, my dear,' Mr. Hatton says. He reaches over and strokes Susan's plump arm. 'You have done us a good turn in finding the girl. Will she sign the bond, do you think?'

"Susan smiles at me and nods. 'I think she will sign. She wishes very much to go to America to find her brother.'

" 'Is that so?' Mr. Hatton raises an eyebrow and looks at me critically.

" 'I was separated from my brother in the fire on the ship,' I tell him. 'Perhaps even now he is being carried to New York on a ship that rescued him and would not turn back.'

" 'But you do not know surely?' Mr. Hatton asks.

" 'No,' I say reluctantly, 'but I will go however I can in hopes of finding him.'

" 'Very nice,' Mrs. Hatton says. 'A nice show of feeling.'

" 'Do you understand what we propose?' Gregory Hatton asks me.

" 'I think so,' I reply. 'You wish me to be Mrs. Hatton's maid, I think.'

"Susan chimes in eagerly, 'They will pay your passage from Liverpool to the city of New York, Mina. They will give you clothing, food, and a place to sleep. In exchange you will work for them faithfully for three years.'

" '*Faithfully* is the watchword.' Mr. Hatton cocks his head and studies me. 'Obedient, hardworking, clean, respectful. That is reasonable, is it not?'

" 'Oh, yes!' exclaims Susan.

" 'But how will I look for my brother?' I ask. I feel tired and upset. My head aches.

"Mrs. Hatton replies in her croaking voice, 'After we have settled in and you know your duties, you will have a few hours each week for your own business. Of course, it will be your duty to report to me where you go and who you see. For your protection I insist on it. America is not like England.'

" 'Or Ireland,' offers Susan.

" 'Mina says thank the Lord for that,' crows little Mr. Hatton, leaping from his seat and twirling me around again.

" 'Will you sign this bond?' demands Mrs. Hatton. 'Let us get the business over with. I am hungry for my supper.'

" 'Yes, you will sign, won't you, Mina?' says Susan.

" 'Let me think,' I say to Susan. My head feels as if it will explode with confusion. I walk away across the room and look into the fire. What can I do? I ask myself. I have no money nor hope of earning it here. Liverpool, from what I have seen, is a filthy, poverty-struck place. Tomorrow I will have no place to sleep. The church offers me the poorhouse. These people offer me passage to America. I am not ashamed to work. I would work for them without a paper. My word would bind me. My word would bind me more than a piece of paper does. Perhaps they do not trust my honesty. I think about it. I do not trust my honesty either. If they are bad people, I will run away from them in America. When I find my brother, he will help me free myself from these Hattons. They are in the right in not trusting me to be loyal to them. I would ask a written promise too from someone I do not know. A log settles in the fireplace, sending up sparks that make me jump in fear. Behind me, Mr. Hatton giggles at something Susan has whispered to him.

"I turn back. 'Yes,' I say. 'I will go to America with you, and in exchange I will work at whatever honest task you ask of me for three years.'

"They all—Mrs. Hatton, Mr. Hatton, Susan—nod and show their teeth in smiles. Mr. Hatton takes a sheaf of papers from an inside pocket of his waistcoat and, wetting his finger, frees one sheet from the others. 'Here,' he says. 'We must just fill this in. Ink and pen, Susan my dear?'

"Susan hurries off to the front of the inn and returns with the materials set ready on a tray. Mr. Hatton, his pink tongue showing between his teeth, fills in lines at the top of the sheet. He blots it carefully and bids me come and look at it. When I stoop over the table to read, he puts a hand on my backside, startling me. I jump and almost upset the ink bottle. 'I am sorry,' I say.

" 'No matter,' says Mr. Hatton. I see that he looks at his wife and winks. He points at the crabbed writing with his freckled hand. 'It is quite simple. All it says is that Mina, Irish spinster, binds herself to work for Mrs. Fanny Hatton, businesswoman of New York City, in such tasks as her mistress shall assign her for a period of three years from today. You see here, I have put the date. And on this date in, ah, 1851 you will be your own master—dear me, I mean mistress—again. You understand?'

" 'Yes,' I say.

" 'Then you can make your mark here,' says Mr. Hatton, pointing with his right hand to the bottom of the page. His left hand rests on the writing at the top of the sheet. He is holding the page steady for me.

" 'I can write,' I say. Like the fool that I am, I proudly sign my whole name, *Mina Pigot,* with a flourish. Susan signs her name under mine as a witness. There is a blank space for a second witness. 'Who will sign here?' I ask, pointing.

" 'Ah, yes,' says Mr. Hatton. 'Just let me do that.' And he signs his name under Susan's. 'Well, well,' says Mr. Hatton when he is done, looking at the names on the paper and then at his lady out of the corner of his eye, 'an educated miss.'

" 'All to the good,' the lady says. I wonder if she means what she says. 'So your name is Mina Pigot,' she adds, examining the papers.

" 'Well,' says Mr. Hatton, rubbing his hands together and then picking up the papers and folding them into an inside pocket of his waistcoat, 'these are your indenture papers, Mina, and I will hold them for you until the ship sails. Then Mrs. Hatton will keep them until your time is done.' He smooths the strands of hair across his pate. 'Here, Susan,' he says. To my surprise, he strokes his hand down her arm again and presses something into her hand. 'This is a good business transacted. I am hungry as a horse and ready for my grub. Bring it on, young Mina Pigot. And then wait in the passageway in case we want you. Your service is begun.'

"After Susan and I have set out the plates of food for Mr. and Mrs. Hatton, we go out into the passageway. Susan stops and gestures me to sit on the little bench behind the chimney. 'If they call, you will hear them,' she whispers. 'When they finish, bring the plates and things down to the scullery and then come into the kitchen and tell me.'

"I do as she bids me. The bench is out of sight of the table where the Hattons sit. At first I hear only the sounds of knives scraping plates and tankards thumped down on the table. When the couple have satisfied their first hunger and begin to speak, I hear their loud voices clear enough.

" 'I do not look forward to the ocean,' Mrs. Hatton says in a complaining tone. 'I wish I had not undertaken this trip. I find I have gained nothing by my mother's death, and my sister was most unwelcoming.'

" 'We have found three suitable girls,' Mr. Hatton growls at his companion. 'Will that content you, madam? You are the one who insists on bringing girls over.'

" 'They are more obedient, Gregory. You know that. The strangeness of the place makes them timid about running off. And I do not want the girls off the streets in New York. They are not clean. Nothing pulls down a house faster than a reputation for uncleanness.'

" 'Cleanliness next to godliness, hey?' replies her spouse. The lady must have looked at him askance, for he adds quickly, 'Ah, a joke, my dear Fanny. A joke.'

" 'Assuming that at least two of them survive the journey, yes, I will be content,' says the lady in her harsh voice, reverting to his earlier comment. 'I shall have to put two of them in the steerage class. I shall have room for only one in my cabin.'

" 'I think this Mina is the most promising of the lot. Keep her with you,' Mr. Hatton says. 'Pass the mustard, dear. I can't eat my beefsteak without mustard to it.'

" 'She's too thin,' the corpulent Mrs. Hatton asserts over the chink of china dishes.

" 'But the red hair makes her interesting.' Mr. Hatton's voice is muffled by the large mouthful he has just taken. There are sounds of vigorous chewing and then he adds, 'They say that red hair is a sign of passion. There are those who pay well in the houses for the appearance of passion, even if they do not get the actual thing.'

" 'Gregory,' says his companion, 'never mind passion. My question is whether she will serve or run away. The red hair suggests a spitfire to me. I dislike it. I see red hair, and I think of the imps of Satan. However, I shall enjoy whipping her when she is disobedient.'

" 'She's signed the papers fair enough,' Gregory says. 'We

have her there. If I were sailing with you, I would break her on the voyage. Even the liveliest spitfire can be tamed if you know how. I would enjoy that as much as you will enjoy beating her.'

" 'But you are not sailing with us,' the lady objects, 'and she will be worthless in New York if she arrives pregnant. Or she might jump overboard. Remember that crazy Molly on the last trip we made together. No, it is not sensible to take risks given the price of her passage. I am glad you are not sailing with us, Gregory. Self-control is not your strength.'

"The man laughs and there is a short silence except for the rattle of silverware, and then the woman says as if she is merely thinking out loud, 'They say virgins go for a higher price in the southern cities. Maybe if I get her healthy to New York, I will sell her south. That little, dark, gypsy-looking one who calls herself Annie has not been with a man, I think, although her friend Rose most certainly has. I must build my resources. Yes, I might sell her. I do not intend to make the voyage again across the ocean you know, dear Gregory. I shall finish out my days in America. You will join me or not as you please.'

"I am struck dumb with horror in my corner by the door. Beat me. Break me. Sell me. I do not understand all that they say, but I hear woe for me and evil in their voices. My head is swimming. At last I rise and creep to the room that I shared with Susan last night. My bed is still there, and the bag of my things. I lie down and wrap my arms about the lumpy sack. I cannot stir or think. When Susan comes to find me, she seems angry at me.

" 'What are you doing here?' she asks. 'What is wrong with you? The Hattons called for you to clear their dishes. They want pudding.'

"I shake my head and grip my bag more tightly. 'I cannot go,' I whisper at last.

"Susan sits on the cot beside me and puts her arm about my shoulders. 'What is it?' she asks in her warm voice. Her arm makes a circle that wards off evil.

"I whisper into her ear the horror I have heard. To my dismay, she does not seem shocked but shrugs her shoulders. 'They are not nice, Mina, but you may defy them later. Only now you have signed a bond to serve them.'

"I begin to weep. 'I cannot look at them,' I say.

"Susan sighs, a sound of annoyance, but her words are not harsh. 'You are young in the world,' she says. 'I will tell them you cannot come just now.' And she withdraws her arm from about me and goes away for I know not how long. I sit huddled where I am. The world whirls in circles around me.

" 'I excused you as ill and exhausted,' says Susan, returning, 'but they are not pleased. Madam says to tell you that you will be punished if you shirk your tasks again. I reminded her that you are but recently rescued from a shipwreck.'

" 'Just the day before yesterday,' I whisper.

" 'Indeed.' Susan pats my arm. 'But, Mina, they are right to expect you to obey them. You signed to be their servant. Their duty is to tell you what to do. They may have just been joking with each other. They have not asked anything wrong of you yet.'

" 'I don't care,' I say. Evil seems to be at my heels now, and I will myself to defy it. 'I will not serve them. I had a bad feeling when the man touched me. They wish to hurt me.'

" 'But you signed the papers.' Susan seems bewildered by the change in me. 'You said you must go to America. Why give up your chance now?'

" 'Did you not understand?' I ask her. My voice rises. 'They will use me as a slave. Mrs. Hatton spoke of selling me. How will I ever find my brother?'

" 'You could run away in New York as soon as the ship docks,' says Susan. Her voice is doubtful. She has already thought for herself of the objections to such a scheme. A penniless, friendless indentured servant in a strange country will not find charity easily.

" 'I must run away now,' I say. Energy floods into me again. I have made a terrible mistake, but I will not bow myself to fate so easily. 'You will help me, Susan,' I tell her with confidence. 'You must know a place that I can go.' I can see in her face that she has an idea that will help me. I think desperately. 'I have a pewter bowl,' I say. 'It is bright and whole.' I dig frantically in my brother's bag for it. 'It came from England,' I assure Susan. 'Here, I will give it to you for helping me.'

"Susan turns the bowl in her hands and strokes its silvery roundness. She smiles. 'Mina, I know nothing,' she says. 'If you were a boy and good with horses, I could send you to my uncle. He complains each time I see him that he has no help that he can trust.'

" 'I can handle a horse,' I say. 'I helped my father and my brother. What I did not do myself, I saw and can imitate.'

"Susan shudders. 'There is something unnatural about a female taking on a man's work,' she says. 'I would be afraid of grooming a horse. Perhaps you should go with Mrs. Hatton, Mina. They say the life for a woman in a good house is easy, with plenty of food and servants. Better to do a woman's work than a man's, I say.'

"I sit on the edge of the cot, brooding over the bag of my brother's things. 'Well,' I say, 'if you cannot help me, perhaps I can sell the bowl.' I reach for it, but Susan pulls back her hand.

" 'Wait!' she exclaims. 'What if you were a boy?'

"I stare at her, amazed. Energy drains out of me. The bag I hug in my arms comforts me. Each lump and bump is familiar. Here are his boots, his trousers, his shirt, his felt cap that was my father's and that we both loved. My fingers grasp the heel of a boot through the rough sacking. I will my brother to speak to me through these things that touched him. I wonder if his boots will fit me.

" 'If my uncle will not take in a girl, then go to him as a boy,' Susan says, turning the bowl in her hands. She laughs, a bubbling sound. 'What a joke.'

"In my daze it takes me a moment to understand her words and meaning. Then the idea floods my mind. 'I can wear my brother's clothing,' I cry. 'Here are the things that will make possible my escape from the Hattons.' I open the bag and pull out trousers, jacket, shirt, and hat. Life has come back to me. I shed my skirts and bundle them into the sack. The trousers drag on the floor, so I roll up the bottoms. 'My brother is saving me,' I exclaim.

"Susan stares at me and then laughs again. 'You need a piece of rope to keep those pants up,' she says. 'And what about your hair? Stable lads don't wear their hair long these days.'

" 'I will cut my hair off,' I say. 'I have a scissors in my housewife. And I will blacken it with soot too. That Mrs. Hatton kept remarking on my hair. I must hide the color as well as cut it short. While I do that, will you write me a note to your uncle and give me the direction?'

" 'He will have my head if he finds out,' says Susan. 'Only it will be a joke on him.' She looks thoughtful for a moment. 'Well, I will do it,' she says. She turns the pewter bowl in her hands and then smooths it against her cheek. 'I like it,' she says, and puts it on the shelf above her bed. 'The Hattons have given me little, after all. They should have tipped me a lot for helping you decide to sign the bond. He did little more than stroke my arm and tell me I am a fine figure of a woman. As if I did not know.'

" 'Please help me,' I beg. 'I need help to cut the back of my hair. And how can I leave Liverpool tonight?'

"Susan, who keeps stopping to laugh, helps me to create my new appearance. It is she who suggests mixing grease with the soot to make it stick better to my hair. She remembers that the carter who brought in a load of strawberries yesterday is sleeping in the stable loft tonight. If I am up before dawn, I may be able to ride with him to Milford. From there, she assures me, it is but two hours' walk to the village of Hay and the great house where I will find her uncle.

"I change myself and make my plan. Susan, chuckling at the pleasure of tricking her uncle—whose name, she says, is John Coates—scrawls a note recommending me. Mr. Coates is a good man, but lazy, she claims. If I show myself willing to work and understanding of horses, he will overlook my Irish ac- cent and my starved appearance, she is sure. The mention of my appearance makes her laugh again. It reminds her also to give me a packet of bread and cheese to eat on the journey.

" 'Well,' she says when all is ready, 'sleep until dawn. Only wear your hat to bed so as not to get grease on the blankets.'

"I do not sleep at all in what remains of the night. I sit on the cot, holding my sack to my breast and listening for any sound from the kitchen. Susan has told me that the carter will come in to drink a glass of ale before setting out.

"When I sense that dawn is coming, I creep out of Susan's room and into the kitchen. By the light of the glowing embers in the grate, I count over the things in my bag. I worry about the skirt. I do not wish to have anything that the Hattons can describe about me. Finally, I cut the ragged cloth into little pieces and burn it in the grate. The shawl that Susan lent me I fold neatly and lay on the corner of the great wooden dresser that holds the cook's pots and plates. My camisole I keep. It is plain linen and of a kind that boys wear as well as girls. My mother made it so that she could pass it down to me when my brother outgrew it. The ruined prayer book, which has my mother's name in it, I cannot abandon no matter what the risk. I find some blacking to polish my brother's riding boots and try them on. They are too large to wear on the journey. I can stuff them with rags or straw when I ride, but I can never walk any distance in them. As I count over the things, I wish for a moment that I had listened to Brewster on the hulk of the dead and taken the comb of the black-haired woman. There is so little that connects us to the dead. Fear drives out memory. The solid object in the hand comforts with its message of the past. We cling not to the thing itself but to the door it opens in the mind.

"As I wait in the kitchen, not quite awake, unable to sleep, I notice some bread laid out to dry on the table. The cook was wanting bread crumbs, I think. Unable to resist, I take a small piece and put it in my bag. I may have need, I think. Dry bread is a protection against the want to come.

"At last the light in the room grays and lightens. The carter comes banging on the door. Susan hurries from her bedroom, all bleary-eyed with her hair still down, to unbar the way. The carter stamps in. I came in from Dublin looking to meet my auntie, Susan lies. My aunt is traveling. She left word that I am to catch up with her in the country near Milford.

"The carter grumbles at the lack of notice but makes no real objection. He gulps his ale and eats his bread and urges me out the door. Susan looks at me and winks. Then she glances at my feet and sees me barefoot.

" 'Buy my clogs, boy,' Susan urges, winking at me. 'I will trade them for the mug in your bag.'

" 'No,' I reply. I keep my voice low, the way I think a lad would speak. 'You have done enough. I am going into the country, where I am accustomed to go barefoot. If I cannot go to America yet, I will go where I can be my simple self.'

"Susan laughs at that. 'Not simple,' she says. 'And you will want shoes before the winter comes. I will see you at harvest time. We will discuss what you need then.'

"I throw my arms about her and cling to her warmth for a long moment. 'Good-bye,' I tell her. 'Thank you and bless your kindness.'

" 'Hurry up, lad,' growls the carter. 'You are much too young to be making a sweetheart of our Susan.' It takes me a moment to realize that he indeed thinks me a boy. When I think it, I feel joy. Perhaps I will be safe from the Hattons in my disguise.

"So I set out for this house in the country. I climb into the back of the empty cart. The driver clucks encouragement to the horse and we are off. We pass through the silent, early-morning streets of the city and out through the ugly suburbs where factories crowd against the shabby homes of workers. At last we come into a road among green fields. As the air smells sweeter and fresher, my spirits rise. I know that I can persuade Susan's uncle to take me on to help in the stables. I will stay quiet in this place where I can work with horses. Next spring, I will ask to earn wages and buy my passage to America. I will be safer as a boy. Wearing my brother's clothes is like wearing a suit of armor as the knights did in olden times. I will not be a slave to anyone. Remembering that

I must look strong and fit for a job, I eat some of my bread and cheese. Hope rises in me and appetite with it."

I cease my tale and look across the space to the other stool where Mr. Serle sits, head bowed, hands clasped loosely before him. "You see, I did not steal except for the one small piece of dry bread. I had to flee to save myself from slavery."

Mr. Serle looks at me doubtfully. "Just slavery?" he says.

I cannot look at Mr. Serle. I feel my face grow hot with an emotion for which I have no name. "When I look back on it, I think they would have forced me to lie with men," I say. "To be like Mary with Tom, for money, not for love."

"Yes, I think they would have forced you to that," Mr. Serle says. "And as terrible as selling your body, they would have sold your innocence. You did right to flee," he tells me. "I understand better now. We may hope, however, that this Mr. Hatton is just passing through Milford and will soon be gone. In any case, no one there knows you."

I think of the priest, Father Foxe. He barely glanced at me. If he were clever, he might connect my story to that of an indentured servant run away, but I did not give my name nor where I live.

"I will stay out of Milford," I tell Mr. Serle.

"You will indeed," he says. "We have hard labor before us. We must feed the harvesters well in the next week. None of us will go to Milford until the corn is in."

Mr. Serle as always is right. When the harvest begins, we rise before dawn and tumble into sleep, dead tired, long after dark. There is no time at all for quiet talk between us in the kitchen now. All is heat and toil.

CHAPTER XV

LABORERS COME from the south, where the harvest is already gathered, and from the north and west, where work is slack in the cities. The local men and women muster carts and wagons, oxen and horses for the battle to bring in the wealth of the land. The master arrives from London. He rises early to breakfast with the factor who manages the farmland. They ride out together and return with handfuls of barley or of wheat, arguing about ripeness and the fullness of the heads. There is a row of makeshift shelters along the far edge of the orchard. Men and women and children all seek employment on the land.

Tom wanders down to escape the heat of the kitchen and to look the women over. Mr. Serle warns me to stay out of the way as much as possible and to speak as little as I can. These are vagrant people, he warns me. They are needy. Because they must live as best they can, they will not hesitate to betray you for a reward, he reminds me. Their need is greater than yours, he says. I heed him and keep my nose turned to my work and my kerchief tied tight over my red hair.

Work and more work. The master here is generous, everyone says. He feeds the laborers at noon each day they work for him. Two women are added to the kitchen staff. No fancy baking or manchet bread is required now. As the lad, I am expected to wash and prepare vegetables, to fetch and carry, and baste and scrub. With all the work, there is little time for chatter, to my relief, for the women ask me my name and comment on my accent. They would engage me in gossip if there were leisure for it. But there is not.

Boards on trestles are set up in the shade of the orchard. There each day we pile meat pies, a ham quarter, basins of vegetables mixed into salads with herring, loaves of the coarse bread from the bakery in the village, gooseberry and raspberry fools in pans. There is a barrel of ale, rolled down the hill by Tom and Mr. Plumb, and great stoneware pitchers of cider and cherry shrub, lugged down by me. As always, the sight of so much food takes all appetite away from me.

The workers come sweating to the feast, with bits of straw in their hair. The pitchers of cool drinks sweat. The ham glistens with fat and sugar. Almost everyone has a cup, a wooden bowl, and a spoon. The few that are too poor even for that take a slice of bread for a plate and pile what they want on it. An itinerant family shares a single cup, while one of our local laborers has a neat kit of utensils and a whetstone for sharpening his pocket-knife and his scythe.

On the fifth day, the sun is strong in the sky above. The air is heavy with the scents of cut grass, of earth, of horses, of human toil. The workers have come late to the noontime meal. There is much to do and clouds are piling up in the west, threatening a change in the weather.

"Shall I fetch more water?" I ask Mr. Serle, who is doling out portions of meat pie with a big spoon.

I do not catch his answer and repeat the question louder. "Yes," he says impatiently. "Fetch it."

As I go down the slope toward the house, I meet Mr. Plumb.

"Good day," I say.

"Did the woman find you?" he asks.

"The woman?" An image of granite-jawed Mrs. Hatton comes to my mind. I feel fear.

"Susan Coates," Mr. Plumb says in his mild way. "She looked for you at the stables, she said, and did not find you. She asked me was the stable lad with black, greasy hair still here. I told her you are a fixture in the kitchen now."

"Where is she?" I ask. Now I am glad. Susan is come for the harvest as she promised.

"Somewhere about," Mr. Plumb says vaguely. "Tell Mr. Serle I have not forgotten the peaches," he says. He plods away toward his gardens.

I wipe sweat from my forehead and knock my kerchief awry. I must stop to retie it. As I return toward the pump in the yard, with the pitcher in my hand, a voice speaks behind me. "Lad, wait."

I turn. A man stands looking at me. He must be one of the harvesters, for his lower face and throat are ruddy brown. His straw hat is in his hand. He has the white upper forehead of one who works in the sun all day and is careful to wear his shady hat lest he be sunstruck. His hair is a dark thatch and his eyes are a piercing blue. Even from the two words he has spoken, I know he is Irish born.

"Yes?" I say cautiously, keeping my voice as low as I can.

He looks at me deferentially. "Forgive my curiosity, lad. I am far from home. Are you by any chance related to the Pigot who comes from the villages west of Follingar? Great horsemen the Pigots were, both father and son. I would not ask except you are the spitting image of a lad I saw a few months back, and I hear in your voice that you are Irish."

I clutch the pitcher, which seems suddenly heavier in my hand. I cannot brain the man in front of such a crowd, but he looms before me as a threat. His straw hat, his worn clothing, his soft voice are familiar. I would weep on his shoulder for the lost home he represents to me. But I must ask myself if he has read the bills that advertise for Mina Pigot. I wonder if this is some trick to catch me and thrust me back into the power of the Hattons.

I answer question with question, the safest way to respond without answering. "Who is the Pigot lad that you know who comes from west of Follingar?"

"Daniel Pigot," he replies eagerly. My heart turns over in my chest.

"And how do you know him?" I say as coolly as I can,

adding, "I must fetch more water. Walk with me if you would toward the pump. I cannot neglect my work or I will lose it."

"I can well understand that," he says, "and for the same reason, I will eat my bread and meat as we walk, so that I will be ready when the bell rings to signal the return to the fields."

"Daniel Pigot?" I prompt him. It is hard to say the name aloud.

Words pour from the man as if he were a bottle and his story cider; someone pulls the cork and tips it over, and out the bubbling liquid froths. I too know this need. "We were on the *Abigail*," he says. "He and his sister sailed in the ship that caught fire. He and I fought the fire with the sailors. When we failed, the fire burned up into the center of the ship. The great mast was a torch to heaven. The people at the front and the people at the back were separated; there was no going between. Daniel Pigot was determined that he would go to find his sister, who was at the front. It was desperate. I seized him in my arms to prevent him from running into the blaze. I jumped with him into the ocean. He came to his senses then. We caught a spar that held us up in the water and carried us with the current away from the destruction. A fishing dory plucked us and three others out of the water. I should have drowned in moments. Daniel Pigot was struggling then to keep both me and himself afloat." He stops, overcome with his feelings.

"Go on if you can," I say. "It is a story I am glad to hear."

He swallows his tears and continues. "The fishing boat was overburdened with us all. Daniel Pigot, after his great effort to save me, sat with his head in his hands. His sister was dead, he said. He had seen her throw herself from the bow of the ship with her clothes and hair all on fire. I believed him that she was most likely dead, although I held back from saying it. Two of the others saved with us had awful burns as well as being half drowned. There was fish underfoot and gear. The two Welshmen whose boat it was were hard put to know which way to sail. The village they came out from was a half day away to the south. Liverpool was closer to the north but, overloaded and with the wind and tide against us, they did not know how long it would take. It was a relief to all when a ship hailed us. The fishermen signaled distress. The *Washington* hove to and put out a lifeboat to aid us."

He pauses and bites into his bread and chews. After swallowing, he grins ashamedly at me. "I do not know what it is," he says, "but since I left home, I am hungry all the time."

"Eat," I say. "It is natural to be hungry after famine and struggle." As I say it, I wonder at myself. I am never hungry. "Go on with your story," I say. We are standing by the pump. I will not draw water until the man tells me what happened to my brother.

"The mate of the *Washington* said that they had seen the *Abigail* on fire and picked up two survivors. They would take on whoever was willing to sail with them to New York, for the captain would not turn back. He had important documents on board that he was bound to deliver with all speed. The two burned men were in great pain, and we judged they could be better served by a doctor on land. I made up my mind then and there that I would never go to America but work in England. I will not trust myself to the ocean again. I must keep land under my feet. Your brother and the other man decided to go. Your brother shook my hand and thanked me. He said that if ever I should have word of what happened to his sister that I should write to him in New York. He wrote the sister's name and a direction to write him in care of the offices of the *Washington* on a slip of paper. The mate of the *Washington* told him what to do."

"Oh." I bite down on the eager words that bubble in me. I struggle to keep my voice controlled and easy. I do not know this man. "Do you still have it?" I ask. "What is the sister's name? Perhaps I might encounter her and give a message," I say cautiously.

The man flushes through the red of his sunburnt face. "I cannot read," he admits. "I lost the paper and never thought about it until now when I saw the way you walk. Then I saw your hair when your kerchief came off and thought of Daniel."

"It is not so terrible," I comfort him. "The brother lives and he can be found through the offices of the *Washington*. That is enough for his sister if you or I find her." I am relieved to hear he cannot read. He knows my brother's name, but he seems to have forgotten mine. Even if he sees the bill advertising for me, he will not be able to decipher it.

"Where will you go when the harvest is done here?" I ask him. It is safer to talk of his concerns than of the things that touch me.

"I will work here in England until I hear the good harvests return at home," he says, "and then I will go back to the old village and the cottage where I was born. When I jumped from the burning ship and clung to a stick in the cold, salt sea, I swore that, if I lived, I would never go across the water again except once to return to Ireland. It is not my luck to go to America."

"I feel for you, wandering away from home and yearning for it," I tell him.

He smiles, a shy smile. "I will survive," he says. "I like to be out in the fields. The English are a sour lot in my experience and suspicious of strangers. I stick with a crowd of us who are working to earn passage back to Ireland or across the sea to the new country. By the end of this season I will have my fare for the ride from Liverpool to Dublin and something over. I will be glad to put my feet on Irish soil again. And then I will never leave nor speak to an Englishman again."

The bell rings to tell the laborers that the time for food and rest are done. I have filled my pitcher with water too late for it to be of use. We walk back down through the orchard.

I gather courage in my heart and speak. "If you see Daniel Pigot ever again," I say quietly, "tell him his sister survived the fire and is safe. She will come to search for him in America, I can promise."

The man regards me steadily and then he smiles, a happy, open grin. I warn him with my eyes not to speak his thoughts aloud. There are people around us. "I will tell him," he says. "I will say a lad with red hair who looked so much like him as to be his younger brother promised me his sister would search for him in America. I am glad to know she lives. I will go my way with a lighter heart."

He shakes my hand heartily and goes away to the fields. By nightfall the grain harvest is gathered in. Tomorrow, early, the laborers will pack up their poor shelters and move on. There are fields to be mowed to the north of us. Then the apple and nut harvests begin, and for those who would go south, the hops will be ripe. In my heart I bless the man who met my brother. Standing in the fresh air of the courtyard before I go indoors, I wish upon the evening star a safe rest for him and for me after all our wandering.

The house servants eat an early, light supper. The master rode out to a neighboring family for dinner, so the evening will close early for us all. Then, just when peace is settling in, several things happen at once. Mr. Plumb brings in a bushel of peaches. Mrs. Bennet has sent word through the master that the peaches must be preserved; half are to be cooked into jam and half scalded and packed in spirits.

Just as Mr. Serle and I are deciding that the half of the peaches that must be preserved in spirits should be sliced and set to steep overnight, someone calls at the kitchen door.

"Is anyone here?" a female asks.

Recognizing Susan's voice, I leap up. "Susan!" I exclaim. "Is it really you?"

"Of course," she cries in her familiar chortling voice. "I am come to see how you are getting on, lad." She puts emphasis on the last word, reminding me that I am not the Mina she knew and helped in Liverpool. I can see that she is looking at the red of my hair, visible at the edges of my kerchief.

"I am well, Susan," I say. "I am the same Paddy you met in Liverpool." I think I am rather clever to find a way to tell her the name they call me here.

"Mr. Plumb said you are in the kitchen, not the stables now, Paddy," Susan tells me. "Is Tom about? I am to come to find him too."

"You know Tom?" I ask. The thought disturbs me.

Susan laughs. "Of course," she says. "We both grew up in

the village here. He is an old, old friend." She pokes my arm and, when I look at her, she winks at me.

"Tom is gone over to the dairy," says Mr. Serle. "I sent him to tell the dairymaid that we will want extra cream tomorrow. The master dines at home with some members of the hunt."

"You look well, Paddy," says Susan. She appeals to Mr. Serle. "May we walk out to the yard for a moment? Paddy needs some air before more work in this stuffy kitchen. He can help me look out for Tom."

"Yes," says Mr. Serle. "We all need some air. I will walk in the orchard myself. But remember," he warns me, "the peaches must be sliced and put with brandy before you sleep tonight."

Susan giggles. "You have a lovely way with words," she says saucily. "I like a foreign accent in a dark man."

Mr. Serle does not answer. We go out into the fresh evening air.

"What brings you to the village now, Susan?" I ask her. "I did not expect you so soon."

Susan sighs, a dramatic gust of breath. "There is the harvest of our home field to help with," she says. "My mother wanted me for a week or two to work with her. She has fruit to preserve, as you do here. Her garden herbs need to be picked and dried. And she wants my help with the cheese. I am tired of the dark and dirt of the city anyway." She laughs, a ripple of music. "This is a good time of year to look out for a husband too. The harvest brings stray sons home."

I see Mr. Serle shrug. I have the impression that even in a few minutes he does not much like Susan. I wonder why.

Susan and I sit on the bench against the dairy wall. Mr. Serle stands by the gate where the honeysuckle is blooming. I can see that Susan is curious. She keeps looking over at him and raising her voice to include him in our talk.

"Where are you from?" she asks him.

"The south," he says laconically.

"The south of what?" she challenges with her laughing voice.

"South of here," he says, and walks farther away into the garden.

"Your Mr. Serle has secrets," Susan says; she pinches my arm affectionately.

"I suppose," I respond. "I confess, I do not know his secrets."

"My uncle, Mr. Coates, is not so fond of this foreigner. But he treats you well?" Susan asks.

"Like the kind Christian that he is," I say. To my surprise, Susan laughs at this.

"What is it?" I say.

Before Susan responds, Mr. Serle walks back from the garden. His head is bent. He has a spray of jasmine in his hand. "Are you all right?" I ask him without thinking whether he will welcome my concern.

"The perfume of the jasmine is too strong for me," he says. "I am reminded of home. I will go in. I will see that the water is boiling so that you can scald the fruit. Rest a little more, but do not stay too long with your friend." He goes before I can answer him.

"What made you laugh just now?" I ask Susan.

"What was it you said about that man?" she asks me as if she is puzzled to remember.

"I said he treats me like the kind Christian that he is," I repeat.

Susan goes off into gales of laughter again. "You ninny," she cries. "That is no Christian. Your Mr. Serle is a Jew, or I will eat my shawl."

"He cannot be," I reply. Susan's laughter is beginning to annoy me.

"Why not?" Susan calms herself, her hand at her breast.

"Because—because a Jew does not look like an ordinary man."

"Oh, I will grant you that. Mr. Serle is handsomer than most ordinary men, but short for my taste. I like a long tom," Susan giggles.

"But Jews are dark and wizened and wear strange clothes and have great hooked noses," I say. "They hate Christians, although they pretend to like them. They lend money and persecute the poor souls who cannot pay them back. They are avaricious and cruel. Indeed, they kill babies if they have a chance."

Before she speaks, Susan looks about to see if anyone is near. Then she says, "Mina, who taught you such ideas?"

"Everyone knows such things," I cry. I am trembling. Mr. Serle has been pretending to befriend me. For what end?

"Who taught you?" Susan asks again.

"Everyone," I say. "The priest told us when we read the Bible about the betrayal of blessed Jesus. Judas was a Jew."

To my amazement, Susan laughs at this. "So were all the disciples, then," she says.

"No," I say. "They were Christians. They loved Christ and obeyed Him. Only Judas hated Him."

Susan laughs and laughs. "Jews are moneylenders, it is true. But Papists are an even more foolish bunch. You think too much about the past," she declares. She lowers her voice to a whisper. "I have heard they are very potent in bed," she murmurs in my ear. I flinch away, and she laughs merrily and hugs her arm about me. It is hard to be angry at her. Her skin has a warm flush; her dark eyes flash with life. Her laughter encompasses me.

"What are you laughing at?" asks Tom, coming to us from the dairy. His hair is tousled and his face is flushed. I think he may have been embracing the dairymaid. He approaches the bench, glaring at me.

"You, of course." Susan looks at him from under fluttering eyelashes. She has dropped her arm from my shoulders. She turns and winks at me. I do not dare to join in teasing Tom. Tomorrow I will pay for any liberty taken today.

"Paddy is telling me what a joy you are to work with, Tom," says Susan.

Her attention is all turned away from me even though she sits in the same position. She puts her hand on my arm, and I can feel that she does it to tell Tom something, not to be close to me. I stand up and move away. "I must go in and finish my work," I say.

Susan stands too and stretches her arms about her head. She yawns and then laughs with her hand over her mouth. "I have had a busy day," she says. "Perhaps I am too tired for this wedding party."

"She's a good lass," says Tom, putting his arm familiarly about Susan's waist. "We are going to dance tonight. You're not too tired to dance with me, are you, Susan? Aren't you jealous, Paddy? Or perhaps you do not like women?"

"He is too young," says Susan. From the look she gives me, I can see that it amuses her to know a secret that Tom does not share.

"Mary—" I boldly begin. Susan cuts me off with laughter.

"Whose wedding do you think we are going to?" demands Tom.

"I do not know," I reply.

"Of course you don't," Tom snorts.

"Mary was weeping on my shoulder as soon as I arrived," says Susan. "She is a fool, but they have found her a husband."

"But Mary said that Tom—" I begin.

Susan cuts me off again. "Mary's mother canvassed the village and the farms for miles around," she crows. "They found a widower with four young children who will take her as she is. He needs the help in the house."

"Her brother raked up a dowry of a gold coin and a solid farm wagon," adds Tom. "Mary is lucky."

"And Tom too." Susan winks at me. "I heard what Mary claimed. He is well out of it. So it's all settled to everyone's satisfaction," says Susan. "And they say there will be plenty of ale and dancing tonight. Her mother and brother are that glad to have her go."

"But—" I want to object. I stop. Susan is giving me a warning look. I see that not only is Tom's arm about her waist, hers encircles his. This is not my business, I decide. Susan knows, and she does not seem to care. Poor Mary.

"Enjoy the dancing," I say.

"Good night, Paddy," calls Tom in his jeering voice. "Come down and dance with the lasses when you are tired of your Mr. Serle."

"Good night," calls Susan. They are through the courtyard

and out the gate to the path through the fields. Susan has left her shawl on the bench where we were sitting. I think of going after them to give it to her and then change my mind. The night is warm and soft. She will not want it. Besides, Tom will think I want her attention.

I stand in the courtyard breathing in the sweet odors of the flowers in Mr. Plumb's gardens. The clouds that threatened earlier are cleared away. Above me, stars prick bright pinholes in the serene dome of the dark. In the still air the sound of music trickles up from the village. Voices and a plaintive tune played on a reed flute come from the camp of the vagrant workers. Tomorrow they will be gone. Perhaps I should follow the sound of the pipe and go wander with them.

Across the yard the light gleams yellow from the kitchen door. Two women from the village who have been helping in the kitchen emerge and make their way toward the gate that Susan and Tom passed through. They too are most likely bound for Mary's wedding dance. Mr. Serle is alone in the kitchen now. I can see his figure cross and recross within the doorway as he finishes the work of today and lays out what he wants ready for tomorrow.

What Susan told me about Mr. Serle cannot be true. Reluctantly, I walk toward the door. I must question him. It will be his turn to tell a story tonight. I ask myself whether I truly wish to hear it.

CHAPTER XVI

IN THE KITCHEN, I find Mr. Serle looking in despair at the bushel of peaches that Mr. Plumb brought in earlier. In the excitement of talking to Susan, I had forgotten it.

"I will get to work right away," I tell him. "This is not your task." I get out a knife and a large basin for the fruit and a small one for the skins and the pits. Luckily there is a bowl of sugar ready-crushed and sieved in the baking pantry. I prepared enough for extra use early this morning and never needed it during the day. Mr. Serle has set out a bottle of the brandy that he keeps in a locked cupboard.

"I will help," Mr. Serle says. "It is sitting-down work. So long as I can rest my tired feet, I am content to work."

"The water is boiling," I say. "Sit while I scald the fruit and loosen the skins."

For a while we labor in silence. My knife flashes in my hand as the rich flesh of the peaches drops into the basin on my knees. As I reach to draw more scalded fruit toward me, I see that Mr. Serle has put the spray of jasmine flowers into a pot of water and placed it beside his array of knives on the worktable.

I nod toward the sweet-smelling flower and say, "Do those grow where you were born?"

"Yes," says Mr. Serle. He does not seem inclined to add anything to the single word.

I search for a way to open a road of talk to him. "What do you think of Susan?" I ask him.

"I see you are grateful to her for the help she gave you," he replies.

"I am," I say, "but what do you think of *her?*"

He considers for a moment. Neat slices of peach fall steadily from his knife into the basin. The kitchen is filled with the smell of the rich heat of summer. "She laughs too much," Mr. Serle says at last.

"Susan said a terrible thing about you," I tell him, looking up from under lowered eyelids.

"Oh?" he says. His face and his voice reflect indifference.

"Shall I tell you what she said?" I ask. I want to ask him, and yet I do not want to.

"If you wish," he replies.

I take a breath. "She says that you are one of the Hebrew race," I say in a rush. "She says you are a dirty Jew."

"Did she say 'dirty Jew' or only the word *Jew?*" Mr. Serle asks. His voice is austere. I ask myself how he can be so calm about insulting words.

"Only the word *Jew,*" I admit. I feel ashamed, but I am not sure why.

"The fruit is ready," Mr. Serle says. "Bring the sugar to pour over it and the scales."

We are both silent as we weigh the sliced fruit and the sugar. I crack four of the peach pits and add the bitter kernels to the fruit and sugar. Then, stirring gently with a long-handled spoon, I pour the brandy in. I will bottle the fruit in the morning before I make the jam. I put a clean cloth over the basin and carry it to a cool corner of the still room to steep overnight. When I return, Mr. Serle speaks before I can find words to apologize to him for my rude question.

"What does the word *Jew* mean to you?" he asks me.

"It means evil," I say. "It means twisted men who live for money and for the great interest they demand for loans. They plot to take over the world's money. It means people who practice a secret religion that is against Christ. Besides, they are all ugly with big noses and long, greasy, dark hair. So I have been taught. I am a faithful Christian and must hate the people who killed my Lord."

"Must you?" says the cool voice from across the table.

"Must I?" I echo. Well, I ask myself, must I? "Must I what?" I hedge.

"Must you believe everything you are taught? Must you hate because someone told you to?" asks Mr. Serle. His voice hides more emotion now. I am not sure whether it is anger or sorrow or something else.

"You are right," I admit. "I do not believe everything I have been taught. And yet, it is hard to turn from the word of the Church." I think then of the priest in Milford and his harsh words. I have not given up the clothing that protects me. "But it is a fact that the Jews killed Christ."

"Is it?" he demands of me.

"I think so," I stammer. "Pontius Pilate asked the people and they said to kill Christ."

"And did they?" comes the inexorable voice.

"Perhaps it was the Roman soldiers who mocked and crucified the Lord," I say, trying to remember the voice of Father Fintan reading in the church on the Friday of Holy Week. I should have paid better attention, I think.

"So the Roman rulers executed your Messiah and all of the people of Israel are responsible?" Mr. Serle says.

"They taught me so," I say. "I have never heard anyone say otherwise. If there is another way to see it, I will try to understand." In memory, I kneel. The priest touches ashes to my forehead. We are all sinners.

Mr. Serle nods. "What can we do but try," he says. I can hear he is not asking me a question. "Have you ever met a Jew?" he adds.

"No," I admit. I think back down the path of the past. "I saw one once at a fair when I was very small and there was food to eat. I had a little pie from a hawker. We were prosperous then. My father still had the care of the horses, and there was money for meat. The Jew wore a black hat. My mother told me to stay away from him. She made me afraid."

"So if I say I am a Jew, you will be afraid?"

"But I know you," I cry. This man cannot be one of those my mother warned me to avoid as she held my hand tight. The memory of my senses tells me she was afraid.

"Will you be afraid to hear a Jew's story?" Mr. Serle asks.

"I have told you my history. I will be quiet to hear yours," I say. I think of the comforting drinks Mr. Serle has given me and the patience with which he has heard my woes. "I will fetch you a mug of cool water," I say humbly. Mr. Serle behaves with Christian grace, and he is the cleanest person I have ever met. I wonder that he can be the embodiment of a great evil. I bring the water, and we sit at the table where the air comes through the open doorway and refreshes us.

"I was born in the Jewish quarter of the city of Rome in the year 1818," Mr. Serle begins. "I mention the year only because my parents reminded me many times as I was growing up that they had waited eight years for my birth, despairing that they would have a child. They had married with hope in 1810, a year of jubilation for my people in Rome. The French took the city. They told the Pope and his minions that they could no longer rule our lives and make us live in shame and degradation. They brought us dignity."

"The Pope could not willingly do wrong," I say. "You should not hate the Holy Father."

"Listen, child, and judge for yourself whether what I say is an insult or the simple truth," he responds.

"Go on, please." I look down sulkily at my hands. He should be fair to my religion. Everyone hates the Catholics here, I tell myself.

"As I said, my parents married in a year of hope and longed for my birth. My people have lived in Rome for thousands of years, for generations always in the same sector of the city. The place is bounded on one side by *il fiume Tevere*—I mean, the Tiber River—and surrounded all about by a wall. Within the wall are seven gates through which we have to pass if we have business outside our permitted place. There is, of course, a fee for passage through the gates. No new houses can be built in the quarter. So, as the population grows or diminishes, we have more or less living space. When families arrive, fleeing plague or injustice, space must be found for them. In years when the fevers do not kill the babies, our families grow and space must be found for them also. Somehow or other, it is always crowded. Rooms are built into and on top of the houses that exist. In places, the buildings lean into each other. There are alleys where young lovers hold hands across from window to window.

"My family, my father, my mother, my younger brother, and I, were fortunate. We lived among other families like ourselves near the Via del Portico d'Ottavia. Our home was on a high floor divided into three rooms in a sound enough house. The house faced on a courtyard, where there was an oven and a firebox for cooking in the summer. When the spring rains came, sometimes the river overflowed its banks and came rushing through the narrow streets and into our courtyard. Then the whole place had to be cleaned of mud and debris. Once after the river flooded, we found a fish in the oven as we were raking out the mess. It was a good joke that the river that tried to kill us also offered to feed us. Unfortunately, the fish was dead when we found it, so we could not eat it." Mr. Serle smiles at the memory, and then his face draws once more into sadness. "I hated the filth and the stench the river left. Even now, it turns my stomach to think of it."

After a pause he continues. "My father imported and sold silk cloth. His firm was begun by my great-grandfather. The office and the warehouse for the goods was in the Christian city, across the river in Trastevere where the firm began back in the days when the Jews were permitted to live in that quarter of the city also. Of course, my father had a Christian partner, for when the firm was founded, no Jew was allowed to possess a business that sold goods to Christians as well as Jews. The families knew each other for many years. Even so, we never went to their house or they to ours. First, we could not eat the unclean food from their kitchen, but also my mother would have been ashamed to bring someone used to luxury into our cramped home with its five chairs—one for each of us, one for a guest. For even though the business was prosperous, my parents, like my grandparents before them, were careful not to make others jealous or to draw the attention of the state. Besides, there was such need around us that much of what we had went to feed and clothe others of the community."

Mr. Serle pauses, and I think of my mother with her bowls of broth and hearth cakes for the neighbors when illness struck or a child died. His even voice picks up the thread of his tale again. "All was well enough as I grew. We ate cakes flavored with anise seed and drank a glass of wine for holidays. My mother had a Christian girl to help her, and they would laugh together as they sieved curd cheese to make *cassola,* and stewed apricots in sugar syrup, and cleaned the house on Friday mornings to be ready for the Sabbath. Clara would appear on Saturday to light the fire in the sitting room, so my father would be comfortable while he read his Bible when we all returned from *la sinagòga*— I mean, our church. After Clara left, my father would take out his book of religious discussion, a work of Talmud written by a Roman rabbi a hundred years ago, which he kept hidden. Owning such a book was forbidden by the Pope. My brother and I would spy every Saturday afternoon to see where he kept it, and every Saturday he fooled us again.

"My father taught me proper Italian, for I spoke a rough dialect in the streets with my playmates. He taught me and my brother mathematics also, all he knew. My mother, who came from an educated family in Venice in the north, taught me French and a little German. For Hebrew and religious studies, I went to the rabbi. He was a stern man, yet wise and kind. I wanted to be like him.

"So I grew. When I was eight years old, I could read and write in three languages. I was careful not to boast of my luck. Many of my companions were illiterate. We kept to the house and the courtyard mostly for our games. The streets were danger-ous, our parents said. We might be stolen away by the Christians to be raised by priests and forced to betray our faith. My parents trusted Clara in many things, but even so, they warned us pri-vately that if she ever splashed water on us, we were to come and tell them right away. Some Christian servants would secretly baptize Jewish children, so the priests could take them, saying that they had been made Christian and must be saved from their Jewish parents. Clara never did splash water on us. Still, it was a part of the uncertain world. She was our servant, but she could become our master by using her religion as a weapon against us."

I wonder that Mr. Serle can call religion a weapon. Prayer is a comfort, and the words of the Bible are beautiful—at least I think so. Perhaps they have evil servants in Rome. I would like to question Mr. Serle but do not dare. I can see in his face and hear in his voice that his story sweeps him away to that distant place. I tell myself to be silent and follow him.

"We knew the walls and the gates that circumscribed our world," he says. "At the age of eight, I had never been outside those walls. My brother and I heard reports of the markets and the Roman ruins and the exotic visitors from foreign lands who crowded the streets that led to the Pope's church, *San Pietro.* Out in the great city was an arch that the boys whispered about. They said it showed the humiliation of the Israelites by the Romans a thousand years ago. To walk under that carved archway, they said, was to curse oneself to be a slave all of one's life. No Jew goes under that arch even to this day. Our friends went out to explore the city, but my mother was always so nervous that some terrible catastrophe would befall us that my brother and I had to promise her not to go."

Mr. Serle pauses, and when he speaks again, his voice is softer, with a longing in it. "My mother was a beautiful woman, with the blue eyes and auburn hair of a Venetian. We adored her and could not bring ourselves to disobey her." He drinks his water and continues more briskly. "Well, we tried to be content to watch the world come to us. We looked in amazement at the costumes and the habits of the foreigners who came within our walls to stare at us or to consult the fortune-tellers. And every day our streets were crowded with those native Romans who had business with the food merchants and the secondhand shops and the tailors.

"One day catastrophe fell on us, not outside our quarter of Rome, but within it. The Pope, Pope Leo, believed that the Jews were becoming too free in the city. The burden of laws that the French had cast away were brought back again. Now Jews and Christians were again forbidden to work together. My father had to give up his business to his partner. My brother and I listened, tense with the fear that we felt around us, our ears pressed to the wall between our bedroom and the sitting room. My father explained to my mother that he trusted his partner. 'He promises to keep me as half owner, but in secret,' he said in a low voice. 'He says when this bad time is over, we will legally be full partners again. He wants me to come to the warehouse twice a week to look at the samples with him. He will give me money each time I visit him. We will not starve.'

"Night after night, my brother and I listened, trembling and silent, looking all our questions to each other with our eyes only, as our parents talked about whether we should move to Alexandria or to Livorno or to my mother's family in Venice. They discussed money. One night we heard the chink of coins as they counted their resources against disaster.

"During the day, no one spoke of the troubled conversations of the night. My mother went her way, serenely attending to the care of the house, our meals, our clothing. Now she had more toil, for it was forbidden to have a Christian servant. There was no fire on Saturday anymore. Strange things happened, however. One cold day a soldier, sent from the Pope's army to inspect the houses of our neighborhood to be sure no Christian servants were about, lit our fire for us just because he wanted to. My mother looked cold, he said. People are ever unpredictable. My brother and I did not care about servants and fires. The change in our lives meant that we could stop worrying about Clara and being stolen by priests.

"All of us had yellow hats to wear when we left the house. It hurt to see the expression on my mother's face as she adjusted the ugly yellow veil over her head and face before she went out. One of our cousins went away to Paris. After a year a letter came back to tell us all that life there was hard but free. He reported that religion did not matter now. He and his wife had decided that true freedom lay in the equality of man.

"On a day soon after that letter came, my father arrived home just moments before the gate to our quarter closed for the night. He was dirty and disheveled, his coat torn and his face bleeding. He had been hurrying through the streets to reach the gate before it closed, when a gang of soldiers came staggering toward him. They were boisterous, linking arms three across and pushing vendors out of their way.

"They surrounded him, joking that they would take him hostage and demand a ransom for him. My father tried to placate them, but they must have thought him not servile enough, for they began to swear at him and shove him against the wall along the street. One pulled his beard, another tore his coat, another knocked the hat from his head and trampled on it. My father tried to seize the hat, because to be in the street without it meant he could be arrested and fined. As he scrambled for it, one of the men kicked him, and he sprawled facedown into dirt and horse manure. The soldiers roared with laughter at that and began to slap each other on the back and congratulate each other for having a Jew at their feet.

"My father wept as he told my mother about it." Mr. Serle pauses and swallows.

"It was not right," I venture timidly. "I am glad he escaped."

"No, it was not right," Mr. Serle says. "And escape? The bells for the evening services began to ring in the city. The soldiers must have had a curfew themselves, for they cocked their ears to the sound. My father ran as fast as he could. One, noticing my father escaping, let out a shout and lobbed a stone after him. The missile caught him on the back of the head and dizzied him, but, terrified for his life, he ran on and lost the men in the turnings of the narrow alleys. As the guard was preparing to swing the gate closed, he came in by the entrance at the Piazza Giudea and stumbled home at last.

"My mother washed him and nursed him tenderly while we watched, wide-eyed with fear. My parents argued long and hard that night. My father knew that by going he would forfeit the business his father and grandfather had created. More than the business, more than hope for the future, his long connection to the place with its smells and colors bound him to the home of his ancestors. The streets were dangerous, but they were his streets, where all the layered memories of his life walked with him every day.

"I will tell you a strange thing that happened at that time. The world was falling in around us. Special taxes, which Christians did not have to pay, burdened us; the rule that ten Jews must appear in one of the churches of Rome every Sunday to hear the Christian service was imposed on us again; no Jew could work outside the walls of our quarter except to collect old clothes or to hawk secondhand goods or food in the streets. The law against owning religious books except for the Bible itself was enforced more and more rigorously. Every day families scraped together what they could and fled. And in their adversity, my people turned against each other.

"We gathered every Friday night and Saturday to worship. One Saturday morning, a man, reading in the sacred scroll, pronounced a syllable in Hebrew in a way that offended another man. I will not trouble you with the details of the matter. One man spoke, the other corrected him, the first objected that his way was right. Soon everyone in the congregation had an opinion. The quarrel persisted week after week, month after month. That syllable and how it should be pronounced became an obsession, a wound in our community that refused to heal."

"Why should a people in trouble make quarrels with each other?" I say in wonderment.

"I have thought about it often," Mr. Serle replies. "Perhaps they feel themselves so helpless against the power that tells them how to dress and where to live and what deference to authority they must express that, like caged birds, they begin to peck at each other. Oppression makes anger, and anger must find a way to show itself.

"The change in the synagogue on Friday nights and Saturdays changed me more than the oppression of the world outside our gates. I was beginning my study of my religion so that I would be ready for the ceremony when I would take my turn to read the Bible for the congregation and be a man among men. I prayed that they would decide what was the correct pronunciation of that syllable, *shewa*, so that I would not have to join in the fights.

"We struggled on, and then the times changed again. They said the Pope was in trouble, he needed money. We felt the press for taxes weigh on us. But when we raised our eyes to the world beyond Rome, we could see that change was coming. Our rabbis wrote letters to colleagues in other cities. Word came from France and Germany that rich Jews with influence had heard of our suffering. A rumor swept through our community that the great house of Rothschild was negotiating with the Pope to buy us our freedom.

"Slowly, a little change began. Trade in old clothes was what most people did. Rags. Rags we wore and rags had to feed us. But when I was eleven years old and preparing to take my place as a man in the synagogue, a school opened for Jews. My parents were deeply pleased. They saw a way for us to rise if my brother and I could become doctors—in our quarter only, of course, for it was forbidden for a Jewish doctor to attend non-Jews. My father's partner was encouraged by the times to give my father more of his share of the money from the business. My brother and I were sent to the new school.

"The students were all Jewish, but the professor was a Christian. I think of that professor with both love and hate. Love because he taught with respect for learning. His face shone with his passion for the Latin of the Roman historians and the brave men and noble deeds they described. Tears came to his eyes when he read the New Testament to us. He held his hand against the black wool coat over his heart as he declaimed Bible passages from memory. With his long legs and long arms and short body, he looked like a great black spider as he patrolled between the rows of desks, monitoring our behavior, ever ready to strike and sting with the ferule he always carried."

Mr. Serle pauses. He takes a fragrant peach from the white bowl on the table. He turns it gently in his hand, then bends his head to inhale its savor. Perhaps the goodness of it comforts him, I think. Silence broods over us. When I fear that he may not speak again, I question him, "At least he had passion for learning and his faith. All teachers are strict, aren't they? How could you hate him for doing his job?"

"Easily," says Mr. Serle. He puts the peach back in the bowl. "He never forgot for a moment that we were heathens to him. He hated us for being what we were. He hated himself for lowering himself to teach us. The only redemption for him would be the triumph of making converts. It was easy to hate him for his desire to make us forsake our very selves." Mr. Serle shrugs his shoulders. "Nevertheless, I learned from him. He loved his books even if he could not love us as we were.

"Every day there was a required reading in the New Testament and a lecture on the benefits of becoming a Christian. At least once a week my brother was whipped for blocking his ears during that lecture. I loved his rebellious spirit, but to my shame, I never had his courage.

"My father was going to the warehouse three times a week now. I did not have much faith in my mother's dream that I would become a doctor. I preferred to understand my father's business, for it connected us to the past and to the other communities of Jews in the north and in the east. The truth is, I loved the fabrics he imported. The heavy silk twills and the diaphanous chiffons pleased my sense of touch. The glinting colors of the damasks with their changing sheen and interwoven gold or silver threads fed the eye with the rich variety that our dark lives lacked.

"The warehouse seemed a safe place to me, even though the journey there through the streets of Rome meant insults and danger. To me, school was the greater assault. The professor sneered at us. He gave little speeches about the moral deformity of the Hebrew race whenever one of us misbehaved. We clenched our jaws and kept silent. We knew because our parents had drummed it into us that the world's refusing us learning was a way to keep us poor. If we followed our hearts and our pride and all together threw our professor out of the window, our parents and our neighbors would pay for our act. So we were quiet. Do not think our silence did not contain our hate.

"We vented our anger in humor sometimes. My brother would amuse us all before class by aping the professor's voice and his spider's scuttling movements. He made us laugh too with fantastical plans for murdering and disposing of the professor without being caught. My brother was a natural leader and a rebel. The teacher tolerated him because he could not keep the class in order without his help.

"In the winter of 1831—I was twelve—" Mr. Serle stops and looks at me. "You were not even born then."

"No," I say.

Mr. Serle looks at me a long moment. I wonder what he is thinking, for he shrugs as if saying something to himself alone before he returns to the past. "That winter, 1831 as I said, a change that seemed to presage hope came to us. In the month of February the people began to gather in groups in the piazzas, whispering. One evening, my brother and I, hurrying home from school, saw our neighbors streaming from their houses. 'What is happening?' we asked.

" 'Follow us,' came the cry.

"We pelted through the turning streets after the mob. People ran to and fro from the dark of the alleys to the torchlit piazzas. The shadows of giants grew upon the walls of the houses and then dwindled down to dwarf size. My brother and I followed a group toward the gate that separated our quarter from the piazza of the fish market.

"The gates that kept us from the city, the gates that closed each night, condemning those locked out to hide in fear in some dark corner or be molested or killed by roaming hoodlums, the gates for which the Christian community demanded a tax from us, were being torn from their posts. Seven or eight of us lifted the barrier free and bore it aloft in triumph through the quarter. Behind us streamed the singing, dancing mob. Old men rushed up to spit upon the splintered gate as it came by them and then fell back, unable to keep pace with us, as we whirled on.

"At the bank of the river we stopped. Some wanted to make a great bonfire, but cooler heads prevailed. There was no safe space for it. Where would our joy be if we set fire to the flimsy, crowded houses that sheltered us? The cry went up to throw the gate into the river. We danced the gate about in a great circle, tearing it to pieces and distributing them in the crowd. Then, shouting curses and prayers of thanks all at once, we advanced to the high bank of the Tiber and threw the hated fabric of our imprisonment into the turbid waters. We milled about in the flickering, uncertain light, shaking each other's hands, slapping each other's shoulders, hoarse with shouting and emotion. I found my brother in the crowd and seized him in my arms. The night vibrated in him.

"When we staggered home, drunk with freedom, my mother made a dish of spaghetti with anchovies for us. We sat at the scrubbed table of cypress wood and ate the hot food, tangy with salt fish and garlic and sweet with oil and toasted bread crumbs. We ate and told her all about how we had tugged the gates apart and thrown them in the river. My brother exalted in his strength, which grew greater as he told the story. He predicted that now that the ghetto gates were gone, the Arch of Titus would soon be reduced to rubble also.

"I listened and laughed and applauded him. But in my heart I doubted. I had heard the men in the synagogue talking about the loan that the house of Rothschild had sent to the Pope—Gregory now. One of the bankers had come to worship with us and to talk to the chief rabbi. Our action had been paid for. No soldiers from the State had prevented us from taking down the gate because they had been ordered to leave us alone. When the money runs out, I thought, when the soldiers are restless, we will be forced to put the gates in place again and pay a fine for destroying them. I held my tongue and ate my meal and thanked my mother.

"The year that I was eighteen, the river Tiber flooded in the spring, not worse than usual, but not much less either. As always, the water scoured out alleyways and brought debris and filth from gutters and cesspools swirling in at our doorways. The floods were followed by heat, and everywhere the palsied hand of fever touched the cheeks of the weak. My parents both fell ill of the bloody flux. My brother and I nursed them as best we could. The doctor who attended our people came and counseled us to feed my parents strong meat broth and keep them warm and clean.

"We boiled and scrubbed endlessly. I learned in those days to be clean above all else. We saved ourselves, but we could not save our parents. My lovely mother died first, worn almost to transparency and yet smiling her love and gratitude to all who helped her. When she was dead, my father gave up. Saying his last prayer, dedicating himself to God, he closed his eyes and gave up his soul."

"God rest them," I say with feeling. Mr. Serle lost his mother and father as I lost mine. I feel for him. I shudder to think of such people burning in hell as infidels.

"I thank you for your thought," Mr. Serle says.

"Your life must have been less without them," I say.

"Yes and no," he replies. "We buried them and said the prayers for the dead. We found such comfort as we could. When the time came to resume life, my brother and I searched our parents' room for the books and money that we knew must be hidden there. We found both, at last, under a false floor in the wardrobe. It was not much, but enough for my brother to continue his studies. We argued about it. Like my parents whispering into the late hours of the night, we turned the future this way and that between us. He wanted to share the money equally; I believed it better to use most of it for his training as a doctor. A small amount I would use to start myself in business as a vendor of roasted chestnuts.

"My brother at last assented to my view of things. I believe that he had a passion to learn. He raged when my parents died, because he did not know enough to cure them. I think the argument that swayed him in the end was that our mother would have been pleased to see him a master of medicine. Unsaid between us was our reluctance to apply to my father's business partner. Surely, we knew, we were owed money from the business in justice if not in law, but we could not bring ourselves to go to him then. We made the best of what we had."

I sigh. "I know what it is to live so," I say.

CHAPTER XVII

M R. SERLE drinks some water and continues. "With sadness and hope, we embarked on our adult lives. I married at the end of our time of mourning. My brother and I went to share the place where my wife lived with her father and an old aunt. Her mother was dead in the fevers that had killed our parents, so we had that raw sorrow among us. My father-in-law sold old clothes, and my wife helped him, as her mother had done, by mending and refurbishing the things. The aunt swept the house and kept the cooking fire burning. She was almost blind.

"This house was not so healthy as the place where my brother and I were born and raised. It was closer to the river. The floods had ravaged the houses there many times, and crooked walls and rotting timbers revealed the damage that poverty could not repair. When my wife became pregnant with our first child, I believed it was my duty to go to my father's old partner to try to reestablish my interest in the business. In truth, I had the welfare of my wife and son to think of, but I also missed the warehouse and the smells of the silk and of the jasmine blooming on the courtyard wall. I thought of all my father had taught me. To work as he had would bring me closer to him again."

I think of how grooming Gytrash and the smell of the stable keeps my brother with me. I watch Mr. Serle across the table. His white shirt is open at the throat. His strong hands are clasped upon the scrubbed board before him and his head is bent over them. He too has wept for his parents, I think. He does not look up and continues to speak.

"One morning I put on my long coat and the hateful yellow hat, for even though the soldiers were less strict just then about enforcing the rules for Jews, I dared not risk a fine. I crossed the river by the island bridges and made my way to the warehouse in Trastevere. It looked the same to me. Guido still sat in the entryway, ready to welcome visitors or to take messages. He greeted me gruffly but not unkindly. When I asked after his father, whom I remembered at his post before him, he kicked his foot in the dirt and said he was dead.

" *'Mi dispiace,'* I told him. 'I feel for you. My father died also this spring.'

" 'I heard it,' he said. 'My condolences.' He jerked his chin in the general direction of the offices on the floor above. 'Your father's partner is gone too. I suppose they never sent to tell you. Things are different here. The son, the young Signorino Raffaello, does things his own way.'

" 'Guido! Guido!' a loud voice called from across the courtyard. 'You are wanted to unload the cart.'

"Guido shrugged and turned away toward the summons. Then he wheeled quickly back. Putting his hand on my sleeve, he looked earnestly into my face. 'Don't expect much here,' he said, his voice a hoarse whisper. 'Signorino Raffaello is not like his father. Nor like yours. May their memory be blessed.' He crossed himself and hurried away toward the storerooms.

"I mounted the stairs slowly and entered the office that my father had shared with his partner. There I had played as a child and been instructed in keeping accounts. Now the son sat at the great table, with the ledger books before him and a mound of fabric samples heaped beside them.

"He looked up at me, nodded, and spoke my name with condescension. 'I suppose you are here to offer your condolences and to see what you can get of spoils,' he said. 'I suppose your father sent you.' I told him that my father too was dead. He shrugged and turned his pen about in his fingers. The son was not the man his father had been. When I said that our fathers had been honest partners and now the business was his and mine in honor, he hotly denied it.

"Well," Mr. Serle says sadly, "I will not repeat the argument we had. He denied my rights; I insisted. At last, he grudgingly conceded that my father had performed services for which he had not been paid. This young Raffaello would examine the books and come up with a figure. In the meantime, I should not come to the warehouse, for it could cause trouble to him. I should come at night, he said, knowing full well that was to risk death. When I remonstrated, he shrugged and said he would do what he could when business improved.

"Disgusted, I turned away. There was no use begging favors from such a man. He would grasp with both hands the treasure he had seized. His defense would be the stronger for the guilt in his heart that what he did was theft. I paused on the threshold. When I looked back to him, he was in the act of making the sign to avert the devil, *le corna*, behind my back. I left without speaking to him further."

"He was not fair," I say. "You should have fought him for your right."

Mr. Serle shakes his head. "You speak like a fool, child. Violence would have led to my arrest and a beating or death for me. That would not have helped my wife and child. It was illegal for me to have an interest in the firm, according to the laws. Only the honor of the elder Raffaello had preserved my father's property. No, I had to grit my teeth and bear it."

"What did you do?" I ask.

"I bought chestnuts and charcoal. I stood on my corner where the sweet smell from the chestnuts on my brazier would waft about to the four winds and draw customers to me."

"And that was enough to live?" I ask.

"Enough when we shared our labors," Mr. Serle says. "My wife, her father, my brother, the blind aunt, we struggled together, and that gave each of us strength. The winter was the best time; the summer the worst."

"How can that be?" I ask. "For us it was the opposite."

"My business was better in the cold months," he says. "Roast chestnuts warm the hands before they warm the stomach.

Clothes sold better then too. Besides, in Rome the summer months bring pestilence."

"But you all lived," I say.

"For a time," he replies, his voice sad with distance. "We followed the news of other countries where many of our friends had fled the tyrannies we suffered under. We questioned the foreigners who came to our synagogue to worship with us. We were proud when we heard of a political pamphlet or a speech that advocated rights for Jews."

I am amazed that news of other countries far away should matter. "Why should you care about France or Germany?" I ask.

"We saw in the freedom of others a chance for ourselves," Mr. Serle replies. "It seemed as if everywhere except in Rome a new age was coming. Workers and tradesmen grew in strength like the new leaves of spring under the sun of freedom. We listened to the rumors of change from the north. At home we saw little evidence of what we wished for. Change may have been seeping beneath us like an underground river, but we did not see it in our daily lives. Those families that had money to spare sent their children north to Livorno and Paris for education and the experience of freedom.

"At last the old Pope, Gregory, died. Rome held its breath, watching the black smoke rise day by day from the chapel next to St. Peter's Church. For the Christian Romans and for the tourists it was a time of gossip and curiosity. For us, it was a time of anxiety. The past had taught us fear. When the new Pope was elected at last, a sigh went through the community that all might be well. He was reputed to be a reasonable man."

I too sigh. "So all was well?" I say hopefully. The turn of Mr. Serle's lips tells me that the memory pouring over him is not of happiness and relief from strife.

"Life went on as ever," he says. "We did not venture to join the celebrating throngs before St. Peter's Church during the coronation of the Pope, another Pius, or go that night to see the fireworks display in the Piazza del Popolo.

"That autumn the rains were heavy in Rome and in the

hills to the north where the river Tiber rises. It rained for days, and then one morning the sun shone weakly through. The river was swollen and moving quickly in glassy heaves and surges. As my brother and I hurried out, we glanced at it, but accustomed to living farther back on higher land, we did not feel the danger. So off we went, he to his work with the physician who had taken him on as assistant, and I to my post selling chestnuts. I was standing at my place when a woman came running by me. I recognized her as one of our neighbors and called after her to ask what was wrong. 'The river,' she cried, 'the river is coming.'

"In haste, I tipped the embers from the brazier into the gutter and hurried after her, lugging my tools. My wife and son were at home with the aunt. In that low place, if the river overflowed its banks, it might come swirling in the doors of the houses. The force of the water could even undermine the timbers of the place and bring all down. It had happened before."

Tears come to my eyes in dread of what I am about to hear. I press my lips together. Mr. Serle must tell his story.

"Four streets from the river where the alleys sloped more sharply, the water stopped us. Already it was knee high and rising. The crowd that had gathered retreated. I would have waded on, but several people caught at me and held me back. I struggled to free myself, dropping my brazier and pan and sack of charcoal and chestnuts. 'Aqua! L'aqua viene!' The cry arose. 'Inondazióne!' Not only before us, but from the west, the water flooded toward us.

"Caught, we moved east and north where the higher ground was, heading toward the steps that led up to the *Chièsa Aracoeli*. Then we were cut off again by water flowing through the streets. A courtyard behind us was open. A crowd of us pushed in and climbed the stairs, up past the apartments and out onto the roof. From there we could look down to the Jewish quarter and to the streets and piazzas in the river's bend.

"The waters had risen halfway up the houses along the river. The *Ìsola Tiberina* showed above the water like a foundering boat, crowded with people and animals and battered by turbulent waters. On the roofs of the Jewish quarter, men and women, children and old people clung to parapets and chimney pipes. Cries for help rose to us from across the city. I leaned against a chimney pot and wept at what I saw."

"What horror!" I exclaim. Mr. Serle seems not to hear me. He is lost in his sorrow.

"As we stood, helpless, the sky darkened, the wind rose, and the rain poured down on us. All that afternoon and night I stood on the rooftop, straining my eyes to see the house where I had left my wife and son, praying."

"I hope your prayers were answered," I tell him. I cross myself for the pity of it.

He does not answer me but says, "A strange thought came to me as I huddled on that stranger's roof in the wet: This is the first night of my life that I have ever spent outside the walls of the ghetto. So this is freedom, I thought. Well—" He breaks off, sighs, and then continues his tale.

"As dawn broke, the rain clouds lifted. A fine drizzle sifted over the city. Through it we could see that boats had put out to take people trapped in their houses to higher ground. The water subsided as rapidly as it had risen, and in a few hours I ventured down to the street.

"I made my way through the muck and slime toward my home. My heart pounded in my chest and the blood rang in my ears. I had to go slowly, but I think that even had the streets been clear and easily passable, I would have moved at a snail's pace. Fear turned my feet to lead weights that my legs could barely shift."

I feel the fear of it too as he tells the story. I clasp my hands tight before me.

Mr. Serle's voice is barely more than a whisper. "As I drew near the house, my brother and then my father-in-law joined me. About us rose cries of joy and wails of grief.

"We found ourselves wading knee-deep as we approached our goal. The rotted door was half torn away from the entrance, and the masonry about the barred windows at the street level was so eroded by the water's force that it was crumbling away. The iron bars hung awry, about to fall.

"All was still within the *pianterréno*. Muck and debris slowed our desperate progress toward the stairway. When my brother, in the lead, put his foot upon the second step, it gave way under him, throwing him back into my arms and knocking me backward into the stinking mud. Grimly, we struggled to our feet. By sticking to the inner, wall side, where the supports for the stair treads still held, we inched our way to the upper floor."

I lean forward. I cannot speak if I would. I look down at my interlaced fingers. We close our hands on emptiness sometimes.

"At the turn of the stair our way was blocked by a sodden bundle of rags. When my brother bent to it, I knew from the stiffness of his back and the collapse of his shoulders that we had found my son. My son. Dead at seven years old. On the step above him, my wife lay like one dead. She gripped our son's arm in her two hands. She must have been trying to carry him up the stairs, to drag him from the dark water that had filled the *pianterréno*. She was alive, but scarcely.

"At last my brother brought her back to a kind of consciousness, but her spirit never truly returned to us. 'I am sorry,' she kept saying. 'I am sorry. Forgive me. I tried to save him. He went back to search for his little cat as I took Guiseppina to the roof. I am sorry. Forgive me. I was not strong enough. I am sorry.' Over and over again, I told her that I understood. I praised her courage. It was speech to a deaf person. Raving the same story again and again, she burned with fever and shook with cold. My brother gave her soothing drafts. He searched his books and consulted his teachers for medicines that might help her. Nothing made her better. She weakened day by day, and five days later, she was dead.

"I bowed my head into her hair, which even in her death smelled of the rosemary she rinsed it with. I remember that sweet odor and then nothing. My heart died with her."

We are silent in the quiet of the kitchen. The cool night air whispers at the door and brings the scent of mown grass and apples in to us. I look at the white bowl of golden peaches on the table, summer's ripeness. It would be an intrusion to speak to Mr. Serle of his loss, to urge him to scratch the scar of his sorrow. I see in my mind the bodies of my parents wrapped in linen, laid side by side. They made light bundles to carry to the church. My brother made a wooden cross for their grave, and we wrote their names on it. I wonder if it still stands. Alone in our sorrows, we sit still, and then, after a while, Mr. Serle speaks as if to himself.

"After my wife's death I was ill with fever for more than a month. My brother nursed me. The old aunt, who had been saved by my wife, tended me when my brother went out to his other patients. Slowly, my body mended, but my mind was clouded. Even as my brother urged me to move from my bed and to sit in the sun each day and to read the journals that were smuggled to us from Paris, I turned my face to the wall and dozed the days away.

"Finally, my brother insisted that I must not lie in bed. Each morning he cajoled me to a bench in the courtyard where I could sit and watch the life of our crowded tenement. I sat there idly day after day.

"Nothing moved me, until one day I heard a woman crying and looked up. It was the old aunt, Zia Guiseppina. For the first time in three months, I looked at her. She was huddled by the brazier on which she cooked the food, weeping and holding her right wrist in her left hand. Her gray hair fell in straggling locks across her cheeks. She had been trying to fry zucchini for *concia* and, almost blind as she was, she had burned herself."

"Zucchini?" I say. *"Concia?"*

"Never mind that," says Mr. Serle. "I talked to her. Since my wife's death, she had tried beyond her strength to do her work. She blamed herself for the deaths of my wife and my son. She felt useless now and, worse than that, a burden and a menace. My wife had set her tasks in order for her, placed the fire where it could not be a danger and the tools where she could find them easily.

"Her sorrow shook me from my sloth. In comforting her, I found the will to act again. I could see also that there was a very real danger for us all in this poor, blind woman's trying to tend the fire without aid. I set myself to help her, and in return she taught me her skills in cooking."

"You learned?" I say, startled from sorrow by surprise. "I thought you always knew."

Even in the sadness of his story, Mr. Serle looks up and smiles. "I learned," he says. "Indeed, I learned. As strength returned, I saw those around me with clearer vision. My brother was worn and thin. He gave all of himself to the ill who needed him. The chaos of our household, with its lack of food and ever-present dirt, took the greatest toll on him. So I began to shop and cook and clean as Guiseppina taught me. And as I learned, I saw that there was skill in choosing produce wisely and preparing it with thrift and art. Banishing the dirt of the city from our rooms gave me satisfaction. Our lives improved. My father-in-law found a woman—a widow—and the rabbi approved the idea of their marriage. They would willingly take Guiseppina with them, but where they could go was a mystery. There was no space anywhere for those who had not money to pay dearly for it. You understand that none of us owned the places where we lived. It was forbidden for Jews. We rented from Christian landlords who cared nothing for our comfort."

"I can understand what that is like," I say, remembering the factor coming to collect the rent and my mother's bitter words at how our labor went to buy luxuries for those who despised us.

"I told my brother we should go to Raffaello," Mr. Serle says. "My brother shrugged his shoulders and made a deprecating face. 'I went to him while you were ill,' he said. 'I spoke to him and was turned away. The papal laws forbid business partnerships between Hebrews and Christians, and your Raffaello is a law-abiding man.'

" 'You were good to try,' I told him. 'I will be stronger soon. Times will improve.'

"My brother patted my shoulder. 'I am pleased with my patient,' he said. 'You are right that times will be better. They say that change is coming. The people have not forgotten the liberty they knew under the French. There is talk of a united Italy. A dream, no doubt. Don't tell anyone I mentioned it.' And he smiled and hurried off to help some other *ammalato*.

"I began to work again, selling fried foods from a little

brazier. Guiseppina had taught me well, and people liked what I made. My wife's father married his widow. They found a place at last and took Guiseppina with them. Now my brother and I could rent a room for the two of us, away from the river in a healthier street.

"We talked of what would come. My brother hoped to marry. He encouraged me to think of it also. I replied that my heart was dead and buried with my wife. He reminded me that marriage is a duty. Soon he would be fully trained in his profession, and then he would marry immediately. He had talked to a fortune-teller about it.

"I do not know what the fortune-teller told him. As we talked that evening, someone knocked on the door. A guard had come to escort him to the house of a rich family. He was wanted urgently at a lying-in. My brother went away, pressing my hand and bidding me not to sit up for him. I never saw him alive again."

"Oh, no!" I cry. I do not want to hear more suffering. It is not fair. It is not right. Mr. Serle ignores my outburst. He is in his own mind again, in another place.

"It was the week before Easter, always a dangerous time for Jews in Rome. My brother was easily identified as a Jew, of course, for he wore the earlocks and the long coat that are common to us. A guard had come to attend him to the family that needed him, but it would be like him to have insisted on walking home alone. 'Dawn is breaking,' he would have said. 'I will bother nobody, and nobody will bother me.' He saw danger only for others, never for himself."

"I don't understand," I say. "Why was he called to danger?"

Mr. Serle looks at me from the faraway place where his thoughts are now. "He was called to a Christian family, but the wife had once been a Jew among us. She was young and afraid and she insisted on someone she trusted," he says. "Our doctors are known through the city for their learning and their skill." He sighs. "When my brother did not return in a few hours, I was immediately alarmed. As soon as full light came, I hurried out into the streets to search for him.

"I asked everywhere. People brushed me away with pitying looks or spoke cruelly. Finally, a laughing boy told me to go ask the *carabinièri* in the Via dei Pellegrini if they had any corpses. Rumor was that a Jew had been caught on the street late last night and got what he deserved. His body was being held until the rich Jews paid for it.

"It was true what the *ragazzo* said. The soldiers in the post on the Via dei Pelligrini had my brother's body. It had been found on the street, they said. Near the entrance to the Jewish quarter. I should be grateful that they had picked it up, they said. I could have it to bury if I brought two gold coins before nightfall. They would send it to the graveyard for suicides and criminals if I was not back by then.

"It was the drop that made the cup of bitterness run over. I swore that I would do two things before three days were gone: bury my brother and leave Rome forever. I made up my mind that I must go to Raffaello, the son of my father's partner. The Hebrew community would help me if it could, I knew. We had done so in other cases over the years. I sent word to the rabbi of my terrible news. I could not give up my brother's body to be thrown in the river or buried in the place set aside for criminals. Yet right demanded that I ask for what was mine from Raffaello before I took the sacrifice of my people."

"You were brave," I say. I am filled with sorrow and yet glad that Mr. Serle talks about his brother with such passion.

"It was easy then," he says, and shrugs one shoulder as he often does. "I had a duty to my brother, and I did not care what happened to me."

"Oh, I hope that, like the good Samaritan, Raffaello helped you in your need," I cry.

Mr. Serle looks at me and lifts an eyebrow. "He was a Christian, to the last," he says, bitterness in his voice. "He rejected me utterly at first. When I humiliated myself and said that I came not on business but to ask for charity based on our fathers' love for each other, he made an ugly face. Then he produced a paper and a quill and said that if I wrote a statement renouncing all claim to the business now and forever and swore never to cross his doorstep again, he would give me money. The sum he named was enough to ransom my brother's body and to bury him as well as to buy my own passage north.

"I sat and wrote what he asked. Secretly, I thought myself lucky to take away anything at all from him. A man like that might have called for his guard and had me thrown out. I wondered if perhaps he knew Guido would not lay violent hands on me. What mattered was not my pride or his in any case, but the dignity of my brother.

"So I gave up the legacy of my father and grandfather. The friendship each had held for his Christian partner was lost and with it the joy of the work. I signed the statement renouncing all and passed it across the table to Raffaello. With a sneer on his lips, he read it through, then rose and crossed to the old iron safe. Carefully, he laid away the paper I had written. I heard the chink of coins as he counted them out from his hoard of gold and silver.

"Raffaello returned and laid out two stacks of coins on the table, one pile gold and the other silver. His stubby fingers lingered over them, patting them into even columns. 'If you are intelligent, you will use this to emigrate,' he said. 'I advise you not to waste it.'

" 'I will bury my brother,' I said, my teeth clenched to control my rage.

" 'Maybe I believe you, maybe I don't,' he said, touching the money idly.

"I could stand him no longer. Rising from the seat I had taken, I moved forward. Abruptly I swept the money from the table, making him start back. I disdained to count it. I could see that it was enough for the ransom. Beyond that, I did not care.

"I bought a fine sheet. I went to the post where the *carabinièri* held my brother's body. I paid the thieves who connived at murder their gold coins. I wrapped my brother in the sheet and carried him in my arms back to the room that we had shared. All night I prayed by him, and in the morning we buried him. As we returned from the cemetery, a crowd of tipsy soldiers reeling by taunted us with cries of 'dirty Jews.' My friends had to restrain me from throwing a stone from the street at them.

"*E se l'è legata al dito,* I told myself then. Like a ring on my finger, I wear this memory. I will remember and avenge the wrong someday. Now, at a distance in time, I am not sure that such terror and cruelty can be repaid or repaired. Only God can exact justice, and He no longer speaks to us."

He rests his chin on his clenched fist and looks with brooding gaze into the dark corner of the kitchen. I wonder if he sees still the faces of men who taunted him over his brother's body. Even the landlord's men who burned our croft were not so cruel.

"But you escaped," I prompt him. I am glad to think of him going from such a place.

He unclenches his fist and wipes his hand over his face as if to raise a curtain on a new scene. "I escaped," he says. "As I left the warehouse in a black rage with Raffaello's money still in my hand, Guido appeared beside me and tugged at my sleeve. In kindness for old times, he opened a way for me.

" 'Are you well, *paesano*?' he asked me in his rough voice. 'You look pale and thin. Has the master upstairs been rude with you?'

"I told him everything. The loss of my son and my wife, my brother's murder. My having come to beg for money to ransom my brother's corpse and bury it. He crossed himself and tears shone on his cheeks. 'They are monsters,' he said. 'A man cannot live among such animals.'

" 'No,' I responded, 'living here destroys manhood. I am leaving Rome. I must go at any cost. I will not see the sun rise and set in the same city with the murderers of my brother.'

" 'You are well out of it, *Beniamino carino,*' Guido growled in his throat. '*Quel culo* is in trouble. No one wants to work for him. No one wants to trade with him. They say he doesn't pay his bills on time. His father and yours would be ashamed of him. *É una testa di cazzo.*'

" 'Hush,' I told him. 'Someone will hear and you will lose your job.'

" 'Eh!' he responded, and made a rude sign in the direction of the offices I had just left. 'I have a new job tomorrow. *Quel culo* will never give me orders again.'

"I congratulated him, but I could not help but sigh that I envied him. 'I too must find a new living,' I told him. To my amazement he offered me a way.

" 'I have a paper,' he told me solemnly, drawing the corner of an official parchment from within his tunic. 'The journey north from here is dangerous for you. There are customs posts and soldiers who take it on themselves to decide who passes on the road. And outlaws too. You must have permits. As luck would have it, my cousin Donato went two days ago to collect his transit papers. He was to travel as a valet for a gentleman, a lord from England. See, I have the lord's letter appointing him and asking him to meet him in Livorno. And here are the permits. You shall have them.'

" 'But what of Donato?' I asked. My head was swimming in confusion.

" 'Donato? The stupid lout met his *innamorata* on his way home. He had a glass of wine or two with her; she took him to the priest. He is a married man now. His wife will not let him leave her sight. What a fool he is for a woman. But see, what luck, he gave me the papers. He thought I might sell them for him, but that I will not do. They are yours.'

"I protested, Guido insisted. I should go immediately, he argued. It was better for me, healthier. I wondered if he had intended to use the papers himself, but he denied it. Fate wanted me to go, he said. The coincidence of my need and Donato's foolish marriage was an omen that must not be ignored. The papers would take me through the checkpoints and borders. I might want to find a more stylish coat, he suggested. Or—he struck the heel of his palm to his forehead that he had not said it first—I could take passage on a fishing boat from the Porta di Roma to Livorno. It would be cheaper and quicker than going overland. His mother's sister-in-law's uncle had a boat, leaving in two days, putting in at Porto Ercole and Piombino. That is what Donato intended, Guido told me. I could even go on to Genoa if I did not wish to stay in Livorno. Donato had been very clever for such a stupid man. Guido advised that I should do what was needful for my brother and my religion and then get away. In short, he had it all arranged.

"In the end, I went to the *carabinièri* to ransom my brother's corpse with my escape from Rome laid out for me. Because of that, I did not throw myself at the soldiers who taunted me. Because of that, I did not throw myself from a bridge into the Tiber. Guido rescued me. And for one silver coin. That was all he would accept, and even that he resisted until I told him it was to buy wine to drink to my safe journey."

"Guido sounds like an angel of mercy," I say. "Or the Samaritan himself." And then, to my chagrin, I yawn prodigiously.

"It is late," observes Mr. Serle. "You are tired."

"No," I protest. "I want to hear more of the story. What happened then?"

"Tomorrow," Mr. Serle promises. He drinks the last of his cup of water. "I can talk no more tonight," he says.

Because I am yawning again, I can only nod in agreement. Leaving Mr. Serle to bar the door, I mount the stairs. I lie down thinking that, after all the sorrow I have heard, I will never sleep. I must lie awake and ponder what it all means. And with that thought I tumble into oblivion.

CHAPTER XVIII

I WAKEN SLOWLY from a morning dream of rain and sadness. From the other side of the curtain, the murmur of Mr. Serle's voice begins. I lie still, wondering what he says. Will he tell me if I ask, or is it a secret rite that my listening violates? I feel unwanted and excluded. His voice pushes me away. I tell myself that this is an unworthy thought and slide from the bed onto my knees. Bowing my forehead to my clasped hands, I begin my own prayer. "Our Father, who art in heaven," I mutter half aloud. If Mr. Serle can pray to be heard, so can I.

I say the words over and then a rosary. The broken beads slide in my fingers. I sigh and heave myself to my feet. My heart feels cold. I am troubled; I want something, and yet no words speak themselves in my mind, no pictures rise, to tell me what it is.

The thump of the lid closing his trunk tells me that Mr. Serle has finished his ritual and gone down to the kitchen. I descend the stairs sleepily. After I have visited the outhouse and washed the night from my eyes with a sluice of cold water in the scullery, I cross the yard to the dairy for a pitcher of milk, another morning ritual.

Susan's shawl lies on the bench where she left it yesterday evening. I pick it up and give it a shake. It hangs damp in my hand, telling me that it has lain out on the bench all night. Susan must have forgotten it completely. I do not wonder at that, for it was a mild night and she would have danced at the wedding until very late or even stayed up for a shivaree early this morning. It is the kind of entertainment both Tom and Susan would enjoy, I think. I shake my head sharply. Like the dew that makes the shawl dank and limp, sour thoughts will weaken my spirit. Poor Mary. Perhaps a shivaree will help her pretend that hers is a marriage of more than desperation. I hang the shawl neatly on the gate where the sun and the morning air will freshen it. It is a fine paisley, not large but pretty with its mix of mossy green and brown threads. I wonder that Susan should possess such fine lady's garb. Stop, I remind myself. My heart is not right this morning.

When I enter the kitchen with the great stoneware pitcher of milk in my hands, Mr. Serle greets me kindly. "Have a mug of tea," he says. "Or draw yourself some ale. You have time to toast some bread and cheese too. There will be little to do today. You must make the fruit preserves. Those peaches are dead ripe. The kitchen smells of them. And when the preserves are done, make a cake, a big one for the larder. That is all. The master is gone to London again with the farm manager and two of the maids. There is a party there tomorrow and business matters to arrange for his daughter's marriage. We will be quiet here for a few days more, and then all descend on us for shooting parties and county balls and family parties to celebrate the girl's betrothal. Have you seen Tom about?"

"No," I say. "Susan never came back for her shawl last night or this morning. The wedding celebration might still be going on. Tom will not leave while there is still ale in the barrel or pie on the table."

Mr. Serle shrugs a shoulder and turns to the fires. I will need a steady heat to cook jam. It will be cooler to work here in the big kitchen instead of in the still room. Slowly, my grumbling mood eases. We spend a day of leisurely business. I cook and bottle the peach jam. I boil the jars and bottle the peaches in brandy that were left to steep overnight. I make a great king cake stuffed with candied fruit and chopped nuts. It cooks all afternoon in the Rumford stove, perfuming the kitchen with its spicy odor. After I take it out of the range oven and it cools, I wrap it in clean muslin soaked in brandy and set it in a covered crock.

Meanwhile, Mr. Serle sharpens all the knives and rubs them with pumice powder until they gleam like old silver. He takes down and cleans the copper molds that hang on the kitchen wall. He boils the cleaning cloths with yellow soap and puts them out in the sun to dry. For dinner the few staff in the house eat cold roast mutton with turnip cakes and pickled beets followed by gingered pears and toasted biscuits spread with fresh peach preserve. Supper is just bread and cheese and salad for those who want it. I am thinking by then of Mr. Serle's tale of last night and feeling the sorrow of it again.

When all is done and the leftover food stored away, the room sparkles clean and orderly. "Did you eat supper?" Mr. Serle asks me. "I do not recall that you took anything."

"I had enough at dinner," I say. "Later I will warm some milk." He shakes his head. "I hope you will continue your story," I tell him.

The night is warm. The door to the courtyard is open again tonight, and the scents of evening come to us along with the sound of distant voices from the stable yard and gardens. Mr. Plumb's children are playing in the orchard. Their treble voices rise and fall, blending with the song of the evening thrush.

We settle in our places. "Where was I?" asks Mr. Serle.

"You were about to sail for Livorno," I remind him.

"Yes," he says. "I went to the Porta di Roma and found Guido's relatives. They greeted me like a long-lost friend. It makes me a little sad now that I could not be more responsive to them. My brother's death took my whole mind. I could barely think of it as real, and yet that morning we had buried him. The sounds and smells of the world came to me from a great distance. I seemed to stand in a dark cave. People called to me from the entrance, from a world where there was light and air, which I could sense but not experience.

"I did something that night that I remember every day. The first night on the ship, waiting for the dawn when we would set sail north for Livorno, I begged hot water from the sailor who supervised the cooking. Sitting on the deck with the full moon to light my hand, I shaved away the ear locks that hung on either side of my face and marked me as a Jew. When the man saw what I was doing, he helped me further to cut my hair short in the French republican style. Now I could go into the world as a man to whom others would have to speak before they judged, I thought. I shook with the anger of it. My faith is all inside me now, not visible. And I have held to that. I say my prayers. I worship with my fellows when I can. I hold to the rules of *kashruth* as best I am able by eating no pig and little other meat. No man will tell me who I am. The yellow hat of the Pope's hate, I have put away in my trunk. It must serve as a reminder of what I have escaped."

"I suppose that it was a little like the freedom I felt when I covered my red hair with blacking," I comment. "Only stronger," I amend.

"Perhaps," Mr. Serle says doubtfully, "but blacking your hair is not a religious action."

I do not tell him of the rebuke the priest in Milford gave me for my disguise. "Go on," I say. "Did you arrive safely in Livorno?"

"I did," he says. "The papers were invaluable. The soldiers at the port looked at them and passed them back without comment. The nobleman who had hired Donato seemed pleased enough to take me when I said I had come as his substitute. I knew nothing of course about what the duties of a valet should be, but the poor man was desperate for help from someone who spoke Italian. He told me what to do and I did it."

"Soon I was managing his life, keeping his wardrobe clean, ordering his dinner, keeping a list of his appointments. At first we spoke French, but then he asked to teach me English. I was glad of the chance, and in return I protected him from the rascally cheats who tried to sell him poorly woven rugs and old paintings, the wood panels of which still oozed fresh sap. When the cook left, I willingly took on those duties. He liked what I made and he told me how to make some of the dishes he missed from England. The poor young man was lonely. He had been sent south by his family for his health. He was leading a miserable existence, writing sentimental poetry at his desk in the morning, sitting in the drawing rooms of the foreign ladies in the afternoon, yawning at musicales in the evening. Eventually, I persuaded him that he would be better off at home."

"Really?" I ask.

"Yes," Mr. Serle says. "His poems were all about a young lady in England. His Aurora, he called her. His health was fine so far as I could tell. He was bored, and that made him think himself delicate.

"I accompanied him as far as Paris. There we parted company, even though he urged me to come to England with him. I felt I should search for my cousins. I had days then when I trembled with dread at being alone in the world. In truth, though, I also wanted to live in the cradle of liberty for a time. Paris seemed a new world to me.

"With the excellent character the nobleman gave me and a note introducing me to his most gastronomically inclined friend, I found employment easily in the kitchens of the best restaurants. I was at Beauvilliers first and then I went to the Chez Grignon, where the great Soyer served his apprenticeship."

"Soyer?" I ask. "Tom mentioned him once, I think. I forget."

"Alexis Soyer," says Mr. Serle. "Alexis Soyer, the master cook who wrote *The Gastronomic Regenerator,* who designed the kitchens of the Reform Club, who invented delicacies to please the palates of the rich and scientific nourishment for the poor."

He pauses and I note the gleam of passion in his eyes. I have no idea what a gastronomic regenerator is or a reform club, but I see that this is not the main story and nod, looking as serious as I can. Satisfied that I am impressed, Mr. Serle continues, "I worked in Paris for several months. I learned—well, I learned everything. And Paris was a revelation to me. I was free to wander where I wished. I sat in cafés on my afternoon of rest. I read newspapers and journals from around the world. Even when I fell ill, I found a friend in the chemist who helped me. He gave me the cinchona powder that has cured me twice now.

"Of course, my illness lost me my job. I was ill for three weeks, and when I went back to the kitchen, they took one look at me and said that I was too weak to take on the lifting and carrying that was necessary. They were not cruel. I received the wages owed me. The manager advised me to go to the country for a rest and apply to them again when I was stronger. With the money I had earned, I could afford to live for a time, and so I took a part of his counsel. I stayed in Paris, though, sitting in the parks and in the sunshine of café terraces, drinking coffee, reading, talking to the other loungers about politics.

"One of my acquaintances found me some light work, cooking the evening meal four nights a week for a famous artist. That gave me enough to go on with. I earned something extra one week by sitting as a model for the painter. I did not care for being stared at so, and I refused when he asked me to pose again. All that summer, I educated myself about the worlds of food and liberty. I joined a club that met in a café once a week to read about America and to discuss the opportunities there. One man subscribed to a journal; another bought a travel book. I bought novels by American writers. We all read what each provided. One week we were enthusiastic about founding an importing firm in the great city of New York. The next week someone would try to persuade us that the French city of New Orleans was where we all belonged. For several weeks, we planned the Utopia we would create on the banks of the great Mississippi River in the heart of the continent."

"It sounds like a good time," I say softly. As he talks about Paris, Mr. Serle leans back in his chair and stretches his legs out. Now he looks like a man at leisure, relaxing at a table in a tavern or café, talking idly with his fellows and at ease with himself and them.

"Oh, yes," he says. "It was a good time. It was a summer of peace at last, although lonely at times and not without care. I could not find my cousins anywhere. And the political journals were full of articles about unrest. Some writers blamed the Hebrew people for the growth of the cities. Our commerce caused ugly change, they said, as if all Jews were bankers and all bankers Jews. Even Paris was not so free of hate as it seemed on the sunny afternoons of late summer.

"In October, I returned to the restaurant, the Chez Grignon, to see if they would hire me back. They had no place, but the manager spoke kindly to me again. The great Monsieur Soyer was in England. He was supervising the most modern kitchens in the world at the Reform Club in London. They had heard that he was hiring staff. The manager gave me a letter recommending me to Monsieur Soyer. I had read in the journals that one of the Rothschilds had been elected to the Parliament in England. I thought I should see a country that elected a Jew to its government before I crossed the seas to America.

"And so I packed my trunk with my books and my other possessions and I came here to England." He falls silent.

"Do you miss your home? Do you miss Rome?" I ask tentatively. Mr. Serle looks stern and angry. Yet, like me, he must dream sometimes of home and his mother's blessing kiss.

"I thought of going back," he admits. "In the winter, just after I came to England, all Paris talked of violence and change. The republic is finally come. They say a king will never sit on a throne again in France. I read in a journal and heard it talked of in the synagogue that they have torn down the walls of the Roman ghetto. Of course, the Pope charged the Jews money for that. Nevertheless, the work we began by destroying the gates is complete at last. The common people advance everywhere for liberty. You must know yourself that the Chartists rallied in Ireland to advance the people's cause."

"The who?" I ask.

"The Chartists," says Mr. Serle. "They believe in the rights of the common people to join in their own government."

I shake my head.

"You never read a journal or talked about the government in your life, did you?" he says.

I admit that is true. "I suppose my father did," I say, "when he drank his toddy with his friends. Knowing the doings of the rulers did not change anything in our lives that I ever noticed. My brother was angry when he saw the ships loaded with grain leaving Dublin's port, but he had no power to stop them."

"He had no power," says Mr. Serle, "but a people united

together may make great changes. Even ships may cease to sail from their ports if the people become one voice. The great Lord Byron wrote that 'Freedom's fame finds wings on every wind.' "

I sigh. I will not go to Ireland to test that belief, I think. I am no Joan of Arc to lead an army into battle. I am no queen in a play by William Shakespeare. "Tell me more of London life," I say. "Did you work for this great Monsieur Soyer?"

"I did," he says. "There is not time enough to tell you of the wonders of that kitchen—the rooms, the spits, the great screens that made it possible to roast meat for a hundred diners and yet prepare a delicate sauce ten feet away without fainting in the heat. I learned every day while I was there. Monsieur Soyer is a great man."

"I never heard of him before I came here," I object.

"You should have," says Mr. Serle. "He feeds the poor. He invents nourishing soups that can easily be prepared and served to the needy from kitchens set up for the purpose. His generosity is inspiring."

"Why, then, did you leave his employ?" I ask.

"London was killing me," Mr. Serle says with a snort of laughter. "The dirt, the damp air heavy with soot, the mean room I slept in. Just after I arrived, I read that Mr. Rothschild had been refused his seat in Parliament because of his religion. I saw Jews cried after in the street, taunted by ragamuffins as Shylocks or Christ killers. I felt I was in Rome again, a Rome with no sun.

"Monsieur Soyer spoke to me. He worried about my health, he said. I had become paler and thinner in the four months I worked for him. He joked about that. 'A cook should be round and smooth,' he said, 'not lean and bony. What recommendation is it if we do not eat our own cooking?' I confessed that it was not the work but the city that took my appetite from me. He said he understood. As luck would have it, a member of the Reform Club had been inquiring for a chef. He would recommend me, if I wished to work in the country for a time. I could come back to London later if the life was too quiet or the man's palate too boring to make cooking for him enjoyable."

"So you came to this house," I conclude.

"I did," Mr. Serle replies.

"You look well enough now," I say. I think back to when I first saw him, lounging outside the kitchen door in the morning sun. He seems strong to me. His skin is ruddy brown and his eyes are clear. He was ill but he is recovered. Life surges in him as a harp string vibrates with music. "Will you go back to the great city, London?" I ask.

"I am going to America," he says. "The months in Paris and in London and then here have given me a chance to test new ways of living and to observe the habits of a variety of men. I will go to a new world. I can work for others all my life if need be. I would rather seek a way to work for myself. I will tell you one great thing: I will never suffer under unjust rule again. I will go where there is prosperity or the prospect of it. I will seek freedom."

"Amen," I say. "Amen to that." We are quiet for a moment, and then I cannot resist speaking. "I do not know your whole name," I say. "You know mine even though you do not use it. May I know yours?"

"My name is Benjamin Serle," he says and almost smiles at me.

"What was the name of your wife? Your child?" I ask. I hope he will trust me with them. I will add them to my prayers.

"My wife is Rachel; my child, Daniel," says Mr. Serle. "It is hard to say their names. It feels like a kind of betrayal of them. By naming them to myself and to someone else, I separate their lives from mine."

"Oh, I understand," I cry out. "His name was Daniel?" I ask in wonderment.

Mr. Serle does not seem inclined to linger over the coincidence of names. "We called my brother Mario," he says. "But his real name in Hebrew was Maimonides."

"You say it all so coldly," I object. I remember how I tried to say my prayers in the morning light and felt a nameless, icy sorrow. "Is it hard to feel for you too?" I ask.

Mr. Serle considers the thought in silence. "Yes," he says at last. "When the skin is wounded, it heals with a scar that shows where the hurt occurred. The scar is a dead place on the body.

Pain is not so acute there. When the heart is wounded, the scars are not visible outwardly, but they are there, nevertheless. I can never again feel so deeply as I did before my wife, my son, my brother were torn from my heart. The scars that heal the wounds make my heart like a clenched fist in my breast."

I drop my head. My hands, my hands that look like my brother's hands, lie clasped on my knees. There is an end to sorrow; it is a dead fire, ashes in the grate. We sit in tired silence.

Mr. Serle breaks into the echoing voices in my head. "Did Susan never come back for her shawl?" he asks. "I suppose if she does not want it, we should put it away. Old clothes have value."

"Like old bread?" I ask. Suddenly I feel the need for air and change. I pick up the poker and thrust it through the bars to stir the last sparks of fire to life.

"Did you ever think to become a Christian?" I ask. Even as I say it, I am bewildered at myself.

"What?" Mr. Serle says, surprise and anger in his voice.

"It would have been easier," I say.

"Easy?" he says. "To turn from my ancestors and my people would be easy?"

"You cut your hair," I remind him.

"As did you," he says. "The outward change does not make you less a female."

I think about that and wonder if his words are true. "Perhaps it does," I tell him. Something in me wants to quarrel—about what I do not know. Old clothes, stale bread, dead ashes in the grate, I push the pain of them away. "Perhaps our inner selves are shaped by our outer appearance. If I live as a man, I will be strong like a man. Since you live like a Christian, why not be saved as we are?"

Mr. Serle looks at me. His eyes are black stones under their hooded lids. I am afraid of his anger, and yet there is something else. In this moment, he is returned from the past to me and the words between us. "When I was a little child," I tell him, "and there was something to spare, I gave a farthing to help the missionaries in darkest Africa. They save the heathens. Our souls are more important than anything on earth."

"Think about this, Mina," he says. "In the name of Christianity, the people of Africa are enslaved. Their owners tell us that servitude is justified because the heathens are taught a new religion. Here is what I think of those who label others heathen, here is what I think of forced baptisms—" and he spits into the grate.

"They say that those who are not saved burn in hell," I cry. "I saw the fire on the ship. Hell must be like that."

I see a flicker of pity in Mr. Serle's eyes. Before he can speak, the loud voices of Tom and Susan interrupt us as they crowd through the open doorway.

"What's going on here?" cries Susan. "We heard your voices clear across the yard." She has picked up her shawl from the gate where I left it. It looks damp again, and she must find it so, for she spreads it out before the pathetic remnants of the fire.

"Nothing is going on," says Mr. Serle. He rises from his chair and walks away into the shadows by the far window.

"We heard you," Susan chortles.

"It was nothing," Mr. Serle says.

"A lovers' quarrel?" asks Tom in a fake, syrupy voice.

"Where were you today?" asks Mr. Serle, his voice cold and hard.

Susan breaks into peals of laughter. "Why, at a wedding," she burbles. Although Mr. Serle addressed Tom, she answers. "We stayed up all last night to help the loving couple greet the dawn. And then we ate the wedding breakfast with them. You should have seen the expression on Mary's face this morning when she smelled the ale and cheese. She ran to the end of the garden to vomit into the currant bushes. Poor Tom was so tired we crawled into a haystack on our way home and did not wake from our nap until the sun went over and I got cold and roused him."

"She did indeed," crows Tom, slapping her on the rump. Susan giggles. They do a jig about the kitchen. They smell of stale beer and sweat.

Mr. Serle stands still in the shadows at the far end of the room. Since he spat into the grate, he has not spoken to me. "Be

on time tomorrow," he says, and walks away down the passageway to lock the larders.

Susan stops their twirling and stares at me. "Did we interrupt you and the Jew?" she asks.

Tom roars with laughter. "They have their bed upstairs and
the comfort of the fire here. Which do you favor tonight, Paddy?"

Susan giggles. "You are a fool, Tom," she says.

"I am no catamite," I say as bravely as I can. I know he
would not speak so if Mr. Serle could hear him.

"Listen to the lad," Tom sneers. "As if I care what a puny
thing like him does for his master. Leave them to each other. It's
all the more women for me."

Susan laughs and laughs.

"Don't let Tom tease you, *Paddy*," Susan says. Her voice
sounds sorry, but her face looks full of the satisfaction of someone holding the power of a secret.

I feel my cheeks crimson with shame and confusion. Tom
makes this spotless kitchen into a dirty place. He makes my only
friendship vile. Why did I want to quarrel with Mr. Serle a moment ago? I wonder. I am ready to weep. But tears will undo me,
and Susan may blurt tipsy words. "I am going," I say. "It is late. I
am tired."

As I flee toward the stairs, Tom puts out a foot to trip me. I
stumble and then right myself. The sound of Tom's laughter follows me as I hurry away.

I settle myself in my cot, but the day's thoughts whirl in
my head. Despite the warmth of the night, I begin to shiver.
The peace of my bed behind the curtain is gone. I have been rude
to Mr. Serle about his religion, and I have fled from Tom's stupid
insults instead of defying him. And Susan stood and watched
and laughed. I am a fool, I think. And yet I am ashamed to go
back to the kitchen. I will think about what to do in the morning,
I tell myself. For now I will be quiet and go to sleep.

Of course, this does not work. Mr. Serle's story, Susan's
laughter, Tom's teasing tumble over and over in my head. Even
holding the lump of my ring in my shirttail does not comfort me
tonight. I hear Mr. Serle climb the stairs. A flicker of light from

his candle shows along the wall where my curtain is not quite closed. That should be a good and a familiar thing. I try to recall the safety I felt here. The feeling is gone.

After I have said the Our Father and a rosary, I say my own prayer to ask forgiveness for my sins and to ask blessing on all the people I know as well as help for my brother, Daniel, in his journey. When I have said it all, I feel better. Then I remember that I asked Mr. Serle his name because I thought to name him and his family in my prayers. What should I say? I wonder. At last, after much thought, I whisper, "And bless Benjamin Serle, who has helped me. And spare his wife and son and brother the flames of hell if that is possible."

Somehow, this does not satisfy me. I am too tired to know what is right and what is wrong anymore. Sleepily, I think of my mother. I wish someone would hold me. I am sad and angry and afraid. The ship burns again in my thoughts. I think of the little girl, a pale, starving thing when she was alive and a few twigs bundled in gray rags when she was dead. She was going to America. There is enough to eat in America, they say.

Stop, I tell myself. Stop. My aunt loved my mother. My mother loved me. Their ring is the circle of their love. We are here and we suffer. Let the priests worry about the meaning of it all. Be where your heart is and rest. And then I sleep a restless sleep at last.

CHAPTER XIX

Tired, I creep down the stairs in the morning. It is bright daylight. I can hear voices—Tom's and Mr. Serle's—above the sound of clattering pots and the chink of the chains for the spits being set in position. If they are still getting out pots, I am not so late as I thought. I hurry to my regular tasks. When the first flurry of morning work is done, the kitchen quiets and the sounds of the hissing fires and the slow clink of the smoke jacks turning make a peaceful background to the tasks of stirring, assembling, and saucing the made dishes.

Mr. Serle looks up from the cutting board, where his knife flashes over a pile of early autumn mushrooms. He must be annoyed that I was not there to wipe them clean when Mr. Plumb brought them in earlier. He does not speak to me.

Tom interrupts what he was saying to Mr. Serle to stare at me. "Standing about, hey, Paddy? That red on your head must be rust."

"What?" I say, startled.

"Rust," he says and laughs. His small eyes with their colorless lashes narrow as he looks me up and down. "Your head is as dense as iron and you don't use it. Your hair is red because your mind is rusting."

"I'm sorry," I say to Mr. Serle, ignoring Tom, who keeps on chuckling at his own joke. "I'm sorry." I try to push meaning into my words. Mr. Serle shrugs his shoulder and goes on with his work.

"What would you like me to do next?" I ask as humbly as I

can. My heart contracts in my chest that Mr. Serle should treat me so coldly.

"Go across to the dairy and get a pitcher of cream," he says. "We have a lot to do. Word came from London at dawn that the family and guests are arriving today, not tomorrow. We must have dinner for twenty ready to send up at half after five o'clock. Get the cream for me, and then see what Mrs. Bennet needs from you. She arrived late last night."

Relief floods through me. He has not shut me out. When I return from the dairy, Tom is telling a story. "One of the guests at the wedding was down visiting from Manchester," he says. "He's a manager in a big mill there. Before we all got too drunk to make sense, he told us some good stories of foreign parts."

"Oh?" says Mr. Serle. To me he does not sound interested; Tom seems to hear the syllable as an invitation to continue. "He was telling us about the problems with the Hebrews they have to trade with for their silk thread. They are a strange lot, it seems. Money changers and cheats, the lot of them. Well, some years ago, a religious man—a Catholic priest, I think it was— disappeared in one of those foreign cities, Demerara, Dimisco ..." Tom stumbles, searching for the word.

"Damascus," Mr. Serle says.

Tom laughs and goes on, "Damascus. They charged the Jews of the city with murdering the man to take his blood for their rituals—some pagan sort of thing. He—the man from Manchester, that is—said he would not travel in strange countries for any money."

"I heard the story too, and it's a lie," says Mr. Serle. He has finished with the mushrooms, and his sharp knife slashes a fat onion to slivers.

"No, no, I swear it's true. I forget the poor soul's name," says Tom.

"Padre Tomaso," murmurs Mr. Serle under his breath, so low that Tom does not hear him. Then he says louder, "That case was settled. There was no murder by the Jews. It is an ugly lie that Jews use blood for any ritual. The truth is that Jews avoid blood. They salt their meat to take the blood from it. If you repeat scurrilous tales in this kitchen, I will ask that you leave."

"I am going very soon anyway," says Tom. "You foreigners are all the same," he adds. "So serious, so moral. It always turns out that it is some imagined insult that you are moral about. Besides, who knows what mischief they do in foreign places. They are not like us."

"Even the Sultan of Turkey knew the tale you tell is a lie. He forbade its repetition in his realm. Perhaps he is more civilized than you are." Mr. Serle speaks coolly, casually. The tone of his voice says that this is an ordinary exchange of opinion, while his words are cutting. Tom seems oblivious. He is having trouble adjusting a chain for the largest spit and goes for a stool so he can climb up and reach the top pulley.

"You are supposed to go to Mrs. Bennet," Mr. Serle says to me. "What are you lounging about for?"

I go to Mrs. Bennet in the still room. As I come in the door, I see her broad rear end bent over. She is stowing one of her bottles on a lower shelf behind the jelly molds. She stands as I speak and greets me as if she saw me yesterday and not months ago. Neither one of us mentions her bottle. Immediately, she sets me to work chopping candied fruit peel for a queen cake. As I pass through the pantries and the kitchen in the course of the morning, I hear Tom's voice running on like water in the brook after heavy rain. He seems to have a lot to say today. Susan's name comes in often. At last, when we gather for the noon meal at the long table in the kitchen, I hear more of what has made him so loquacious.

I sit on a stool near the end of the table, nibbling on a crust of pastry from the mutton pie Mr. Serle made for the servants' dinner. I have a mug of ale. As always when there is food piled everywhere in preparation for a feast, I lose all appetite. My eyes and my nose feed me without need of putting anything in my mouth. The abundance overwhelms and sates me. I have to remind myself that I had no breakfast. I will be dizzy before the day is over if I do not eat. Mr. Serle has taken his piece of pie outside to eat, with the excuse that he needs a rest in the sunshine before the final labors of the day. I would have liked to go with him, but I am afraid that Tom will make some remark. I do not want to be thought a catamite.

"So you have found your woman at last?" Mrs. Bennet teases Tom. "Those other lasses will be disappointed."

"Susan will have my head if I don't give them up," he says in a satisfied tone.

"Forswear all other, eh?" someone volunteers.

"I'll miss the fun of it," says Tom. I am amazed that he sounds genuinely sad.

"So, will we all be dancing at your wedding soon?" asks Mrs. Bennet. "Are the banns to be read this Sunday?"

"Not so fast," Tom objects. "Susan and I might marry here or later, in the city. I am not a man to be rushed, even when I have found the warmest bed I ever knew." They all laugh at that.

"Has Susan gone back to Liverpool, then?" I ask. Heads turn in surprise. This is the first time I have spoken at the table.

"Paddy has a tongue," comments the boot boy, who has returned from London with Mrs. Bennet.

Tom is chewing his meat and mustard. He has cut a slice from the great roast of beef that is meant for the gentry's sideboard tonight. Even now it is turning on the spit. After Mr. Serle left the kitchen, Tom cut his piece from the bottom, where it will not show. "Liverpool? Susan is never going back to Liverpool," he says. "Just now she is off in Milford on some business. The city I mean is Manchester. We go there in a day or two. Together."

"Isn't that like your selfish way, Tom," says Mrs. Bennet, and takes a swallow of her ale. "Here we are with a great party coming any hour now and you are full of talk about running off to make your fortune in the city. You'll lose your job."

"To the devil with the job," says Tom. There are indrawn breaths around the table.

"Shame on you, Tom," says Mrs. Bennet. "The master treats us well here."

"The pay is better in the mills," says Tom. "The man from Manchester—"

I do not sit to hear more but go out for some air and sunshine before the afternoon's labors. Mr. Serle is before me, sitting on the bench against the dairy wall.

"Are they almost finished?" he asks me.

"Yes, almost." I could tell him about Tom and the roast beef, but it seems unimportant in the great whirl of other things. Besides, nothing can be done about it now. I summon my courage. "I am sorry I quarreled with you last night," I say. "I thought argument would push away pain."

"It never does," Mr. Serle tells me. He does not sound angry.

"It is hard for me," I admit to him. "All through Lent after I received the ashes on my forehead and on Good Friday too in Holy Week, I heard our kind priest tell us the story of how the Jews killed our Lord."

Benjamin Serle looks at me with sadness. I cannot interpret the feeling in his dark eyes. "Even if some Jews did agree with the Romans long ago, what should it mean to us? Were you there? Was I?"

Before I can reply, we are interrupted by a call from the kitchen door. The women from the village who are to help with the extra work tonight have arrived. Mr. Serle must come and set their tasks. He goes ahead of me across the yard. Soon enough, the servants' meal is cleared away and all is bustle and confusion in the kitchen and the pantries.

Mrs. Bennet and I finish our work promptly with the help of one of the women from the village. We are setting out no sweets that need last-minute finishing. Mrs. Bennet goes to look over the preserves and fruit syrups that we made in her absence. I go to assist in the main kitchen. Mr. Serle sends me to the gardens to find Mr. Plumb, who promised a basket of lettuces by mid-afternoon.

I find Mr. Plumb beyond the dairy, beside the chicken coops turning a compost heap. He looks happy in the mild afternoon sunlight. His shoulders bend to his task. When I greet him, he smiles broadly at me. He has a smear of dirt across his cheek. He admits cheerfully that he has forgotten the promised lettuces, and so I fetch a basket and hold it as he cuts me a dozen perfect, pale green heads. The air is welcome and so is the stout presence of Mr. Plumb, who says no word more than is needed.

I walk back slowly to the kitchen. There are at least six people hurrying to and fro. The savors of simmering fish soup and roasting beef permeate the air.

Mr. Serle says in his calm way, "I want you to make a dish of salad with those lettuces and toasted walnuts."

Even though I am tired from my restless night, the work in the kitchen steadies me. There is so much to do. At last the soup is poured, steaming, into the great tureens and taken upstairs. After that, the roasts and the made dishes, the sweets and the savories are sent up in four waves of courses. The gentry sit at their dinner for three hours. By the time they have begun their sweets, we are cleaning the kitchen and the scullery. While the gentlemen are drinking their port, the mistress sends a note down from the drawing room to tell Mr. Serle and the kitchen help that she is mightily pleased. After that, the village women, cheered with a glass of cider, finish their tasks and go. Mr. Serle and I are alone. I finish the scouring of the worktable while Mr. Serle sharpens the knives. Then we will bank the fire and go to rest. Tomorrow will begin early, with manchet bread to set and servants needing breakfast before their masters and mistresses rise.

We will be hard put to do it all. I think I will have to build the fires in the morning, for Tom has not been seen since just after noon when he said he had a call of nature to attend to and disappeared. One of the women from the village reported at the end of the day that Susan Coates had appeared in the courtyard and beckoned to Tom. But no one else had seen it, and since the woman said that Susan appeared like some "demon lady from a fairy tale tempting a man to his doom," we were inclined to laugh at her for dreaming.

I turn toward the scullery with the wash rag in my hand when we hear voices in the courtyard. Tom and Susan. I go into the scullery and rinse the cloth and hang it by the warm boiler to dry. I wash my hands. As I dry them, boisterous laughter echoes from the kitchen. I consider not going back but instead climbing the stairs to my bed. Curiosity drives me to look in on what they are doing. And the hope that Tom may be planning to work tomorrow. I am not fond of laying the fires, even though I am no longer so afraid of lucifer matches. Besides, I wish to stay awake and talk with Mr. Serle.

When I enter the kitchen, neither Susan nor Tom sees me. They are standing facing Mr. Serle with their arms about each other's waist. Rather, Susan has her arm about Tom's waist, and Tom rests his hand low on Susan's hip. Her hair hangs in a thick brown braid down her back. Here and there curls escape from its twists as if they had a vital life of their own. Tom and Susan lean into each other like a couple of tipsy dancers.

"We have our golden egg," Tom is crowing. "Susan here has got money out of that devil Hatton, and I have my wages."

"Mr. Hatton?" Mr. Serle says. He sounds startled. I hold my breath for fear.

"You wouldn't know him. This Mr. Hatton Susan knew in Liverpool has been in Milford for a few days doing his bit of business. Susan encountered him, and Susan knows what to do with Mr. Hatton," says Tom.

"Really," Mr. Serle replies in his most neutral tone.

Susan seems to hear this as a question or a challenge. She laughs and then says, "Not to shock you, sir, but our Mr. Hatton is a gentleman who likes his simple pleasures."

"Really," says Mr. Serle again in his tone of cool disinterest.

"Tell him, Susan," Tom chortles, and I see his hand squeeze her hip. "I like to hear it."

Susan titters and says, "He's an old gentleman who doesn't ask much of a girl. Just a good scolding for his naughty ways and a vigorous thwacking on his bare bum with the handle of that little whip he likes to carry. He pays well for the service. I saw him this morning, and he paid me for his little beating and then again for some information I could give him. He is still desperate to have that girl Mina."

Tom laughs heartily. "I have heard about Mina," he cries. "I was so sure the girl was a down-cheeked lad, I never saw what was before my eyes. You and your catamite!"

Although he does not speak, Mr. Serle must have looked his anger, for Tom's voice changes. "You cannot blame me for mentioning it," he says in a placating voice. "It is such a joke on me that I was blind."

I summon my courage. I must face them and learn what Susan has said to Mr. Hatton if I can. Mr. Serle is there, I tell myself. They will not hurt me.

"He is such a fool," Susan cries.

Mr. Serle speaks above the laughter of Tom and Susan. He sounds angry now. "I have no need to hear this," he says.

"Nor I," I say, and step into the kitchen as boldly as I can.

"What! You are here, Mina?" cries Susan. "I thought you would be asleep by now."

My heart thumps in my chest. "You sold the tale of where I am to Mr. Hatton?" I ask. My voice shakes.

Susan purses her red lips; she could be kissing the air. Her look is sly, as if she feels ashamed and yet enjoys what she has done. "I helped you in Liverpool, didn't I?" she says.

"You helped me, yes," I reply, "but you have acted as if helping me gave you a right to own me. Have you told Mr. Hatton where I am? I thought you were my friend."

"I have got a little money from him," she says. "But I fooled him. I told him you went back to Liverpool. I saw Mr. Hatton merely by chance. He always comes for the Milford fair. We are old acquaintances. It just happened."

"But why would you say anything?" I cry.

"I need the money," Susan says in a sulky voice. "And I lied for you. You are not hurt by it."

Tom looks me up and down. His stare is dirty. "I should never have known," he says. "You can't be much of a woman. There's hardly a bump where bumps should be under that smock. More of a broomstraw." He laughs. "What a joke on me!"

Susan seems more intent on her own affairs than on my person. She has no interest in my anger at her. "We are leaving here," she says. Her voice is no longer sulky but bubbling with her accustomed energy. "There are jobs in Manchester, good jobs. We will live in a house in the city. We will work and earn good wages. We will buy baker's bread and butcher's meat. I am sick of harvesting the wheat, taking the corn to the mill, slopping the pigs, and salting hams. I am sick of carrying chamber pots in the inn or slaving at home. In Manchester there are drinking houses with music and singing. We will work all day and enjoy ourselves all night."

Her bubbling, happy voice, which once I loved, enrages me. "You sold me," I scream at her. "You sold me for the chance to labor in a mill and to drink in an ale house."

"Don't be so bitter," says Tom. "Susan did right. She lied about your whereabouts, after all. Mr. Hatton deserves to be lied to. And there is profit in it." And he bursts out into heehawing laughter.

"Well, it's a good joke all around," says Susan with satisfaction. "I am four times lucky. Mr. Hatton paid me to get you to sign the indenture papers, you gave me a fine pewter bowl for helping you disguise yourself, Mr. Hatton paid me for his little bit of fun, and he paid me again for a hint about where to find you. I have as much money from Mr. Hatton as I think I can ever get. And still, Mr. Hatton does not have you. The joke is on him."

"You betrayed me," I say. It is hard to make myself speak to her. Susan does not seem the least sorry for her treatment of me or her debasement of herself to serve Mr. Hatton either.

Susan looks speculatively from me to Mr. Serle and shrugs. "Don't sulk," she says. "Whatever happens, you are here for now. Food and a warm bed are more than you had six months ago, I wager. You are lucky too." She smiles at me. I do not smile back. "You will do what you like, Mina. You and your Jew will know what that is, I am sure."

I am ashamed to look at Mr. Serle. He does not speak but continues silently to lay out the knives and spoons and bowls for tomorrow morning's work.

"Our luck is with us in every way. The master was on the terrace smoking when we came up tonight. He seemed glad to hand over my wages," Tom boasts. "He shook hands and wished me luck at parting."

"I told you to ask as soon as we saw him." Susan pinches

the roll of flesh at his waist. He pulls her thick braid from her back and loops it across her throat. They seem to be performing a show for our benefit, oblivious to our silence.

"You are right as always, my love," says Tom, tickling her until she squeals.

"You are finished here," says Mr. Serle. "Be on your way, so I can lock the doors."

"We'll leave you to your beds, or bed," says Tom. "You have been clever, I will say. Trying to murder me because I called the girl your catamite. That was a joke on me."

"Out," says Mr. Serle. He has picked up the big butcher knife from the table.

"Don't you threaten me," Tom says, falling back a step. "I don't work for you anymore, but I can still go to the master and tell him about your dirty ways. He won't like fornication in his kitchen, and he won't like being fooled by such as you."

"Out," says Mr. Serle. He moves toward the end of the table as if he will come around it with the knife in his hand.

"Let's go, Tom," says Susan, pulling him toward the doorway.

"I could fight this lizard, this toad of a foreigner," Tom boasts, even as he lets Susan pull him through the door. "I could smash him."

They are out the door and in the courtyard. I fly forward and push the door closed and slide the bar through its iron staples. From the yard, I hear singing begin, some obscene ditty that fades away into the night.

"They are gone," I say to Mr. Serle.

"They are drunk," he says, putting down the knife in its place. The tension eases from his shoulders. "They deserve each other."

"I thought Susan was my friend," I say. "Now I am afraid."

"Let the evil go," Mr. Serle tells me. "You are done with them, and if Mr. Hatton looks for you in Liverpool, he will not find you. Feel sorry for them. They will find out what hard labor is when they face the great machines in the mills of Manchester."

"But what if she has lied to me also? What if she said that I am here?" I could cry with the fear.

"Let it go," Mr. Serle says again. "Lies trip over themselves in her mouth."

Here is another part of my heart to be sealed off. Even as Susan cut my hair and wrote her uncle's name for me, she reserved to herself her right to be my enemy. I want to erase her face and her voice from memory. Perhaps, I remind myself, I should be grateful that she sent me here. It was not unkind. And yet, like a spider wrapping its prey in silk against the hour of hunger, she gave me a hiding place in preparation for her own time of need. It is no thanks to her that I am safe still—at least I think so.

We finish the preparations for tomorrow and go to our beds. I have trouble falling asleep. The wind has risen and a branch taps the wall. I doze a little and then awaken suddenly and sit bolt upright in my bed. I have dreamed that Tom and Mr. Hatton are climbing the stairs to seize me. I tremble and pull the blanket up around my neck. I think I should get up and put my pants and my shirt on again. I could put my kitchen smock on also. In my dream they wanted to take my clothes and turn me naked to stand in the cold to be laughed at by strangers passing by.

Beyond my curtain, Mr. Serle snores in his bed at the other end of the attic. The soft rhythm reminds me that I am not alone. Anyone mounting the stairs will have to pass Mr. Serle. And I barred the kitchen door myself tonight. I am myself, I think, feeling sleepy again. I have made friends with Mr. Serle despite our differences; Mr. Hatton will not find me. I will not sell my soul.

I sleep, and a strange dream comes to me. I am in the loft over the stable, nestled in the hay. Four women step through the window in the loft and walk down the hay as if they trod a set of marble stairs. They stand before me, silent. All four are beautiful. The first is slim and dark, the smallest of them. She wears a high-necked gown of brown stuff. In her hands she holds a wooden spoon. The second wears her honey-brown hair in smooth, thick braids that make intricate loops about her ears and then are pinned up to the top of her head to form a sort of crown. Her dress is blue. The neck is low but filled in with a fine white kerchief edged with lace. She cradles a baby in her strong arms. The third wears her blond hair in a springing halo of ringlets. Everything about her is abundant—the panels of her rustling, scarlet silk gown, the great diamond pendants swinging at her ears, the mounds of her white breasts bulging in her low-cut, straining bodice. She toys with a string of fat pearls, running them through her fingers and raising them in a gesture of caress to her red lips. The last is garbed in the long black robes and white wimple of a nun. A rope, from which hangs a rosary of wooden beads, girds her waist. The face framed by her wimple is pure and beautiful. Her soft eyes gleam in the starlight.

I open my eyes wide. The light is dim, and I would see four such beautiful beings more clearly. "Who are you?" I ask in wonderment. "Tell me who you are." In the way of dreams, I know that my words make no sound in the dust-filled air between us and yet are heard and understood.

The small, dark one speaks. "I am a good daughter and a loyal sister to my brothers," she says. "I make the house, I tend the fire, I mend the clothes. My father and my brothers bring food into the house. With my spoon, I stir meal into the bubbling water. I serve out what is needful. I conserve. Strong men protect me, make me safe. I serve them because it is my duty."

There is a silence and then the second speaks. "I am a true wife and a loving mother," she says and smiles from a place of infinite grace. "Through union with a man, I experience the highest calling of a woman. Men exalt me. I serve them with love." She nestles the heavy child more securely in her arms and coos to it in a wordless bubble of sound.

I turn my open eyes to the third woman, who stares at me boldly. Her look makes me feel naked, and I pull my blanket tightly about my shoulders. Seeing my movement, she smiles, a cruel curving of her pouting lips. "Men need me," she says. "Our congress is a fair bargain. I enjoy the weakness that draws men to me. My days are pearls that I can hoard or spend. I pretend to serve men because my power over them is infinite. I enjoy the joke."

The fourth woman raises her white hand in a gesture of blessing. "I serve the spirit needs of men on earth," she tells me, looking deep into me. "The authority of the Church guides my every step. I am the bride of Christ, and his priests minister to me. I am admired by all men and yet safe from them."

I look at these four beings and ponder their words. Are these angels come to help me or devils come to torture me? I wonder. Their moist lips part. The fourth one speaks again. "Give up the world and its sorrows. Save yourself," she says gently. "Men need your prayers." "Every woman wants my power," says the third one, tossing back her rich tresses and showing her smooth breasts. "Every woman wants to be me," says the second. Her smile is in her eyes, not on her lips. "Every woman is me," says the dark one. Silently they turn away and mount their invisible stairway. At the top, they face me once more and each holds up her burden: the spoon, the child, the necklace, the rosary. As they came, they step out through the window and are gone.

I am awake in the dark. The women frightened me. Which one am I? I ask myself. Which one would I wish to be? But I am none of them. How can I be when I have no man to serve or to minister to me as they each do? Tears of self-pity spring into my eyes. Wait, I tell myself. If none of these is what you would choose, wait. Hide in your brother's clothing until the choice is clear. No hurry. Someday you will be in America. Decide there. My soul is my own. And souls are not men or women, I think. Relieved, I fall asleep and do not wake again until Mr. Serle calls me at dawn.

CHAPTER XX

T HE FOLLOWING DAYS are so busy that I have no time for philosophical thoughts about my soul or fears about Mr. Hatton's coming to find me. Mrs. Bennet complains that her legs cannot stand the strain of so much work, and I have some of her baking to do as well as tasks for Mr. Serle. But the labor will be easier very soon. Indeed, several of the houseguests and their servants left today. There are just ten places for dinner tonight upstairs.

Today dawned clear and cool, a perfect morning, Mrs. Bennet asserts, for spinning sugar nests to decorate the meringues in custard she is making for today's dinner. Mrs. Bennet is making jellies as well as her custards, so Mr. Serle undertakes to teach me the technique of spinning sugar wreaths. The master wants plain roasts of meat and spitted game birds, batter puddings, and chopped salads for the main courses—an old-fashioned dinner, and easy for Mr. Serle and me to prepare after the servants' noon meal.

We work in the main kitchen because, Mr. Serle explains, there is not room for spinning sugar in the cold pantry or the still room. He binds two forks together with the tines outward and greases them lightly. He wraps me in a large, clean flour-sack apron and spreads an old sheet on the floor in front of the worktable. Two oiled broomsticks project from the edge of the worktable over the sheet. They are held in place by a cutting board weighted with heavy iron pans. We set a large pot of water on the range and a smaller pot with crushed sugar. On the table a clean platter lies ready for the sugar nests.

Mr. Serle sets a low stool for me to stand on, facing the broomsticks. The method is easier, he claims, if one has some height from which to throw the sugar syrup. Then we watch as the sugar melts, clears, browns. When it cracks, Mr. Serle sets the small pan within the larger pan of hot water. I stand on the stool, dipping the double fork into the sugar and flicking back and forth, back and forth, spinning out fine threads of sugar. Of course, I have difficulty finding the trick of it at first and fling a few hot blobs of syrup about. Soon the air is filled with the pungent scent of caramel.

When I have successfully spun out a skein of filaments, Mr. Serle dips his hands in a basin of ice water, shakes them dry, and then gathers the brittle threads into an airy ring, which he sets on the platter laid ready. We make two; a disaster of blobs falls to the sheet on the floor, and then we spin five perfect ones. We pause to cook more sugar.

"I like this," I say, peering into the pot. "Do they really decorate their sweets so in France?"

"You are doing well," Mr. Serle says. "You have the knack. Some pastry chefs build palaces in sugar."

"Will you teach me?" I ask eagerly. I imagine a structure of latticed grace, a tower with a cloud of golden sugar threads like a halo at the top.

"I can't teach you," Mr. Serle says. "This is the limit of my knowledge."

I am surprised. It seems to me that Mr. Serle knows everything. In the pan the heated sugar changes its nature; fire transforms the solid grains into a translucent white sand, which melts into one mass and then clears to glassy transparency, tinged with gold. The gloss of it reminds me of the bright halos about the heads of the angels in the picture Father Fintan kept in our church.

After we have spun ten more sweet, fragile nests, we stop and clean up the kitchen and ourselves. The platter is full, and I carry it away into the cold pantry. Mrs. Bennet will be content.

"I need water," I say when I return. "All this sugar has made me thirsty." We rest for a few minutes, and I drink my water. "I think you have sugar in your hair," I tell Mr. Serle.

He does not answer me. Instead, a dreaming look comes into his eyes. "I have been thinking about going to America very soon," he says. He is sitting at the table with his chin propped on his hand. "There is a place I will search for. I dreamed of it last night."

"What place?" I ask.

Mr. Serle reaches under his apron and takes one of his favorite books from his pocket. He holds the small volume balanced in his left hand; the supple fingers of his right hand flick over the pages. I rest and sip my water as he reads a little to himself.

"Ah, here it is," he says at last, and begins to read to me. "Listen to this," he says. " 'On a level with the point lay a broad sheet of water, so placid and limpid that it resembled a bed of the pure mountain atmosphere, compressed into a setting of hills and woods. Its length was about three leagues, while its breadth was irregular, expanding to half a league, or even more, opposite to the point, and contracting to less than half that distance, more to the southward. Of course, its margin was irregular, being indented by bays, and broken by many projecting low points. At its northern, or nearest end, it was bounded by an isolated mountain, lower land falling off to east and west, gracefully relieving the sweep of the outline. Still the character of the country was mountainous: high hills, or low mountains, rising abruptly from the water, on quite nine-tenths of its circuit. On all sides, wherever the eye turned, nothing met it but the mirror-like surface of the lake, the placid view of heaven, and the dense setting of woods. The hand of man had never yet defaced or deformed any part of this native scene, which lay bathed in sunlight, a glorious picture of affluent forest-grandeur.' Is it not wonderful?"

"A glorious picture indeed," I say. "But I would be lonely there. Where are the people?"

"I will make a place of peace and plenty. The people will come to us," he says. "Enough. Not so many that they disturb my view of the lake and the mountain. I will search for it."

"Will you really be happy in such a place?" I am puzzled. "What about the restaurant in the city you have talked about?"

Mr. Serle laughs aloud. I think it is rare to hear him laugh free and easy. "You are right, child," he says. "I am a contradiction. The roar and diversion of the city and the silence of the wilderness. I want them both at once. Truffled paté on a gold-rimmed porcelain plate and a handful of fresh blackberries still warm from the August sun. Where can I eat them both at the same meal?"

"Nowhere," I say. "It is honest oat cake and fresh berries or else cream reductions laced with brandy, kickshaws, and trifles. But your restaurant. Will there be work for me there?"

Mr. Serle puts his book away. "Can you brave the ocean once more? Do you truly wish to go to America?"

"Yes," I say. "Of course, I must go. Only I am afraid to go all alone. Will you help me find passage? In America, I will find my brother. I will tell him I am safe, and then I will work for you."

"We will go," Mr. Serle says. "I can help. Only you will not work with me if your brother does not approve it."

I stop and look at him. My heart stops and then starts with a thunder in my chest. "We are going to America," I say. "I can go with you? In truth? When?"

"Very soon," he says. "If we are going, we must go soon. We will talk about it."

Just then someone looks in to ask whether the noon meal is ready. I hurry to stir the stew simmering on the back of the range, and Mr. Serle empties a jar of chutney into a bowl.

A few days later, we have at last a quiet evening for talk. The family and all the guests that remain have gone to a dinner and ball at one of the great houses in Milford. The ladies' maids and the coachmen are all gone as well. The servants remaining have an early supper and then sit in the housekeeper's room or go early to their beds. Everyone is glad of a few hours of respite from the bustle of the past weeks.

When the simple servants' supper is done, Mr. Serle and I clean the kitchen. I take the plates and cutlery into the scullery, and we sit at the scrubbed table and drink our tea when we are finished.

"You do not eat enough, Mina," he tells me. "Again tonight, I noticed that you ate only a little bread and salad. Food connects us to the pleasure of the world."

"I am not hungry," I say. "Working where there is abundance every day keeps the opposite before me. I feel as if I am taking food from my sister's mouth when I put a heap on my plate. I love the world. I like the taste of things, but there is always too much. It makes me want to weep."

Mr. Serle nods. He does not eat so much himself, I think. I change the subject to ask him a question that has been nibbling at the corner of my mind for days. "I have worked and had my room and board here," I say. "Now I must have money for the passage to America. Where will I find it?"

"But you have wages owed you," Mr. Serle says.

"I do?" I ask.

"Of course you do," Mr. Serle assures me. "When I hired you away from Mr. Coates, I entered another kitchen assistant on the estate factor's book."

"You did!" I exclaim. I am overcome with surprise.

"I did indeed," he says. "I thought you knew. You will have enough for your passage with a little left for provisions, I imagine. And I have six months' wages owed me. I command a high price from the master here. That will pay my fare with plenty left for a lodging while I find work. You will go to your brother or perhaps find work also."

"I hardly dare to ask for wages," I say. "I do not know how to do it."

"I will manage it," Mr. Serle tells me. "Very soon."

"I am grateful," I declare. "I hope the ship we find is sound." I do not like the thought of the sea.

"The future will bring what it brings," says Mr. Serle.

"The passage across the ocean must be cold in wintertime," I say, imagining the wind and ice.

"You are right. Autumn is coming," Mr. Serle says. "If we

do not leave soon, it will mean waiting until next spring for safer passage. I do not like the cold."

"I am ready to go," I say. "My brother must be wondering why I have not come to find him."

"He—" Mr. Serle starts to say something and then stops. "It is time," he begins again. "In my religion the celebration of the New Year comes soon. I would like to mark it by beginning on a new life."

I summon up my courage. "Will we really go together in the same ship?" I ask him. "I will feel safer if I know someone out of all the strangers."

"Of course," he says.

We sit silent for a time, thinking of the change that is coming. I break the quiet. "What food do you miss the most from the past?" I ask.

Benjamin Serle looks thoughtfully at the stove. Then his nostrils widen as if a good scent assailed them from some dream kitchen. *"Frittèlle,"* he says. "You would not know what they are."

"What are they?" I ask, of course.

"A soft dough of yeast and flour and water," he says, "flavored with anise seed and dark raisins, cut in the shape of diamonds, fried golden in olive oil, and then soaked with a syrup of honey and lemon and eaten warm. Nobody made them as well as my mother did.

"And you?" he asks after a pause while he tastes the food of memory, and I try to imagine it. "What will you miss?"

"I will miss potatoes," I say. "Not the potatoes of England, but those of my childhood before the hunger came to us. My sister would milk the cow. My brother would fetch the biggest potatoes from the storage shelf. We would bury them in the ashes of a turf fire. Then, when the praties were ready, white and fluffy inside and crusty outside, I would run out in the rain to pull green onions from the garden. My mother would split the potatoes open and pour in fresh cream from the cow and mash in the green onions I had cooked in butter in the iron skillet."

"That is something you will be able to eat in America," he says. "They certainly have potatoes there and cream and onions."

"I do not think that it matters that the ingredients are to be found easily or not," I say. "The fire will not be of peat turfs dug by my father and brother; it will not be my sister's hand that milked the cow and set the potatoes to bake. I will not look over to see my mother's smile as she sets our food before us. There are meals that we will never eat again." I think to myself that I am sorry I broached the subject.

"Better to remember than to starve ourselves of the happiness of the past," says Mr. Serle.

"I feel hungrier now than I did at suppertime," I tell him. "Talking and the thought of travel seem to give me appetite."

"Good," he says. "We must set up a tray with cold meat and cake. The housekeeper gave directions that the family will want light refreshments when they return from their ball. When that work is done, I will make you a second supper."

I build up the half-dead fire in the range again, and Mr. Serle assembles what he needs. As he cooks, he talks to me about the kitchens he has worked in, the change that the liberation of the people brings with it. Where there is freedom, he says, there are cafés and restaurants. Groups of friends gather to eat and talk. "Where there is freedom there is civilization," Mr. Serle says. "I do not mean the effete whipping of chocolate in porcelain cups, but order and proportion. A great meal brings together a balance of meat and produce, the piquant, the hearty, and the sweet. Spices and herbs matter. The textures of substance, crispness, smoothness matter. Likewise, the balance of people around the table must reflect the opinions of the day. The knowledge of the head must be balanced with the knowledge of the heart." He pauses and looks up from the bowl of eggs he is beating. "Take a cup and go steal a little of Mrs. Bennet's rum," he bids me.

I am amazed he knows. When I return, he is heating a frying pan on the range. As I watch, he adds the rum to the batter he has made and beats it. Then he uses a feather to film the surface of his pan with melted butter. He pours in a spoonful of batter and fries pancakes, so thin they are like lace, one after the other as he continues talking. "At the perfect meal," he says, "there is no excess and no greed. Those without appetite are pitied and treated gently. Each one at the table attends to each of the others. The temperature in the room is moderate, the decoration comfortable without ostentation. The dishes on the table provide variety of colors, textures, seasonings. The palate is stimulated with subtle combinations. Nothing is overdone, nothing is bizarre. The food nourishes the body without sating it; the conversation nourishes the mind without overwhelming it."

"It sounds like a very paradise," I tell him.

"Perhaps," he says.

He folds each pancake around a spoonful of pot cheese softened with cream and a spoonful of raspberry jam thinned with a little more of Mrs. Bennet's rum. He sets six pancakes on a dish and sprinkles sugar over all. Then he wraps his hand in a thick cloth and takes the iron from the back of the fire where it has been heating. He holds it low over the dish until the sugar crackles and glazes. Then he divides the dish onto two plates. "There," he says, "sit at the table and eat."

As I nibble at the mix of buttery pancake, tart and sweet fillings, and brittle shards of glassy sugar, I think about America. "I will write a letter to Father Hugh Fintan, the priest of our village," I say. "I will tell him where I have been and where I am going. If he hears word from my brother, he can tell him where to look for me."

"Very sensible," comments Mr. Serle. "Do you like your *crêpes*?"

"Oh, yes," I say. "This is delicious. What did you say it is called?"

"The French call the pancakes *crêpes*."

"Is Paris really a city where all are equal?" I try to imagine Mr. Serle walking in a great city. His slim figure moves gracefully among crowds of people and then is lost from my sight.

"No," Mr. Serle says. He looks somber. "There are lords and footmen, beggars and ladies who twitch their skirts from them lest they be soiled. They talk of equality. Still, some have pantries stuffed with food and some starve."

"Why is there no justice in the world?" I cry.

"Justice?" says Mr. Serle. "I have given up on justice. Hope for a better time, yes. Always hope. Put your heart there."

"Hope?" I say. I look at him and remember standing on the deck of the ship in Dublin harbor when the man said to my brother, looking at the ships laden with wheat, that there is no justice. I remember the anger in my brother's eyes. Benjamin Serle looks not angry but sad. Maybe anger is stronger than sadness because anger fights for change and change is hope.

"I am going to hope for justice and fight for it too," I say.

Benjamin Serle smiles at me.

"Will Tom go to the master and tell him I am female?" I ask.

"Tom is too lazy to make a fuss," Mr. Serle reassures me. "There is no profit in it for him now."

"I will be glad to go away from this country," I sigh. "I dream sometimes that I return to my village and find my mother and father and sister and brother all seated by the fire. I stoop a little going in at the doorway, for I am taller since I left them. They look up at me and smile a welcome. There is no surprise. They know always and forever that I will return to them. I have never left."

"Do you mean you wish to go back to Ireland, then?" Benjamin Serle asks me. "Would the priest you mentioned help you?"

"I do not even know for certain sure that he is there himself," I respond. "He talked of migrating. I think that, dream as I will, there is no going back. What could I do? I would live out my life scrubbing pots in some English landlord's scullery and tending my parents' graves if I can find them. The past is a living death. No, I must go to America. But it is hard."

"We will think of ourselves as pilgrims," Mr. Serle says. "Our homes exist only in our hearts. We will value them for what they were and leave them behind us. The cottage you grew up in is burned. The room where I was born and where my mother loved me is someone else's now. My wife and our child are dead. Suffering lies everywhere behind us. Those places and those people we love are destroyed in this material world. They are our past, and now we will go west across the ocean. Why not?"

"But—" I know that there are indeed "why nots" to be set out.

"You and I are but a pair of infinite isolations," he says. A sad idea, I think, and yet he says it as simple fact, not sadly. "What we are to each other, what we can be, what we cannot ever be, only you and I need know. We will make a simple story for the world."

"Yes," I say, "the world will ask for a story."

"So we will provide one." He smiles at me. "What would you have us be, Mina?"

There is a long silence. Each of us retreats into our own thoughts. Perhaps, I acknowledge to myself, I am afraid of the choice before us.

Mr. Serle must be thinking similar thoughts, for he says, "Father and daughter will not do. It would let me protect you sometimes, but if we are challenged we will have no proof; then you will be taken for my mistress. Some would be angrier for having thought the first before the second." He shakes his head, as if rejecting some disturbing idea.

"You could marry me," I say.

Mr. Serle looks shocked and then sorry. "You cannot mean that," he says.

"It would be safe," I say. "It is the usual story." It feels suddenly like the only way. After all, if Mr. Serle is married to me, he cannot betray me as Susan did.

"Let us be clear," Benjamin Serle says, his voice stern. "I will never marry a Christian. I will never marry out of my faith. I will not marry a convert either."

"I am not intending to become a heathen," I say. "I am thinking of convenience and independence from society."

"It is certainly not independence to tie yourself to a man twice your age who does not share your religion or the habits of thought and belief instilled in you from birth by your parents and neighbors. And there are other aspects of marriage you know nothing about, child. Your convenience is a fraud."

I hang my head. What are these aspects of marriage I do not know? I wonder. I sigh. "You are right," I admit. But I rebel. I am not his child. "Marriage is safer," I insist.

"Safety is not everything." Benjamin Serle's dark eyes regard me steadily. "In my faith, children take the religion of their mother. If the mother is not a Jew, the children cannot be Jews. I did not suffer under the edicts of the popes to turn away from my responsibility to my people and to my children. I will not marry where my children will be born aliens to me. You do not mean ill, but you are wrong to suggest it."

"It is not my fault the popes were unjust," I object. "I wasn't there."

Mr. Serle actually smiles. He is not really angry, even though his voice is strained with feeling. "I pray every morning that I will be worthy of being one of the nation chosen by God to live out His precepts on this earth," he says. "Despite my imperfections and the cowardice I have shown in setting aside the outward signs of my religion, I pray that I may remain loyal to my people in my heart."

"I pray too," I counter. "I pray that the souls of all the worthy will be saved and that the wicked and the heathen will turn to the truth of Christ's love."

"Our prayers are true within us, and yet we contradict each other," Mr. Serle says.

"Can you see who I am?" I ask. "Can you see me and not see the Church that speaks against your people?"

"I try," he says. "You were taught hate, not born to it, and so was I. Can we be friends?"

"I think so," I reply.

"Good," says Mr. Serle quietly.

I look down at my empty plate. "So we cannot marry," I say.

"We cannot marry. That is true. There is no shame for either one of us in that. And yet," he says, "I am drawn to your sadness. I will protect you if I can."

"Will you ever marry again?" I ask.

"I do not know." He bows his head. His face is hidden from me. "My wife, my Rachel, weighs on my heart. I could not save her from her death. If I love a woman and lose her like that again, it will kill me."

"Is it wrong for me to talk of marriage?" I ask him.

"No," he says. "After so much loss, you want to be safe. You may think that love and safety and marriage are necessarily linked together. They are not, but even if they were, you are not ready to love anyone yet."

What he says is a strange relief to me. I am not ready. The time is out of joint, I think, hearing an echo of my father's voice. I do not love him and he does not love me. This feeling is something else. I am the beginning, not the end, of a story.

"Well, we will find a way," Mr. Serle sighs.

"On the ship that burned," I say reluctantly, for it seems bad luck to mention it, "my brother thought that he could earn some money by working. We might be away from those with leisure to ask questions if we work. Perhaps you could find passage as a ship's cook, and I could be your assistant."

"Clever child," says Mr. Serle approvingly. "Yes, I can seek work, and you can be my young cousin or my nephew going out to join some other branch of the family. Perhaps we can find a great ship that carries the gentry traveling on business as well as those like us who seek our fortune. If we are lucky, there will be a berth for the cook near the kitchen instead of in the crew or passenger quarters."

"Oh, yes," I say, and clasp my hands tight together. "I will not have to stifle among the women below the decks doing nothing, and you will have all your wages saved for your restaurant. Let us try."

"I will write the letters tomorrow," Mr. Serle says. His voice is cheerful.

"I can go as I am," I say. "I will wait to be a woman. I feel safer in these clothes."

"I can well understand," Mr. Serle says kindly. "Yes, maybe it is best if you remain a lad a little longer."

"Indeed," I say. "I am so glad to be going to America."

"Can you resign yourself so quickly to be a pilgrim, Mina?" says Mr. Serle in his quiet voice. "Can you hold the good of the past in your heart and return to it only in your dreams?"

"I do not know," I say. "How can we know what we are until we are tested?"

"I have asked you the wrong question," he says. "I should ask rather if you are willing to make the trial, to be tested?"

"Yes," I reply. "My answer is yes. I hope that in the wilderness of America I will find sustenance."

"Ah, yes," says Benjamin Serle. "Manna in the desert. We will pray to be fed."

"I will not pray to be fed," I say, "although I shall indeed pray, I am sure. I shall work hard and feed myself with the pay for my labors. Perhaps I will find work as a pastry cook. Do you suppose they like sweets in America?"

He laughs and says yes, he thinks that they do.

Just then the clatter of hooves sounds from the stable yard. The family is returned from their dinner and dance. Mr. Serle stirs the fire and sets wine to heat. A footman hurries in to fetch the tray of food that has been waiting all prepared with a clean linen cloth over it for this past hour or more. All is bustle again for a while.

Then the house settles down for the night. In the kitchen, the fire is banked, the door barred. Mr. Serle has yawned and gone up the stairs. I stay to wash my hands and face in warm water in the scullery. The day's sugar clings to my skin. Coming out of the scullery, I pause at the foot of the stairs. The moon is full tonight and high in the sky. Silver light pours in at every window. The shapes of things are clear and yet drained of color. The world is silver and gray. Nothing is distinct, nothing has substance. I feel my way up toward my bed with my hand on the wall. I need the touch of rough plaster under my fingertips to anchor me, else I would float away in the moonlight.

CHAPTER XXI

SUMMER IS PASSED, and Mr. Serle has completed his last task, supervising the beer-making for the estate. After weeks of preparing our departure, we leave the kitchen and the attic tomorrow. The master has given us our wages and letters attesting to our characters. The day before yesterday, when the house party broke up at last and the family went visiting, we were free to go. We are staying until tomorrow, however, so that we may leave the kitchen in perfect order and pack our bags carefully. Mr. Serle is pleased, for he has fulfilled his promises and inconvenienced no one by his actions. Since I made no promises to begin with, I have no need of such qualms.

Tomorrow we will be in Liverpool, preparing for our new posts. We are a cook and a cook's assistant on a ship called the *Victoria*. Its kitchen will be very small compared to what we are accustomed to. The letter we have says that we will be expected to sleep on bunks in the storeroom next to the cookhouse to guard the supplies against theft. This sounds frightening, but Mr. Serle thinks it will be better and healthier than sleeping below the waterline in such narrow, crowded bunks as I saw on the *Abigail*.

Mr. Serle's friend in Milford has recommended us to a family we will stay a night with in Liverpool. We are spared the expense of an inn. As we prepare for our journey, I try not to think of America too much. It brings unsettling dreams in which I search for my brother and fail to find him.

The strangest thing for me is that I have a new name. When

Mr. Serle asked for the money and the letters for us, the master said he did not know my name. Mr. Serle told him it is Daniel Serle. He apologized to me when he came down to the kitchen after.

"I did not know what to say," he confessed. "I realized that I had to give you a boy's name and, in truth, Paddy stuck in my throat. The way Tom said it always made it an insult to you. I suppose that if I had my wits about me, I would have said Daniel Pigot. Even so, you have nothing, I believe, that says who you are. And I have the paper attesting to my son's birth. I have always kept it."

"My brother had the letters and the paper from our priest, Father Fintan, that says I am baptized," I say. "My brother had them all when we were separated."

"I hope you are not angry that I named you without your choosing." Mr. Serle looks uncomfortable, even a little guilty.

"I am not unhappy," I assure him. "Daniel is the name I treasure above all others." I wonder if, by giving me this name, Mr. Serle has in a strange and subtle way adopted me. I do not mention it, for I admit to myself that it would hurt me to hear him deny it.

I cannot talk to him about it, for today Mr. Serle is spending from dawn to dusk in Milford with others of his kind. He has to observe a great religious holiday, he told me. He will not eat all day, only worship with the other Jews. They do not even have a minister in Milford, he said. He has a duty to go so there will be enough men to make a congregation. They conduct their service together, reading their Bible and saying their prayers for the dead. After, he will break his fast with one of the families and return late in the evening. I thought of walking to Milford with him and going to church myself. I could show him that I too am devout. Not so devout, I scold myself. I have not taken holy communion since I left our village and Father Fintan. The memory of the plump priest in Milford stops me. I cannot make confession to him. He would tell me again to change my clothes, to give up everything. He would refuse to bless my journey.

I pray for strength for the days to come and then complete

the few kitchen tasks that Mr. Serle has left for me. Mrs. Bennet is already complaining that she is overworked without us. In the afternoon, I go down to the gardens to say good-bye to Mr. Plumb. He is in the orchard, raking up windfalls under the apple trees. His attire is as worn and earth-stained as ever. It is warm today, and he has pulled a battered straw hat and not his shapeless felt one about his ears. He greets me kindly and leans on his rake to talk.

"I am come to say good-bye," I tell him. "I am going to America."

"I heard the news," he says. "Tomorrow, is it?"

"Yes," I say, "tomorrow, early."

Mr. Plumb reaches up and puts one hand under an apple that remains among the leaves on the tree. As he holds his hand still below it, the fruit detaches itself and falls to him. I exclaim in wonder at the chance.

"Look at that," he says, turning the red and yellow globe in his hand. "It took its time, clinging to its mother tree until it knew itself ripe and ready. It is the last, I think"—he cranes his neck to see if there is fruit higher among the branches—"yet not the least. The time came, and we were both ready for the moment."

He hands me the apple. "For you," he says, and his smile splits the moon of his face.

"Thank you," I reply.

"Eat it," he says. "Do not store up for the future the taste of today. What is crisp and sweet now may be stale tomorrow. That is how some things are."

"I will eat it," I assure him. "But first I must thank you for your kindness. You helped when Mr. Serle was ill. You have treated me kindly. I will remember peace in your gardens."

"Perhaps," he tells me, "the peace was not in the garden but in you when you escaped the house. Secrets are hard things to bear in company."

I look at him sharply. He does not speak but smiles at me. I see the knowledge in his eyes. "Thank you for keeping my secret," I tell him.

"Nature has no secrets," he says. "There is the seed and the soil. There is the sun and rain. In their due time things sprout, ripen, and decay. What is exists, and time reveals it as nature wills."

"Good-bye," I tell him. Tears brim in my eyes. I will never again see his stout figure stooping beside a rosebush. I will never again see his idiot's smile contradicted by the shrewdness of his blue gaze.

"Godspeed your journey and bring you safe to your goal," Mr. Plumb tells me. It is a benediction.

"Thank you," I say. My heart is humbled. "May you live out years of contentment in the beauty of your gardens."

Mr. Plumb smiles and waves to me and turns back to his raking. The winey odor of decaying fruit fills the air. As I walk away, I bite into my apple. The flesh crunches crisp and sweet between my teeth just as Mr. Plumb promised. I eat it down to the core. The shiny black seeds are visible in their translucent compartments. I tie three of them into the corner of my kerchief before I take the remaining core to Gytrash. I lean on the paddock fence and stroke her gray velvet nose and say good-bye to her.

In the morning we put our bags and Mr. Serle's trunk into the back of the cart that takes us to Milford. We are taking a train—a train—to Liverpool. This is the start of Mr. Serle's new year. It begins a little awkwardly. The pony cart is going to Milford with our baggage and some sacks of turnips for the market. Mr. Coates has sent one of his stablemen to drive. As we prepare to leave, the man invites Mr. Serle to climb up on the seat beside him. One look at Mr. Serle's face reminds me of his fear of horses. There is nothing I can do to help him. As a result, Mr. Serle bounces miserably in the front seat of the cart, nervously watching the rear quarters of the pony, and I bounce miserably in the back of the cart, watching the dusty road behind us.

The train is a fearful experience. Mr. Serle purchases the tickets while I guard the baggage. During the wait for the train, we sit on a bench without speaking. There is a tea cart with a woman offering tea and sweet cakes, but neither one of us is hungry. At last the ground trembles and the air fills with noise and dirt. In a cloud of steam and cinders, the locomotive lumbers past us and groans to a halt with the squealing, swaying cars bumping behind it.

We see our baggage loaded and find a place together. The hiss of the engine startles me to utter a prayer, and then the car jerks forward and back and forward again. The noise of the piston-driven wheels pounds in my ears. Conversation is not possible. Mr. Serle reads quite calmly in one of his books while I look out the window and worry that we will hit something or run off the track into a field. I plunge my hand into my jacket pocket and find the packet of sugared almonds Mr. Serle's friend gave me at the warehouse in Milford weeks ago. Silently, I hold them out to Mr. Serle. He smiles and takes one and continues reading. Tentatively, I put one in my mouth. The crunch of sugar coating and the mealy nut blend together in my mouth. The flavor heartens me.

Nevertheless, I am glad when the smokestacks of the city begin to blur the horizon. Soon we are running past kitchen gardens and houses and then factories and tenements piled up against each other. The station at Liverpool is larger than that at Milford and crowded with people. From the chaos Mr. Serle subtracts a porter with a hand cart to assist us.

We find our way to the house where we will stay the night. The family are all out. The maid directs us to leave Mr. Serle's trunk and our bundles in the hall. She offers us refreshment, but Mr. Serle is in a great hurry to go down to the shipping offices. He must look over the business of the trip, he says, and be sure that all is satisfactory.

We make our way through the streets toward the river. There are the same dank passageways and the white faces peering out at us that I remember. I look at them with pity. At the wharves a great ship is being loaded. We skirt the tangle of passengers and cargo and find the warehouse with the offices of the *Victoria*. There we sign our names to the list of crew. No one pays much mind to us. We are a small part of the bustle and routine of preparation for a voyage. Mr. Serle asks a question of one of the clerks about the rules for distributing provisions to the steerage passengers. An officer is summoned, and I am sent to sit on the bench outside the warehouse door while Mr. Serle and the officer review manifests and contracts.

For a time I am content to watch the movement of the crowds about me. The air smells of tar and coal and river muck. Mr. Serle is taking his time. Restless, I rise and begin to read the notices attached to the warehouse wall. Ships' sailing dates are announced. Passenger lists are posted. Gentry advertise for servants willing to go to America or the Indies. People come and go. I saunter along the wall feeling like an adventurer, a traveler of the world. I push my cap back on my head in imitation of an errand boy I see hurrying by with a bundle of ribbon-tied papers in his hand.

A glancing blow from behind me knocks my cap completely from my head. I wheel to defend myself from attack and face Mr. Hatton.

"Mina, Mina Pigot," he cries triumphantly.

"No!" I exclaim and move to run.

Stupid with fear, I am not quick enough. Like a toad flicking its tongue at a fly, Mr. Hatton reaches out and grasps my arm just above the elbow. His small hand grips like iron. He still wears his neat black frock coat buttoned tight over the round ball of his belly; he still wears his hair combed in strands across his bald pate. He leans his face into mine, pokes the stock of his whip under my chin to lift it, and speaks so only I can hear him. "I would know those red curls anywhere," he says. "Your lad's clothing does not fool me. I recognize your walk." His teeth are gray and small.

For a frantic moment I think he might bite me and I pull away, stumbling as I try to kick at him. He evades my foot nimbly and seizes my arm again. When I try to pull out of his grasp, he raps me on the side of the head with his whip.

"See," he says. "See who is master. You ran away. Susan told me to look for you dressed as a lad. Now it is my duty to punish you and make you return to your service."

"No," I cry, "I will not be a slave for anyone. You cannot

make me." I am dizzy from his blow. I cannot think clearly what to do. I pull my arm free and again stumble back from him. I cannot seem to clear my head to flee.

My struggle with Mr. Hatton is attracting attention. I hear voices, laughing and shouting. The loungers of the dock are gathering to see what is happening.

"Kick him harder, lad," cries one.

"Whip the scoundrel," cries another.

"Is he a thief, sir?" calls a deeper voice.

I cry out Mr. Serle's name. Desperately, I twist away from Mr. Hatton and run. Hands grasp at me. Beside me, the mouth of an alley opens between dark buildings. Ahead is a crowd of laughing men. I turn into the alleyway. It is a short passage into a courtyard where privies with broken doors let out their dreadful reek. There is no way out save up the stairways of the buildings. Mr. Hatton's whip slashes at my legs.

I wish that I had run the other way to the docks. I wish I were mounted on Gytrash, riding down the water meadow and away up the hill. I would feel the air blow about me and the power of the horse between my legs. If he tried to stop us, flying through the streets, Mr. Hatton would fall beneath Gytrash's flashing hooves and be destroyed. No one could catch us.

The whip slashes to the left and to the right, driving me back toward the wall, making it impossible for me to break and run. Now I am backed up against the stone wall of the alley. Mr. Hatton presses toward me, showing his nasty teeth.

"You cannot make me go with you," I say with a defiance that I do not feel. My voice strangles in my throat. My words are barely audible.

"I will enjoy making you." He smiles into my face. "My wife bought a ticket for you. That was money wasted." He taps me with the stock of the whip on the side of the head. "My wife had to sail without a servant to attend her. That annoyed her, and I paid the price of her anger." He hits me again. My head is swimming. I cower back against the wall. If only the stones would yield and let me melt into them. "You do not know what it is to be a slave, my dear. Not yet. You have a lot to learn, you harlot." He raps me with the whip butt and at the same time reaches out and pulls me to him. His round belly presses on me, his wet mouth leeches onto mine.

"Oh, yes," he says, letting go with a sucking sound. "You are no boy inside those clothes. You and I are going to have such fun being naughty together." With his whip hand he seizes my hair. With the other hand he pushes his hand into my jacket and gropes at my chest and through the fabric of my shirt pinches the nipple of my breast so it hurts.

"You are growing," he pants into my ear. "You are not so flat as when I first saw you. Now a little tickle will help make you a complete woman." He rubs my breast roughly with his palm. I think I will faint with horror. He pushes my head back against the stone wall and pushes his mouth into mine. Like a fat slug, his tongue squirms against my closed lips.

As I struggle, he bites my lip. This startles me so much that it breaks the spell that made me voiceless. Breaking loose from him, I scream and kick at him fiercely. I punch at his soft, paunchy belly and make him gasp. He loses his hold on my hair.

Even as his whip slashes sideways at me, I have broken away from him and I am running toward the alley's mouth. Rough arms seize me and I scream again.

"Child, child," says a familiar voice.

"Let go of my servant," says Mr. Hatton.

"Who are you?" says the stern voice of Mr. Serle.

"I am Gregory Hatton, and this is my bound servant who has run away," says Mr. Hatton, pronouncing each word loudly and distinctly. "She pretends to be a boy so she can escape."

"You are mistaken, sir," Mr. Serle asserts politely. "This is my kitchen apprentice, Daniel. I have employed him this past year."

"You lie," Mr. Hatton sneers. He flicks his whip. The lash cracks above my head.

Mr. Serle pushes me to the side. His hand goes down, and I see the flash of a knife blade as it rises again. Mr. Hatton flicks his whip again, and I cry out as he slashes down toward Mr. Serle. But Mr. Serle holds his knife ready in his outstretched hand. The lash severs itself upon the razor-sharpness of his blade. In the instant, Mr. Hatton stares at the bare whipstock in his hand. The thong lies like a dead snake in the mire at his feet.

There are cries from the mouth of the alleyway, where a crowd presses. Mr. Serle folds his knife and puts it away. "Now we can talk," he says. "But let us take our business to a quieter, cleaner place."

Mr. Hatton nods, speechless for the moment. "After you," Mr. Serle says courteously, gesturing Mr. Hatton to precede him. As we emerge, Mr. Serle seizes Mr. Hatton's arm in his and walks him close beside him through the crowd. To all but me they must look like friends who have made up a quarrel. The loungers disperse, murmuring disappointment that there is no further fight to cheer.

Mr. Serle and Mr. Hatton stride out across the roadway, past the carts and milling people. I hurry after them. We make our way to the quiet of a vacant pier.

"Now. What is your business, sir?" asks Mr. Serle, folding his arms across his chest and looking Mr. Hatton up and down. Mr. Hatton is puffing from the brisk pace that Mr. Serle has set him.

"I am here to take my indentured servant, Mina Pigot," says Mr. Hatton. "She signed a bond with me for service, and I intend to see she honors it. Surrender her, or I will have the law on you."

"I see no Mina Pigot here," says Mr. Serle.

"Do not provoke me," says Mr. Hatton. "Give over my servant or face the law."

"You made a spectacle of yourself in the street just now," says the cool voice of Mr. Serle. "So far as I know, it is not permitted in this country for men to make love to men in public, or in private even."

"She's a female," says Mr. Hatton. He is trying to sound superior. "Go back to your own business, sir, and leave me to mine."

Mr. Serle laughs, but he does not sound amused. "The magistrate will not be pleased to be told of respectable Gregory Hatton trying to rape a kitchen boy."

"I have searched for months for my bound servant who ran away," says Mr. Hatton. He sounds angry, not like a man who will give up a lost battle. "I heard that there was a chance she had returned to Liverpool. I spent money in Milford to paste up notices. I paid a reward to someone who guaranteed I should find my quarry here. I want what I have paid for."

"I am sorry that you have been to such expense for nothing," says Mr. Serle.

"I intend to press my case," Mr. Hatton snarls. "I will be satisfied, sir."

There is a long pause and then Mr. Serle speaks again. "Before we call a constable, let us consider," he says thoughtfully. "I concede that there is value in a trained servant. I can understand that one might wish to sign indenture papers with an apprentice to whom one was planning to teach valuable skills."

"I see you are a businessman," Mr. Hatton replies. He too sounds more thoughtful than before.

"If I train a kitchen assistant," Mr. Serle says slowly, as if he is thinking out a problem as he speaks, "I would expect to have at least three years of service in exchange. I would need to teach my assistant many skills, such as the methods of roasting, broiling, sautéing. There are secret formulas for sauces, some of them my own invention. After three years, someone trained in my kitchen learning my techniques would be equipped for life. I would set the value of my teaching at twenty-five pounds. Not more, of course, but not less either."

"I think you underrate yourself," Mr. Hatton's tone is unctuously complimentary. "Thirty would be closer to the value of all you can impart. That's thirty guineas, of course."

"Yes," says Mr. Serle. "I can say yes to thirty guineas. I would value my teaching so high as that."

"Done," says Mr. Hatton, quick as a blink of the eye.

"I would have to see the bond, of course," Mr. Serle says.

"I just happen to have it here," says Mr. Hatton. "Of course, I am concerned that the sum you mention will not completely recompense me for what I give up. This particular servant had great potential in the service I planned for her."

The paper rustles in Mr. Serle's hands as he looks at it. "Come, Mr. Hatton," he says. "If you are not satisfied with my offer, I know a lawyer here who will tell us whether this document is legal."

"No, no," says Mr. Hatton quickly. "I accept your offer. Two honest men such as ourselves have no need for lawyers. If you have the money ready to hand, I will sell you the bond and be on my way."

Mr. Serle reaches into the inner pocket of his coat and takes out a soft leather pouch. "I have the money," he says.

"I will just hold the indenture paper while you count it out," comes the smooth voice of Mr. Hatton.

"Of course," says Mr. Serle. I recognize the tone of irony he uses when Tom or I say something that reveals our littleness.

I hold my breath for fear at what is happening. This is the money that Mr. Serle has saved for his beginning in America. He is spending his restaurant to save me. It is not right, and yet I want so desperately to be free of Mr. Hatton.

"Here you are, sir," says Mr. Serle. "Your price."

The sounds of the city and the wharves are distant murmurs. The chinking of the gold and silver as it changes hands and the rustle of the paper as Mr. Serle folds it and puts it in his breast pocket roar in my ears.

"Shake hands and part friends," says Mr. Hatton.

Mr. Serle's voice is cold. "No," he says, "I will not shake hands as if we were *both* gentlemen. Our business is done. You have the money and I have the bond. Go. My nephew and I have business to attend to."

"Enjoy her," says Mr. Hatton. "I envy you the taming of her."

Mr. Serle says nothing. There is a pause. Mr. Hatton turns and makes his way back along the pier. I feel the blood beating in my ears.

"You can breathe, Mina," says Mr. Serle. "He is gone."

Mr. Serle has turned away. He stands with his back to me, looking out over the river where the gulls wheel and dive. Water laps under the pier. Fear leaves me like mist burning away in the morning sun. Now I feel ashamed at what has happened. I would like to fall on my knees and seize his hand to kiss it. Instead, "Thank you," I say. My voice shakes. "I owe my life to you."

Mr. Serle shrugs his shoulder as he always does when he does not want to talk about a subject. "Don't worry about it now," he says.

"How did you know I needed help?" I ask.

He looks surprised. "You screamed my name," he says. "Just as I came out the door, I saw you run into the alley. I saw the man chasing after you."

"You saved me." I begin to weep. I feel so stupid and helpless. And I feel dirty too. The places where Mr. Hatton pawed at me will never be clean.

Mr. Serle touches me gently on the shoulder. "Do not weep," he says. "You saved yourself. You ran."

"But you made him go away," I say. "You bought the paper." I raise my hand to wipe my tears away and see that there is blood as well as water on my face.

"Look, there is a pump. You will feel better when you rinse your face and brush yourself down," says Mr. Serle, not unkindly. We walk across together to the place, and when I have cleaned and composed myself, he asks me, "Are you well enough to stay with me, or will you return to the Pimintel house to rest? I have errands still to do."

"I will stay with you," I say.

"Your cap is gone," he says. "We will find a respectable place where you can buy yourself a new one."

CHAPTER XXII

THE FAMILY we are staying with are the Pimintels, and they are all at home when we at last walk up their street into the setting sun that dazzles us. The father is a tall, dark man whose beard is touched with gray. Although he looks aloof, his manner is kind. He shakes my hand when Mr. Serle introduces me as Daniel without mentioning a second name. Mrs. Pimintel is a slight woman with a graceful way of moving and a shy, small voice. There is a son, Lionel, and a daughter, Edda. They have their father's height and their mother's softer coloring and physical grace.

They show us to the room where we will spend the night, Mr. Serle in a high, narrow bedstead and I on a cot set under the window. Mrs. Pimintel tells us the family supper will be served as soon as we are ready. As I am about to wash, Mr. Serle, who has refreshed himself first, detains me. He asks if I am recovered from the shock of my encounter with Mr. Hatton.

"Yes," I say, but when I begin to thank him again he hushes me. He wants to tell me that these are pious people we are staying with. They will say a prayer before we eat, he says. It will be in the Hebrew language, a simple blessing of the bread and the wine. He hopes that I will repay this family's hospitality with courtesy and respect for their ways.

I am hurt that he should doubt me. Mr. Serle is nervous, I tell myself.

"You have a smut on your nose," Mr. Serle informs me. "Wash your face. I am ready and will go down now."

Left alone, I take off my shirt and wash thoroughly all the places Mr. Hatton touched me. I scrub my mouth until it hurts. I feel not clean enough but cleaner as I hurry down the stairs.

The calm routine of this household calms my heart. As Mr. Serle said would happen, there are prayers. The son, Lionel, opens a drawer in a chest and takes out four small, saucer-shaped hats. He gives them to his father and to Mr. Serle and to me. Copying the others, I place the thing on my head. Mrs. Pimintel wears a lacy house-cap over her hair. Only the daughter, Edda, is bareheaded, her smoothly braided brown hair twisted into a great knot on the back of her head. To my eyes, she seems to wear a crown.

Everything in this house is simple and yet pleasing. There is a servant to bring in the dishes and to clear them, but Mrs. Pimintel serves us. We eat clear soup followed by fried fish accompanied by shredded cabbage and fine noodles cooked together and flavored with caraway seeds. I remember how I thought the seeds looked like mouse droppings the first time I saw them, but I do not say so. After that we eat stewed plums, served in thin glass dishes, and sweet almond cakes.

During the meal Mr. Serle and the professor talk calmly about Amsterdam, where Professor Pimintel and his wife were born. I half listen as I eat and observe Edda and Lionel. Lionel is the most beautiful young man I have ever seen. There is something in the turn of his head and the definition that his close-trimmed beard gives to the line of his jaw that fascinates me. His coloring is all golden brown; even his eyes are like dark honey. When he leans forward to direct his words to his father at the head of the table, I can see his face bright with thought and feeling. He cannot be many years older than I am, and yet he seems to belong to the world of adults while I am still a child.

The men talk with passion about the rights of working men and freedom of speech.

"All Europe is changing," Lionel tells Mr. Serle. "I wonder you do not wish to work here to speed the change."

"Hush, Lionel," says his father. "Do not be rude to our guest."

"It is a fair question," Mr. Serle observes in his quiet way. "I have asked it of myself. It comes down at last to one thing. In my discussions with others in Paris, I learned much about America that I had not known. We talked of ordinary life in America, but we also read descriptions of its government with deep care. Listen: Congress—that is the governing body, you see—shall make no law respecting an establishment of religion, or prohibiting the free exercise thereof. I have lived all my life under laws that give individuals liberty or not according to religion. I cannot wait for freedom here. I must experience it in my life, now. Perhaps it will prove a chimera. Perhaps no matter what the laws say, people find ways to hurt each other. I will find out. I have no ties to keep me on this side of the ocean. I will risk the New World."

Mr. Pimintel responds thoughtfully. Then Lionel raises his voice to say, " 'Tis liberty alone that gives the flower of fleeting life its lustre and perfume, and we are weeds without it," and I understand that he is reciting a poem.

Mr. Serle praises his words and says something that also sounds like poetry, in a language I do not understand. I have no need to speak during the meal except to express my thanks at the end.

When the meal is over, we are invited to sit quietly as guests in the parlor while the family attends to their evening tasks. The oil lamps are lit. There is a fire in the grate to take away the evening damp. All is peace and domesticity. A student has knocked at the front door, and the professor gives him a lesson in his study. Lionel has gone out. From the kitchen below, we can hear the distant sounds of running water and the murmur of voices as the women clear away the supper and prepare for tomorrow. Mr. Serle is looking over his little collection of books to decide what he wants on the voyage and what he will pack away in his trunk to go into the storage hold of the ship. He has already laid out the notebook in which he collects recipes.

"I shall want to continue my work on this," he comments, patting its stained buckram cover. "It is a memory book as well as a means to teach others what I know."

I can no longer sit in silence when the events of the day weigh on me still. "I am truly your servant now," I say to Mr. Serle. "You have purchased the pledge I signed. I am glad to serve a just master."

He puts aside his notebook and looks at me. "I am not your master," he says.

"But you must be," I insist. "You bought the bond." Fear fogs my mind again. If he bought me, he can sell me, I think in panic. He could give me up to someone worse than Mr. Hatton. I so want him to keep me. "I will try to be obedient," I say hesitantly and, ashamed. "For thirty guineas, you have the right to rule me."

"What?" he says. I look up at him from under lowered lashes. He seems annoyed. There is a flush of red high on each of his brown cheekbones. "Do you think I am a beast, child?"

"No," I whisper.

"I am no master to you, except as you choose to work with me," he says. "The bond you signed is not legal. I had forgotten it." He draws the paper from his shirt where he put it after Mr. Hatton gave it to him. "See. Mrs. Fanny Hatton is the owner of the indenture. Susan Coates is the first witness, but two witnesses are required and the second is Gregory Hatton. He has signed across two lines, the line for the second witness and the line of the document that is indicated for a magistrate's signature and seal. There is no magistrate, no seal. No one would hold you to this."

"I see," I tell him. Tears blur my eyes as I look at the hateful paper.

"Besides," continues Mr. Serle, "you told me several times you signed indenture papers for three years. It says here five years. The Hattons are frauds all through."

"I remember he put his hand down on the paper when I tried to read it," I say. "What a fool I am."

Mr. Serle regards me with a steady gaze. He seems to be trying to decide whether or not to agree with me. When he speaks, he surprises me. "I am hurt that you do not know me better," he says. "We have spent many hours together. You nursed me when I was ill. I have kept your secrets. In all that time, I have not treated you as a man treats a woman either in word or deed. You are a child, unformed. I would not prey on you. I take no credit for it. My wife occupies my dreams. There is no space for another."

"But you bought the paper from Mr. Hatton," I say. "Why did you do it?"

"Why?" he seems surprised at the question. "It seemed the reasonable thing to do."

"You gave the money knowing he had no right to it?" I ask. I am bewildered. The feel of Mr. Hatton's grasping hands and mouth overwhelms me again. I scrub at my lips with the back of my hand and shiver with remembered fear. What if I am wrong about Mr. Serle as I was about the fraud Mr. Johnson, and the Hattons, and Susan? Can I trust my own thoughts?

"Certainly these indenture papers are a fraud." Mr. Serle taps them with his finger.

"But you have given money for nothing," I say.

"I do not wish to be delayed in Liverpool. Besides, I dislike suffering," Benjamin Serle speaks abruptly. He glances at me and then away. He compresses his lips as if he wills himself not to let anything more escape.

I hear the compassion in his words despite the curtness of his speech, and now my cheeks flush with shame that I have ever doubted him, but my heart leaps in my chest. It is my own fear that keeps me from knowledge of what is before me and from trust. I remember that Mr. Serle told me that when the heart is wounded, its scars are not visible outwardly. A fear inside keeps me from truth. This must be what he meant. And more than that, perhaps, if I can be brave, if I can know my heart, slowly it will heal. Truly, this good man is my friend.

The fire whispers to itself in the grate. Together, we sit silent in its warmth. The paper lies on the table before us.

"Well," Mr. Serle says, "enough of this. The bond is yours. Do you wish to keep it?"

"No," I reply. "I hate it. I will burn it." If it burns, it will no longer exist in this world. It can be like ashes in my memory. Not gone, but reduced and easier to cast away.

Benjamin Serle rises and stirs the fire. The flames dance up, blue and red. "Whenever you wish," he says.

I take the paper between thumb and forefinger and carry it to the fire. I drop it onto the hot coals. For a moment it seems as if it will not burn. Then the paper browns and twists in the heat. The black ink of the names writhes. Mina Pigot, Fanny Hatton, Gregory Hatton, Susan Coates dance for a brief moment above the flames. Then a corner of the paper flares up. The whole catches, burns bright, dies. Standing close beside me, Mr. Serle takes the poker and stirs the ash to nothing in the coals. The warm light bathes our faces.

"Poor thing," he says. "Poor thing, to think that any man has a right to buy you."

"If the papers had been legal," I say, "he would have bought me."

"Certainly not." Mr. Serle is distressed. "You can sell the labor of your hands; you can sell your attendance to another for a space of time. You cannot sell your person, what you are, your very self."

"You mean my soul?" I ask.

"Yes," he replies, "I mean your soul."

"People sell their souls to the devil," I tell Mr. Serle.

"That is another matter entirely," he says.

"But I have heard that it happens," I insist.

"Only in old stories," he reassures me, seating himself at the table again.

I can wait no longer. "I have one last secret," I tell him humbly. "I have the ring that my mother gave me. See here it is, sewn up in my shirttail." I pull it out to show him.

"Yes," he says. He barely glances at it.

"Look at it," I urge. I pull apart the threads that hold the ring sewn into my shirt. "It is the ring that my mother's aunt gave her and that my mother gave me. See how the red stone flashes in the light. The ring itself is gold. See." I hand it to him.

"It is pretty," he says, turning it in the light, "and it must remind you of your family."

"Is it valuable?" I ask. I think that gold must be of value.

He looks at the ring more closely. "I am no jeweler," he says, "but, of course, it is worth money. How much I do not know."

"I will sell it," I tell him. "I will sell it to pay you back for buying me from Mr. Hatton. I will add to it the money from my wages. Here." I scramble in my pocket for the coins. "Here is what is left after buying my cap." I put the silver and copper on the table. "And I will give you the three sovereigns of my wages I sewed in my shirt for safety." I pull at my shirt again. "You gave money that you saved for your restaurant. I must repay you."

"I can earn money," Mr. Serle says, "and so can you. So first, I will take no money from you until you are safe in America and able to repay me easily. We will settle any debts we have then. The ring I will never take. Your mother and her aunt before her wore it. You brought it with you through shipwreck and sorrow. I counsel you to keep it."

"But I owe a debt," I say. The ring glows red and gold in the palm of my hand.

"Wait," Mr. Serle says. "Keep the money you earned through hard work, and the ring that your mother gave you. If times are desperate, these will be your resources. Keep all safe against an evil day."

I think about what my mother and my father might want for me. Debt is dangerous. And I owe Mr. Serle a great, great debt. Yet he is right, the ring is my connection to the past. It would be very hard to give it up. "I am not sure," I say.

"I am." Mr. Serle speaks firmly. "Wait. You have trusted me with knowledge. Try not to fear. I will not abuse your trust."

"Oh!" I exclaim. Benjamin Serle seems to read my mind. It shocks me that another person can read me so. Perhaps age brings wisdom with it.

"I am grateful to you," I say. "I will work for you until my debt is paid and more. I am grateful. And yet the deepest feeling I have is always fear. I do not ever seem to leave its shadow. There is an empty place where my heart once was. I saw Susan and Tom hug and tickle each other. They talked of love and laughed together. I wondered: What is it that they feel?"

"I would not envy what Susan and Tom feel for each other," Mr. Serle says. His lips turn up in his ironic smile.

"But they feel something," I say. "I want to feel something."

"You do," Mr. Serle says. He sounds surprised. "You feel more than you may know just now. Wait. Be patient."

"I will try," I say. "But sometimes I am empty inside and then I am afraid."

Mr. Serle looks thoughtful. "It is a feeling," he says. "It is a feeling."

"Not a good one," I complain.

"Not everything in this life is good," he counters. "You share that with the rest of us."

"Well, now I am free," I say. "I have no secrets now."

Mr. Serle looks at me skeptically. "There is the matter of your dress," he says.

"But that is not a secret from you," I tell him. "It does not matter anyway. What I wear is just a convenience. The ancient knights wore armor. I have seen a picture in a book of a knight in metal casing from head to foot. He carried a sword and a banner. I am simpler. I wear a boy's trousers and jacket and cap. They are my armor against the world."

"The knights wore armor to protect them in battle," Mr. Serle objects.

"You don't think I have done battle with the world?" I ask him.

"I am corrected," he says. "You have done battle indeed."

I nod and return to my struggle with the journals that the Pimintel family have laid out on their parlor table and invited me to read. I pick up something called *The Jewish Chronicle* and am surprised to find it is written in English. I set it down, however, because the journal lying under it, *The Illustrated London News,* has an account of starvation and rebellion in Ireland. Some of the grand folk seem to believe that food exports should be stopped. My brother would be glad to know of this, I think.

There is silence for a time. I attempt to understand the

political news. Rights have been denied my people. The jails are filled. I ponder the meaning of it and wonder what my brother would want me to do. Perhaps I should go back to Ireland and find out what is happening instead of going to America. The thought frightens me. I know so little. I turn from the dangerous present and the incomprehensible future to a moment of goodness in the past.

A question comes into my head. "Why did you help me that morning when the pony stepped on my foot? Why did you give me work?" I ask Mr. Serle.

He sets down his book and looks at me. "You looked desperate, child, and infinitely sad. I watched you groom the gray horse before you brought out the pony. You moved with a skill and a confidence that amazed me. The animal looked huge next to your frail figure, and yet you had a power that mastered it."

"So it was the horse that made you see me?" I ask.

Mr. Serle looks thoughtful. "Life is never this or that only," he says. "I disliked John Coates. I could see he wanted to get rid of you, and I wanted to annoy him by taking you in."

"Thank you," I tell him. We are silent until Mr. and Mrs. Pimintel come in. Their evening tasks are done. They begin a conversation with Mr. Serle. I excuse myself and go upstairs, where I sew my ring into my shirt again and then sit, holding the lump of it through the linen and thinking of those I love.

CHAPTER XXIII

I AWAKEN in the night and am disappointed it is not dawn yet. I want to be gathering my bundle together, setting out. I am ready to go down to the docks and board the *Victoria*. I want to see her with her flags afloat on the wind. I wish that I had a green ribbon and could tie it in my hair. I would have a flag of my own.

Mr. Serle lies asleep across the room. He snores in a low rhythm, peacefully. I toss on my bed under the window. Strangely, what disturbs me is not the horror of my struggle with Mr. Hatton, or the excitement of tomorrow, or the nearness of Mr. Serle without the familiar curtain to separate us. The disturbance is in the sense I have that this is the old way, the feeling of going to sleep in the cottage where I was born with my sister beside me on our pallet, my brother barely an arm's reach away, and our parents across the room on their low bedstead. This is the way it should be. This is the safe place. The familiarity of it excites and troubles me.

Silence grows around me. As the rumbles and cries of the city recede in the night, the rhythm of the train enters my head. I feel my body pulse with the remembered motion of the iron wheels. *You will change, you will change, you will change* becomes a song inside me.

I fall asleep at last. In the dark a dream comes to me. I walk out from the door of our whitewashed cottage. I have been churning the cream until the butter is come, and I am warm from my work. I climb the stile in the stone wall and am away up through the fields. The land is green, green, green, like a velvet gown laid over a curving body. Cows in the pasture lift their moody heads to look at me and lower them again to the grazing. I am running now, up the hill. The wind rises, lifting the damp tendrils away from my forehead and blowing my skirts. Now I am at the crest of this hill, which is the first rise toward the greater mountains that lie, blue-gray in the distance, to the north of us. Behind me a hawthorn blooms white among the green leaves on its thorny gray branches. Along the road below me is the straggle of white cottages that make our village.

The air I breathe is moist with fine rain. The stirring wind seems to blow it away about me so that I see it and am yet not wet. This is my country, I say to myself, this is my birthright. I want to stoop and pull handfuls of the green grasses laced with tiny white flowers and the darker green of clover. I will cram the green of it into my mouth and chew the essence out of it. As I am about to bend to seize the grass about me, I see a procession of people walking up the road.

From behind the cottages, walkers flow in an endless line. They wear gray, hooded cloaks that cover them from head to foot and shield their faces. As I watch, the first turns and crosses the yard beside our house, just as I did. One by one by one, the gray figures follow. Across the stile they climb, each turning to give a hand to the one behind. They glide through the pasture. As the thin streamers of cloud that we call mares' tails move silently through the blue acres of sky, the figures float across the green fields and up the hill where I am standing.

I brace myself against the shock of their approach. There is an army here that will overwhelm me. But, like water breaking around a rock in the streambed, they part around me, flowing not up the hill behind me but into the earth. Endlessly they come, divide about me, are absorbed into the land on which I stand. And now a low humming begins beneath me. They are singing as one voice. I strain my ears to learn their song. It strengthens, fades, strengthens again. If only I can hear it, learn it, I will be safe forever. Teach me, I cry desperately in my dream, teach me. I can make no sound. In the way of dreams, my voice is imprisoned in my throat. Only the faint humming of the earth vibrates through me one last time, and then the green fields and the hills fade to nothing.

I awaken. A bird is singing in the twisted city tree outside the window. Mr. Serle is gone from his bed. I rise and wash myself thoroughly. There is warm water in the big pitcher on the stand. When I am dressed, I venture out into the hall. Edda is coming up the stairs with a basket of clean clothes.

"Good morning," I say with my most careful manners.

Edda stops and sets down her basket. "Today you leave." She embarks on conversation without preliminary. "I am so amazed. You are my age, I think, and you are going to America. You are the bravest person I have ever met."

Her eyes are the same strange honey color as her brother's. When I look at her, I see him too and feel doubly awkward. "I am not so brave," I mumble. "And Mr. Serle helps me, so I am not all alone."

"No," she insists, "you have courage. Mr. Serle told my mother at breakfast this morning that you were almost killed when the *Abigail* burned. We heard about it, of course. Anyone who can sail again after that experience must be brave. Besides, you are handsome. I never saw such beautiful hair as yours. I will think of you every Friday when I polish the brass candlesticks until red glows in their gold."

I am struck speechless.

"Remember me," she says. To my surprise, she leans to me and kisses me softly on the cheek. "When I am grown, I hope to marry someone brave and handsome like you."

I stand and stare at her, confused and overcome. She blushes crimson and, picking up her basket, hurries away down the hall. "Thank you," I call after her, summoning my wits too late. She does not turn. I have to admit to myself that it is just as well.

I go down the stairs cautiously and am glad that only kind Mrs. Pimintel is in the dining room to oversee my hasty breakfast. She tells me that Mr. Serle has gone out to purchase more cheese, fresh beef to go in the ice chests, and a variety of spices. He studied the supplies list again this morning and became concerned at the overabundance of salt pork and the lack of other necessities. He hopes to find fresh apples as well as oranges and lemons. The owners of the ship have not planned carefully for the tastes of the important cabin passengers we are hired to serve. As soon as Mr. Serle returns, we will leave.

I am beginning to fidget and think of repacking my bag one last time when Mr. Serle returns laden with his purchases. We secure the supplies in two cloth sacks Mrs. Pimintel gives us. Then, with Edda's gentle farewell kiss on my cheek, I follow Mr. Serle and the carter, who pushes a hand truck with our trunk and bags on it, through the streets to the docks. I am going to America.

At the dock, the ship's boat is waiting for us. It rides low in the water, loaded with boxes and bales. The ship itself, the *Victoria*, is anchored in the river for tonight. Our baggage is lowered down to the boat, and then Mr. Serle and I clamber down the slippery ladder and take our places facing the two sailors who man the oars. Mr. Serle sits directly in front of me. I am wedged in the stern beside his trunk and my bag. Someone shouts a warning on the dock above us and a serpent of rope comes snaking down, half in the boat, half trailing in the water. One of the men catches it and coils it in the bow, as the other plies both oars to keep us from bumping the dock pilings. Then each man takes an oar, and we are pointed out into the river and under way.

The sky is overcast but mild. A shiver of wind makes waves ripple across the river. The ships rock at anchor. The cleats on the ropes that run along their masts ring against each other. The calls of men and birds, the bells of the warning buoys, the shrill whistles from barges and ferries echo about us. As we pass from the protected water near the shore, the waves splash a little higher, and I push my bag down beside me to protect it from the wet. In front of me, Benjamin Serle hunches his shoulders and lowers his dark head against the wind.

With my right hand I hold the edge of the boat beside me for balance. Soon hand and sleeve end are drenched. I shake my hand and watch the drops fly from my fingertips. The surface of the river is so near that I can scoop a palm full of silvery water and let it flow away again, back into itself. I think of the maid, Clara, whom Benjamin and his brother feared when they were children. I have it in my power to splash some water and whisper some sacred words. It would be so easy, I think, so easy. He would be saved. My heart rises at the thought—if the ship founders, I will see him in heaven.

Words speak themselves in my head. For a moment I am in the whitewashed church set in a green field with the small gray stones of the dead leaning over the graves. Just inside the entrance of the church is the stoop of holy water. Father Fintan's voice says quickly, *"In nomine Patris, et Filius ..."* and dies into a whisper of wind across the water. I let drops of water trickle from my fingertips. I will not do it. I cannot do it.

The sailors ply their oars, the wind freshens across the water. Mr. Serle turns his head to the right to look back at the dark city slumped by the river. I see the pure profile of him, the high forehead, the dark brows, the bright ray of thought from his eye, the curve of his lightly compressed lips, and the proud set of his head. He dips his hand in the water and lets the drops trickle down as I just did. A memory of the day I first watched him knead bread, a dusting of flour caught in the black hairs on the backs of his hands, returns to me. His hands are beautiful. He glances back at me and smiles. "It's a good morning, isn't it?" he says.

I nod, speechless. When he turns back in his place, I dip my hand in the water once more and make the sign of the cross on my own breast. We must save ourselves each in our own way. And all that day, as we sort and stack and label supplies and worry at the little space and the unknown demands that will be made on us, I feel inexplicably happy.

It is harder the next afternoon when we leave the port. The poor souls whose deprivation shows in their drawn faces have been herded down beneath the decks to claim their bunks. The rich people have watched their servants load their trunks and boxes and unpack what is needful for the voyage. Again we all assemble on the deck to see the ship cast off for the journey. Again the ship drops down the river with the flow of the tide. Again the wharves and houses and the plumes of dark smoke over the city fade from view. The ship dips south and west into the sea. As daylight fades, Mr. Serle and I stand on the gently rocking deck outside the cookhouse and the storeroom where we will work and sleep for who knows how many weeks to come.

England, Ireland, Italy, France, all fall behind us into the past as we move across the trackless waste of water. I worry that the ship will founder in a storm. The faint odor of smoke from our cookstove makes my heart turn over in my chest. The wind, which smells of salt, lifts my hair from my forehead. The light of the setting sun tracks gold across the black water. I do not want this life to end yet. "I am afraid," I whisper to Benjamin Serle.

"Think of your grandfather's family," he tells me. "You said they are seafaring folk."

"You remember," I say. "I had forgotten."

"Don't forget," he admonishes me. "Carry it with you. Let it make you brave. Because," Benjamin Serle says, quoting another of the novels he loves, " 'Difficulties are conquered where mental courage combats disappointment, and keeps the untamed spirits superior to failure and ever alive to hope.' "

"Hope," I reply. "Hope again. The rest sounds noble, yet I do not believe it expresses how we think in our real lives. The words are too grand and too neat. Besides, we both know that difficulties are not always conquered." I remember Mr. Serle's brother, but I do not speak the sad thought.

"But I find the point well stated, even if not true," says Benjamin Serle, and he smiles.

I laugh out loud. "You are too old and too serious," I say. "It will not be hard to call you Uncle Benjamin."

"Uncle Benjamin?" says Mr. Serle. He sounds startled. The ship dips a little into a wave, and he steadies himself, resting one hand near mine on the railing. "Uncle. Of course."

"Of course," I say. "Only read me the adventures of these novels you treasure and spare me the morals." I push my hands into my trouser pockets as a boy would and squint my eyes toward the horizon.

The sea, which we both fear, may confound us, the fire within us, which sustains our hope, may burn to bitter ashes. No one knows the future. And yet—where the sun is sinking toward the west, a world lies all before us.

AUTHOR'S NOTE

The fiction of Jane Austen, Charlotte Brontë, Emily Brontë, Frances Burney, William Carleton, James Fenimore Cooper, Benjamin Disraeli, Maria Edgeworth, Gustave Flaubert, Catherine Maria Sedgwick, and William Makepeace Thackeray, and the poetry of Shakespeare, Milton, Cowper, and Byron inspired and informed the narrative of *Mina*. The reader will find references to many of these authors' works in names, menus, and descriptive details and, occasionally, in direct quotations. In addition, I owe a great debt of thanks for historical, cultural, and factual information to the following works:

Brillat-Savarin, Jean Anthelme. *The Physiology of Taste: Or Meditations on Transcendental Gastronomy.* Trans. and annotated by M. F. K. Fisher. San Francisco CA: North Point Press, 1986.

Davies, Jennifer. *The Victorian Kitchen.* London, England: BBC Books, 1989.

Dumas, Alexandre. *Alexandre Dumas' Dictionary of Cuisine.* Edited, Abridged, and Translated by Louis Colman from *Le Grand Dictionnaire de Cuisine.* London, England: Spring Books, 1964.

Laxton, Edward. *The Famine Ships: The Irish Exodus to America.* New York NY: Henry Holt and Company, 1996.

Machlin, Edda Servi. *The Classic Cuisine of the Italian Jews: Traditional Recipes and Menus and a Memoir of a Vanished Way of Life.* New York NY: Everest House, 1981.

Vogelstein, Hermann. *Rome.* Trans. Moses Hadas. Philadelphia PA: The Jewish Publication Society of America, 1941.

Web Site of the Society for the Study of Nineteenth-Century Ireland. www.qub.ac.uk/english/socs/ssnci.html/. Viewed March 2000.

Finally, even more important than the books that teach us are the people who know and sustain us. My love and gratitude to Mary Lyon Manson, who believed in the project from the beginning; to Robert Ceely, who, as always, gave support in crisis as well as joy; and to my parents, to whom this book is dedicated.

ABOUT THE AUTHOR

JONATHA CEELY grew up in Canada and has lived in Turkey and Italy. She is a former teacher and administrator who lives in Brookline, Massachusetts, with her husband, who is a composer and teacher. She is currently at work on her second novel.